In the Arms of the Heiress

MAGGIE ROBINSON

BERKLEY SENSATION, NEW YORK

THE BERKLEY PUBLISHING GROUP
Published by the Penguin Group
Penguin Group (USA) Inc.
375 Hudson Street, New York, New York 10014, USA

USA | Canada | UK | Ireland | Australia | New Zealand | India | South Africa | China

Penguin Books Ltd., Registered Offices: 80 Strand, London WC2R 0RL, England
For more information about the Penguin Group, visit penguin.com.

IN THE ARMS OF THE HEIRESS

A Berkley Sensation Book / published by arrangement with the author

Berkley Sensation Books are published by The Berkley Publishing Group.
BERKLEY SENSATION® is a registered trademark of Penguin Group (USA) Inc.
The "B" design is a trademark of Penguin Group (USA) Inc.

For information, address: The Berkley Publishing Group,
a division of Penguin Group (USA) Inc.,
375 Hudson Street, New York, New York 10014.

ISBN: 978-0-425-26581-9

PUBLISHING HISTORY
Berkley Sensation mass-market edition / July 2013

PRINTED IN THE UNITED STATES OF AMERICA

10   9   8   7   6   5   4   3   2   1

Cover art by Judy York.
Cover design by George Long.
Interior text design by Kelly Lipovich.

ALWAYS LEARNING   **PEARSON**

Chapter

❦

1

Nice, France
Early November 1903

Dear Aunt Grace,

*It is with the heaviest of hearts I write to tell you my
beloved husband Maximillian is dead—*

"You are *killing* him?"

Her maid, Kathleen, had the most annoying habit of
sneaking up behind her when she least expected it.

"It's not as if he even exists," Louisa Stratton replied,
wiping up the splotch of ink.

Kathleen opened the terrace doors to the Mediterranean, and a chill, damp breeze almost blew Louisa's letter
away. It was supposed to be warmer in the south of France.
It was not.

"How did he die, then?"

"I don't know yet. Avalanche? Train wreck?" Maximillian might be a mountaineer when he wasn't in museums, clad in tight leather, his face burnished by the great out-doors. The tender lines around his cerulean blue eyes from squinting at the sun would fan out like ecru lace. Louisa would trace them with a fingertip as he hovered over her—

Kathleen slammed the doors shut. "Both would have been all over the newspapers."

"Damn it." She should have thought of that.

"Indeed. You'll have to find something less sensational. A heart murmur, perhaps. A septic finger."

Louisa brightened. "Yes! He was picking late roses for me and caught a thorn. Such a tiny thing, yet so dangerous. You know how he spoiled me—fresh flowers every day, no matter the season. The man should have been wearing his gloves. His hands were so lovely. Long and smooth, with hardly any hair on his knuckles. He could do *anything* with them." She gave Kathleen a naughty smile.

Kathleen tsked. "None of that talk. It still won't work. After all, Maximillian Norwich is supposed to be an important man. You've made him so. You know your aunt always reads the obituaries, and she'll wonder why you didn't put the notice in."

"I was simply prostrate with grief. Half out of my mind. She thinks I'm mad anyway."

Louisa usually had an answer for everything. If there *had* really been a Maximillian, she was sure she'd show all the proper feeling for losing the love of her life. She probably wouldn't rise from her lonely bed for weeks, per-haps months. Years. She'd rival the late queen in her long-ing for Albert, only she'd be far more attractively dressed.

There would be an alp of crumpled handkerchiefs and untouched dinner trays. Kathleen would call her a lost cause, and Louisa would simply turn her face to the wall in a melancholy fever. Watch the wallpaper pattern blur through unceasing tears. Listen to the siren call of the sea outside, which might tempt her to sew rocks into the hem of her nightgown and drown herself.

Of course, Kathleen would catch her at it before she

pricked her fingers too bloody—Louisa had little experience sewing despite Aunt Grace's attempts to turn her into a lady. Doctors would be consulted—perhaps Kathleen would even send all the way to Vienna for Dr. Freud.

"You'll have to go to Rosemont in full mourning if you kill him. You know how black washes you out, if I may be so bold as to remind you."

"As if I could stop you." Bold didn't begin to describe Kathleen's tongue. After five years of service, she was more friend than maid to Louisa. Over the past year of freedom they had shared several hair- and skirt-raising adventures that had cemented their bond even further.

But lately, Kathleen had become very cranky. Louisa suspected the cause was some useless man. Before they'd run off to the Continent, the new Scottish chauffeur, Robertson, had been making sheep's eyes at Kathleen. True, he was a braw lad, but Kathleen should not give up her independence for a few minutes of clumsy coupling. Intercourse, in Louisa's opinion, was much overrated.

"And your aunt would see to it that your social life be curtailed completely, just like she used to," Kathleen continued in her usual role as the voice of reason. "A full two years of mourning. No visits. No concerts or lectures. I doubt she'd even let you go to London for the day to get a tooth pulled. You'd be bored to tears in no time. And wearing black to boot."

"Too true." Louisa nibbled at the end of her gold-plated Conklin Crescent Filler fountain pen, which was already cratered from previous unhappy letter writing. What a bloody nuisance it was that she'd had to invent Maximillian in the first place. But Aunt Grace had been beyond horrified when Louisa left for a motor trip across the Continent with only Kathleen for company, inundating the travelers with telegrams and letters at every poste restante, outlining in gruesome detail what might happen to two innocent young women alone in Evil Europe.

Well, Louisa was hardly innocent, as Grace well knew.

But she was *absent*, and out of Grace's reach. The letters had ceased abruptly once Louisa informed her family that she'd met the magnetic Maximillian Norwich beneath an especially dim and muddy Rembrandt in the Louvre, then married him after a whirlwind courtship.

But then the letters resumed with tepid congratulations. Louisa must come *home* and bring her *husband*.

Rosemont had not felt like home for some time, but after a blissful year of adventure and non-marriage, Louisa acknowledged it was probably time to return. Kathleen was sulking. Driving about in an open motorcar all winter might give them both chilblains. There had also been some difficulty with Louisa's bank lately that had to be straightened out. And according to letters from her wretched cousin Hugh and even Dr. Fentress, it was Aunt Grace who might be really dead soon—not that Louisa believed it.

Grace was much too spiteful to die. The woman had never even had a head cold the twenty-one years Louisa had lived with her after Louisa's parents died. From the age of four, Louisa had been relentlessly upbraided by her guardian for every small infraction. Her inevitable big infraction had hellish consequences.

Well, perhaps the devil wanted Grace after all.

"What do you suggest, Kathleen? Should I tell the truth?"

Her maid raised one gingery eyebrow. "You? Tell the truth? I might faint."

"You never faint. You are the only female I know who can keep her head in a crisis. Besides me, of course."

If Kathleen disagreed with the compliment, she had the good sense to say nothing. When pressed, Louisa would have to acknowledge she had gotten into more than her fair share of scrapes the past few months. It would have been handy to have a husband or two to help her out of them—not that she had plans to ever marry. Why should she? She was an heiress, independent, unfettered. Louisa didn't need a man to boss her around. She'd had enough rules at Rosemont growing up, spending over twenty years of her life like a nun walled in a convent.

Of course, Rosemont was far more luxurious than any convent Louisa had ever seen in her travels, with its thousand-acre park flush with fauna, its fifty rooms glittering with gilt. For an untitled gentleman—just like Mr. Darcy!—Louisa's father had been hideously rich, and he'd married well, too. Her American mother had a fortune even greater than his. Unfortunately both her parents had died in a boating accident when she was very young. If their portraits had not hung in the Long Gallery, she might have forgotten what they looked like.

"We have to go home sometime," Kathleen said. "Don't you ever miss Rosemont?"

No, she did not. Grace and Hugh were there, as well as a few other dependent relatives, and somehow Louisa could not seem to get rid of them. Grace had returned to her ancestral home to serve as guardian when Louisa's parents died, and the others had just hunkered in. It was easier to run away when she came into her funds last year than to butt heads with Aunt Grace and try to throw them all out of the house.

Louisa did not like to think she was a coward. She *would* go home, *would* confront them. Some of them, anyway. She had no objection to her mother's cousin Isobel hovering in the hallways. They had come to England husband-hunting together in the late seventies, but only Louisa's mother had been successful.

If one could call drowning after less than five years of marriage successful.

Louisa needed some success of her own. She would bribe Grace and Hugh with whatever inducements she needed to once her banking problems were solved.

She'd have someone at her side when she did it. A help-meet. A handsome, sophisticated man of the world who had swept her off her feet in the Louvre and who had been making sweet, sinful love to her with finesse and flourishes ever since with his long, smooth hands—at least in her fervid dreams. Maximillian Norwich would come to Rosemont with her, even if she had to bribe him, too.

Louisa tore up the letter to her aunt. "Kathleen, what is the name of that agency your brother used last year to get his new job? Evening something?"

"Evensong, Miss Louisa. The Evensong Agency. On Mount Street. Works wonders, Mrs. Evensong does. That's where Rosemont's new chauffeur came from, too. Why do you ask? You're not planning to fire me, are you?"

"Certainly not." Louisa did not know what she'd do without Kathleen, even if she'd been a bit prune-faced lately.

"Well, that's a great relief. Do you want me to bind your breasts for our jaunt this afternoon and brush off your trousers, or are you wearing your corset and carriage dress?"

"Trousers, I think. It's damned cold out," Louisa replied, reaching for another piece of hotel stationery.

Chapter

❧

2

Tuesday, December 1, 1903

$\mathcal{M}$rs. Mary Evensong really wished she could hold her nose indefinitely, but alas, one had to breathe. Instead she fished a perfumed handkerchief from her needlepoint purse and held it to her face. One could not surpass the scent of Blenheim Bouquet—lemon, lime, and lavender. Three delightful things. Penhaligon's new fragrance had quickly become her favorite, even if it was intended for gentlemen, and once she was done with this distasteful task she would stop by the Jermyn Street shop just to inhale more of it.

The bundle of rags on the sprung sofa shifted, and Mary narrowed her eyes behind her smoke-gray spectacles. Captain Charles Cooper was a long man lying on a short couch. It appeared he had not bathed or changed his clothes in some days, and the patch he wore over one eye had now migrated and partially covered a somewhat blunt nose. His dark hair was shorn, and his face would have been clean-shaven if he'd bothered to run a razor over it the day before yesterday.

Mary approved. London was positively teeming with fur-faced fellows. The fashion for beards had always eluded her. In fact, she believed most men sported them to hide their weak or double chins. And it was ever so unpleasant to get a mouthful of moustache when one kissed a gentleman—not that she had occasion to know lately.

There was a distinct aroma of cheap gin and male sweat in the room, and once again she was forced to gulp into her handkerchief.

"Captain Cooper," she said in a rallying voice when she had tricked herself into thinking of citrus fruit and Spanish sunshine, "wake up."

"Don't want to."

Well, that was much easier than she thought. She would hate to have prodded him with her umbrella.

"I am Mrs. Evensong, proprietress of the Evensong Agency, and I have a proposition for you, sir. Mr. George Alexander has brought it to my attention that you have recently resigned your commission and are in need of work."

"No." Captain Cooper still reclined on the couch, his eyes closed.

"I assure you I spoke with him myself." The employment of Captain Cooper was not the only thing they had discussed. Mr. Alexander was a businessman of many interests, and he had piqued Mrs. Evensong's interest with a possible investment opportunity. She would look into it with her usual thoroughness.

Cooper sighed. "I don't care who you are or who you've talked to. I don't need any charity job from George. He's done enough."

"This is not charity, Captain, but a paid position. Mr. Alexander has very little to do with it apart from mentioning your name." Mary Evensong was not going to tell the captain that if he signed his employment contract, she would be paid by both the industrialist *and* Miss Louisa Stratton. There was no reason to explain the ins and outs of her business, for they frequently changed with each individual case. She was nothing if not flexible, both in her professional and personal life.

"There is a young lady who wishes to engage your services and will make it very worth your while to rise from that vile sofa and find the nearest bathtub."

Charles Cooper struggled up on one elbow, pushing his patch over one sightless blue eye with a shaking hand. Mary had read the reports and seen the commendations, talked to enough of his superiors and schoolmasters to have formed an opinion of the man who looked extremely unheroic and unintelligent at the moment despite their effusive praise. Heavens, he looked as if he'd like another drink soon to begin his day, and she did not want to be present to watch him throw his life away.

"A young woman, eh? I gather you're not talking about yourself."

Mary stiffened but inclined her elaborate black velvet hat in his direction.

"You intrigue me, Mrs. Evensong. I haven't fucked a woman since I came home from South Africa. Where is she? I'm more than ready."

"If you think you can put me off with your crudeness, you must know nothing of the Evensong Agency," Mary said, unruffled. "I always accomplish my missions, and you, sir, are one of them."

"I'm past being saved, Mrs. Evensong. Do us both a favor and get out."

He sounded so weary, and looked worse. Mary tossed a dirty shirt on the floor and sat down on the only chair in the room.

"I didn't ask you to sit, woman."

"No, you didn't, and your rudeness will have to be remedied before you meet my client. She is most particular.

You've been to public school. You've been an officer. Surely you have not forgotten how to treat and speak to a lady." Mary folded her gloved hands primly in her lap.

"As I just explained, I've had very little to do with ladies lately. Does your client like a bit of rough? I can't imagine why else she would be interested in a factory foreman's son."

"My client is a very discerning young woman who need not know of your early years; though if she were to find out, I doubt you'd shock her too much. She's very— democratic."

"A socialist, eh?"

"I don't believe she's political at all, except when it comes to the rights of woman."

Cooper grimaced. "Oh, spare me from a bloody suffragist. Whatever she wants, I am not her man, Mrs. Evensong. I can't drive her to Mrs. Pankhurst's meetings and rallies—I'm half blind, remember?"

"Miss St—that is, the young lady drives herself, Captain Cooper." Mary had also read the police reports from several European nations detailing Louisa Stratton's driving skills. They left a little something to be desired. What the young woman needed was a good chauffeur, and Mary knew there was one at Rosemont, a steady young Scotsman she'd placed there herself.

"Does she now? Well, I suppose you'd better go on and tell me what she wants before my landlady gets suspicious about why I am entertaining an old trout like you in my room."

Mary Evensong hoped her gray wig was on straight. But why wouldn't it be? She always paid attention to every detail of her appearance, to show the world what they expected to see.

"Your landlady will think nothing. She was very handsomely compensated to let me in, and by the way, once she saw the state of the place she requested that you pack your things at the earliest opportunity and vacate the premises."

Not quite true, but Charles Cooper didn't need to know that, did he? It gave him one more incentive to agree to her plan.

She always had a plan, and several alternates should unfortunate circumstances prevail. Mary rather thought she had Captain Cooper's full attention now. He glared at her with one bloodshot blue eye.

"Go on," he barked, in much the tone he'd probably used to command his troops in the Transvaal.

"It's simple, really. My client is in need of a handsome, cultured gentleman to pose as her husband during the Christmas holidays at one of the premiere country houses in England. Rosemont. In Kent. Have you heard of it? It was featured in the December 1900 issue of *The English Illustrated Magazine.*"

"I'm afraid I wasn't in the country at the time to read any society magazines, Mrs. Evensong," the captain said dryly.

"Of course you weren't. I know you were serving honorably in Africa. I simply mention it because it is a very grand property and it will be a privilege to call it home for a month."

"Till death do us part, or just thirty days? Why does this girl need a fake husband?"

"She has had some difficulty with her family. It seemed a good idea to her at the time to invent a husband." Privately, Mary thought that Louisa Stratton had been just a little too madcap for comfort, but one couldn't undo the past unless one was very clever. Which Mary was. Over the years, she'd rescued several young ladies from their ill-advised activities and no one was the wiser.

Cooper rubbed his stubbled chin. "How much?"

"I beg your pardon?"

"What's the pay? I have family, too."

Mary Evensong knew. Two older brothers, their wives, and their numerous offspring, most of them working in one of George Alexander's pottery works. Cooper would likely be employed on the factory floor beside them had not Mr. Alexander plucked him off it when he was a lad of twelve and sent him to school. George Alexander had seen promise in young Charlie Cooper, and Mrs. Evensong squinted at him to try to do the same. Mr. Alexander was a perspicacious gentleman, with a finger in many pies and a fortune that was not to be sneezed at.

She quoted the price she and Miss Stratton had agreed upon. Captain Cooper turned the color of the dingy shirt on the floor.

"For a *month*? Are you serious?"

Ah, that made him get up and start pacing about the room in an agitated fashion. He must have been quite handsome marching about in his uniform—it was a pity that Maximillian Norwich was an effete art connoisseur and not a soldier.

"Perfectly. The Evensong Agency has been in business since 1888. We have never broken our word once," Mary said, lying just the tiniest bit. "There will be a proper wardrobe for you, too. One cannot go to a house like Rosemont in a celluloid collar." She reached into her handbag and pulled out the business card of a discreet tailor and handed it to the captain when he shuffled by her. Mr. Smythe could give any haberdasher on Jermyn Street a run for their money for quality at less than half the price. "You have an appointment at noon tomorrow. I shall escort you. And I must have your promise. You will give up your drink. Maximillian Norwich would never swill cheap gin."

"Who?"

"Did I not mention that is the name of my client's imaginary husband? You shall have to answer to it."

Charles Cooper's weathered face broke out into a grin. His teeth were remarkably good for a man of the lower classes. "Mrs. Evensong, for the amount of money your idiot client is paying me, I would answer to Fido. Max it is."

Miss Stratton might insist on *Maximillian*—she'd seemed especially enamored of the name—but Mary did not want to press her luck. There was a great deal to be done in the next few days and a cheerful Charles Cooper was far superior to the morose man she'd first encountered.

In fact, perhaps she should help him pack his few belongings and offer him the spare room on Mount Street. She and her staff could keep a watchful eye over him to ensure he kept his appointment tomorrow in a sober state. He looked as if he needed a good meal, too, and Mary's cook was one of the best in London—even if she'd spent her formative years as a whore.

She made her second proposition of the morning. Captain Cooper made no objection. Yes, the agency's motto, "Performing the Impossible Before Breakfast Since 1888," was on its way to being fulfilled.

Chapter

❦

3

*T*hey were all cracked, talking about him as if he couldn't hear. It was his eye that was injured, not his ears. Charles was sick to death of being poked and pinned by the bald little Mr. Smythe and his assistants, who had crawled over him like ants at a picnic for over an hour.

"I say, are we done?" He sounded posh, a regular Harrow boy, if he did say so himself. No one would suspect he'd been raised in George Alexander's workers' village. George was a generous employer, a benevolent man. Some might even say that because he stole young Charlie away from his family and civilized him, grown Charles owed him his life.

Well, his life wasn't worth much. George had got a poor bargain.

"Almost, Captain Cooper. You've been very patient," the tailor said.

He'd been very *bored*. And he was damned thirsty. If he couldn't have gin, Charles wondered if he could talk the old Evensong biddy into giving him some wine at lunch.

If they ever ate some. Breakfast was but a distant memory. Good as the meal had been, Charles's stomach rumbled and the tailor's assistant gave him a cheeky grin.

Charles had been lectured at length all morning by Mrs. Evensong as to what his duties and responsibilities would be as Miss Louisa Stratton's temporary husband. She had even pressed a lavishly illustrated art book in his hand, as this Maximillian fellow—Maximillian!—was supposed to be some sort of expert. As Charles didn't know a Rembrandt from a Rousseau, he expected he'd have some studying to do.

It would be just like old times, when, as a scholarship boy, he'd outshone the scions of the best families in England. No one could call Charles stupid, or remain standing very long if they did. He'd been as good with his fists as with his figures.

School and the army had polished some of his rough edges, but at twenty-seven, there were still a few splinters that poked through. He hoped Miss Stratton wouldn't be too sorry once she finally met him.

But really, what did he care? He was to be a well-paid lapdog to a silly society bitch. He could put up with most anything for a month for the exorbitant fee. This Louisa must have several screws loose and way too much money.

A sheltered little princess like her would have died on the spot if she'd seen what he had in Africa.

Charles hopped off the box he was standing on and shot his cuffs. He'd worn a uniform for ten years, and he barely recognized his reflection in the triple mirror. The new suit, well, suited him. Mr. Smythe, the tailor, was even going to make him new silk eye patches, which would be a vast improvement over the itchy one he'd been given in the field hospital.

To look at him without it, you'd never know he'd lost

most of his vision. But he'd gotten headaches trying to stare through the blur of broken blood vessels and floating bits. His mates teased him, saying the eye patch gave him a piratical air that would be useful with the ladies. But he hadn't bothered to find out if they were right.

Charles had not been able to think of women in a sexual sense after he'd helped bury hundreds of them and their children, their naked bodies blistered by the sun, malnourished, skeletal. Kitchener's troops had set up a vast network of internment camps to imprison the Boer women, tents springing up like mushrooms in the dry ground. Food and water routinely failed to reach them, the English supply and communication lines to the refugee camps broken by their own South African countrymen. As special cruel punishment, those wives and children whose husbands and fathers were still fighting received smaller rations than the others. If the families didn't starve to death first, then measles, typhoid, and dysentery finished the job.

There were times when Charles wished he'd lost vision in both eyes to save witnessing the devastation.

South Africa was the real world, its heat and blood pulsing up through the cracked earth; England was just a flimsy false stage set, populated by those who had no idea what their heroes were capable of. He'd be in the footlights soon himself, playing a role before his curtain dropped.

Damn, but he was hungry. Not as hungry as the doomed Boer women must have been, but it was best he not dwell on the past anymore. Maximillian Norwich would not care about slaughter and death—there was no such thing in his elevated existence. *His* life was all about his silly heiress and her shiny motorcar, champagne, and caviar.

Charles stumbled on a bolt of cloth. Blast. In Mrs. Evensong's rush to remove and improve him yesterday, he'd had left his journals under the floorboards of his room at the boarding house. Mrs. Jarvis had probably lined up a new tenant already—the woman would not let an opportunity go by to make more money, even though he'd paid the rent through to the new year. He wouldn't miss the grime or smells, but he really would miss his journals.

His family would understand once they read them.

He turned to Mrs. Evensong, who was examining a figured maroon waistcoat as though she'd discovered the Holy Grail. What an odd woman she was. "I have to go."

She looked up, frowning. It was hard to see her eyes beneath the gray-tinted spectacles, but he'd bet they were shrewd. "Why? Where are you going?"

"I forgot something at my old lodging. Don't worry. I'm not going to the corner pub. I gave you my word."

"Yes, you did, and I expect you to keep it. Very well, Captain. You'll return to Mount Street once you're done?"

"Of course. I don't suppose that cook of yours can fix me a sandwich?"

"We can do much better than that," Mrs. Evensong said smugly. "Don't be too long. I'm expecting Miss Stratton to stop by this afternoon."

Damn. He really wasn't ready to meet his "wife." But if clothes made the man, he was presentable enough. Mr. Smythe helped him into a charcoal tweed overcoat to guard against the wind and handed him a top hat. It had already been decided that his bespoke clothes and extra hats would be monogrammed and inscribed with his new name or initials and ready by tomorrow morning. Mrs. Evensong thought of everything.

Charles hailed a hansom cab with the money she had advanced him—not quite enough to get in trouble with, but certainly adequate to get to a less desirable part of town and back. His ex-landlady, Mrs. Jarvis, pretended at first not to recognize him, and he had to drop a few of his ill-gotten gains in her grubby hand before she let him into his old room, dogging him like a terrier. Did she think he'd steal the broken curtain rod? She watched as he pulled up a warped floorboard and retrieved the marble pasteboard journals.

"What are them books?" she asked.

"My history, Mrs. Jarvis—every battle and wound and

woman. It will make for fascinating reading on a cold winter's night." He imagined his brothers turning the pages once he was gone, forgiving him a little between his words and the money he would leave them. Tom and Fred would understand. They had to.

Suddenly the old building shook from an explosion below on the street. Without thinking, Charles tackled Mrs. Jarvis and rolled onto the floor with her, shielding her scrawny body with his.

"Get your paws off me, you looby," she shrieked, struggling under him.

His response had been instinctive. Mortars. Grenades. But there could not be shells falling in the middle of the old neighborhood, could there?

"It may not be safe. What was that noise?"

"Who knows or cares? Get off me now!"

Charles could not remember the last time a woman lay beneath him. Mrs. Jarvis was certainly not a candidate of choice, and her screams rang in his ears until he thought they might bleed. Charles put his hand over Mrs. Jarvis's open mouth, only to be rewarded with a vicious nip. "Shh. I hear someone coming."

The stairs creaked ominously and Charles tucked the woman between his body and the wall. He'd keep the damn harpy safe even if she didn't appreciate it.

"Hullo? Captain Cooper, are you in there?"

A woman.

"I don't like the looks of this place, miss. It smells dreadful."

Another one. Neither one of them sounded like Mrs. Evensong.

"Hush, Kathleen. You're such a snob. I'm sure those who are less fortunate are delighted to have a sound roof over their heads. Sir? Are you decent? May I come in?"

Holy mother of God. Charles unclamped Mrs. Jarvis's mouth and braced himself for her bloodcurdling yelp. He did not have long to wait.

"Help me! He's gone mad!"

Charles leaped to his feet just as his door pushed open. Mrs. Jarvis remained on the floor, frantically pulling her skirts down.

The women's eyes widened in shock as they took in Charles's little blunder. He brushed the dust from his new coat and tried to fix a smile on his face that would not frighten the young ladies. If they'd join Mrs. Jarvis by screaming along with her, he'd be deaf as well as blind for sure.

"C-Captain Cooper?"

The blonde was extraordinarily pretty, although she was as white as her ermine coat and matching muff that covered her hands. Charles wished there was a little pistol hidden inside it with which she could shoot him to put him out of his misery.

"Miss Stratton, I presume."

"Oh, Miss Louisa. He *can't* be the one. How can Mrs. Evensong have made such a mistake? She's supposed to be infallible," the little redhead said.

"Hush again, Kathleen. I'm sure there's an explanation. Isn't there?"

Her eyes were bright and golden brown and focused on his lips, waiting for him to explain. As if he could.

She was a golden girl from tip to toe. Miss Louisa Stratton looked like money, honey, and double cream. Charles had never seen anyone like her.

Mrs. Jarvis grabbed his bad knee as she dragged herself up. "He tried to rape me!"

Before Charles could protest, the golden goddess spoke. "Don't be absurd, my good woman. You are old enough to be his mother. You are not *that* sort, are you, Captain? I've always thought Oedipus to be a very repulsive myth. But if you're afflicted with that complex, I'm sure I can find you a good doctor. They are making all sorts of progress with the study of the human mind in Vienna, you know. We were there last spring, weren't we, Kathleen? The pastries were *wunderbar.*"

Mrs. Jarvis was right. He *had* gone mad. He needed a glass of white satin. Nay, a bottle.

"There was a loud noise," he said lamely.

"Oh yes. I'm afraid that was me—that is to say, my automobile. Something's gone wrong. A piston misfiring perhaps. We'll have to have the car towed to the local garage. There *is* a local garage, is there not?"

Charles limped to the smudged window and looked down. Keeping a safe distance, a dozen awestruck street urchins ringed Miss Stratton's smoking motorcar, but they wouldn't remain awestruck for long before one of them decided to remove a headlamp. He opened the window.

"Iffin any of ye little bleeders lay so much as one filthy finger on that car, ye'll find yourselves in a nasty jar."

"We's just inspectin' 'er, guv. No 'arm done," the leader of the little pack shouted back.

"See it stays that way, or none o' ye will live long enough to razzle-dazzle."

"Aye aye, Cap'n." The brat saluted him.

"Mrs. Jarvis, I do apologize for the misunderstanding," Charles said, returning to his more mellifluous tones.

She nodded, looking at him with pity, damn her. "'Twas the war, I expect. Some men come home off their onions. I reckon you're one of them."

"Indeed. Miss Stratton and—Kathleen, is it?"

"Yes, sir."

"I believe we should continue this conversation downstairs and make some arrangements for your conveyance. It will not be safe here for long."

Miss Stratton looked dreadfully out of place in his old lodgings and would stand out even more outside in the street. What was she thinking to drive here in that ridiculous vehicle wearing a white fur coat? He noted the goggles dangling from her neck like an ugly necklace. It was *she* who was off her onion.

"How did you find me?" he asked as they trudged down the stairs.

"I stopped at the Evensong Agency. The young man there gave me your direction."

Charles was somehow glad it wasn't Mrs. Evensong who'd betrayed him. He had come so far in life, but was almost right back where he'd started in this rackety building.

"I am staying there now. At Mount Street. Mrs. Evensong is tutoring me as to proper husbandly behavior, but I'm sure you can instruct me far better."

"Oh, I don't have the first idea what a *real* husband does. Maximillian has ruined me for any other man," Miss Stratton said sweetly. "He is entirely considerate of my feelings, always at my elbow ready to be helpful. We discuss art and history and philosophy and he takes my opinions as seriously as his own."

Aye. The girl was definitely off her onion.

Chapter

❧

4

*H*e did look promising in his stiff new clothes, Louisa thought. She hadn't expected the eye patch, but it gave him a rather dashing air.

Maximillian might have lost his eye in a fencing accident. He fenced divinely, all muscle, nimble on his booted feet, bare-chested and glowing with healthy, unusually aromatic perspiration. There was that intriguing little trail of dark hair that arrowed down below the waistband of his trousers—

But one instant of distraction, and tragedy struck. How brave he'd been. How stalwart. It was a shame the unfortunate event had occurred before Louisa met him, as she would have made an excellent nurse. Unruffled. Serene. Ready with encouraging words and caresses for her poor darling. But Maximillian would not have wanted her exposed to any unpleasantness.

Yes, that story would do very well. Louisa tucked both hands in her fur muff and shivered. It was cold out, and the mechanic was taking an age to hitch the car to his team of horses.

Captain Cooper had urged her to go home, which meant her suite at Claridge's at present. But she'd refused, seeing the job to the end, and Kathleen remained stubbornly by her side. Her maid was boring holes into the captain's back, examining every inch of him as he bent to help fasten a chain to the bumper of her poor little Cottereau.

"Do you like what you see?" Louisa hissed.

"He's not *my* husband now, is he? But I bet he's got a nice bum under that coat."

"I'll never find out." Louisa decided she could feel slightly sad about that. The captain was tall and well formed, his skin still bronzed from his time in Africa, his one visible eye the color of cornflowers. He was going gray at the temples, though, which was surprising for such a young man—he was twenty-seven, only a year older than she according to Mrs. Evensong's file.

"Really, have you thought this through? You're still on your honeymoon. Your aunt will put you in your parents' room. You'll be expected to be sharing a bed to beget little Norwiches."

Bother. It was ridiculous in a house the size of Rosemont that her parents had shared a bedroom. Everyone knew fashionable people simply didn't do such a thing, little Norwiches or not. "He can sleep in the dressing room on a cot."

"He may have other ideas about that, Miss Louisa. You saw what an animal he was with his landlady."

"He explained all that," Louisa said with impatience. "He reacted to the explosion, thinking it was a bomb or something. The man was heroic under fire in his attempt to save the woman from harm."

Kathleen sniffed. "Don't say I didn't warn you when he tosses you down on the floor at the least little noise. You'll be black and blue—you know you bruise easily, being so fair. I don't trust him. Did you hear how he spoke to those children? If he's a gentleman, my name isn't Kathleen Carmichael."

"Mrs. Evensong claims he went to Harrow. Don't you have a middle name?" How odd Louisa didn't know that—Kathleen had been with her since they were both twenty-one. Her own was Elizabeth, after her mother.

"No, Miss Louisa. One was enough. My parents had twelve children and they'd run out of names they liked by the time I came along."

Twelve children were a great many. Louisa had been an only child, not counting the proximity of her cousin Hugh in the nursery. It would have been fun to have had a real brother or a cousin who didn't torment her with impunity.

"How much longer do you think, Captain Cooper?" she called from Mrs. Jarvis's doorway. The least the woman could have done was offer them a cup of tea while they waited. But it probably would have been served in a dirty cup and taste like ditchwater. Louisa was very unimpressed with Mrs. Jarvis's establishment.

"We're about done, aren't we, Joe? Miss Stratton is staying at Claridge's Hotel. She'll expect to have her car delivered there tomorrow morning."

The man scratched his head with blackened fingers. "I don't know, sir. That's a French car. I may not have the parts. And iffin I do, it will be an expensive repair job."

"Do what you can then, but let Miss Stratton know as soon as possible. She'll have to make alternate travel plans."

Louisa was fairly sure that Charles Cooper whispered "Lord, I hope so" after his admonishment to the mechanic. Unsporting. She and Kathleen and the Cottereau had been inseparable since Louisa purchased the car in Paris after her original English mode of transportation tapped a recalcitrant brick wall. It was hardly her fault the brakes failed.

"Let me escort you ladies back to the hotel."

"Actually, Captain, Mrs. Evensong is expecting us for tea. I was supposed to meet you at her office for the first time this afternoon. But I couldn't wait." Louisa had wanted to see the real man in his native environment. She was now more confused than ever. Charles Cooper was a very odd sort of fellow, smooth one minute, scratchy the next.

"The best laid plans." He gave her a slow smile, and Louisa's heart did a little flip. His nose was not aristocratic, but his teeth were excellent. Impulsively she wound her arm through his.

"How far do you think we'll have to walk in this ghastly neighborhood before we come upon a hackney?"

"A little ways. Miss Kathleen, may I offer you my other arm?"

Well, that was charmingly done of him. He *was* a gentleman, no matter what Kathleen said.

They walked a few shabby blocks before they found a cabbie, who sighed at the great distance he'd have to drive them.

"Do you not wish to earn money, sir?" Louisa asked tartly. "What is this country coming to? Things have changed for the worse while I've been away. When I left last year, people still liked to eat, and one cannot do that without sufficient coin. Shall we find a more ambitious fellow?" she asked her companions.

"He's only trying to drive up his price, Miss Stratton. I'm sure he's as ambitious as the next driver. More so, probably, and you've given us away. How much will you charge us?"

The man named his price. "Highway robbery!" Louisa cried. People always took one look at her and tried to take advantage. But she'd be damned if she'd don burlap and sackcloth to throw them off the trail.

"Get in, Miss Stratton. You're attracting attention."

It was true. A few people had clustered on the corner to watch her argue with the jarvey. Louisa held fast to her muff, where her fat billfold was tucked into a pocket. She was an heiress, with not only a fur muff but a fur coat and a diamond pin in her veiled driving hat. She'd learned this past year to be careful, but all her good sense had deserted her today.

Perhaps it was doubly Captain Cooper's fault. She'd dressed to impress him, and it was difficult to think with his blue eye upon her.

"Very well," she said, raising her chin, and allowed him to lift her into the carriage.

She and Kathleen sat side by side as Charles Cooper sprawled opposite, his long legs inevitably taking up some of their space. He was so silent Louisa felt obligated to speak.

She didn't like silence. She'd had way too much of it growing up at Rosemont with no one to talk to and no one to listen. Quiet made her—nervous.

She searched for a neutral topic, something natural where Captain Cooper wouldn't think she was prying too much, when all Louisa really wanted to do was ask him a thousand questions. How had a decorated soldier wound up living is such a shithole? She wouldn't say *shit*, of course. She still had some vestiges of ladylike behavior left. Who had broken his nose? Was Africa worth visiting? Did he have a sweetheart stashed away somewhere?

She opened her mouth but Captain Cooper beat her to it. "You needn't worry. That cot is fine. I won't share a bedroom with you, Miss Stratton. Neither one of us would get much sleep."

Louisa felt her blush rise. "You have very acute hearing."

"I do. It's rather a miracle. A lot of soldiers go deaf. War is noisy. All that exploding ordnance."

"It's very quiet at Rosemont." Too damn quiet.

He shifted in his seat. "Doesn't matter. I don't sleep well."

"Are you troubled by bad dreams?" She'd tried to read Dr. Freud's very interesting book about dreams in the original German, with a German–English dictionary at hand, which really had not helped much.

His face was unreadable in the shadow of the cab. "You might say that."

"I can call upon the family doctor. He can come to Rosemont and give you something for your nerves."

"My nerves?" His voice was ice-cold.

"You know. To help you sleep," she said hurriedly. Men never liked to admit they had any weaknesses. "When you are unsettled. Cannot get something out of your head. Dr. Fentress was very useful when my aunt wouldn't let me have my debut. I had vexed her over something, I cannot remember what, and she punished me by canceling the whole thing. I couldn't sleep for days until Dr. Fentress came with his elixir." Oh, Louisa could remember perfectly well what she had done, but she wasn't about to tell this stranger. She could still smell the lilies before they'd been shoveled out the door. Just one whiff of lilies had made her sad ever since.

"Your *debut*."

She refused to flinch. "Yes. You must know how important it is for a girl to be fired off into society. One really cannot find a husband without the Season. Not that I want a husband *now*. I did then, though." Louisa had really wanted her freedom and money more than she wanted any man, two things Aunt Grace refused to grant her. As her principal guardian and trustee, Grace had discouraged every male within miles of Rosemont from setting foot on its doorstep. By necessity, Louisa had become very inventive in seeking them out instead.

For a while. And then the bars had dropped and she'd become a prisoner in her own home.

"Let me see if I understand you, Miss Stratton. You took drugs to help you sleep because you couldn't wear a fluffy white dress and dance all night and bag some rich nincompoop. Boo hoo."

When he put it that way, she did sound awfully spoiled. But spoiled was the very last thing she'd been. "You're a man—you wouldn't understand!"

"Miss Louisa," Kathleen cautioned.

"Hush, Kathleen. I have a perfectly good mind and I believe I'm allowed to express it, especially to an employee. And that is what you are, Captain. You'd best remember it."

Louisa expected a blast back, rather like what happened to her unlucky car. But the man's lips thinned and he said nothing.

There was that devilish silence again. "I've offered you help, and you have mocked me. That is not very gentlemanly of you."

"Ah, but your maid, Kathleen—Carmichael, isn't it?—is right, Miss Stratton. I'm no gentleman. And I have no idea what my arse looks like, but you are both welcome to inspect it at any time you wish. I am, after all, your employee."

Kathleen choked beside her. Heavens, the man had the ears of an elephant. Louisa would have to be careful in the future.

They were getting off to a very bad start. She should have been patient and waited to meet him at Mount Street over the tea tray, but patience was not her virtue. She'd exhausted it long ago.

Louisa was not going to let him goad her, however. "I shall keep that in mind. While we're on the subject, I won't return the favor. You are to keep your eyes and your hands to yourself unless I instruct you to show some minor affection in front of my family. Maximillian would never be indiscreet in public. *He* is a consummate gentleman."

"My eyes?"

The man could do more with two words than anyone she'd ever met.

"You know what I mean. I am truly sorry for your infirmity. How did you lose your eye?"

"I didn't lose it. It's still there."

"Well then," she said in somewhat confused triumph, "I was right."

"I'm sure you always are, Miss Stratton. You're paying me well enough to say so."

"I don't expect you to always agree with me," Louisa said, beginning to have an odd feeling in her chest. "You're a man."

"I am."

Well, that was that. Louisa would have to adjust to the silence all the way to Mount Street. She, Louisa Elizabeth Stratton, could not think of another thing to say.

Charles did not think he'd be able to go through with this, money be damned. The girl was impossible, bossy, a man-hater, and too pretty for her own good. Now that he'd gotten a better look at her—with his *one* eye—he could see that her mouth was too wide (*"The better to nag you with, my dear"*) and there was a witch's mark in its left corner, but she was still very attractive. Every time her fur coat flapped open, he could see her narrow waist and the hourglass shape of the rest of her that seemed to be all the rage. He wondered if she could breathe through her corset, then decided she'd had plenty of air with which to harangue him thus far.

He felt a little like a prize bull at the fair, only he wouldn't be getting the bonus of getting cozy with the cows once he'd won his blue ribbon. A day under Mrs. Evensong's roof had not been sufficient to rope him back into civilization, and he was making a hash of this husband business already, unless they were to be a bickering couple.

That he thought he could manage. This Maximillian sounded like a moony moron that bore no resemblance to anyone he knew, and Rosemont was bound to be perfectly awful. He'd probably break the china and piss in a corner before it was all done.

If only he'd found the courage to kill himself the other night, he would not be bumping knees in this poorly sprung carriage with Louisa Stratton and her outspoken maid. He'd always had a passion for redheads, when he'd felt passion. But somehow Kathleen's blond mistress appealed much more to his lower nature.

Charles wondered what the heiress would look like when her corset was unstrung. He pictured bright pink lines on milk-white skin, bountiful breasts bursting into his rough hands, her waist as small as a child's.

And then he saw himself lacing her back up, pulling the strings so tight she could barely move. Barely breathe. He would put his hand around that tiny waist and keep her still. He could do anything he wanted to her then, and she would be unable to resist. He'd pluck the pins from her pompadour and use her golden hair to guide her down—

He was a beast. Miss Stratton was not that kind of girl, and he wasn't that kind of man, was he? He'd never felt such unnatural desire in his life—to subdue. To control.

How odd that modern women spent a fortune on corsets to contort their bodies to such unnatural shapes. A few months in a Boer concentration camp would have whittled their waists down to size at no expense at all.

Charles shut his eyes. He could pretend to sleep until Mount Street. Maybe Miss Stratton was right. Charles would see this Dr. Fentress. Swallow bottles full of his elixir if it would make the nightmares stop and the days clearer. If he was to do without gin, he would need a bloody miracle.

Chapter

5

Thursday, December 3, 1903

*T*he next day, Charles was both ginless and lacking in any sort of miracle. The princess had kept the porters busy at Victoria Station. Charles did not understand how one woman could fill so many trunks. And how could they all have been stuffed in her little motorcar during her travels? But apparently Louisa had sent them along with her car by steamship across the Channel. The car, thank the powers that be, would remain in London until the proper parts were found for it.

Charles might not value his life, but he had no desire to end it in a ditch on the road to Rosemont, and he was grateful to sink into a somewhat tattered first-class compartment of the Chatham Line. The railroad company had the reputation of being a somewhat shaky enterprise, but at least its trains always arrived on time.

In Charles's case, he was not sure that was altogether a good thing. He'd gotten ahold of that magazine from

Mrs. Evensong yesterday after tea, had seen photographs of Rosemont's turrets and vast expanse of lawn running down to the sea. Charlie Cooper was going to be very much out of place.

He'd had hopes that he'd be left to himself on the train with the ladies in an adjacent compartment, but that was not to be. The maid Kathleen made a great show of taking out a book so as not to participate in the conversation between "husband" and "wife." Charles shut his eyes at the blur of gray sky and bare trees beyond the window, but he couldn't shut his ears. Louisa Stratton was chattering incessantly as she was wont to do.

"Chattin' Stratton," he mumbled.

"I beg your pardon?"

"Are you never silent? You're giving me the devil of a headache."

"I suppose I'm a bit nervous about going home," Louisa said, surprising him. "I haven't seen my family in over a year. And it's absolutely essential you understand the role you are to play. I thought we just might brush up on the details we discussed with Mrs. Evensong."

"Rembrandt. Louvre. You were the most beautiful girl I'd ever seen."

Her golden brows knit. "I'm sure I never told you to say that."

"It's my own invention. You want Max to be your devoted dog, don't you?"

"Not at all! I would never want a man who could be led around on a leash. Maximillian is much too much of a man to allow me to dominate."

Charles flashed back to his mental image of a near-naked Louisa, her creamy flesh encased by a rigid corset. Bound. Helpless. Perhaps with a gag over those lovely ever-mobile lips. He shifted in discomfort on the seat. What the hell was she doing to him?

"Fine. Then we will discount your looks. Did I marry you for your money?" Charles was sure this girl had been hotly pursued for her face and figure—the fortune was just a bonus.

"Maximillian has his own independent income. A substantial one."

"How did I earn it?"

Her tongue poked into the corner of her lush lips before she spoke. "You didn't. You inherited it."

"Just like you, then."

"Surely you know women are limited in their choices of profession," she said. "And in so many things. You men control the world, and a bloody mess you've made of it."

Louisa Stratton didn't know the half of it. "I cannot disagree. So, my income is enormous, because I've invested wisely and am a genius with numbers."

"Are you?"

"I was always good at maths. I could be, if I had any money to play around with. But I don't. You saw where I lived, Miss Stratton."

Louisa gave a delicate shudder. "Maximillian was raised in wealth in the French countryside."

"Some château or other, I believe you said."

"Château Lachapelle. It was once a monastery, and the Dark Monk is reputed to haunt the corridors."

Charles laughed. What a fantastic imagination the idiot heiress had. "You have been reading too much fiction. I don't believe in ghosts."

"Very well. You don't have to mention the monk if you don't want to. I just thought it added a soupçon of interest to your childhood. Your parents were English expatriates who ran away from arranged marriages. Very romantic."

A load of rubbish in Charles's opinion. "There's the tiniest glitch, Miss Stratton."

"You must remember to call me Louisa! We've been married happily for months now."

"I don't speak French well, *Louisa*. I took it at school and pretty much left it there as well."

She waved a gloved hand. "Oh, that won't matter. We'll

just say your parents were eccentric and preferred to converse in their native tongue. You were tutored at the château. No one in my family will quiz you—they loathe the French as all good English people do. A few days in Paris to shop is one thing, but my aunt Grace never permitted me to go abroad even for that."

"Poor little rich girl."

Louisa's cheeks turned pink. "You may think you know all about me, Mr. Cooper—"

"Max," he reminded her. "We're so happily married."

"—but you don't, *Maximillian*. I'm not saying I've had a horrible life—I know I've had advantages some can only dream about. But it was not a bed of roses at Rosemont."

Charles laughed again. "Quite the turn of phrase, dear wife."

Her blush deepened, but she soldiered on. "You collect art, and the château is filled with wonderful things."

"Like the Dark Monk and my eccentric parents?"

"I'm quite sure I said they were dead, too—didn't I, Kathleen?"

The maid did not look up from her book. "As doornails. So your aunt wouldn't write to them."

"Just so. While you are an esthete, you are also an athlete."

"You rowed her on the Seine on a moonlit night, Mr. Norwich," Kathleen said, turning a page.

More rubbish. Where did girls get such ideas? From unrealistic romances like Kathleen was reading, no doubt. Charles had never rowed anything or anyone in his life—now if she had him bowling a cricket match or playing rugby, he was her man.

"And what is the story behind my deformity? An oar in the eye?" He had suffered damage to his left eye when a shell exploded rather too near him. Once he'd come to, the doctors told him his vision might improve with time, but Charles saw no evidence of it so far.

"I don't suppose you fence."

"I do not." He could hack his way through underbrush well enough, but the army had given up its swords for the deadly precision of automatic weaponry. Maxim machine guns were all the rage on the veldt.

Louisa was thinking, her pink tongue curled into the corner of her lips again. Charles had noted the habit and was hoping that tongue might be persuaded to do something else. "Do you box?"

He'd scrapped with his brothers growing up, and had held his own at school. "Yes, although I'm not one for the Queensberry rules."

"Well then. You received an unlucky blow in the ring. That's when you broke your nose, too."

Charles kept his hand from touching the bridge of his nose, flattened courtesy of his brother Tom for some childhood infraction he couldn't recall. "Won't your aunt think I'm a savage?"

"Oh, no. Her son Hugh fancies himself quite a pugilist. He made a name for himself at Oxford. But if he challenges you, you must decline. I have a horror of the sport." Louisa wrinkled her nose. "You gave up all that violence for me when we married."

"No fighting. What else is forbidden?" Charles wished he was taking notes. He had a feeling the list was going to be a long one.

"You may not smoke. You *don't* smoke, do you?"

"Filthy habit."

"I'm so glad you agree. I understand it's very difficult to give up once one's begun. No drinking to excess, but I believe Mrs. Evensong covered that with you already. You must keep your wits about you at all times. My family is . . . difficult, and though they may test a saint's sobriety, it is vital you don't let them send you over the edge."

What had Mrs. Evensong told Louisa? Not too much, he hoped. He'd enjoyed his pint in the past, but no more so than any other bloke. It wasn't until he'd come home from the war that he'd let his demons loose and tried to drink himself into welcome oblivion.

"You are to ignore Cousin Isobel if she seems a bit too . . . friendly. Isobel still thinks there's a chance for her to make a good match and will pump you about your bachelor friends. Make up something amusing but vague. She and Mama came to England from New York to marry titled gentlemen, though neither one succeeded."

"That's why you are not Lady Louisa."

"Correct. Mama fell in love with Papa, and that was that. Of course, he had a fortune and didn't need hers, so my American grandparents were somewhat mollified."

"Are they still alive?"

Louisa shook her head. "They died when I was fourteen—a boating accident, like my parents. My relatives are very unlucky on water. I'm almost afraid to take a bath."

Dear God. The thought of Louisa Stratton wet and naked in a porcelain tub was almost too much to contemplate. Charles took a deep breath.

"So, no fighting, drinking, smoking, and no flirting with Cousin Isobel. Have I got it all right?"

"It's a start. We'll have to be nimble as we go—the sands are always shifting at Rosemont."

"Well, it is on the coast."

"Why, Captain Cooper! I believe you've made a joke."

So he had. A faint ray of sunshine seemed to be piercing his gloom. How could he fail to appreciate the improvement in his circumstances? Once the month was over, he'd have a substantial nest egg for his brothers and a harmless adventure with a very pretty girl to remember while he spent eternity in hell.

The train meandered through chocolate-box villages and gentle hills, Louisa talking all the way. Charles was getting used to her nervous energy. She seemed to have an opinion on everything and was not shy about expressing it. Poor Maximillian Norwich would never have a moment's peace.

The real Maximillian would have strategies to quiet his voluble wife. He might give her a smoldering look across a room, inveigle a way to get her alone and kiss her until she was witless. Finger that intriguing mole at the corner of her mouth that her pink tongue always touched when she was thinking. Capture one of her demonstrative hands and place his lips on her palm. Nip a jeweled earlobe, breathe the scent of crushed violets from her long white neck.

"Captain Cooper—Maximillian—have you heard a word I've said?"

"Of course. I shall endeavor to do everything you say." That was easy enough, wasn't it? He had nothing better to do. But he had a nagging feeling he'd missed something important.

"Now, tell me about *your* family. I've told you all about mine."

Had she? He couldn't very well tell her he'd stopped paying attention some miles back.

"There's not much to say."

"Come now, don't be shy. Just because *you* were not brought up in a château doesn't mean I shall judge you."

Charles could not picture ermine-coated Louisa Stratton in the humble kitchen that served as sitting room and occasional bedroom to his family. "My parents are dead. They both were employed by Alexander's Pottery Works. My brothers and their wives work there now."

"Oh. Pottery?"

"I don't expect Alexander dishes are on your dining table at Rosemont. George Alexander produces unembellished, practical items, from teapots to chamber pots. For the lower classes. Just like me."

He caught Kathleen's brief flare of triumph across the seat.

"I—I thought you went to Harrow," Louisa said doubtfully.

"And so I did. George sponsored me—took me right off the line and paid for my education." Tom and Fred had resented Charles's elevation. Ah yes. His nose—he remembered now.

"I have nieces and nephews, but I'm not close to my family anymore. I probably couldn't tell you all their names if you put a gun to my temple. I was away a long while."

"I see."

"I hope you do, Miss Stratton. I may not turn out to be the right man for your job. Maximillian and I don't have much in common—I'm bound to put my foot wrong somewhere. I've not visited too many châteaux or museums."

Try none.

There was her tongue peeking out again. He waited for her to tell him to get off at the next station. The silence lengthened—in fact, this was the longest time in their brief acquaintance that Louisa was not talking his ear off.

"You *were* an officer."

"I rose on merit. And have a chest full of medals, for what they're worth."

Not much.

Louisa sighed. "Well, I'm sure you'll try your best. Everyone swears by Mrs. Evensong, so she must have confidence in you. She simply raved about you, you know. I confess I *did* wonder why you were agreeable to do this. I was looking for an actor. Someone with experience. You don't strike me as one who will stick to the script."

"A little improvisation might come in handy. I'll try not to disappoint you."

"Fingers crossed then." Louisa gave him a bright smile. "We get off in three more stops. I expect Robertson will be there to meet us."

Kathleen dropped her book to the floor. Charles bent to pick it up and handed it back to her, but not before reading the green and gold cover. A CHECKED LOVE AFFAIR. *Spare me.*

"Thank you, Mr. Norwich."

"Think nothing of it. Who is Robertson?"

"Our chauffeur, though I think he doesn't get to drive the Daimler very often. Aunt Grace hates it. But all that will change now that I'm back home."

Charles didn't trust her gleeful smile. "What is your fascination with automobiles, Louisa?"

"I don't know, really. I do so love the wind in my face."

"And the bugs and dust," Kathleen added. "You'd best let Robertson do the driving, Miss Louisa. I hear he's thought of putting in his notice. No man likes to feel useless."

"You *hear*? Did a little bird tell you, Kathleen? So that explains all the mysterious letters you received from Rosemont. I swear, you got more mail than I did, even with Aunt Grace hounding me at every turn." Louisa turned to him and winked.

The redheaded maid put her book in her carpetbag and snapped the clasp with finality. "As far as I know, it's not against the law to write letters."

"And if it was, you'd do it anyway. Do you drive, Cap—Maximillian?"

"I have not had the opportunity." He'd been perfectly satisfied with horses all his life, and his cavalry career confirmed his expertise.

"I'll teach you then."

Kathleen snorted and looked out the window.

"It will be fun!" Louisa insisted. "There's nothing like the freedom of the open road."

Charles would reserve his opinion on that. There had been a time when he'd sought freedom—from George Alexander's well-meaning mentorship and his family's resentment. He'd turned down the chance to go to university for the army, and he now wondered if his quest for independence had not backfired rather spectacularly.

Everyone knew war was hell, but Charles had not expected to plummet so deep into the devil's environs.

Louisa concentrated on teasing Kathleen about her chauffeur for the rest of the journey. The train rolled into one more charming station after the other until it got to Stratton Halt. A flock of seagulls that had been perched on the red tile roof of the tiny whitewashed building squawked and circled away as the train pulled in.

As soon as Charles stepped onto the platform, the scent of salt water enveloped his senses. He'd not been a good sailor during any of his transports, so there was no danger of following in Louisa's relatives' footsteps. In any event, it was coming on winter, not ideal for testing the waters.

But he'd always appreciated the sea, its vastness and power. He would be seeing it safely behind glass soon. Rosemont was set atop a white cliff overlooking its own shingle, according to *The English Illustrated Magazine*. Louisa may have had her reasons to run away from home, but it hadn't been for lack of a view.

A couple of men and a horse-drawn wagon were waiting to collect their luggage, and a young man in livery, presumably Robertson, stood near a dark green Daimler. If Kathleen was expecting a kiss from her sweetheart, she must have been disappointed. Apart from a tip of his cap to the ladies, he was all that was proper, helping the men with the trunks in efficient silence before he got back behind the wheel.

It was not an effusive welcome for any of them, and Charles felt a prickle of unease. Even Chattin' Stratton seemed subdued. What exactly had he got himself into?

Chapter

❦

6

$\mathscr{L}$ouisa had wished for flags and flowers and a little crowd at the train station. She'd read of such welcomes when heiresses arrived from their honeymoons, but Aunt Grace would not condone such frivolity. Just as well, really. If she ever came back from a real honeymoon, that greeting would be special.

"Good God."

They had finally turned into the drive, Robertson driving far more slowly than Louisa ever would. She tried to see Rosemont with Captain Cooper's eyes. Eye. She'd have to be careful regarding his injury. It was just like her to ask a person in a wheelchair if they'd like to go for a walk in the garden—she meant to be kind, but her foolish tongue constantly tripped her up.

To her two eyes, the house looked as tall and forbidding as it ever did. It was built in 1856 by her grandfather, George Stratton, a banker who had delusions of grandeur more suited to a peer of the realm. Of brick construction, it was an odd mix of Gothic and classical, with pitched roofs and turrets and too many windows to wash. Snarling gargoyles perched on every peak and pediment. When she was a little girl, she had named them all.

"Home sweet home," she said lightly.

"It looks like a prison. Or an asylum."

"There are plenty of inmates within who would argue they are as honest and sane as you and I." And they would be lying, Louisa thought. "It looks nicer in the summer when the roses climb over the façade. Rosemont, you see. We are missing the mountain, but my grandfather was very fond of his roses. The aspect is lovely, don't you think? But it was still a lonely place to live in."

The gray-green sea was flat today, but Louisa remembered when it roiled. She took a deep breath of salty air. "It's too cold to swim now, of course, but perhaps we can walk along the beach later once we get settled." The car rolled into the courtyard, and in less than half a minute, the staff emerged from the front door and lined up. Beside her, Captain Cooper gave an audible gulp.

"They're all here to meet you, Maximillian," Louisa whispered. "Begin as you mean to go on."

"What in hell does that mean?"

"Hush. Maximillian doesn't use vulgar language in the presence of a lady. You must accept their deference as if you're used to it. Remember the château staff attended to your every whim, not that you were hard to please. But don't be *too* friendly—the servants will think less of you. Don't be too cold, either. I never would have married a snob."

"I'll aim for 'just right' then. Goldilocks would have had a regular field day breaking beds and chairs in a pile this size."

Captain Cooper had seemed weary on the trip, but suddenly his chin lifted and spine stiffened as he climbed out of the car. He extended a hand to her to help her down and she gave it a gentle squeeze. "Showtime. Break a leg! Good afternoon, everyone!" she said with false cheer. "I'm so pleased to be home." Louisa clung to the captain's arm as an affectionate—but not *too* affectionate—new wife would. "May I present my husband, Mr. Maximillian Norwich?"

Louisa performed the necessary introductions and accepted the earnest congratulations. Several of the servants were unfamiliar to her, but Griffith, the butler who'd been here since her grandfather's day, provided assistance. Captain Cooper nodded and smiled in a most dignified manner, not showing too many teeth. He made a striking impression in his new clothes. Aunt Grace would not be able to fault the man on his fashionable appearance.

"How fares my aunt, Griffith?"

The butler clucked. "Not well, Miss Louisa, not well. Oh! I should say Mrs. Norwich. I daresay that will take me a little to get used to. Mrs. Westlake has not left her bed this age. She's most anxious you go straight to her apartments to see her, once you've refreshed yourselves, of course."

"And my cousin. Is he about?"

"In London, madam. On bank business. We expect him back any day."

Well, that was one good thing. Louisa did not relish the prospect of Hugh inspecting Maximillian Norwich just yet.

"Lulu, darling!"

The man at her side twitched. "*Lulu*? Really?"

Louisa stifled her groan and urge to elbow Captain Cooper for his mockery. Isobel flew out the front door, dripping in pearls and trailing sleeves and scarves. Louisa found herself embraced in a quantity of silk heavily scented with patchouli. She stifled a sneeze, too.

"Is this divine creature your husband? I quite see why you eloped, dear heart. What shoulders!" Isobel was actually running a hand over one of them while Captain Cooper looked somewhat ill at ease. "I am Lulu's second cousin, Isobel Crane. *So* delighted to meet you. Now, you must tell me exactly how you charmed her. We'd given up that any man could do so."

"Isobel, do let go of Maximillian; you'll bruise him. We'll have plenty of time to talk later. I'm sure my husband wants to see our rooms before we go to Aunt Grace. Griffith, where did Mrs. Lang put us?" The housekeeper had not been present in the line of employees.

"In your parents' room, Mrs. Norwich. Mrs. Lang wished me to apologize for her. Her mother's funeral was yesterday and she is not yet back."

"Goodness, how awful." Louisa wasn't sure if she was commenting over the death or being forced to share a bedroom with Captain Cooper.

"Cot," Cooper muttered.

"Shh. I'll see to it, if Mrs. Lang hasn't already. She does tend to cover all the bases." Louisa didn't much like Mrs. Lang, but she recognized the woman was an excellent housekeeper.

They trooped up the front steps behind Griffith, passing into the enormous entrance hall. An arrangement of hot-house flowers stood on the center table. Louisa had spent much of her time growing up hiding in the conservatory, and she recognized the plants as Rosemont's own—she'd tended them herself. "Lovely," she said to the butler.

"Your aunt Grace did them herself to welcome you home."

Louisa was surprised. It was not like Grace to be crafty or kind. "Got out of her bed, did she?"

"No, Mrs. Norwich. Everything was brought up to her and then carried down."

The Chinese urn weighed a ton, even empty. "How annoying for the servants. I'll be happy to do the next one. It will be time for pine boughs and holly soon, I think."

"Yes, madam. May I say how delighted we all are to have you home for Christmas. Last year just wasn't the same without you."

It hadn't been the same for her, either. She and Kathleen had dined on roast duck and champagne in a French country inn, warm and snug in the charming little dining room.

There had been no interminable Christmas lunch with twenty courses and Aunt Grace giving her the gimlet eye.

"I hope you and Mrs. Lang will help me when it comes time to get presents for the new staff, Griffith. There are quite a few new faces."

The butler cleared his throat. "Yes, madam. Your aunt insisted on replacing those staff members she felt were inefficient."

Grace really had no right to do so now that Louisa was officially in charge. But how had Louisa exercised her authority? By running away.

"Well, thank goodness you're still here. I don't know what Rosemont would do without you."

"You'd all manage, I'm sure." But Griffith looked pleased with the praise. "But speaking of presents, we have a small wedding gift for you and Mr. Norwich from the staff." Griffith snapped his gloved fingers. There was no noise, but a footman raced in with a very large beribboned box. The servants had followed them into the hallway and stood expectantly.

Captain Cooper stared. "A *small* gift?"

"Oh, Griffith! You shouldn't have! How very kind of you all. Help me open it, Maximillian. Darling."

"Of course, Louisa. Darling." The captain pulled one end of the silver ribbon while Louisa pulled the other. They tussled with the box top. Inside a cloud of tissue was an ornate ceramic planter.

"To pot one of your orchids, Mrs. Norwich. We know how you love your flowers."

"It's lovely." Louisa stifled her impulse to kiss the old butler on his cheek. The impropriety of it would horrify him. "I cannot wait to fill it. Thank you all so very much."

There was a smattering of polite applause. Everyone had contributed out of their hard-earned pay, Griffith more than his share, no doubt. Louisa was sure Aunt Grace was not a generous employer and resolved to do something about that as soon as possible.

"You needn't accompany us up the stairs, Griffith. I know my way. Come along, Maximillian, dear."

"Yes, Louisa, dear."

Louisa looked over her shoulder. The captain was wearing a deceptively meek expression. That wouldn't do at all. Maximillian was forceful, always in command, except of course when he deferred to her superior sensibilities.

"Stop that," she hissed.

"Stop what?"

"Looking like that—so, so—milksoppy."

"Is there such a word?"

"You know what I mean."

"Yes, dear."

Oh, this was not going to be easy. Louisa rued for the hundredth time that she'd ever created the impossibly charming, impossibly perfect Maximillian Norwich. What man could ever live up to him? Certainly not Charles Cooper, who seemed determined to drive her the slightest bit crazy.

She passed by her old bedroom with regret and continued around corner after corner to the end of the hall. The double doors to her parents' suite were open. More flowers graced the sitting room mantel and tabletops, and a lively fire warmed the room. The cream and gray wallpaper was new, and the furniture had been reupholstered in dull grayish jacquard fabric that reflected the present color of the water. Not very cheerful. Louisa sensed Aunt Grace's grim decorative hand. She walked to the bank of windows and set the new planter down on the sill. "I never get tired of watching the waves."

"Impressive."

The captain had come up behind her, his single word tickling the back of her neck.

"Yes, isn't it? This suite has a sea view from all the rooms, even the bath."

"I trust the seagulls won't tell any tales when I'm scrubbing away."

Louisa had a quick mental flash of a burnished man lazing in the bathtub—his chest slick with silver beads of water, his head thrown back and eyes closed—and shook it out of her head. She was not going to see any of Captain Cooper's exposed brown skin if she could help it, no matter how curious she was. "You can close the shutters for privacy if you like."

"I don't think so. The view's too beautiful."

Louisa nodded. "We can agree on that at least. But you mustn't be *too* agreeable. No more of this "Yes, dear" nonsense. I would not respect a man who doesn't stand up for himself, and neither will my aunt. She already thinks I'm much too headstrong and need the firm hand of some man. But that's nonsense. Maximillian and I have an equal partnership."

"Do we indeed? That's not very likely, particularly for two spoiled only children. I grew up in a castle, after all."

"It was a château, and I wasn't spoiled!"

"Oh, come now. You grew up in all this splendor. I'll have to drop bread crumbs like Hansel and Gretel to find my way back here."

"I can draw you a map."

"I may take you up on that. My entire family lived in a cottage half the size of this room."

It was true that the sitting room was very large. The bedroom was even larger. Louisa supposed she should get the inspection over with. The door to it was set flush into the gray-painted paneling. Really, if she was truly married, she'd feel like she lived in a battleship. If she stayed in these rooms for any length of time, they'd have to be done over. What had Aunt Grace been thinking?

Louisa knew very well. Apart from the flowers, which the servants had probably placed, this sitting room did not say "Welcome home."

The bedroom was at least as her parents had left it, its furnishings quite faded from years of morning sun. She had only the dimmest memories of cuddling on the glazed chintz window seat with her mother, and even those memories were more likely wistful wishes. Louisa bustled through to her mother's dressing room, the cupboards standing open and empty, and threw open the bathroom door. The black-and-white tiles sparkled, but she had no interest in refreshing herself just yet.

"God blind me! The tub's the size of a swimming pool."

"Never mind that. We are searching for your cot, Cap—Maximillian." It was going to be dreadfully hard to remember to call him by the correct name. She should have practiced more on the train.

Another door led to her father's dressing room. *Dressing room* was a misnomer. It was really a small bedroom, complete with a single bed, a fireplace, and a comfortable leather club chair beside it. It had its own exit to the hallway, so the captain would not have to wander through the bath, her dressing room, and her bedroom and catch her in a state of dishabille. A stack of books lay on the bedside table. Had her father ever read them? Louisa knew so little about her parents' habits.

Captain Cooper sat down on the mattress and bounced. "Hard. But better than sleeping in a trench. And you'll be far enough away so my restlessness won't disturb you."

Ah yes. His nightmares. She would have to send for Dr. Fentress. "I'm glad it suits. I really haven't spent time in here in years and had forgotten what was in this room. The doors have always been locked."

"How old were you when you lost your parents?"

"Four." She had her mother's jewelry, of course, but nothing else. Aunt Grace had stripped the rooms of all personal effects. Were her parents' things in the attics? How nice it would be to imagine her mother in one of her Worth dresses.

"So young. My mother died when I was fifteen."

"Is your father still living?"

"No."

Captain Cooper did not elaborate, and Louisa left the

unhappy subject alone. They were both orphans, and Maximillian Norwich was as well. Killing off inconvenient make-believe people was not difficult, but living with real loss was.

"Our trunks should come up any minute. Do you wish to use the—" A real wife might not be shy about her husband washing and doing other things involving plumbing, but she was not a real wife.

"Ladies first. I'll wait here." He folded his long body into her father's leather chair and shut his eye.

Good heavens. She hoped he didn't hear her as she relieved herself. To make sure, she turned on the taps and hummed. It was a bit early for a Christmas carol, but she had never kept the rules of Advent and would not now. In her opinion, all those mournful hymns were best left unsung.

After a few rounds of "Good King Wenceslas," she washed her hands and face and checked her teeth for any remnants of their lunch on the train. It couldn't be put off any longer. It was time to see Aunt Grace.

But when she returned to her father's dressing room, she found her "husband" sound asleep in the chair, snoring softly at regular intervals. Louisa didn't have the heart to wake him up—the past few days had been exhausting for her, too. Tiptoeing out of the room, she decided to make his excuses to her aunt. A few hours' delay would make no difference. Captain Cooper was hers for the whole month, and would have plenty of time to suffer under Aunt Grace's gorgon-like stare.

Chapter

7

The blue velvet drapes were closed against the thin afternoon sunshine, but the room did not smell of illness or pending death. Aunt Grace sat up straight in bed in a lacy bedjacket, her reading glasses slipping down her nose, her faded blond hair rolled up neatly. A pile of society newspapers were littered across the counterpane. She set the *Tatler* down and stared over her lenses, her dark eyes sharp.

"Ah, niece! So nice to have you back with us after all this time. I suppose we must put an announcement of your marriage in the papers. It is really quite shocking that we have not done so already. I imagine they'll want to interview you, too, though of course we will shun the publicity. What has it been now—almost four months of wedded bliss?" She peered into the gloom behind Louisa. "Where is your young man?"

Oh dear. Louisa hadn't planned on announcements or interviews. "He sends his regrets, Aunt Grace. I'm afraid his old injury is troubling him."

"Injury? What injury?"

"I may have neglected to mention it. His eye was damaged in a youthful boxing match and I'm afraid he gets dreadful headaches sometimes. Travel has been a strain for him."

"You've not gone and shackled yourself to some weakling, have you, Louisa? From your letters, I was under the impression Mr. Norwich was perfection itself."

"Maximillian *is* perfect, truly. I could not ask for a better husband."

"Your loyalty does you no credit if the man is unworthy of you and your fortune. All this nonsense about art. What kind of man spends all day looking at pictures in museums? He's not a molly, is he?"

Louisa choked back a laugh. Captain Cooper was definitely not effeminate in any way. "Of course not. He collects art for his château and is regarded as quite an expert in certain circles."

"I suppose you'll want to settle in France then and leave me the running of Rosemont."

Well, that didn't take long. "I'm not sure what our plans are." It suited Louisa to be evasive. If all went according to plan, she'd dislodge Grace and Hugh and make Rosemont her own at last, or at the very least be back on the Continent next year enjoying her freedom. "And I shouldn't like to tax you, Aunt Grace. Hugh wrote that you've not been well."

Her aunt waved a white hand, her diamond wedding rings glittering. She had married the younger brother of a viscount, although the marriage had not lasted long before the man got lucky and died. "Oh, pooh. A few fainting spells here and there. It was my own fault—I flirted with a new diet for a little while. One hates to lose one's figure as one ages, as you will one day find out if your reckless behavior doesn't lead you to an early grave. Dr. Fentress has given me an iron tonic and I'm getting stronger every day."

Louisa curbed her reckless tongue. "I'm glad to hear it,

but it's time you took care of yourself. Perhaps a smaller house would suit you better."

"A smaller house? What nonsense! Rosemont has been in my care for over twenty years. You'll not find so much as a speck of dust under your bed. I hope you do not think I've shirked my duty."

Grace was certainly not crawling under furniture with a duster herself. Louisa did not want to argue quite yet with her aunt, although it was clear she was spoiling for a fight. The woman had never met anyone she hadn't tried to dominate, and for far too long she'd intimidated Louisa. But no more. Louisa was twenty-six years old, practically ancient. She'd crammed a lot of living into the past year of independence and was not about to cave under Grace's scrutiny.

"I don't want to tire you out, Aunt Grace. We can talk tomorrow."

"Tomorrow! Why, I've arranged for a welcome-home dinner for you tonight. I've asked Dr. Fentress, the Merwyns, Mr. Baxter, and a few others. I hope your husband's headache clears up—everyone is just dying to meet him."

Damn. Louisa had hoped for more time before she threw Charles Cooper into the brine of the Rosemont social sea. Mr. Baxter was her man of business at the bank. He was not going to make some sort of legal fuss about her marriage, was he? She hadn't thought to ask Mrs. Evensong to forge a marriage certificate for her, not that the woman seemed likely to participate in a real fraud. "Oh, you shouldn't have gone to the trouble. Are you well enough to come down to dinner?"

"Of course I am! I hope you can say the same. It's not as if you're fresh off the boat," Grace said. "You spent several days in London at Claridge's, didn't you? Hugh heard you were driving around in your awful little car frightening the horses."

Hugh. Louisa had made a lucky escape there if he was in London and hadn't tried to see her. It would have been awkward to produce Maximillian at the dock when she hadn't even met him yet.

"Yes, we stayed in town for a few days. Maximillian had business to attend to." Louisa had seen the tattered journals he'd tucked under his arm when he left his boarding house, and she was curious about them. They were probably buried beneath his new clothes in his trunk, but it wouldn't be sporting of her to go digging for them.

Would it?

Louisa acknowledged she found Captain Cooper to be a bit mysterious, and it wasn't only because of his eye patch. He'd easily confessed to his humble roots, so his past was clear enough, but there was something—

"Are you listening to me, Louisa? Either you're chattering like a magpie or off in your own little world. I swear you will be the death of me yet."

No such luck. "I beg your pardon, Aunt Grace. I was remembering Monte Carlo."

"Gambling with all those foreigners. How vulgar. What about Monte Carlo?" Grace asked crossly.

"Oh, nothing of importance. I shall see you tonight." Louisa bent to give her aunt a reluctant peck on the cheek and then made her escape. She didn't return to her parents' suite but to her own rather humble girlhood bedroom. Things were exactly as she left them last fall, a silver hairbrush black with tarnish on her dressing table and a stray bit of ribbon sticking up from a drawer. So much for Grace overseeing domestic perfection.

Louisa's small dressing room held dresses seasons out of date. Aunt Grace had said it was a waste to buy new clothes when Louisa never went anywhere except to church. She had more or less lived under house arrest until her twenty-fifth birthday, going only to the home of the elderly Merwyns for the occasional dinner. There were plenty of people under her own roof, so she she'd never lacked for company—just *select* company.

She'd give all these dresses to Kathleen to sell. Louisa

had lots of elegant Parisian clothes now and would be spoiled for choice tonight. But damn. A dinner party to ready herself for, and ready Captain Cooper, too. She really had to think of him as Maximillian, and was wishing she'd named her husband something simple.

Like Charles.

She wandered the twisting corridor and opened the door to her sitting room. Charles Cooper was in his shirtsleeves, both stockinged feet on the gray sofa. He had the illustrated art history book Mrs. Evensong had given him across his lap, but he rose instantly. "Where have you been?"

"Do sit down. I went to see my aunt. You'd fallen asleep, and I didn't want to disturb you."

"You should have woken me up. What must she think?"

"She thinks you had a headache from traveling."

He looked as though she'd insulted his manhood. "From a few hours on a train? What a poor sort of fellow I'd be."

"I blamed it on your eye, if you must know. I didn't want her to be surprised when she meets you later and have her ask rude questions about it. She can be very . . . formidable."

"Is that your way of saying she's a right bitch?"

Louisa grinned. "What a way with words you have, though Maximillian would never use such a pejorative."

"I figured she had to be a dragon if she drove you across the Channel."

"She likes to have her own way, and so do I. Our relationship became more difficult as I grew older. She wanted me to marry my cousin Hugh, and when I refused, things went from bad to worse."

"So I'll have competition." He waggled a dark eyebrow.

"Of course you won't! We're already married."

"Somehow I don't think that will stop your cousin from paying you compliments. Marriages can be dissolved, you know. Especially ours, as it doesn't really exist."

"Which reminds me. My banker is coming to dinner

tonight, along with several other exalted personages that Aunt Grace has invited. I'm afraid we're about to have our trial by fire."

Not a flicker of emotion crossed the captain's face. "I'm ready. A whole army brought up our trunks and unpacked everything. That's what woke me up."

"Are you? I'm not. I'd hoped to have a few more days to prepare you. Be wary of Mr. Baxter. He's been in Aunt Grace's pocket for years. Something fishy is going on with my bank, and I plan on asking him about it."

"I thought you have control of your inheritance now."

"I do. But everything goes to Mr. Baxter first, and then he's responsible for making deposits to my account. There's not as much there as should be."

Captain Cooper shrugged. "Some investments lose money."

"I know that! I'm not some empty-headed nitwit."

"No one said you were. Well, if we are to impress the masses tonight, who gets first dibs on the bath?"

Louisa knew she was blushing. "You go first. I want to visit the kitchens. I'll have some tea and sandwiches sent up. Or do you want a whiskey for courage?"

Captain Cooper closed the book. "No whiskey. Wasn't that one of the rules?"

"*I'd* like one," Louisa said.

"None for you, either. We've got to keep our stories straight. A moderate amount of wine at dinner will have to do."

"I suppose you're right. We keep country hours, here, Captain. Dinner will be at six. Oh! I really *am* a nitwit!"

"Why so?"

"You haven't a valet. Maximillian Norwich must have a valet."

"Don't you remember? The poor soul—Antoine, I believe—broke his leg climbing all those stairs at Château La Whatsis right before we were ready to sail. He is recuperating."

"Lachapelle. You're rather good at this, aren't you? Thinking on your feet."

"Some might call it lying, Miss Stratton. I should call you out."

"You might not win. I'm very good with a pistol."

He looked startled. "Are you really?"

Louisa nodded. "Papa had a gun collection." She wasn't going to tell him *why* she'd found it necessary to familiarize herself with it.

"You are full of surprises, my dear. Off you go. Find me a valet in your travels, although I'm sure between the two of us we can manage to get me dressed. I take it all I need to do is turn on the taps for hot water?"

"Yes. Rosemont has all the modern conveniences."

"What a treat. *À bientôt,* Louisa."

"You don't speak French, Maximillian."

"Surely a word or two would not go amiss, *ma belle.*" He winked and gave her a very warm smile.

Oh dear. Charles Cooper was turning into Maximillian Norwich right before her eyes and she wasn't sure she had the fortitude to resist her "husband."

Chapter

❦

8

Louisa had found a ruddy-cheeked young footman who had made Charles as presentable as possible—which, Charles had to admit, was very. The mirror told him he'd never looked more elegant. Hell, he'd never been elegant in his life, not even in uniform.

Elegance wouldn't get him very far with his brothers. If they saw him now, they'd howl with laughter, then decide to beat him up for rising above his station again. Though they were all much older now—maybe bloodshed wouldn't be called for. In any event, it was this faux elegance that would keep them comfortable in the future—not only would they have Charles's salary, but they could sell off all the posh clothes.

Charles twisted a worn gold signet ring Mrs. Evensong had thoughtfully provided in his Norwichian trousseau. There was a horned bull and sheaves of wheat, indicating what he hadn't a clue. A Latin phrase was inscribed beneath, too faint to make out. He'd have to ask Louisa what his family motto was—"Bread for All"? "Hung Like a Bull"? He chuckled at his inanity and gazed out the window as he waited for Louisa to emerge from her dressing room.

It was full dark, so he really couldn't see a thing, not even any stars over the sea. The vast blackness suited his mood. But soon he'd have to turn on the charm. He hoped he remembered how.

Louisa had listed the cast of characters who resided at Rosemont—not that he had kept them straight. There was the flirtatious middle-aged American cousin Isobel, who was more pathetic than predatory. The dragon aunt Grace and her feckless son Hugh, who apparently wasn't at home. A small crew of other relations and connections, all much older than Louisa. She'd said she had a lonely childhood, although with the number of people in the house, Charles could not imagine how.

He supposed one could find lots of quiet corners in a house this size to escape from annoying relatives. There had been no such escape for Charles when he came home from school holidays. After a while, he simply stayed at Harrow with the boys whose families were in India or some other exotic destination.

He'd had exquisite privacy in the modern bath this afternoon, with plenty of hot water piped in. The rest of the house was not as up-to-date, the furnishings harking back to the era in which it was built half a century ago. No one had thought to retrofit it with an electric circuit, either, as far as he could tell. The sitting room was lit by a profuse combination of oil lamps and candles, but it was still damned gloomy. Or so he thought until Louisa cleared her throat behind him and he turned.

She was in blond lace that matched her hair exactly. Unlike so many of the fashions of the day, the dress hadn't an extra ounce of flounce or trim, but it didn't need any. Louisa was poured into it, and its severe lines emphasized her narrow waist and abundant bosom. Her shoulders were bare, bands of puffed and pleated lace serving as sleeves. There were pearls and topazes around her long white throat and pinned into her hair. She was, quite simply, the most breathtaking beauty he'd ever been near enough to touch.

And he wanted to. Charles had not felt desire for anyone or anything since his crack-up in Africa. Louisa Stratton, despite her runaway tongue, might prove to be the trigger to dispensing with his self-imposed celibacy.

But no. He was the hired help, and the ground rules had been clear. He couldn't even find any satisfaction with someone more suitable—one of the housemaids, for example; he was a man still considered to be on his honeymoon. How disloyal Maximillian Norwich would be if he betrayed his lovely heiress. The irony of his sudden lust almost made him laugh.

She waited at the threshold of her parents' bedroom, expecting her due. Charles unstuck his tongue from the roof of his mouth. "You look nice, Louisa."

Her brows were several shades darker than her champagne-colored hair, and they knit briefly, then relaxed. "Thank you, Maximillian. You look nice, too."

"Any last-minute orders?"

"I haven't ordered you about, just made suggestions. It will be very like a minefield down there. Cook says the table is set for twenty. You are likely to be grilled like the Scotch salmon we're having for the fish course. Just be . . ."

Her unfinished sentence hung in the air. "Myself?" he supplied helpfully.

"Don't be ridiculous. You needn't volunteer anything, but do speak when spoken to. And mention Lachapelle."

"Loire Valley."

"Exactly. Ready?" She floated toward him and held out a kid-gloved hand.

They made it down the central stone staircase without incident. Louisa led him to a reception room the length of a cricket pitch. It was crammed with tapestries, Chinese jardinières, spindly French gilt furniture, and most of the dinner-party guests. At the center of the room, in a throne-like Louis the Somethingth chair, sat a woman whose resemblance to Louisa was unmistakable. Somehow Charles had been expecting a lumpy gray-haired dowager, but this soignée blonde must be the dreaded Aunt Grace. Charles thought she must be more than halfway from forty to fifty, yet her trim figure and unlined face made her look like Louisa's older sister.

She didn't rise. "Mr. Norwich! How delighted I am to meet our Louisa's husband at last."

Charles knew what he had to do without Louisa's little push. He crossed the carpet and bent to kiss the woman's extended hand. "Not as delighted as I am to meet Louisa's beloved aunt. Do please call me Max."

"Max, is it? I understand your given name is Maximillian."

"But quite a mouthful, yes? My friends call me Max. I've been trying to persuade Louisa to follow suit, but you know how stubborn she can be."

Grace gave him her first genuine smile of the evening. "I do indeed. We are depending upon you to teach her all the errors of her ways."

"I can find no real fault with her, ma'am. One could not ask for a more dutiful or beautiful wife."

"Very prettily said. Louisa, you claimed he was handsome and charming, and I see that was not one of your usual exaggerations. Do forgive me, Max, for not leading you around to our guests. Dr. Fentress's orders." She smiled up at the older gentleman who stood by her chair. "But Louisa will perform the introductions. You haven't forgotten who we are, have you, my dear, after all your time away from home?"

"Not at all, Aunt Grace. Who could forget such distinguished company? *Max*, darling," Louisa said with special emphasis, "this is Dr. Fentress, who tells me he's known me since I was a baby."

"How do you do, sir?"

"Quite well, quite well, Mr. Norwich, now that I know little Louisa is in good hands. Your wife ran harum-scarum as a girl, you know. Mrs. Westlake had her hands full, didn't you, Grace? And going off to the Continent unchaperoned except for an Irish maid—I won't tell you how many sleepless nights we've passed worrying about little Louisa."

Little Louisa bristled next to Charles, but somehow kept her mouth shut, rising in Charles's estimation. In a minute of conversation, she'd been portrayed as thoughtless and heedless, a liar and a hoyden, all by people who allegedly had her best interests at heart.

"Louisa's free spirit is what first attracted me to her," Charles said, earning a grateful squeeze to his arm. "There is no one like her."

"Spoken like a man besotted with his wife! See, I told you, Grace, all would be well. You raised her right."

"I did try." Grace Westlake gave a world-weary sigh, as if to say she wasn't sure her efforts had been successful. "Max, dear, we don't wish to monopolize you. Louisa, introduce your husband to our guests."

They took a grateful step backward. "Dismissed," Charles whispered into Louisa's ear.

"She likes you. Or seems to. That's a first," Louisa whispered back.

"You sound annoyed. Did you wish her to take me in dislike?"

"No, of course not." Louisa suddenly gripped his arm in a stranglehold, and it was all he could do not to yelp. "Oh God. How *could* she?"

"What is it?"

"She's invited Sir Richard."

"Who's that?"

"Sir Richard Delacourt. The man standing next to the vicar. He's a n-neighbor."

Charles looked for a man in a dog collar, then at the tall, brown-haired man beside him. Sir Richard was a decade older than Louisa, with a neat reddish beard and pale gray eyes. Handsome, Charles supposed. "He doesn't look especially dangerous."

"He—I—oh, it's complicated. I was only seventeen."

"Ah."

"Oh, don't make it sound like that," Louisa said, objecting to his one syllable.

"Confess later. I promise to be sympathetic. We were all seventeen once. Who is this woman bearing down on us with all the teeth and feathers?"

They spent the next five minutes circling the room, avoiding the vicar's corner as long as they could. Everyone seemed pleased to see Louisa, but there was an undercurrent of negativity beneath their inconsequential conversation, as if they did not want to appear *too* pleased. Several of her relatives—an odd lot they were—darted nervous glances at Grace Westlake, who sat in her throne surveying all.

Charles could tell Louisa was nervous—there was a light sheen of perspiration at her hairline and her gloves were damp. The introduction was inevitable, and the vicar, Mr. Naismith, pumped Charles's hand with enthusiasm and kissed Louisa's blushing cheek.

"We do look forward to seeing you both Sunday. No one has been able to do the altar flowers for us like you, Miss Louisa. All those colors thrown together so unexpectedly! Singular, quite singular. We've missed you in these parts."

"Thank you, Mr. Naismith. Sir Richard, how do you do? May I present my husband, Maximillian Norwich?"

If Louisa had been seventeen when they had their fling, Sir Richard must have been old enough to know not to trifle with a virgin. Charles felt himself carefully assessed by those silvery eyes, and somehow found wanting. Charles couldn't see the appeal of the man in front of him, either.

Though he was not a sheltered young girl. Perhaps Louisa had been intrigued by his title, or just the very fact that he was a *man*. Sir Richard might even be responsible for the fact that Louisa no longer held men in any kind of awe.

"Norwich, good to meet you." Sir Richard sounded bored, deliberately so. His handshake was as brief as it was civil. "Do you shoot? It's a Delacourt family tradition at the Priory on New Year's Day. You both could join us. It would be like old times, wouldn't it, Louisa? Your aunt has already agreed to join us."

Charles had not pointed a gun at anything but a human in his life, and he truly did not want to blow some poor bird to bits to prove himself to anyone. His aim would be off now anyhow. He brought Louisa's hand to his lips and gave her a heated look. "I'm not sure what our plans are, Sir Richard. My wife might want to return to France directly after Christmas. I have a small château in the Loire Valley and we both may be homesick by then."

The gray eyes narrowed. "Ah, France. But you are English?"

"Yes." Charles was saved from dragging out the dead expatriate parents and his odd upbringing by Griffith's announcement of dinner.

A strict order of precedence into the dining room was orchestrated by Grace Westlake, and Charles was separated from Louisa. He found himself escorting Isobel Crane into a banquet hall big enough for all the crowned heads of Europe and their entourages. There was a blinding array of silver and crystal on crisp white linen, and epergnes filled with lush hothouse flowers and fruit. Quite an impressive show for the boy who once worked in a pottery factory. Charles's stomach clenched at the heavy scent of lilies. Somehow they always reminded him of death—not that he needed much reminding.

This extravagance was ridiculous. For a mad moment, Charles wanted to sweep the china and glassware to the floor. While these pointless people had been cosseted by such luxury, he had been burying and burning the emaciated corpses of women and children.

But Maximillian Norwich knew nothing of such things. He lived safely in his château in the Loire Valley, surrounded by beautiful paintings. He would think nothing of fishing out the fish fork from the rigidly arranged place setting and sipping fine wine. His pretty young wife was an heiress and his days were filled by one pleasure after another.

But night would come.

Chapter

❦

9

$\mathcal{A}$unt Grace was a fiend. She had placed Sir Richard at the head of the table, with Louisa seated to his right. Charles—Maximillian—Max!—was all the way down at the other end, sandwiched between Grace and dotty Isobel. She hoped he'd hold up to her aunt's scrutiny and her cousin's likely under-the-table squeezing. Louisa couldn't even catch his eye—Grace had them on the same side of the table. At least she lucked out with her other dinner partner—it was Great-Uncle Phillip, who was mostly deaf and too indifferent to be bothered to do anything about it. He gave her a nod and then dug in to his first course.

"I thought you were on the outs with my aunt," Louisa murmured to Sir Richard.

"So did I. What has it been—ten years since I was invited to Rosemont?"

"Nine. I'm surprised you came. After all, we're just jumped-up bourgeoisie. We made our money in *trade*." Louisa tried to keep the bitterness out of her voice. If it wasn't for her grandfather's bank, she would not be spearing her oysters with a silver fork.

"You haven't forgiven me, I see. You must realize I had an obligation to the ancient Delacourt name. I hear one can buy a title now—the king is most accommodating. Maybe you should look into that for your new husband. Where did you find him, anyway? Does he know about us?"

"There is no 'us,' Richard."

"Not for lack of you trying. You were like a little spaniel, all brown eyes and golden curls. You rolled over, but you certainly did not play dead."

Louisa examined her knife and wondered if it were sharp enough to cut through Richard's evening clothes to his heart. Not that he had one.

"Do you intend to blackmail me, Richard? I thought Lady Blanche solved your financial difficulties."

"Poor Blanche. She was quite overset she couldn't join us tonight."

Lady Blanche Calthorpe, now Richard's wife, had once been Louisa's school friend. During the one glorious year she had been sent to Miss Edwin's Seminary for Young Ladies in Bath to be "finished," they had formed an unbreakable bond.

Or so Louisa had thought.

"Is she ill?"

"Let's not talk about her. We have a great deal of catching up to do."

"I have no interest in your life at all, Richard."

"I see you haven't changed a bit. Rude as ever. How did you manage to capture this Maximillian fellow? Ah, but perhaps he values a lady of experience. Some men don't mind another's leavings."

Louisa set her wineglass down. "It is the twentieth century, Richard. Women have as much right to enjoy themselves as men, not that being with you was remotely enjoyable. I know that now, after all my *experience*. You should really get a few tips from Max. I'm sure Blanche would appreciate it."

Richard's face darkened to the color of his wine. "You bitch."

"Well, you did call me a spaniel. I really don't see how we are going to be able to get through the next seven courses, do you? Which of us shall leave the table? I can plead exhaustion from my travels, or you can pretend to be concerned for Lady Blanche. Or we'll vow to stop speaking altogether—I *am* hungry and the food is always good at Rosemont even if the company isn't."

"You'll pay for your insolence. Do you think just because you ran away for a year that people have forgotten your reputation? Don't think you can come back here and start fresh."

"I have no wish to remain at Rosemont under the present circumstances. Max's château is heaven on earth."

Richard snorted. "I almost feel sorry for him."

"Oh, don't bother—he's a *very* happy man, if you know what I mean. Thank goodness. Here is the footman with the next course. Work your charm on Mrs. Naismith and I'll watch Uncle Phillip chew."

How had she ever found Sir Richard Delacourt attractive? Louisa had no excuse for herself, except that she'd been trapped at Rosemont with little to amuse her and she had been hopelessly young. Seventeen-year-old girls were idiots, full of romance and possibilities that had no relation to the real world. Richard had been tall and didn't have that horrid curly red beard then, and his haughty gray stare had made her want to appear worthy of him. However, getting down on her knees and getting caught was not the way.

Oh, it had been so mortifying. Aunt Grace had been wild with fury. Dr. Fentress was called for to examine her in the most humiliating way. Her party was canceled and her freedom curtailed. Louisa had not even been allowed to ride for fear she'd venture onto Priory land and disgrace herself further. She was locked in at night, although eventually Louisa escaped now and again.

Grace had blamed it all on Louisa's "American blood," although the Americans Louisa had met in her travels were nowhere near as stupid as she had been. In fact, she had admired them. They were fresh-faced, confident, lively. Courageous, too, for leaving their homes in Boston, New York, or Philadelphia to marry some impoverished, inbred lord. Money for a title—it's what her mother Lily and her cousin Isobel had been after two decades ago in that first wave of American brides. Byron Stratton had no title but captured Louisa's mother's heart nonetheless.

Maybe Louisa should reverse the trend and go to America, find a nice young man from a good middle-class family and settle down in one of the leafy suburbs that were springing up. Garden cities, where everything was new and one did not have to get tangled in the past.

Once she got rid of Maximillian Norwich. Max would eventually have to die as originally planned, perhaps tumble down the château stairs like Antoine—only he'd break more than a leg. It did seem a shame to have to get rid of him, though—Captain Cooper was a very dashing man. She hoped he was enduring being partnered with Aunt Grace and Isobel. Between the two of them, he was earning his hefty fee tonight alone.

The table was suddenly quiet, and Louisa looked up from her champagne sorbet. All eyes were upon her. Now what?

"Louisa, your husband was just telling me the most shocking story about your stay in Monte Carlo. Do tell me it's not true," Aunt Grace said in ringing tones.

Louisa leaned forward but could not catch a glimpse of Charles. "M-Max is generally truthful, aren't you, darling?" She sat up as tall as she could and could see only the top of his dark head over Mrs. Merwyn's feathers.

"I only lie when you instruct me to, my love," he replied, turning so she could see him. Louisa could only describe his expression as naughty, and knew at once she was in trouble.

"Why don't you tell me what you said, and then I can attest to your veracity."

"Oh, you tell the story so much better than I, *mon ange*."

Louisa was going to kill him off right here at Rosemont. She wondered if he could hold his breath long enough to fool the undertakers.

"She wouldn't tell me earlier, and now I can see why," Grace said.

"Oh, it wasn't as bad as all that, Mrs. Westlake. In fact, it was rather endearing if you think about it."

"Come Louisa, don't hold back," Sir Richard sneered. "We all want to know what you were really up to while you were away."

"We—we spent our honeymoon in Monte Carlo," Louisa began. At least that's what she'd written to Aunt Grace.

"We met, you know, at the Louvre," Charles interrupted. "Under that ugly, dark Rembrandt, isn't that right, *Lulu*?"

Oh yes. Death to Max, and possibly even to Charles Cooper.

"Anyway, neither one of us could see a damn thing— pardon me, ladies—a blessed thing in it. What was all the fuss about, anyway? All that brown and black paint, as if we were staring into the bottom of a barrel. We had a few laughs over that, and one thing led to another. I was the happiest man in the world once I convinced her to marry me, and we headed to Monte Carlo directly after the ceremony."

"Where was the ceremony?" Mrs. Naismith asked, just as a good vicar's wife should.

"St. George's on the Rue Auguste Vacquerie," Charles answered promptly. "It is the oldest Anglican church in Paris, although of course the building has not always been on that site."

So he *had* been paying attention. "Louisa drove, of

course. I must say I was tempted to kiss the ground once we got there. What a little daredevil she is behind the wheel, but I have limited peripheral vision—she'll wear the goggles in our family."

"I would never permit my wife to drive," Sir Richard said.

"As if *my* wife would ever ask for permission," Charles said, chuckling. "She is a very modern, independent woman in every respect. An original."

Louisa could almost forgive him, but she had no idea what was yet to come. So she reserved her beneficence and examined her sterling-silver spoon. What an ornate pattern, so very many nooks and crannies. It must be a trial for the footmen to clean and get it to gleam so.

"Get to the heart of the story, man!" Dr. Fentress urged.

"Ah yes. The heart. How fitting you should mention that, Dr. Fentress, for it was hearts, or lack thereof, that caused the whole thing. We were playing bridge in our hotel suite, you see. Just a friendly game with another couple we met, Baron and Baroness von Steuben."

"Germans?" Aunt Grace made a moue with her carmine lips. She might serve German Mosel wine at the table, as was the fashion, but she held the country in contempt.

"Austrians, I believe. Charming couple, weren't they, Louisa?"

Louisa had never played bridge in her life. She knew it was gaining popularity and similar to whist, but she didn't play whist, either. She had no head for cards—she'd spent most of her time in Monte Carlo admiring the jewels and dresses of the other travelers and sticking her toes in the sand instead of gambling.

"Very nice. Although Hans was a bit of a bore." She might as well get into the spirit of things.

"But Minna made up for him, don't you think, darling? What a little *apfel strudel*. Anyway, hearts were trump, but Louisa miscounted. She lost the last three tricks and was forced to pay the forfeit."

"Someone could have seen you." Grace clutched at her heart.

Goodness. Now Louisa was interested in finding out exactly what scandalous thing she'd done. "Max, you'll have to say it. I'm much too embarrassed."

"Nonsense. You're among family and old friends. Nothing you could do would surprise us anymore, Lulu. You are so like your dear mother," Isobel trilled. "Such a scamp."

Charles came to her rescue at last. "It's all right, darling. I'll finish the story. We had a wager—the loser was to do something outrageous in a public place at the winner's bidding."

Louisa shut her eyes. If Charles Cooper had her dancing the cancan, she would kick him in a *private* place when she got him alone later.

"The baron insisted," Charles continued, "that she sneak onto the stage of the Opera de Monte Carlo and sing one song. Of course, the building was quite empty, save for the cleaners. But they put down their brooms and mops and swore Louisa rivaled Nellie Melba. They had never heard 'Good King Wenceslas' sung with such panache."

Really? That was *it*? Louisa was sorely disappointed in herself.

"A Christmas song in August. How brazen, my dear," Mr. Naismith said, teasing. "You will get your chance in a few weeks to sing carols to your heart's content." He lifted his wineglass. "A toast to the return of the prodigal daughter and her new husband! Cheers to Mr. and Mrs. Maximillian Norwich. May you share many happy Christmases ahead."

"Hear, hear!" Even Uncle Phillip raised his glass. Charles rose and moved down the table until he was behind her, his warm hands on her bare shoulders. "My own songbird. Thank you all for your welcome. I find I'm quite overcome, so overcome I want to kiss my wife in public, even without the Baron von Steuben's urging."

Louisa twisted her head to stare up at him. She wanted to beg him to please sit back down at once. But she wasn't fast enough. He bore down on her with all the graceful intent of a practiced predator, and his lips touched hers.

All right. This wasn't so bad. A brief, dry peck—

And then his tongue insinuated itself between the seam of her mouth.

Oh. This wasn't so bad at all. Her eyelids fluttered shut and she leaned into the kiss against all good sense. Well, Aunt Grace said she didn't have any, so why fight it? Captain Cooper was the most marvelous kisser, gentle yet firm, his mouth moist without being mushy. He seemed to know just where to touch her tongue with his, and she felt herself melting like her champagne sorbet.

Golly, but this felt divine. She hadn't let a man come anywhere close to kissing her in ages. Louisa flushed hot and cold, which had nothing to do with the temperature of the dining room. Her hand lifted from the tablecloth so she could touch his face, feel the dark bristles that were already colonizing his jaw despite his afternoon shave.

The sound of silver spoons against crystal reverberated around the table but failed to break the captain's delicious, insidious spell. Louisa knew she should stop, but she couldn't think how to begin to retract her tongue, to shut down the sweep of sensation that tingled down to her toes. Couldn't think at all. Might never want to think again.

Oh, damn. This kiss meant nothing to him—he was just earning his pay. But wasn't he so very good at his job?

Chapter

❧

10

*S*he smelled of violets and tasted like wine. Charles knew he was breaking all the rules, and he didn't much care. She had told him no public displays of affection, but these people needed to be taught some kind of lesson. They'd all underestimated her, still saw her as the incorrigible hoyden she was as a young girl. How could they not see that she'd grown up and had a good mind of her own? Yes, she talked one's ear off, and perhaps they didn't like all the things she believed and said.

But they were here on her sufferance, living in her house, eating her food, drinking her wine. And nearly every word he'd heard most of them speak of Louisa had been somehow dismissive. Belittling. Even Isobel, who seemed to hold Louisa in some affection, had blurted out things she shouldn't.

He'd been a bit mischievous setting her up with that Monte Carlo story, but Mrs. Westlake had badgered him about it in her poisonously sweet way. Charles had to think of something, right? The few times he'd been able to swivel around like a doorknob to see her, Louisa had looked miserable sitting down at the other end of the table. Charles didn't care for the way that blighter Sir Richard was talking to her, either. He could tell from the man's expression that whatever had once been between them was still festering. Louisa must have said something to the baronet to finally put him off, for he had devoted himself to the vicar's wife for the last three courses.

Charles was more than a bit mischievous now. He steadied himself on the back of Louisa's chair, for he was in danger of sliding down to the carpet and bringing Louisa with him. He could not recall when a mere kiss had been this explosive.

Of course, he couldn't remember when he last kissed a girl—

Oh, yes, he could. Charles wobbled and carefully withdrew from Louisa's upturned face.

She was flushed pink, her brown eyes unfocussed, lashes batting like butterfly wings.

"Mr. Norwich!"

"Oh, Grace, don't get your feathers ruffled. They're newlyweds, after all." Isobel laughed, but Charles could hear an edge of hysteria. It must cost the residents of Rosemont to go against Grace.

"Please forgive my shocking behavior. I have no excuse, save that I'm in love with my wife," Charles heard himself say.

"Bah," the old gentleman next to Louisa grumbled. "You're delaying the next course, young man. Sit down, sit down."

"I'm sorry," Charles whispered to Louisa. "I don't know what came over me."

She straightened, reaching for her water glass. Her hand was trembling. "Think nothing of it. I don't."

Liar. But neither of them could risk another kiss.

Charles returned to his seat, prepared to be manhandled by Isobel and reprimanded by Grace. He did not have long to wait. Once he shifted so that his leg was nowhere near Miss Crane's clutches, he turned to Grace Westlake.

"I suppose you think I am a bounder for behaving so improperly."

"A bounder?" Grace wiped her lips on a lace-edged serviette, leaving a crimson stain. Some poor laundress would have a time getting it out. "No. More like a fool. Someone should have warned you about my niece before you married her, Mr. Norwich. You young people are so impetuous. You think you know everything. Louisa has been difficult all her life. When she ran away, I truly feared for her mental stability."

"I beg your pardon?"

"She has always been headstrong. I should think after one evening here you have discovered what her family and friends truly think of her."

"I've discovered that she has precious few *friends* in her family," Charles said baldly.

Grace sighed. "It may appear that way to you. You're a stranger and know none of us. I daresay you don't really know Louisa."

"I know her well enough."

"Oh. Passion." Grace waved a dismissive hand. "That won't last. And when it fades you'll realize you've shackled yourself to someone who cannot bring you true happiness. She's incapable. Irrational. All this talk of getting a job, of women's rights, of freedom, whatever she thinks that may be—she will not make you a comfortable wife, Mr. Norwich."

"Comfort is highly overrated." It was true Louisa had already tilted his world, though not for the reasons Grace Westlake stated.

"You say that now. Talk to me in a few months when your château has lost its allure and she wants to go to India or Africa or some such hideous place."

"Travel is very broadening, Mrs. Westlake." It had certainly opened Charles's eyes.

"You have an answer for everything. You're very smooth, Mr. Norwich. I'll give you that."

Charles snipped the last thread of his patience. "There's something I don't understand. Louisa told me your son wanted to marry Louisa. If she's so . . . difficult . . . why would that be?"

"Her family knows her best, and can protect her from her baser impulses. It would be a sacrifice for poor Hugh, but he was ready to do it. Still is."

"Louisa is *my* wife," Charles said firmly.

"But you needn't hold yourself to a mistake, Mr. Norwich. I'm prepared to offer you generous terms to end the marriage. It's a pity you were married in an Anglican church, but these things can be arranged for a price. Everyone has one, don't you agree? I'd planned on speaking to you privately tomorrow, but now is as good a time as any. Isobel is flirting with old Mr. Baxter and cannot hear us, though he knows my plans already. That wretched woman will throw herself at anything in trousers, even a man old enough to be her father," Grace said with disdain. "Dr. Fentress can present Louisa's medical history to you. She was not a virgin bride, as you must know. You've been duped, young man, enticed by a pretty package that's rotten within."

Charles threw his napkin down on the table. "If you will excuse me, Mrs. Westlake. I am feeling unwell."

She gave him a sly smile. "I imagine you are. Think about what I've said. I'll expect you in my suite at eleven o'clock tomorrow morning. We have much to discuss."

Charles got up unsteadily. Louisa looked up with consternation, probably expecting him to wander down and give her another kiss. He gave her an apologetic shrug.

"Headache, I'm afraid," he said to the table at large. "Do forgive me."

It was all he could do to muster the dignity to walk out of the cavernous room when he wanted to run shrieking. After a few wrong turns down dark corridors, he was back in their rooms and dying for a drink. But a drink would not erase the evening.

What had he fallen into? And how was he to extricate himself from it? He rubbed his temples, for in truth he really was getting a headache.

Poor Louisa. Or maybe not. Maybe she deserved the opprobrium from those downstairs. Only her maid Kathleen and the old butler seemed to genuinely like her—everyone else had kept a little distance from her.

That disparagement could be due to Grace. She did seem to rule the roost, and everyone looked to her rather than Louisa for direction. Louisa should have been sitting at the head of the table. Hell, Charles himself should have been sitting at the foot instead of Sir Richard Delacourt.

He didn't like any of this, but he really didn't know who had the truth on their side. He'd thought Louisa to be spoiled and rackety himself. Was there really something "wrong" with her?

Charles didn't think so. But his judgment had been impaired for some time now. Wherever the truth lay, he needed to tell her he was about to be bribed to "divorce" her.

If he had no honor, he wouldn't say a word, just take what Grace Westlake offered and disappear. Louisa had already paid half his fee—a small fortune—and the sum was sitting in his new bank account collecting interest. Maybe Grace could be cajoled to match what was yet to be earned, and Charles would save himself the effort of continuing this charade.

He loosened his tie and sank down in a gray chair before the fire in the sitting room. How soon would Louisa make her escape to check up on him? If she was indeed so unconventional, the guests might not expect her to stick around for tea and gossip while the men drank their port and smoked their cigars.

The stitching on his new silk patch was irritating the corner of his eye, and he pulled it off. Everything dimmed instantly, with whorls of blood and shadows obscuring his vision. He covered half his face with his hand and waited for the room to right itself.

The door burst open and Louisa entered, all lace and violet scent and umbrage. "How dare you leave the table!"

"Shh! Sit down and we'll talk like civilized people. You wouldn't want the company downstairs to think we're having a lover's quarrel."

"They can't hear anything—we're miles away. Anyway, Mrs. Naismith is playing the piano while Mr. and Mrs. Merwyn are singing."

"I'm sorry to miss it." He tried to imagine the stout Merwyns singing a duet together and failed.

"Oh, no, you're not. No one would be. Neither one of them can carry a tune, but it's tradition here for them to perform at dinner parties. Why did you leave?"

"Your aunt said any number of things I found objectionable. I found I could not be a good boy and listen."

"I *told* you she was challenging. If she was easy to deal with, I would not have had to invent a husband."

"You'd better sit down, Louisa." He took the eye patch out of his pocket and tied it back on. Louisa came into focus, pale and obviously agitated. He didn't want to have to add to her upset, but he felt an odd loyalty to protect her. "Grace has offered—or will offer—me a substantial sum of money to end our marriage."

Louisa slid into the chair opposite. "Oh."

She didn't sound surprised.

"She's in cahoots with the banker. And Dr. Fentress, too. They plan to tell me tomorrow you are a few sandwiches short of a picnic, and that I'd be better off without you. It's all about your fortune, isn't it?"

Louisa shook her head. "It's really about the power. Grace has plenty of money of her own. She hates me; she always has. No matter how good I was, it wasn't enough. After a while, I decided to be bad. Why not? Behaving got me nowhere. Then she really turned the screws and cut me off without so much as pin money. I could go nowhere. Do nothing. If she could have figured out how to stop my inheritance, she would have. Sometimes I thought she might have me declared mad. And sometimes I thought I *would* go mad."

Charles gave a low whistle. "Good Lord, you really *are* a poor little rich girl."

Her lips trembled. "Are you mocking me?"

"No, I'm not. What will happen if they discover that we're not really man and wife? This scheme might be considered proof of your insanity."

Louisa's brown eyes widened. "Do *you* think I should be institutionalized?"

"I wouldn't wish that on the other patients. Now, don't kick up at me—I'm only teasing."

Charles was just realizing this hoax was very dangerous indeed. While he didn't think what they were doing was precisely illegal, it was scandalous nonetheless. Hell, they were sharing a suite of rooms. Louisa may have an iffy reputation, but discovery of their unwed state would put the final nail in her coffin.

"There's no reason for anyone to suspect anything," Louisa said, sounding like she was trying to convince herself. "You've been a model husband so far, except . . . toward the end."

He thought she might mention the kiss, but she did not.

"I'm sorry. I should have stuck it out downstairs."

"Yes, you should have. Grace always gets what she wants. She's ruthless. But you must deflect her. When you meet with her tomorrow—"

"You want me to go through with that?" asked Charles, incredulous.

"Absolutely. I'd like to know what she thinks I'm worth."

He reached across and took her hand. It was cold as ice despite the warmth of the fire. "You are priceless."

She snatched her hand away and buried it into the lace on her lap. "Save that kind of talk for when it counts and there are people around to hear it. If Baxter is siding entirely with Aunt Grace, she might be behind the bottle-neck to my funds. That's really why I came home. Don't worry! I can still pay you."

Charles felt a flare of annoyance. "I don't care about the money."

"*Everyone* cares about money, even me. Money is freedom."

Money was also food. Health. Most people Charles knew would rather eat than be free, whatever free meant.

"All right, boss. What's our strategy?"

Louisa's tongue was peeping from the corner of her mouth again. "I don't know yet. Let me think."

"Two heads are better than one, or so I've been told. Do you trust me?"

"I have to, don't I? Oh, this is so much more compli-cated than I expected."

"It's only a month. We can endure anything for thirty days." Charles had seen much, much worse than Grace Westlake and her minions.

Chapter

11

*L*ouisa had expected the worst, but not within less than twenty-four hours of her arrival. Wasn't Aunt Grace more subtle than that?

Apparently not. Imagine. Talk of her dishonor and bribery at the dinner table. No wonder Captain Cooper got up and left. What must he think of them all? His own family might not be very grand, but they surely wouldn't be so vicious with one another.

And . . . Sir Richard Delacourt. Grace had been making her point inviting him after all these years, had she not? Louisa was never going to escape from her youthful indiscretion if he was thrown at her at every turn. Grace planned for them all to spend New Year's Day at the Priory? Unthinkable.

She punched her pillow down and stared at the shadowed ceiling. When Kathleen had come in to help ready her for bed, Louisa enlisted her to keep an eye out belowstairs. The servants always knew everything before anyone else did. She wondered how often Mr. Baxter visited— she'd have to find a new bank officer if he was representing

Grace's interests rather than those of the Stratton heiress. The Strattons still owned the majority of shares in the family bank, and there must be someone there she could talk to besides Hugh or Mr. Baxter.

Louisa's father, Byron, had been a great sportsman, rather in the mold of Sir Richard, now that Louisa thought about it. He'd been far too busy amusing himself and his pretty young American wife to pay attention to the family bank, Stratton and Son. Her grandfather must have been disappointed, but the business continued to prosper without Byron in life, and certainly after his death. Under Grace's careful stewardship, Louisa had been stunned to learn the amount that came to her when she turned twenty-five.

She'd been giddy. Now no one held any legal authority over her or her finances, though nothing had stopped Grace from inserting her opinions into everything anyway. So Louisa had simply left, and proved to be every bit as wild as her aunt had always said she was.

She was beginning to think she should not have left, or been so wild. Too late to cry over spilled milk, however. She had a strange man two rooms away from her who could either help her with her future or ruin it forever, but she was praying for the former.

Sleep would not come. Louisa longed for her old room—her girlhood bed, her familiar books, the botched watercolors she was forced to paint as Grace tried to turn her into a demure young lady. There were lovely vistas here at Rosemont, but Louisa had succeeded in making everything look smeary and dull.

Her parents' room had better pictures on the wall. Louisa lit a lamp and got up to examine them, as an art connoisseur's wife might. She did love art, even if she had no talent for it herself. Her father had purchased several works by the American marine artist Fitz Hugh Lane, among the other seascapes. They were restful, really—calm water and sun and sky, harbors that Louisa had never visited. Why had she not thought to go to America last year? The Atlantic was a bigger barrier to contain her past than the English Channel.

That's where she'd go once she was done here, even if she did dislodge the Westlakes from Rosemont. She'd explore her American roots, walk the fashionable New York streets where her mother had grown up. There might be some distant cousins to meet, maybe someone her own age to befriend. She hadn't had a real friend in years. Except for Kathleen, who was as dear to her as a sister, but as different from her as chalk is to cheese.

Louisa could hear Aunt Grace's disparaging tones now. *"One doesn't get too familiar with the servants."* It had been a miracle that Kathleen wasn't sacked when she and Louisa grew close in their isolation. But Kathleen was always punctilious in front of Grace, appearing meek and properly cowed. Once Louisa's bedroom door was shut, it was altogether another thing.

Louisa wondered where Kathleen was now. She'd declined to sleep in Louisa's dressing room, saying it would cause talk if she were to be a human shield between her mistress and Maximillian Norwich. Maybe Kathleen was rendezvousing with Robertson in his room above the garage. He'd been hired not long before Louisa had bolted, but he had apparently been here long enough to impress unimpressable Kathleen. The man hadn't said so much as boo when he'd picked them up at the station today, but he was only keeping to his place in the Rosemont pecking order.

It was clear Grace was still queen.

No doubt her aunt was sleeping soundly, pleased at the mischief she'd made at dinner, confident she could bribe Louisa's new husband to sue for divorce. On what grounds, she wondered. Insanity? Louisa *did* feel unbalanced now that she was home again. She supposed a criminal conversation charge could be trumped up if the price was right— some poor fellow might be persuaded to lie and say he'd slept with her and made her an adulteress. It was almost funny—if Charles Cooper really was her husband, he might be eager to get out of his marriage now that he'd met his in-laws.

Louisa sighed. This worry was getting her nowhere. Whatever Grace was up to, she'd be foiled—Charles seemed unbribable, unless he really *was* a good actor. Mrs. Evensong had picked well. Louisa had confidence in his honor and honesty—he didn't have to tell her what Grace had said, but he had. It would have been easy for him to betray her— he didn't owe her anything, really. Didn't even know her.

She touched her lips. He had not kissed her as a stranger.

She extinguished the lights and climbed back into bed, her thoughts jumbled. Louisa had been kissed before. And more. She'd not been as much of an idiot lately as she'd been with Sir Richard—she liked to think she'd learned her lesson, and a hard lesson it had been. But there had been a few times over the past year when she considered giving herself away again, this time with no expectation of marriage. She would *never* get married.

Louisa shut her eyes, pulled up her nightgown, and touched herself. Who needed a man when she had fingers? She eased into her mattress, circling damp flesh, willing herself to relax.

Relaxation, like sleep, was difficult. Was it because Charles Cooper was just yards away? There were three doors between them. But had she locked her dressing room door to the bath chamber?

He was not the sort of man to enter a bedroom without an invitation—she would stake her life on it. So why was she so nervous? Was she afraid he'd discover her in her shameful attempt to reach bliss?

No. It was not shameful—she did not care what any book or anyone said to try to frighten her with to control and diminish her. She was human. She had needs, and it was ever so much easier to do for herself than place herself at any man's mercy. Men didn't care for anyone's satisfaction but their own. Charles Cooper was probably just like that, brutish in the bedroom. Taking. Staking.

But what if he watched her at a safe distance, his blue eye smoky with desire? Louisa pictured him at the doorway, his dressing gown unbelted, his chest bronze in the firelight. He would direct her from afar, his voice thick with arousal. Tell her where her hand must go next, instruct her to remove the nightgown that suddenly felt so hot and scratchy. She would listen carefully and obey, as white as the linen sheet she lay upon, wet with her own dew. A small cry escaped and she plunged into herself, frantic to keep flying, so close, so close—

And then she heard a crash. A low, agonized groan. She snatched her hand away and listened to the real world around her. The wind was blowing outside as usual, rattling the mullioned windows. Her bedside clock was ticking, the fire rumbling down. And two rooms away, Charles Cooper was shouting, barking out orders to phantom soldiers.

He had warned her. She covered her ears with her blankets, but it was no use. His agitation was rising, his voice ragged. Someone besides herself was bound to hear him, even though they had privacy at the end of this wing of the house.

Louisa would have to wake him. Perhaps offer him a spot of medicinal brandy to soothe his nerves. He had nerves, no matter what he thought. There was brandy in the sitting room cabinet. They could build up the fire in there and talk till his night fevers passed.

She plucked her satin robe from the foot of the bed and hurried into it, not pausing to put her discarded nightgown back on. Louisa flushed, thinking of her fantasy. It had been very diverting inserting Captain Cooper into her little ritual. Which was only fitting, as he was taking mythical Maximillian's place. When she'd conjured up her "husband" as she sought her pleasure in the past, his physical details had been sketchy.

She knew what he would look like now.

She lit a taper from the fire and swept through her dressing room and bath. The shouts were muted now but somehow more desperate. Louisa rapped once on the thick oak door and turned the handle.

The little room was a shambles. The bedside table had tipped over and her father's books were scattered half open on the floor, along with all the bedclothes. The fire had gone cold, but she could see the captain thrashing on his narrow bed. She swallowed hard. He was as naked as she had been a few minutes ago.

She straightened the table and closed its empty drawer, then set the candle into a brass holder she found on the carpet. "Captain Cooper. Charles. Wake up."

He gave no indication that he heard her, and how could he? Her words wavered between a croak and a whisper. Louisa took a step forward and placed a hand on his muscled arm. "Charles—"

Oh Lord, a mistake. He pulled her down on top of him in a swift, violent embrace. Before she could gather her wits, Charles Cooper had flipped her on her back and rolled over on top of her, one of his broad hands perilously close to pressing all the air from her throat. Louisa's fists flailed at his back. His body was hot and heavy against her, his manhood pressing against the bare skin her disarranged robe had exposed. She had never been in such a position of intimacy before—her previous encounters had lacked finesse. And a bed as well.

"Captain Cooper! Wake up now! You are hurting me!" She didn't dare to scream, couldn't have, really.

His eyes opened and he stared down at her without any recognition, not relaxing his hold an inch.

"It's all r-right. You were dreaming."

He was still. Hard and still, like a slab of granite that had toppled upon her. She couldn't mistake the prod of his penis against her belly—it was becoming more granitelike as the seconds ticked by.

"Charles?"

He shook his head, like a spaniel emerging from the

water. "Who are you?" His voice was rough, but there was fear behind those three words.

"Louisa Stratton. We are at Rosemont, my home."

"Good Christ." He released her and scrambled off the bed. My goodness but the man was beautiful, long and very lean, although there were red marks and divots on his skin. Battle wounds, she guessed. He bent to pick up a sheet to cover himself. It was a shame Louisa could not tell Kathleen about the very perfection of the man's arse.

He didn't meet her eyes. "I'm sorry," he said, gruff. His fingers were clumsily fastening the sheet low on his hips. It was all Louisa could do to ask him to leave it and come back to bed.

"That's quite all right. You weren't yourself. And you did warn me there was difficulty at night."

"I did, didn't I? And now you have all the proof you'd ever want. I'll leave in the morning."

"No!" Louisa sat up, oblivious to the fact that her dressing gown covered very little of her at the moment. "You can't go! We have a plan."

He collapsed in the chair next to the fireplace. There was no warmth there, and the man looked like he needed some to recover. He was shaking from cold—or something else. He stared at his feet, which were long and oddly appealing in their nakedness. Much like the rest of him.

"I didn't mean to startle you, but you were crying out. Why don't we go into the sitting room? Have something to drink. We've both had a shock."

"Don't pity me. I can't bear it."

"I'm not pitying you. One might think you were very clever—you got me in your bed, did you not, after I expressly forbid such familiarity. Why, you might have ravished me and no one would be the wiser." She pulled the folds of her robe tighter.

Charles's lip curled. "I could claim I was exercising my rights."

"You know perfectly well you have no rights. Come. Let's go where it's warm. Your room is like an icehouse."

How could he have thrown the covers on the floor? Louisa swore she could see her own breath.

"I'll be all right."

"At least let's do something about the fire in here then. I'll fetch the brandy." She slid off the bed and stood up, a little shaky herself.

He looked up. "Didn't Mrs. Evensong tell you about my problem?"

"I only know of your bad dreams, and you told me about them."

"I drink, Miss Stratton. As much and as often as I can. I promised her I would try to do this job sober. I wouldn't be plying me with brandy if I were you. There isn't enough in the house for me once I get started again, and I might not remember I'm supposed to be a gentleman. Next time you come in the room in the middle of the night, I really might ravish you."

"Oh." *Oh.* Charles Cooper was no sort of white knight at all. "Then what can I do? Shall I ring for tea?"

"Do whatever you want. You're my employer, after all."

He looked so bleak and miserable in the dim room, the candle guttering with each draft of wind from the uncaulked windows. Louisa would see to getting that fixed.

Someone would still be up in the house—Grace prided herself on round-the-clock service. And if she had to, Louisa could manage herself. She'd spent most of her lonely childhood in the kitchens with the servants. "I'll rustle up a tea tray. You tend to the fire. Or do you want me to?"

"There are some things I can still do myself, Miss Stratton. But you're safe from me. Bedding a woman is not one of them."

Chapter

✤

12

*C*harles opened the window wider to clear his head. He estimated he was up high enough in the house so if he threw himself out the rattling window, he'd fall to his death. That wouldn't do much for Louisa's reputation, but it was a tempting thought nonetheless. He was sick of being sick, driven mad with dreams of carnage and his complicity in it.

After the injury to his eye, he'd been sent to one of the concentration camps to "tidy" it before it was inspected by members of the do-gooders of the Fawcett Commission. Word had spread that something was seriously amiss in Kitchener's army, finally reaching Parliament and the public. Somehow he and his ragtag team were supposed to convince the visitors that the brutal conditions of the Boer women and children were not as bad as initially reported.

No. They had been worse. A full quarter of the inmates under his brief tenure died. The simplest hygiene was non-existent. His own men died as well—more soldiers were felled to disease than battle. Charles had felt as though he was swimming against an impossibly polluted tide, where death by drowning would be a welcome thing.

The clean sea beyond the ledge outside Rosemont beckoned. But again, he couldn't do that to Louisa. What sort of husband sought to end his life when a new one was just beginning? He felt protective of her in this gilded snake pit, even if their relationship was a sham.

He shuffled to the chair and sat down. He shouldn't sit here wrapped up in his sheet like a wrinkled Roman emperor. Louisa would return soon with her bloody tea and sympathy and he would have to pretend to be civilized. He'd already behaved like a beast, crushing her under him before he knew who she was.

On the whole, she'd been remarkably calm about it. And naked and soft under that pink silk robe. They had been flesh to flesh, like a true husband and wife, but he'd awakened before he could do too much damage. Not that he was capable anymore—he'd tried a time or two after he got back on British soil. His cock had denied him when presented with a real live lady, not that the women he'd sought comfort with could be described as such. Thank God his hand still worked on those very rare occasions his mind cooperated with his need.

Really, what did he have to live for? He couldn't fuck, did not want to fight ever again. He was done, washed up at twenty-seven. At least he'd go out in a lark as Maximillian Norwich.

Charles was just rising from the chair when he heard the click of the door to the hall opening behind him. Goodness, service in the old ancestral pile was spectacular. She'd left only a short while ago. He settled back in the chair and waited for the tea and some of Louisa's bracing conversation.

What he got instead came as a surprise before the dim room darkened completely.

*T*wenty minutes later, Louisa struggled up one of the narrow back stairs with a tea tray. The gleaming white kitchen had been scrubbed clean and was completely deserted—unusual, but then the kitchen staff had worked hard for her homecoming dinner party and deserved the respite. The stove had been slow to relight and her favorite tea hard to find—Cook had put it in a different canister from a year ago. Louisa still thought a drop of brandy in the tea might not go amiss. If the captain did not want to join her out of moral principle, that was all right.

She'd seen enough red bulbous noses, broken veins, and paunches on the Continent. Not all Frenchmen and Austrians and Italians were handsome and debonair. But Charles Cooper did not have the look of a souse. If anything, he was too lean and ascetic. The hair on his head was shorn as any monk's, and he rarely smiled. There was something very grave about his demeanor that intrigued her.

And she didn't believe he had no interest in sex. Even if he'd been more or less unconscious when he'd attacked her, his anger had rapidly turned to arousal. She'd seen the paintings and the statues. Had unfortunately seen Sir Richard. Charles Cooper would fit right in to any museum, his lengthening manhood an improvement over those mysteriously attached fig leaves, at least from an educational perspective.

Louisa rounded the last corner that led to their suite. The captain's bedroom door was open, but no spill of light fell on the carpet. Had he left to go in search of her? Did the foolish man not start a fire first? She was cold herself now in her flimsy robe and couldn't wait to pour herself a cup of tea.

"Here we go, Maximillian," she said, pausing in the doorway, as if someone might be around to hear her. "Max?"

A gust of air blasted from an open window straight across the little room. The candle she'd left had gone out, but she could see the bed was empty save for two plump pillows. He must have gone to the sitting room after all. Louisa was tired of balancing the tray and decided to set it on the bed so she wouldn't have to struggle with closed doors. It was then she heard the faintest rasp coming from the floor.

A prickle of unease took hold of her. She bumped up against the club chair that was no longer angled next to the hearth. It was so damn dark in the room, she was afraid she'd trip. There had been books all over the floor, so she scuttled carefully around the chair. "M-Max?"

A groan. Then her bare foot encountered ice-cold flesh and she gave a little shriek. The captain was lying face-down on the floor in front of the fireplace, still wrapped in his temporary toga. Louisa sank to her knees. Her hand hovered over a shoulder, but she was afraid to touch him after last time. "Charles," she whispered.

He couldn't be asleep in this extraordinary position—no one liked sleeping on the floor when a bed was so handy, did they? Though perhaps his soldiering had inured him to discomfort and he actually preferred some hard surface. How odd it would be for the maidservants to find him like this when they lit his fire in the mornings.

She would leave him sprawled out, half on the carpet, half on the hearth tile, but she could shut the window—the poor man would be covered in frost by morning if she didn't. He might catch his death, and it was much too soon to rid herself of Maximillian Norwich.

Besides, Louisa had never seen a real dead body and had no interest whatsoever in doing so. It was one thing to kill off Max in concept; to do the actual thing to poor Captain Cooper seemed very unsporting.

She rose to tiptoe around him, but his hand shot out and clamped her ankle, pulling her down to his level in an exceedingly graceless tumble. Louisa felt rather like a loaf of braided bread, all twisted around herself. They were eye to eye now, although he hadn't moved except to blink once as he realized whom he held captive. The bristly carpet nap pressed into her cheek and his hand was like an iron cuff on her leg.

"Not again. Really, Captain, this has got to—"

"Shut. Up. Is there anyone else here?"

"Of course there's no one else here! I had to make the tea myself. It's on the bed if you want some. I'll be happy to pour if you'd only let me up. What peculiar habits you have, lying on the floor like a mastiff. This is most unpleasant."

They were so close she could see his lips quirk in the gloom. "I daresay. Did you hit me, Louisa?"

"Did I *what*?"

"Hit me. With a brick or a shovel or something equally 'unpleasant,' as you might say. Whatever it was, it knocked me off my chair. I only just woke up."

She squirmed under his hand, but he held her fast. "I—I—of course I didn't do any such thing! How could you think it of me?"

"Well, you did tell me on the train coming down here that eventually Maximillian Norwich had to die. I thought you might be getting an early start."

"I'm not really going to kill *you*," Louisa huffed. "I'm going to kill an imaginary man. And not with a shovel or a brick. He'll have a death befitting his station, something dignified." She hadn't decided Maximillian's denouement yet, except to rule out train wrecks, mountain climbing, and flower picking. Now that she'd met Charles Cooper, it was impossible that a mere thorn could kill him.

He relaxed his grip, but only just. "Very well. I suppose I'll have to believe you."

"Of course you do! I never lie!"

He said nothing, but the silence spoke volumes. Louisa supposed he had a point. What was all of this between them but one gigantic lie? "Someone really hit you?"

"Yes. I think I may need some nursing. How are you at the sight of blood?"

Blood? Was he lying there *bleeding*? It was too dark to tell. "Do get up!" Oh, what if he couldn't? "I mean, *can* you get up?"

He grunted. "I can try. You'd best light some lamps."

He released her ankle and she scrambled up. The match safe had fallen to the floor with the books, but she found it and lit the wick of the lamp on the fireside table. Charles was still prone on the floor, his short dark hair encrusted with something darker. "Oh my God."

"While I'm sure prayer can be effective, I'd prefer some sticking plaster," he grumbled, hauling himself up on his haunches. He swayed and caught himself on the chair.

"Oh yes! Of course. There must be something in the bathroom. Stay right there."

"Not going out dancing." He slumped against the chair. "Dizzy."

"I'll send for Dr. Fentress."

"No!" He winced at the sound of his own voice. "No. No doctors. I'll be fine. Give me a cup of that tea before you go."

Louisa poured a cup with shaking hands. "It's probably gone cold by now."

"Doesn't matter." He took a loud slurp, something Maximillian Norwich would never do even if he had been hit with a brick or a shovel. Maximillian did all things in moderation.

Except in the bedroom. There, he was fiendishly artful, a sleek animal with endless, inventive sensual appetites.

"It's good. Thank you."

Louisa hesitated, feeling a swell of some unidentified emotion as she stood over him. The sheet was still mostly around his hips, and his torso was dusky in the lamplight. This was *exactly* how she pictured imaginary Maximillian, and Louisa wanted to examine real Charles further. But the poor man was bleeding, for heaven's sake. "I'll get the bandages. And some carbolic."

He made a face but said nothing, and she stepped into their shared bathing chamber. It was lit by a flickering glass lamp in case of nocturnal need. Louisa turned the wick up and began to methodically search through the drawers of the long dresser set under the windows. She found bars of soap and sponges, embroidered hand towels, face cream, balls of cotton. It wasn't till she reached the bottom drawer that she found a first aid kit with bandages and scissors and labeled brown bottles. She blessed the staff for their attention to detail, for everything in the dresser was new and neatly arranged. Louisa filled a small basin with warm water and pulled some squares of flannel from the open shelves near the tub.

"Ah. Florence." Charles Cooper gave her a lopsided grin from the chair. He'd gotten himself back up and was fiddling with the draping around his waist. A drip of blood crept down his neck.

"This is just awful," she said as she dumped her equipment on the fireside table. "Who would do such a thing to you?"

"Any one of the dinner guests. They struck me as a rum lot," he said, more cheerful than he had a right to be.

"They've all gone home. It's just the family left."

"Even worse, you must agree."

"Don't tease, Charles. Someone at Rosemont tried to kill you!" She dabbed his head with the wet washrag and heard his swift intake of breath.

"Surely not. Death is so final. Perhaps they meant to warn me off. Send me back to the château so they can get their hands on your money."

Money. Louisa hoped it wasn't about that. Human greed knew no boundaries. But somehow she couldn't picture Aunt Grace whacking Maximillian Norwich in the head before she tried to bribe him tomorrow.

Today, actually. It was after midnight.

Aunt Grace didn't need her money—she had plenty of her own. Hugh would inherit a fortune, so he didn't need it, either. Besides, Hugh was in London and not wandering around Rosemont in the middle of the night.

Could one of the servants have done this, perhaps to commit robbery? Louisa looked around the room, but all drawers were shut, and the only mess was the books Charles had knocked over himself in his fevered dream.

"Ow."

"Sorry. I think it's clean enough now. The wound is deep but I don't think it needs stitches. Hold still. This may hurt." His fingers dug into the arms of the chair while Louisa swabbed his scalp with carbolic. It was the only indication that he felt anything at all as he sat in otherwise rigid control. She stuck the plaster on as best she could, hoping it would stick to the short strands of hair. "There. Good as new."

"Except for the bloody headache. It never pays to fib. Now I've got one in truth." His accent had roughened, his roots emerging. My goodness, she was alone with an uncouth, half-naked man in a dimly lit bedchamber, and she had no desire to flee.

"Shut the window, why don't you. I don't guess my assailant climbed down the drainpipe?"

"I shouldn't think so. We're awfully high up. And anyway, your bedroom door was open when I came back from the kitchen." She fiddled with the clasps of the casement and locked it. "You'd better lock the door to the hall from now on, too."

"Jesus. This wasn't a once-in-a-lifetime opportunity?"

Louisa's tongue curled into the corner of her mouth. It was horrible to think she had brought Captain Cooper here to be bludgeoned nightly. "We can't know. I expected to be on my guard against gossip, but not this sort of thing."

Charles rose unsteadily from the chair, clutching his sheet. "Thank you for patching me up."

"It was the least I could do. I—I don't think I should leave you alone. People with head injuries are supposed to be monitored."

He pretended shock. "Why, Miss Stratton, are you proposing to sleep in my bed? I don't think we'd fit."

"I thought you could come to my room. I can watch you from the chaise." Despite the long day and even longer night, Louisa did not think she'd be able to fall asleep. Her mind was in turmoil. Someone had attacked the captain.

Would they attack her next? Growing up, she'd spent most of her time at Rosemont in her room or the kitchen or the conservatory, under a kind of voluntary house arrest, even before Grace restricted her movements. She didn't relish the thought of spending the next thirty days in the gray sitting room even if she did have a gorgeous man for company.

"Your room." Charles sounded hesitant.

"Yes."

"I don't think that's a good idea."

"Whoever did this to you could have a key to get in again. You might fall asleep and never know what hit you. That is, if you ever woke up again."

"You think they're coming back to finish me off?"

"I—I don't know. This seems much more than a prank."

"My head agrees with you. Mrs. Evensong did not say the job was going to be dangerous. But I brought my pistol."

Louisa felt her knees buckle. "Your p-pistol?"

"Years of training. Force of habit. One never knows." He shuffled over to the bedside table and pulled open the drawer. "Blast. It's gone. I guess we want to watch for bullets now as well as bricks."

Chapter

❦

13

$\mathcal{C}$harles spoke lightly, but he was troubled. His army-issue pistol had been with him for a decade. It was an old friend, and he had use for it if he ever worked up his courage. He crouched down on the floor and looked under the bed, remembering that he'd knocked into the table in the night. Perhaps the drawer had opened and the pistol had fallen to the floor, miraculously without firing. If it had, all his indecision would be moot and Louisa Stratton Norwich could have claimed her widowhood.

There was nothing to see, not even a ball of dust. There wouldn't be in a house like Rosemont.

Charles was beginning to think that Louisa Stratton should have stayed in France. Something was truly wrong here. It was one thing to think of killing himself, but he discovered he didn't much care for the idea of someone else putting him out of his misery.

"All right, let's go to your room. But you needn't sleep on the chaise. The bed's big enough for two or three as I recall. I swear I will not test its limits."

Louisa blushed. She probably didn't know what a

ménage à trois was. But if she *was* his wife, he wouldn't want to share her with either gender. He guided her out of his arctic room with a hand placed on her lower back. The silk was slippery against his rough fingers, and he wondered how soft her skin was beneath it. Very soft, he decided. White and pure. Though now that her face was scrubbed clean of powder, he noted she had a tiny constellation of freckles across her cheek and nose. Probably from driving that car of hers all around the countryside. Give him a horse any day.

"Do you ride?"

Louisa stumbled on the bathroom tile. "I beg your pardon?"

Ah. He'd mentioned the size of the bed. She thought he was now talking positions in it. The image of Louisa naked over him, her golden hair streaming, stirred his recalcitrant cock. "I thought perhaps after I keep my appointment with your aunt, we could explore the estate on horseback."

"Oh. Yes, of course I ride. Or used to. My aunt forbade it the last several years I lived at home. She was sure I'd run to—" She bit off words that were to follow.

"Sir Richard," he supplied helpfully. They had traversed the bathing chamber and her dressing room, locking all the doors behind them, and were now in the enormous bedroom. Her fire needed feeding, too, else they were bound to stay cold. "Get under the covers. I'll see to the coals."

He thought she might object but heard her slide into the bed and punch up the pillows. He was conscious that his pajamas were still in a dresser drawer. They had been Mrs. Evensong's idea—lately Charles had slept in his clothes or in the nude, being far too drunk and uncivilized to care about changing. He should go back into his room and get them.

And Louisa should put on a nightgown, something that went straight up to her stubborn chin. That dressing gown of hers was not going to stay put as she lay beside him.

He'd seen the slice of thigh as she walked, the curve of a breast as she bent. Her white throat was visible and kissable above the robe's deep V.

Jesus. His mind was traveling into unfamiliar territory, or at least territory that had not been explored in a good long while. That hit on his head must have dislodged some memories of when he was a normal man. When he could see and touch and taste, his most pressing thought being how to get himself inside soft female flesh quickly and spend.

Charles realized his eye patch as well as his pajamas were in the other room, but the light was low enough for him to ignore the floating debris that bedeviled him so in the daytime. He'd close his eyes soon enough, will the throbbing at the back of his head to lull. He'd best roll onto his side, back to Miss Stratton. Pretend she wasn't there.

Impossible.

The fire caught. There was no reason to remain huddled in front of it poking, delaying the inevitable. Charles would spend what was left of the night lying next to a beautiful woman. Hopefully he wouldn't slip into a coma and miss the experience.

Louisa could throw water at him to wake him up. Whiskey would be more welcome, he thought ruefully.

Feeling a bit like an African native, he tied the sheet firmly to his waist and padded across the thick carpet to the enormous four-poster bed. Louisa had staked claim to the far, far edge. There would be no "accidental" brushing against her plush curves. Charles didn't think he'd be doing much sleeping anyway—his skin felt stretched too tight for his bones, every inch alive with something not quite painful but present.

Alive. He felt alive, for the first time in over a year. How ironic when someone had tried to kill him, or at least warn him away. And now his gun was stolen as well as any peace of mind he might have secured pretending to be the hoyden's husband.

He could ask Louisa for an increase in pay. He hadn't signed the contract with Mrs. Evensong to get shot at. Charles had had quite enough of that, thank you very much. If anyone was doing the shooting, it would be him.

He wasn't safe here, but then neither was Louisa. Sharp tongues could be superseded by sharp objects. He felt a surge of protective concern for his poor little rich girl.

Feeling a little under siege, he stared across the dark room at the door to the sitting room, wondering if that was locked, too. He would get Robertson to drive him to the nearest gunsmith, and not leave his weapon in a drawer this time.

There was a rustle behind him. A sigh. Another. Resolute, Charles shut his eyes.

"There is a gun room here. My papa had a collection, as I told you. We can find something to replace your pistol tomorrow."

Charles had not expected so practical a discussion, or the fact that she was reading his mind. He rolled over. "Indeed? I wonder why mine was stolen then if there are weapons at hand."

"To disarm you, of course. To leave you vulnerable. At their mercy." There was bitterness in her voice. She was not really speaking of him.

"I recall you telling me you're a fair shot."

She nodded. Tension emanated from her, despite the fact that she'd drawn the coverlet up to her chin and had angled a pillow so it would prevent him from touching her.

Charles had promised to be a gentleman, and he kept his promises. Mostly.

"Well, that's convenient. I think you should arm yourself as well. And we should stick together. Louisa, do you have any idea who would try to harm me? I assume it's a way to hurt you—I'm just the collateral damage."

Her tongue teased the corner of her mouth. "Do—do you want to resign? I don't want anything awful to happen to you."

"I don't want anything awful to happen to *you*, and I'll stay at Rosemont to make sure of it. You can kill me off later when things are settled. Do you have a will?"

"Mr. Baxter was after me to make one before I left, but no. I just couldn't face it. Silly of me, I know. We're all going to die, aren't we? I could have cracked us up a hundred times this past year—cars can be so unreliable. And the roads! Nothing but mud and ruts. If anyone deserves my fortune, it's Kathleen for what she put up with. But as yet, there is no one who will benefit directly from my death."

"Except your husband. By law, your fortune would come to me even without a will, would it not? Kill me first, kill you next, and your closest relative—Grace, I presume—inherits."

"Oh! Oh, Charles, I am sorry for putting you in this predicament." She looked at him earnestly, her dark eyes wide.

She was scared stiff, and so she should be. Her house was a viper's nest.

"Let's not worry ourselves anymore tonight. I'm exhausted." He made a show of stretching and yawning, then turned away from her shadowed face.

The room was alive with noise—the fire hissing, the clock spinning, the windows quaking with wind, the water choppy beyond. Charles waited to hear Louisa's steady breathing, but instead he heard a ragged hiccup and an unladylike sniff.

Damn. She was crying. Bold, brazen Louisa Stratton was within arm's reach, and she needed to be comforted even if he'd promised not to touch her. He warred with himself for only a few seconds before he rolled and reached for her, dragging her to the middle of the enormous bed. She buried her damp face on his bare shoulder, heedless of snot and tears, her body jumpy against his. Charles stroked her back as if she were a nervous woodland creature, settling her at his side, kissing the top of her golden head. Her hair was plaited to her waist and he stroked it, too—it was heavy and smooth and needed to be unraveled. She smelled of violet eau de cologne and soap, clean, sweet.

They should have had their tea and talked companionably in front of a fire before they'd attempted bed, but the pot must be stone cold now. So Charles was left with a weeping woman in his arms, her salty tears and lips against his skin, her body stirring what had long been dormant— no, dead—inside him.

"I'm sorry," she mumbled into his chest. "I don't know what's come over me. I'm usually not such a watering pot."

"Hush. The concept of mortality is enough to drive philosophers and priests mad. I'll hold you until you can sleep."

She blinked up at him, her cheeks wet. Her gilt-tipped lashes were dark, spiky, reminding him of a fawn. But Louisa Stratton was no weak baby deer—she was a madcap heiress who did as she pleased.

Until she returned to Rosemont. Charles had watched the liveliness drain out of her hour by hour.

She frowned. "I'm supposed to be watching over you."

"We can watch over each other." Charles cupped her cheek and wiped a tear away with his thumb.

"Just like a real married couple," she whispered.

"Almost." He wasn't about to frighten her with what he suddenly wanted to do as her pretend husband. She looked up at him with such trust, his heart squeezed. She shouldn't trust him, didn't have a clue what he was capable of.

He would not take advantage of her misery, or any woman's. He had once, and had hated himself ever since. He had done Marja no kindness in the end, and she had died like all the others, no better off for his touch.

"Th-thank you." She stilled, then took a corner of the sheet and wiped the moisture from his shoulder. "I've made a mess of you."

"I've endured worse, believe me."

Louisa settled into the crook of his arm, her body close and hot against his. He imagined she was imprinting him with the pattern from her figured silk robe, branding him with vines and leaves. Charles refused to let himself look down at the creamy skin of her décolletage or the innocent hand that was placed across his chest. She had capable hands, he recalled, hands that moved expressively as she chattered on, hands that could light stoves and shoot guns and drive cars.

And drive a man wild with their light touch upon his skin.

He had only himself to blame for this torture. It might be better to go back to his room and wait to be clubbed to death.

"Charles?"

"Yes?"

"This is very comfortable, don't you agree?"

Not at all.

He gave a grunt that could be interpreted any which way. He should feign sleep, begin to snore so she would stop trying to talk to him. No such luck.

"I've never slept with a man before. In a bed," she amended, in case he had doubts about her virginity. "Isn't that ridiculous? I'm twenty-six years old and ruined anyway, at least according to Aunt Grace. It's not as though I can get my purity back, is it?"

Charles had no answer for her. His throat was a desert and his tongue glued to the roof of his mouth.

"It's rather silly, isn't it—my avoidance of intimacy, I mean. I'm a modern, free woman. Why should I obey society's stringent rules? What's good for the goose and all that. Although it really should be 'what's good for the gander is good for the goose' in this case, shouldn't it? Why should men have all the fun? Of course, in my experience men have been disappointing. Starting with vile Sir Richard. But I haven't yet been able to convince myself of the efficacy of sapphism."

Charles choked. She was babbling. Well, she'd had a shock, although it should be he who was incoherent after getting whacked on the onion.

"I don't suppose you're in the mood to kiss me again, are you? I really don't think I'm sleepy at all."

"K-kiss you?"

"As you did at dinner. I'm not asking you to act as a petticoat-pensioner—you needn't go beyond a kiss. If you don't want to. Although, if someone is trying to kill us, I suppose carpe diem should figure into our thinking."

Was she saying what he thought she was saying? The blow to his head must have scrambled his brain. Charles had had enough. He released her and tumbled backward. "I might not be able to stop myself, brute that I am. I'm as vile as Sir Richard. More so."

"I thought you said I was safe from you." The damn girl gave him a look that said she didn't *want* to be safe.

"I lied." By God, he *had* lied. He was as hard as a rock.

"Well, that's all right then. But I don't think I'd mind at all if you—if we—if—you know."

"No, I bloody well don't!"

"Acted as man and wife. Just for tonight. Who knows what tomorrow will bring? We may be murdered in our sleep." Louisa gave him a dazzling smile, as if the prospect of future death was quite delightful.

"You should be locked up."

"I was. For years. It didn't really work. I am as hopeless as ever. If you agree to perform this extra duty, I will of course make it worth your while financially."

Charles's mouth dropped open. "You will pay me to fuck you?"

"Don't be so rude. Maximillian would never say *fuck*."

"I am not Maximillian. There *is* no Maximillian. By God, your aunt was right to try to contain you. You're mad."

Louisa poked a finger into his chest. "Don't you dare side with her! I am not mad. Just curious. You're right here, I'm right here, and we both need some comfort. It has been a very trying day, you must admit. You needn't do anything out of the ordinary—just the basic shag."

Charles sat up and knocked his shoulder into the headboard. "You do not know what you are saying. Are you sure someone didn't hit *you* in the head?"

"I am perfectly sure this is what I want. I don't know why I didn't think of it before. But then," she mused, "no one I've met before has been as suitable as you for a liaison. You are very handsome, you know. And sufficiently distant. I don't sense you want something from me that I can't give. All my other beaux have been so *grasping*, but my fortune doesn't seem to impress you in the least."

"Believe me, I want your money, or else I wouldn't have agreed to this crackpot scheme," Charles growled. "Do not cloak me with an honor I do not have."

"Oh! But you are honorable. I'm sure of it. The very fact that we're having this argument proves to me you are *just* the man to take me to bed. Now," she said, rising up on an elbow, "let's stop talking. Kiss me, please." She shut her huge brown eyes and pursed her lips.

Devil take it. How could Charles hold out against such baffling logic? He was only a man. In fact, he was relieved to discover he was *still* a man. He would kiss her. He didn't have to go beyond a kiss. She'd said so.

Carpe diem indeed.

Chapter

❦

14

*L*ouisa realized she probably looked like an ornamental goldfish with her lips pursed, so she parted her lips a little, hoping she appeared somewhat kissable, and opened her eyes a fraction. She really was out of practice.

Louisa was not entirely sure what had set her on the path to seduce Captain Cooper this evening. She'd been very stingy with her favors this past year, eluding all sorts of Continental rakes and rogues. A kiss was one thing, but she'd permitted no one to take liberties with her person. Sir Richard's fumblings were still fresh in her mind even after all these years, and she'd not been eager to repeat her foolish mistakes. She was impervious to concupiscence. Invulnerable. A shielded and belted goddess of belated chastity.

But there was something about Charles Cooper that pierced her shield and drove straight into her heart. Maybe it was his reluctance. His natural reticence. His crooked smile. Whatever it was, she felt a connection with him that she'd never expected.

He'd said he drank to excess. That he was doing this for her money. Every step of the way he'd been self-deprecating. Too honest. Yes, he was perfect for this job.

If Louisa looked deep inside herself, which she was loath to do most days, she was terrified of making another mistake for "love." True, she'd been only seventeen when she embarked on her ill-fated affair. When one was seventeen, one knew very little of lasting value, and certainly nothing of love. Her judgment had been execrable. She'd actually thought Sir Richard would marry her!

She'd been consumed with such longing, such *wickedness*, she hadn't spared a thought for everything her aunt had drilled into her from childhood. As easily as she'd bundled up dirty stockings for the laundry maid, Louisa had tossed her virginity away as a despised inconvenience.

Her good sense as well.

Lust was not love. She knew that now, and could be perfectly satisfied with lust for the time being. Lust felt *delicious*. Her body thrummed like a well-oiled engine as she gazed up at Charles Cooper. He was so very attractive. Had done something useful with his life, too, unlike the dilettantes she'd encountered in Europe. It was clear he did not want to overstep his bounds, but it was time to redraw the lines.

Charles did not disappoint, drawing her up into his lap. He stared at her for a few seconds, his eyes blazing bright blue even in the firelit dimness of the room. And then he took utter control of her, one hand delving into her hair while the other skimmed the edge of her robe. She was frozen in place, right where she needed to be. His mouth bore down with just the right amount of pressure, his lips firm and dry. The kiss was commanding, yet still questioned. Louisa sensed she could break it off at will, but that was not the answer she gave him.

She eased into his broad chest, feeling remarkably comfortable despite her very wanton request. She had not wanted a man this close to her in ages, and now she felt as if she'd like to crawl right into him. She let her tongue tease against his, then boldly thrust it inside his mouth, claiming the kiss for her own.

He responded, and they chased each other back and forth until neither was in charge. And wasn't that wonderful, this shared game? No matter who won, they would both benefit.

Sensation washed over her, prickling her scalp clear down to her toes. Louisa was simultaneously cold and hot, her nipples peaking beneath his nimble fingers, which had somehow slipped under the robe. Charles's touch was unerring. Electric. Her breasts ached with unfamiliar need. She'd never paid them much mind before, but suddenly all she wanted was Charles's mouth on her nipples.

That would mean the cessation of this glorious kiss, however, and Louisa was not ready to surrender any part of it. Her body would have to wait to be worshipped. They had all night. The rest of their lives.

Her breath hitched. Where had that thought come from? She mustn't be vulnerable again. This was just lust. Everyone succumbed to it eventually. It was her time. For now.

If his hands could roam, so could hers. His shoulders were broad, his cheek rough with stubble. The knot at his waist was impossible, but she found a slit in the sheet and ventured in.

Mercy. He was huge and hot and temporarily hers. He surged up in her hand, his kiss becoming urgent.

An hour or so ago she was touching herself, and with any luck she could make him do her work for her now. She begged silently for him to reciprocate, and it didn't take him long to push her robe apart. His hand moved from her belly to her nether curls, heading straight for her pulsing center. Her startled—grateful—cry was muffled by the endless, enveloping kiss. She was cocooned in pleasure, in wet and warmth. Charles seemed to know where to touch her. How to touch her. She hoped she was returning the favor, doing justice to the hard velvet cock in her hand.

Perhaps he'd think her clumsiness was simple enthusiasm. It was hard to concentrate when he continued to stroke and swirl over her most sensitive flesh. But he seemed to have no objection to what she was doing, so Louisa tried to match his rhythm and intensity.

It was working. The kiss lost its focus and Charles withdrew, gasping against her throat, sending shivers down her body. She nipped his shoulder, trailed tiny kisses everywhere she could reach. She was still sitting across his thighs and wondering when he would tip her down to the mattress when the spurt of hot liquid spilled over her hand. She stiffened in surprise as he pushed her away, removing his magical hand and leaving her bereft of her own climax.

"Jesus," he said raggedly, looking chagrined. "I'm sorry. I'm like a schoolboy. That was unforgivable." He wiped her hand with the sheet he still had wrapped around him.

"What's unforgivable is that I did not join you in your bliss."

He looked at her and burst out laughing. "You look so damn prim. And here you are asking me to finish you off. Give me a moment to catch my breath and I'll get to it."

His reaction was so very strange. Almost manic. "Never mind. I can take care of myself."

"The hell you will! I'll go mad if I have to watch you touch yourself. I'm sorry, Louisa. It's been a very long time for me. To have a woman in my bed. I've said as much to you. I thought myself—incapable. But tonight I never thought once about—" His smile disappeared as if it never was.

"What? Or should I say who?" She straightened the folds of her robe. "Who is your lost love that's ruined you for other women?"

"It wasn't like that." He swung his legs off the bed and sat at the edge, his back to her. Louisa saw a scattering of light scars down one side of his back. Shrapnel, she decided. Poor Charles.

"What *was* it like?"

"We should go to sleep. I'll go back to my room and pray someone puts me out of my embarrassment. Brick. Shovel. Whatever's handy."

"So you'll renege on your promise?"

He turned to look at her over his shoulder, his face in deepest shadow. "What do you mean?"

"You were, as I believe you put it, going to 'finish me off.' I'm holding you to that. It's not at all fair, what just happened. It's been a very long time for me as well."

He was silent so long she wondered if he remembered how to talk.

Then he sighed. "You are a most unusual young woman, Louisa Stratton. One underestimates you at one's peril."

"Thank you, I suppose. Some might just call me a hoyden."

"That, too. Lie down then and make yourself comfortable. I aim to earn my keep."

"This isn't about money," she said, unable to keep the annoyance out of her voice. "I think we're beyond that, don't you?"

He settled his long body down beside her. "Miles and miles beyond. You look adorable when you're angry."

"I'm not angry. Just sexually frustrated. Dr. Freud believes—"

"Hang Dr. Freud and all the other charlatans." Charles kissed the tip of her nose, causing her to go cross-eyed for an instant. His face was still close when he finished, his breath warm on her cheek. "Don't you want to unbelt that robe?"

"When you remove your sheet."

"Very well." He gave a tug and the linen slipped from his hips. His member was in a state of repose against a nest of black curls, but still quite fascinatingly large. Much bigger than Sir Richard's, she realized with a trace of dismay. She should not be thinking of that man now, even if Charles was recalling an old amour. "Your turn."

Louisa fumbled with the silk and Charles had to help her. The fabric parted under Charles's intent inspection. "You are beautiful. Much too beautiful for the likes of me."

"D-don't be silly." Louisa was not completely at ease with Charles's direct gaze.

"No. Really. Your waist is so tiny. How did you manage that?"

"Waist training. From the time I was a little girl. I slept in my corset for years. Aunt Grace's doing. There were times I thought I couldn't swallow a bite."

He traced a finger down her breastbone to her navel. "Torture. Torment."

"Yes, but now my figure conforms perfectly to the fashions. I suppose I should thank her." Louisa wondered what might happen if she ever became pregnant, but that was not likely to happen. She'd have to find a husband first, and she was not looking for one.

Good heavens. Had Charles Cooper ever had a wife? Was he some sad widower who went off to war, leaving her behind to die alone? "Tell me about this woman."

"No. Not now. I'm going to be much too busy." He bent and pressed his lips on the broad curve of her hip. Then he moved down her thigh, feathering her skin with tickling kisses. He was so awfully close—

"W-what are you doing?"

"Pleasuring you, of course. Has no one tasted you before?"

"Tasted me? I'm not a foodstuff."

"That's where you're wrong. The nectar of the gods is right here."

And then his tongue—his tongue!—swept into the crevice of her mons veneris and she screamed.

"Hush. We don't want to disturb the household. I am not hurting you, am I?"

Oh, he was evil. The smug look on his face told her he knew exactly what effect he was having upon her.

How stupid she was. Louisa should have realized men could do this to women, just as women could do it to men. How lovely would it be if they could do it to each other at the same time. Was that even possible? Louisa would ask once Charles had finished, because clearly she could not speak a word at the moment.

His mouth was incomparable. Teeth and tongue and fingers helping. Plunging. Tugging. Doing things Louisa did not know the verbs for. Some pressure on her pubic bone, a flick and she was shattering, legs splayed, her back arching off the bed in exquisite agony. And still he didn't stop until she rose twice more to the impossible peak of perfection.

"Nectar," he said, as he moved up the bed. "See for yourself." He covered her mouth with his and she felt a hot flush of arousal course through her body. This could not be proper at all. But when had she given a fig for propriety?

Louisa kissed him back, having lost her mind and whatever scruples she'd ever possessed. Charles Cooper was a demon. And he was *her* demon for the next thirty days.

She reached for his manhood, thrilled to feel it, too, had responded to Charles's miraculous kiss. Louisa was greedy. She wanted more. She wanted it all, every messy, sweaty adventure he was capable of giving her. They might only have tonight, for someone was out to hurt them. She really, really should release him from his obligation and face Rosemont and its residents alone. Maximillian could be called away on business, or they could quarrel as husbands and wives did. He would be safe.

But not tonight. She was too selfish. And stubborn. She wanted to erase whatever memory Charles had that brought that bleakness to his eyes. She would banish that ghost if he let her.

She broke the wicked kiss. "Make love to me," she whispered. His cock jerked in her hand. *"Please."*

Charles looked at her, his eyes black with desire. "It wasn't enough?"

"Nothing will ever be enough. You've corrupted me."

"Good," he said, and proceeded to corrupt her further.

Chapter

❧

15

This was folly. But Charles was every bit as swept away as the foolish woman in his arms. Someone had to see reason, but he was very much afraid it wasn't he.

Louisa Stratton was his employer, but that trifling detail had nothing to do with his current confusion. He wanted her, wanted a woman for the first time in months. But what if Marja came between them, a wraith reminding him of his guilt?

No. Not now. There was no one in his senses but Louisa, whose taste and touch and scent had driven him delightfully mad. There would be consequences, but for this night he would pretend he was normal, pretend he was Maximillian Norwich, engaging in church-blessed carnal relations with his lovely, rich wife. There was nothing sordid or salacious about sticking his needy prick in her smooth wet passage and bringing them both to ecstasy.

Louisa parted for him and he pushed in, grateful there was no barrier of resistance. She was not a virgin, a fact that didn't trouble him beyond wishing she'd given her virtue to someone more worthy than Sir Richard Delacourt. She was right—women deserved their satisfaction as much as men. He might not support the suffragist cause, but why should one half of the population be denied what physical comfort God had given humans? Most lives were brutal and short—one almost had an obligation to snatch happiness where one found it.

Of course, there was pregnancy to fear, and Charles cautioned himself to withdraw when it was time. But until then he would savor every inch of friction, every sigh that escaped Louisa's lips. He rose over her, feeling strong and almost certain of the rightness of this act. They had well pleasured each other, but now the experience was mutual.

Her response was everything he could hope for as they found their sensual path together, meeting and parting until he drove into her with no further thought of teasing escape. She was crying in earnest now, wild, swallowing him up inside the hot core of her womanhood, her fingernails raking his back.

He canted his body until he knew his cock brushed against her clitoris, grinding against her, going deeper with every circling of his hips. She was helpless, wordless, her mouth begging for a kiss. He obliged, leaning down and using his tongue as a weapon of victory. She splintered beneath him, rocking up under him in broken waves, rising, falling, rising up again. Her orgasm was as undisciplined as her driving—Louisa had lost all control.

If he was not careful, he would do the same. With the utmost reluctance, he withdrew and pushed his cock hard against her, spilling onto her smooth white skin. It was almost enough, but he groaned in frustration anyway at being denied the ultimate satisfaction. To be totally accepted. To mark her inside and out as his own. Something primitive blossomed within him and he bit a spot above her collarbone, sucking the flesh between his teeth as she gave a little scream beneath him.

Charles had hurt her. Louisa lay breathless beneath

him, her body shaking. Her eyes were dark and wide, finally seeing him as he was.

He was a beast who took advantage of those weaker than he. Why, he could snap Louisa Stratton in half, get hold of her by her tiny waist and squeeze the heedless, vibrant life out of her.

As he'd done once before.

He shut his eyes against her accusing beauty and rolled away, leaving her to the mess on her stomach. He couldn't touch her again.

"Charles, what is it?" Her voice was soft. A balm. One would never know she'd been shrieking like a wild cat moments before.

"This—this wasn't right. None of it. I'm sorry I . . . defiled you. I will leave in the morning."

Louisa gathered up the covers with unnatural calm. "You are rejecting my friendship?"

His mouth twisted. "Friendship? Is that what silly society girls call this? Pardon me. I call it fucking, Miss Stratton. We've satisfied the itch now. There's no need to drag it out any longer and repeat the mistake." His head ached. She looked so innocent amidst the jumble of sheets and pillows. So fresh, a living rebuke to his darkness.

"Stop talking such nonsense! Tell me what is wrong."

What wasn't? Though at least Louisa wasn't dead.

"There's nothing wrong. There's nothing right. I suppose I must thank you for tonight—I never expected to have relations with a woman again."

"Why not? You're not attracted to your own sex are you?"

"Jesus Christ." He laughed in spite of himself. "Not guilty of *that*."

"What are you guilty of?"

She was like a terrier after a rat. Charles supposed he qualified as the rat. So she thought she wanted to know more about the man she'd hired to debauch her? She wouldn't like what she would hear.

He'd never spoken of what happened, not to his friends or his doctors or his family. It was all there in his journals, though, which were now buried beneath his new underwear in the top drawer of his dresser. Maybe he should fetch them and she could read a paragraph or two. Charles would watch her fascination turn to disgust, then horror. She would understand why he had to leave, why Maximillian Norwich, and certainly Charles Cooper, had to die.

He would tell her, and then he would go. She'd push him out the door herself.

"There was a woman. A girl, really. In the concentration camp I helped to administer. You've heard of the Fawcett Commission?"

Louisa nodded, her face grave.

"You cannot imagine the conditions the women and children endured there until it was turned over to the civilian authorities. It was—it was hell on earth. Sickening. You don't know the barbaric cruelty that permeated the army. Scorched earth. Britain's glory days are well behind us all. No wonder people want revolution." He would never believe anyone in authority again.

"Did you love her, this girl?"

Charles shook his head. That was really the worst of it. He hadn't known Marja at all. "She was dying. And she didn't want to die a virgin."

"Oh, Charles." She reached to touch his hand, but he snatched it away.

"I fucked her, Louisa. Oh, not fucked. She was too weak and I was too frightened of discovery. We were quiet. Quiet as death. I was consorting with the enemy, don't you know. A girl in my care to boot. Someone I was responsible for, though God knows no one truly cared what happened to the women in that camp. I'm a man with no honor, a man who did nothing to change the circumstances I found myself in."

"What could you do, Charles? You were just one person."

"That's no excuse. I should have killed myself rather than take part in it all. Instead, I killed her."

"You didn't."

"I did. Or may as well have. She died minutes after we had sexual congress. Had a heart attack. She was so tiny. Skin and bones, but stronger than I was."

Marja once must have been a beautiful girl. She was a rich Boer farmer's daughter who had been educated—she spoke English better than half of Charles's men. He hadn't been in the camp ten days when she sought him out, her yellow hair in broken tufts around her skull. Her eyes were the color of the endless African sky, and they bored holes straight into Charles's soul. She had been moved from camp to camp, watched her mother and sisters die. When she'd made her proposition, Charles knew she had doomed them both.

"I can't forget the look on her face when she—when she died. Almost . . . happy. Lucky to have escaped the disease and degradation. I envied her." He ran a rough hand over his head, forgetting the bandage. Louisa was quiet beside him, staring into the fire, her profile limned like an Italian cameo.

"No one knew what had happened—I covered my tracks well. She was just another dead Boer. But I knew. I—I did things. Said things my superiors didn't want to hear. They put me back in the hospital, then shipped me home. I couldn't stay in the army, so I resigned." His bitterness curled inside him like a living thing, tainting everything he touched. How could he have let himself get into Louisa Stratton's bed?

He took a breath. "So you see, the fabled Mrs. Evensong made a terrible mistake hiring me. *You* have made an even worse one bedding me. There's no excuse for what I've done. What I am."

"I agree." Her voice was clipped, devoid of the sympathy she'd shown all night. It served him right. "You are surely the stupidest man in creation! You did a kindness to that poor girl at the expense of your career, and now you're going about like the bloody voice of doom. War is awful, Charles. Everyone knows that, even 'silly society girls' like me. I read the papers and know they don't tell the whole truth. Is this story what's in those journals you were clutching at your boarding house?"

Charles's jaw went slack. Perhaps she wasn't so silly after all.

"I can see from your face I am right. Be careful when you next play cards at Monte Carlo, Mr. Norwich—you will fool no one. You should publish your experiences so that nothing like it ever happens again," Louisa continued, putting an arm into the sleeve of her discarded robe. "There will be other wars. There always are. Men make sure of that, don't they? And we women have no say except to weep over our dead lovers and children."

"Louisa—"

She held up a hand. "There is nothing more you can say to me unless it's to tell me you have reconsidered and will be staying here at Rosemont. If you cannot promise me the month I've hired you for, you might as well slink away tonight. I can tell Aunt Grace about the attack on you. People will understand that you don't want to lounge about, waiting to be assaulted again."

"You think I am a coward."

"Maximillian might be a coward. I don't think you are, Charles."

She was covered up now. A damn shame. Her braid had come loose and a torrent of tangled fair hair fell to her waist. Louisa Stratton would need no false hair or pads for her pompadour, or any paint for her flushed face. She was lovely, and Charles had ruined their extraordinary moment. The woman had given herself to him, and he'd proven by every word and deed he was unworthy. What kind of man made love to a woman and then confessed to the death of another? What could he say now to dig himself out of this wretched hole?

He'd been in torment for months, but somehow Louisa Stratton had cut right through it all. She folded her arms across the pink robe and watched him expectantly. He was going to disappoint her.

"I don't know what to do."

"You dream about this girl."

Charles nodded. "Among other things. There's no shortage of bad memories for me to mine."

"Then we need to give you good things to dream about. I'll confess I don't want you to go. I have need of you here to help with Aunt Grace. You needn't come to my bed again if you stay at Rosemont—I agree this was probably very unwise. We can chalk it up as the capstone to a very odd evening all around."

It was ridiculous to feel hurt when she'd only expressed his own opinion. "Let me sleep on it. If I can."

"Perhaps you should go to your own room after all. We can talk at breakfast. I've arranged to have it delivered up here. Everyone thinks we're still honeymooning, you know," she said, wistful.

She had not been shocked by his tale. Only . . . irritated. Annoyed that his past infused his present so thoroughly. She'd called him the voice of doom. Cheeky baggage.

Louisa Stratton made it all sound easy—he was simply to forget the ugliness and move on. Write an account of the camp and publish it! As if he could purge himself of Marja's ghost. He had tried to drink her away and that hadn't worked.

But when Charles finally succumbed to Morpheus sometime close to dawn, he dreamed of a cream and gold creature, her hourglass body beneath him. Above him. A kiss on her wicked lips and mischief in her dark eyes. The scent of violets and sex.

He slept on.

Chapter

16

Just his bloody luck. Mrs. Lang had gone off for her mother's funeral, so there was no one to sheepdog after the maids to keep them safe in their own beds. And here was Kathleen in his. But would she let him stay there with her for a kiss and cuddle? Bloody hell, but no.

Robbie Robertson crept back up the dark stairs to his little apartment over the garage. He was not feeling particularly proud of himself. Their little plan—really, Kathleen's little plan—had been risky in the extreme. The damn house was like a giant rabbit warren, and any one of three dozen servants could have come upon him as he navigated Rosemont in the dark. What reason would a chauffeur have for being upstairs near the master suite? And holding a truncheon to boot?

Kathleen was reading a green book by lamplight. "Did you see anything worth seeing? And did you put a stop to it?" she asked, turning a page.

"Aye, you daft woman." Robbie Robertson threw himself down on his narrow bed, where Kathleen had already made herself quite at home. Her freckled shoulders rose above the coverlet, and with a naughty smile she put down the book and pulled the coverlet aside, revealing a pale breast that fit perfectly in his hand. He'd missed that breast and its match. But now she was home and not going anywhere if he could help it.

"Your reward."

"I'm not sure it's enough. He was all by himself, probably minding his own business with not a thought to ravishing Miss Stratton. I may have hit him too hard. They could arrest me for attempted murder."

Her green eyes widened. "Hush now! You never meant to really harm him!"

"Tell that to the poor bloke's head when he wakes up. And will you testify in my trial, lass? No, they'll be arresting you, too."

"No one is getting arrested," Kathleen sniffed. "As long as he couldn't have his wicked way tonight with Miss Louisa, we've both done the right thing. I heard all about that kiss at dinner from the footmen. Shocking, it was, in front of all those people when he's being paid to behave. He's a dangerous man—I can feel it."

"You may be right there. Look what I almost tripped on." Robbie pulled the captain's gun from his coat pocket.

Kathleen's freckles stood out against her white cheeks. "Is it loaded?"

Robbie shrugged. "Not anymore. Why would the gentleman bring a gun to Rosemont?"

"You see? He *is* dangerous! And he's no gentleman. I saw where he lived, remember. What kind of decent man would hire himself out as he has? He's after something. For all her wild ways, Miss Louisa is such an innocent. Look what happened with that rat Delacourt. It was before my time, but everyone knows how hurt she was. She needs a keeper."

"And you've appointed yourself to that role. Who will take care of her after we're married?"

Kathleen sprang away. "Why shouldn't I still work for

her? Don't tell me you'll forbid it! I'll not take orders from you or anyone!"

"Didn't you say she'll leave Rosemont again if she can't get rid of her aunt? I'll not have my wife gallivanting all over creation in someone else's motorcar. I might get so lonely I'd have to find a sweetheart."

Kathleen punched him in the chest with a little fist. "Damn you, Robbie Robertson! Don't joke about such a thing."

He grabbed her arms with both hands and looked into her face as earnestly as he knew how. "Kat, you were gone thirteen months, two weeks, and four days. I was true to you even when my cock ached so bad I was afraid to bring myself off. I put up with that bitch of an aunt sneering at my car and my driving all that time, twiddling my thumbs while she had Thomas hitch up the carriages. I got so bored, every inch of that car was like a mirror, it was so damned shiny."

"I know. You wrote me."

He dropped her back into the pillows and stared out the tiny dark window. "I've got no reason to stay here, Kat. We could go somewhere else, make a good life for ourselves. Cars are the future, you know. I can fix them. I can drive them. Maybe even build one of my own someday. I'm a fair mechanic. I don't have to be a chauffeur forever. You don't have to be a maid."

He felt a soothing hand on his back. "There's nothing wrong with being in service, Robbie. I'm not ashamed I work for Miss Louisa."

"No one's saying you should be ashamed. But don't you ever just want to be free? Have the wind in your hair and the sun on your face?"

"What, and get my hair all ratty and even more freckles? You're a dreamer, Robbie."

His Kathleen was tart-tongued and invariably sensible. He sighed. "Aye, I am."

"And you're a *man*. It's fine to talk of freedom, but if

we marry I'll be bearing one baby after another like my mother did, and who will be free then? Neither one of us."

"If we marry? It's when, Kat. *When.* You talk to Miss Stratton. I'm ready to call the banns."

"First we've got to make sure she's safe from that man. Just because he's got a pretty arse—"

"Kathleen Carmichael!" Robbie spluttered.

"I'm not blind like he is. He's a good-looking man, and my mistress is vulnerable. No one's ever treated her right, not even her own family. Poor girl. So, tell me. You hit him with the truncheon?"

"You are a bloodthirsty little thing."

"Was he in bed?"

"No, sitting up in a chair in his room. It was an awful mess, stuff everywhere. A gun on the floor! Imagine. I did him a favor picking it up. He never saw me, but I'm worried just the same. What if he's dead?" Robbie didn't think he hit the man that hard, only enough to prevent him from enjoying Miss Stratton's bed, but he had fallen face-first on the floor. Robbie had been too scared to check for a pulse.

"He's not dead. We'd know." She was so stubborn in her righteousness. Maybe he'd be better off with Kathleen far, far away. She was bound to lead him a merry jig when they married.

"How would we?" Robbie asked patiently. "Miss Stratton's asleep. No one will find his body until the morning when they come in to light the fire in his room."

Kathleen bit a lip. "Oh, stop, Robbie. You're making me nervous."

"As you should be. Wait! Where are you going?" Kathleen had scrambled out of bed, her slender body lovely in the lamplight. So many freckles—he'd like to lick each one.

"I'd better go up and check."

"Now?"

"Of course now. Neither one of us will be able to relax

until we know he's all right. Alive, at least. I'll be right back."

She pulled her shift over her copper hair and was dressed before he could talk her out of going. "Be careful."

"I'm always careful." She waved and disappeared out the door.

Damn. The evening was in no way progressing as he'd hoped. When Kathleen had climbed his stairs, his heart had leapt with joy. Until she told him what she wanted him to do. Robbie couldn't make her see sense. She was a loyal little thing, he'd have to give her that, so worried about Louisa Stratton it had been easy to promise to incapacitate Maximillian Norwich for the rest of the night. No, what was the man's real name? It didn't matter. Kathleen had sworn him to secrecy. The whole scheme was proof that Miss Stratton was light in the brain-box.

Robbie undressed, folding his uniform carefully on a chair and locking the captain's old pistol in his trunk. He fed a few coals into the stove in the corner of the room. He didn't want Kathleen to be cold when she came back, though he planned other ways to warm her up.

He'd been celibate for over a year. It was unnatural. The other men on Rosemont's staff had teased him unmercifully, but he had an understanding with Kathleen, and he meant to keep his word. They'd fallen in love quickly last year—a risk for servants who were at the whims of their employers. But before he knew it, she was gone. Weekly letters were no substitute. She was finally here now, or would be once she'd determined he wasn't a murderer.

He should have gone with her, but he'd made one escape from the house and didn't want to press his luck. It was very late, well past midnight. And colder than a witch's tit outside with the wind blowing up off the Channel. Naked, he got under the covers and waited to hear Kathleen's footsteps on the stairs.

And waited. What was keeping her? Had she decided

not to come back? Robbie hoped that was not the case—once the housekeeper Mrs. Lang came back, the maids would be locked in at night and let out in the morning only to perform their drudgery. He and Kathleen would have very few chances to be alone, and Robbie had been counting on tonight to last him for weeks.

He heard the soft thud of the door below and smiled. At last. He was just sitting up when one of his boots sailed through the air, missing his head by inches.

"Oi! What was that for?"

"Well, the bastard is not dead, you'll be happy to know."

Robbie felt the knot of worry unravel. "Isn't that a good thing? How inconvenient it would be if I had to go to the gallows."

"Oh, I don't know. I'd like to hang you myself. Captain Cooper is not asleep."

"Oh? Did he bother you?" Robbie was prepared to hit the fellow on the head again if that was the case.

"He's not bothering *me*. He and Miss Louisa are fornicating even as we speak."

Kathleen looked fit to be tied. It was too much to hope for that she'd been inspired by witnessing this unexpected event. "What? Are you sure?"

"Quite. She is mewling like a cat. He is panting and grunting like a savage. The bedsprings are creaking like a badly tuned violin. I could hear them through the sitting room door. I didn't go in, of course."

Her cheeks were as fiery as her hair. "Did you by any chance look through the keyhole?" he asked.

"What if I did? The room was too dark to see anything, but I have ears. Robbie, how could you?"

"I hit him; I swear I did."

"Not hard enough. Poor Louisa. We'll have to get rid of him some other way."

"All you have to do is tell the truth to Mrs. Westlake. He's not Maximillian Norwich, now is he? Not really her husband or anybody's."

Kathleen sank down on the chair that held his clothes. "I couldn't do that to her. She'd be mortified, and her aunt would never let her hear the end of it."

Robbie patted the mattress. "Come to bed, Kat. There's nothing else we can do tonight."

"I won't be able to sleep a wink."

Robbie grinned. "No, you won't. I'll make sure of that."

He caught the other boot before it could do any harm.

Chapter

❦

17

Friday, December 4, 1903

*L*ouisa buried her face under the blanket and groaned as Kathleen drew back the faded chintz curtains.

"Good morning to you, too, Miss Louisa. *Mrs.* Norwich," her maid said tartly.

"What time is it?"

"Time for you to get up. They're setting up breakfast in the sitting room right now as you requested. You wouldn't want your eggs to be cold."

Louisa had no interest in eggs, cold or hot. "Is my husband awake?" she asked loudly for the benefit of the servants on the other side of the door.

"Dead to the world. Neither one of you woke up when Molly came up to light the fires." Kathleen bent to retrieve Louisa's nightgown from the carpet. "Exciting night?"

"Give me that!" Louisa grabbed it from her maid's hand and pulled it over her head. Sometime in her restless night her robe had untied and she was naked again.

Did Kathleen suspect what happened? She seemed very grumpy this morning. "I'll just wash up and wake him myself," Louisa said, climbing out of bed. She took a step and realized she was sore between her legs. Captain Cooper had been deliciously rough, but he was not apt to repeat himself.

Louisa entered the gleaming white bathing chamber and turned on the taps of the sink. She didn't dare look in the mirror to see the aftereffects of last night. Were her lips still swollen from kisses? She washed her face, then lifted her nightgown and sponged her body, wiping away the dried evidence of her folly. An atomizer of violet scent sat on the dresser under the window. Louisa spritzed herself in all the relevant places, ran a brush through her knotted hair, and then tapped on Captain Cooper's door.

"Go away," he mumbled.

Louisa turned the doorknob. The room was no longer locked. Charles Cooper was fully dressed, standing before his windows. He had tidied up the room. All the books had been returned to their stack and the bed was made up as neatly as if one of the maids had been in.

"Did you sleep at all?"

"Some."

She lifted a brow. "Well?"

"I'll stay."

That was that. He did not elaborate.

"Excellent. Breakfast is ready if you are." Louisa was suddenly aware she stood in the doorway in her white batiste nightgown. "I'll join you in the sitting room in a minute."

He knew to go out the door to the hallway to give her some privacy in her dressing room. She pulled a heavier brocade robe from the wardrobe and caught a glimpse of herself in the mirrored door. A livid bruise stood out at the base of her throat, nearly matching the deep garnet color of the dressing gown. No wonder Kathleen had given her that sour look. What would people think if they saw it?

That she had been well loved by her husband.

She buttoned up the nightgown. Louisa would have to turn her mind to how to make herself a widow soon. Maximillian must perish in some dignified way, and thus far she had no clue how to accomplish that. Captain Cooper looked too young and healthy despite his recent history of drinking to succumb to illness. It would have to be an accident.

If he was bashed on the head again, it just might come true.

Louisa was disturbed by the act of violence. Frightened, too. Rosemont had taken a sinister turn in her imaginings. They would have to get to the bottom of last night's mischief, but first Charles had his interview with her aunt.

Louisa gave up trying to do something with her hair and let it fall over her shoulders. She was, she realized, hungry despite her earlier distaste for breakfast. Whether she could swallow a morsel facing Charles Cooper was another matter.

Resolutely, she walked through to the sitting room. Charles sat at the round table in front of the window nursing a cup of coffee, but he rose immediately when she entered. He was handsome in his new clothes this morning, his eye patch in place. "Good morning, my dearest Louisa," he said, a hint of amusement in his voice.

"Good morning, my dearest Max." Louisa turned to the footman for whose benefit this display of affection was intended. He hovered near a large cart laden with silver-topped dishes, enough for Charles's regiment. It must have been a devil of a job getting it all upstairs and rolling down the hallways. The kitchen was out to impress the new master. "I think we can serve ourselves. William, isn't it?"

"Yes, ma'am," the young man said.

"William, please tell Cook she has outdone herself again. Thank you."

Louisa waited until William was gone before seating herself. Then she popped back up. "May I fix you a plate?"

"Like a good wife?"

"Like a good hostess." She could feel the warmth on her cheeks. Captain Cooper unsettled her, now more than ever. He had seen her. All of her. And she had seen him, too. Louisa knew exactly what lay underneath all those fine clothes.

But they had agreed that last night had been a mistake. It seemed Louisa was specializing in mistakes that resulted in carnal knowledge with the wrong man. One would think after Sir Richard that she would be immune to a man's charms.

But Charles had been charming in his way. He had needed her last evening as much as she had needed him.

Now that the sun was trying to peek out behind the clouds, the threat of bodily harm to either one of them didn't seem so dire. She reached for the silver coffee pot to top off the captain's cup.

"What if the food's poisoned?" he asked conversationally.

Louisa set the pot down with a clank. "You don't think—"

"It's hard to know what to think. The coffee seems fine. My head's not swimming—I can see you clearly. That's a very pretty robe you're wearing, by the way."

"Th-thank you. I am a little underdressed. You look ready to meet Aunt Grace. How is your head?"

"Tolerable. I thought it best to get ready before you woke up. Isn't it odd that your parents shared a bathroom? I thought toffs kept separate quarters."

"Most do." Louisa looked at the cart with dismay. "Poison? Really?"

"I'm game if you are. We should eat exactly the same things so we don't have a Romeo and Juliet scenario. Might as well pop off together."

"You are taking all of this remarkably well, I must say."

"It's not the first time people have tried to kill me." Charles rose from the table and lifted the lids. "Looks good. Doesn't smell funny. Kippers?"

Louisa shuddered. "No. Nor kidneys or bacon. I don't usually eat meat in the morning."

"Well, if you survive breakfast and I don't, I guess we'll know the reason why." He heaped his plate with an unconscionable amount of food, then spread a linen serviette on his lap and tucked in.

Louisa was slower to choose. Now that the possibility of poison had seeped into her mind, she evaluated each item. Strychnine in the pot of jam? Rat poison in the eggs, posing as pepper? She placed a slice of dry toast on her plate. It seemed safe enough. Cook liked her—she'd spent quite a bit of her childhood in the kitchen when she wasn't hiding in her room or the conservatory. But certainly the food could have been tampered with as it rolled through the corridors.

"We should just leave," she said, staring out at the glistening waves.

"You want to turn tail and run?"

"I never wanted to come home in the first place. Hugh wrote that his mother was dangerously ill, and so did Dr. Fentress, but we've both seen for ourselves that she's perfectly well as long as she's skewering me. The real reason I came back was to straighten out some issues with my bank. And also Kathleen was homesick. Lovesick, more likely. She and Robertson have formed an attachment."

"The brawny Scots chauffeur?"

"Aye, laddie." Louisa took a reluctant bite of toast. For someone who had been hungry, she had a great deal of difficulty chewing.

Charles noticed. "You'll have to eat more than that. Look, I'm still alive." The captain's plate was nearly empty.

"It might be a slow-acting poison. You could topple over hours from now."

"I knew I could count on you to brighten my day."

And your night. Now where did that thought come from? Louisa was not going to warm Charles Cooper's bed again, or he hers.

Though it had been rather splendid. Even his confession did little to spoil the feeling of repletion and well-being Louisa had at the end. If he had been half as masterful with the poor prison camp girl, she had died a happy woman.

Louisa startled at the warm hand that closed over hers across the table. She looked up, and he gave her a crooked smile. "I think we should be honest with each other, don't you? Us against the world and all that."

She nodded, wondering what else he had to tell her.

"Thank you for last night. For your understanding afterward as well. I was churlish. A boor. You gave me your greatest gift and I'm afraid I was too sunk in my own misery to appreciate it."

"Y-you already thanked me."

"But I didn't mean it as much as I do this morning."

"Maybe you *have* been poisoned."

"No, more like hit on the head. Maybe it's time to"—his eye slid from hers to the sea below—"accept, I suppose. I cannot go back and change anything I did, for good or bad."

"No one can rewrite history." If she could, her parents would not die, and Aunt Grace would be a safe distance away from Rosemont.

"Oh, can't they? The winners always glorify themselves."

"I suppose that's true." His hand was still on hers, and Louisa felt no need to pull away. It was very companionable, sitting at the little table together, a brisk fire going, crumbs and coffee cups between them. Like a real married couple.

"Well, anyway, I want you to know that last night was . . . important to me, and I'll do everything I can this month to be a proper consort in front of your family. No more stolen kisses and so forth."

Louisa felt a brief pang of regret. But surely that was the sensible solution to carrying out their masquerade. She nodded.

"Well, now that that's settled, let me fix *you* a plate. That toast's not enough to keep a bird alive."

Louisa made no objection. She watched as he dropped small, precise spoonfuls of food on a plate—some stewed apples, scrambled eggs, the deviled kidneys that she would not eat. He buttered another piece of toast lavishly and topped it with strawberry preserves, then placed it all before her. To her amazement, he refilled his plate and kept her company. He was on the thin side, but if he continued to eat like this she'd have to roll him out of Rosemont after Christmas.

"Should I tell your aunt about last night?"

Louisa swallowed hard, then realized he meant the assault. "Maybe. If she was behind it, you might warn her off. Talk about going to the authorities."

"Who are the local authorities?"

Louisa made a face. "Sir Richard is the magistrate. I really don't want to have any more to do with him if I can help it."

"I concur. Oily fellow, isn't he?"

"The oiliest." Louisa wondered how her old friend Lady Blanche was faring as his wife. She had always been delicate, but they had been married for almost nine years now, so Blanche must be made of hardier stuff than Louisa supposed. They had several children, too, and by all accounts from the servants' gossip Blanche was a devoted mother. Louisa did not know this for a fact, as all contact had been cut between the Priory and Rosemont years ago. She could have used a friend, but Aunt Grace had forbidden visitors after the disgrace.

Then again, Blanche would have been unlikely to visit her husband's paramour. Louisa's affair with Sir Richard had been brief and before the marriage, but it was a well-known scandal. Both Sir Richard and Grace had seen to that.

Gosh, she was falling into a funk about her own past after she'd chided Charles. She pasted a smile on her face. "Are you ready for the Inquisition?"

"I am wearing chainmail armor under my coat. I trust I'll still have my fingernails after Grace is done with me."

"She won't be done until you agree to give me up." Louisa set her fork down. She really was too agitated now to eat.

"Why does she dislike you so?"

"I haven't any idea. Well, no, that's not true. I know she disliked my mother. But I look nothing like her."

Charles cocked his head and studied her. "No, your resemblance to your aunt is most remarkable."

"Don't remind me. It's a little like looking at a mirror that's going blind. The same, but different."

"She must resent you for being so beautiful while she is fading."

"B-beautiful?" Louisa knew she looked well enough, and her French clothes were certainly as flattering as money could buy, but beautiful? She had freckles, her mouth was too wide, and she had that wretched brown mole in the corner of her lips.

"Beautiful. And I'm not saying that because you are my employer."

For a moment Louisa had forgotten their true relationship. Charles felt like a friend, though he was both more and less than that. "Thank you."

Charles pulled a chased gold watch from his waistcoat pocket. Used, but heirloom quality. Mrs. Evensong had an eye for detail and had kitted him out flawlessly. "It's nearly time. Let me go brush my teeth again so I may smile at the old biddy without fear."

"You'll have a lot to fear if you call her an old biddy. She's only forty-six." Hugh had been born when Grace was just seventeen, and she was widowed by twenty-one. So much responsibility at such an early age. Louisa supposed that might account for her sour disposition. Louisa's own youthful antics had not been helpful in sweetening her aunt's mood, either.

Maybe her aunt really wouldn't have been such an ogre

if she hadn't been stuck with two wild little children in this gargoyle-infested house, barely more than a child herself. If Grace had had someone to love her, Louisa's upbringing might have been very different.

Ah, she was allowing sympathetic sentiment to enter the picture. Aunt Grace would not approve—she didn't have a drop of emotion in her.

"Good luck, Charles. I mean Max."

He rose from the table and leaned down. "Give us a kiss then for that luck."

She shut her eyes to that looming presence and lifted her face, expecting a peck on her cheek.

And that was exactly what she got.

Damn.

Chapter

❦

18

With the help of one of the ubiquitous footmen, Charles located Grace Westlake's suite of rooms. It was in a tower—Rosemont had six of them, all ringed with menacing gargoyles—and Charles was relieved and a little out of breath when he finally reached the top step. No wonder Grace was ill, if she had to make the climb several times a day.

He knocked on a cruciform door and was admitted by a stringy middle-aged woman in a maid's uniform. Grace was seated on a wing chair in the sunny parlor, her feet up on a tufted cushion. She wore a ruffled peach peignoir and matching slippers, but her face was carefully made up and her hair coiled in a neat chignon—she had not recently risen from her bed. She was a very pretty woman for her age—for any age, really—but had none of the sparky liveliness of her niece.

"That will be all, Perkins. Tell Miss Spruce to bring up the correspondence in an hour, and when dear Dr. Fentress arrives have him sent right up. Do sit down, Mr. Norwich. Or did we decide on Max?"

"We *are* family." Charles gave her an insincere smile.

"Are we? For the time being at least, though you strike me as a sensible young man. Surely you are giving the information I told you last night serious consideration."

"Mrs. Westlake. Aunt Grace. It does not matter one iota to me that Louisa was not a virgin. Neither was I. We fell in love, and love overcomes all obstacles, don't you think?"

Charles was talking out of his rump. He'd never been in love, not even when he was a moonling. Love was a luxury a poor boy like him couldn't afford.

"I don't believe in love, Max. Love is for the lower classes. People like us marry for position. Connections. Money."

He was not surprised she was a snob, even if the family had made its fortune in banking rather than inherited land. It was often the upper-middle stratum who was the worst, anxious to leave behind any trace of the shop. England really was an upside-down place, valuing idleness over honest labor.

"Maybe I'm a rebel," Charles replied.

"Yes, I understand your upbringing in France was most unusual. Your parents are deceased?"

Charles nodded, trying to remember fictional facts about his French château.

"Lucky for Louisa. I'm sure they would not approve of her."

"Oh, I don't know." Charles was becoming very annoyed. "She's beautiful. She's rich. Knowing them, they would think I'm the lucky one."

Grace Westlake's eyes grew sharp. "I understood from Louisa's letters you have no need of her money, that you have sufficient assets of your own."

"That's right. But a little extra income never hurts."

"Well then. Perhaps you'll be amenable to my proposition after all."

Charles leaned back in his chair and waited to hear her terms. It was lushly padded, devilishly comfortable, and he was exhausted after his misbegotten night. What would Grace Westlake do if he fell asleep as she attempted to bribe him? He struggled to keep his eye open. "Fire away."

Grace steepled her multi-ringed fingers together. "I don't expect Louisa told you of her youthful indiscretion before you married. She threw herself at our neighbor, Sir Richard Delacourt. He could do nothing but catch her. He's just a man, after all, and men have their appetites."

Charles did not feel obliged to defend all men against the woman's generalization. In his experience she was, regrettably, more or less accurate. "I was curious as to why he was a dinner guest last night."

Grace's cheeks took on the faintest color beneath her maquillage. "Why, he's our most prominent neighbor, and fences have since been mended. One cannot really blame him for my niece's impetuosity. I discovered Louisa's disgrace myself. Fortunately, I hushed it up as best as I could."

Charles knew she was lying even if her face was a serene mask. "But you punished her."

"Of course I did! One's chastity is precious, and since Louisa had relieved herself of it, what was to stop her from engaging in affairs with every male she could get her hands on? Footmen, stableboys, and the like. The girl has no discrimination. None. She's always been overfamiliar with the servants." Her lips twisted in disgust.

"So I canceled her presentation, and kept her close to home, hoping she would see the error of her hoydenish ways and repent. I controlled her purse strings, you know, and the staff at Rosemont views me as its legitimate chatelaine. There was no question my rules were to be obeyed. She lived very quietly, fooling us all, when all the time she was planning to run off to France and who knows where else at the first opportunity!"

"She had eight years of quiet living, if I can count correctly. Quite a sentence for a foolish mistake in judgment. She was twenty-five when she left, ma'am."

"But still a willful child! Hugh and I tried our best to

reason with her. As I said last night, he offered her marriage to protect the family's reputation. Several times. The boy has always had a soft spot for her, though I cannot see why."

"You forget you are speaking of my wife, Mrs. Westlake." Charles did not suggest that maybe Hugh had a mother complex, as Louisa's Dr. Freud was apt to say. Louisa was close enough to her in looks to be her younger twin.

"She doesn't have to remain your wife, Mr. Norwich. Mr. Baxter and I have discussed a very generous settlement should you come to your senses and renounce her. You may not need the money, but neither do you need an untrustworthy wife who will betray you once she tires of you. She's—she's unstable. Volatile. Needy. Even as a little girl she thought she could do just as she pleased without consequences. I blame my brother. He and his American wife spoiled her dreadfully."

Charles pictured Louisa as a little orphan, pinafored and pigtailed, trying to squeeze an ounce of love out of her aunt. Doomed to failure. Mrs. Westlake was a cool customer.

Frigid.

She must have sensed Charles's abhorrence and waggled a hand at him. "I'm not a monster, you know. I tried my best; truly I did. Hugh will tell you I never played favorites with the children. He's still a bit cross with me about that. But I took my responsibilities seriously, even if I was unable to mold Louisa into a proper young lady. She's incorrigible."

"And I like her for it." Charles rose. "I'm afraid I'm going to disappoint you, Mrs. Westlake. I have no intention of divorcing Louisa. You'll have to get used to me. Although I should warn you, I don't take kindly to your method of getting rid of me."

"You said yourself extra income was always welcome."

"I'm not talking about the bribery. Someone came into my room last night and tried to do me harm. What do you know about that?"

Grace Westlake's rouged mouth fell open. "I? Why, nothing, of course! I assure you I've never resorted to violence in my whole life."

"What, you've never spanked a naughty little girl?"

"No, I never did," Grace said with considerable indignation. "Louisa was isolated when she misbehaved."

"Locked in her room with bread and water—if that—I imagine. Things are going to change here at Rosemont, Mrs. Westlake. For the better, for they certainly couldn't be any worse."

"W-what do you mean?"

"This is Louisa's house, is it not? Every stick of furniture, every carpet, every painting belongs to her. You are here as her guest, aren't you? I wouldn't count on remaining so much longer."

Louisa's aunt gripped the arms of her chair but she didn't get up. "How dare you! If I hadn't come when my brother and his stupid wife died, Louisa would not be in the enviable position she's in today! Ask Mr. Baxter—thanks to my wise investments, I've quadrupled her fortune!"

"We thank you. But Louisa does not need a guardian now. She has me."

"And you—a foreign stranger no matter who your parents were—think to swan in here and usurp my authority. Well, it won't do, young man. Louisa must have some sense of gratitude beneath her ramshackle ways. She won't allow you to uproot me from my home."

"We'll see about that," Charles said. He might have stepped into the shit with this—Louisa had not told him how she was going to ask her aunt and cousin to leave. But here he was in the dragon's den, and he might as well make himself useful. Better take the brunt of Grace Westlake's wrath than have it directed at Louisa.

Charles realized his first impression of a spoiled, care-free rich girl had been very far from the truth. He may have grown up in reduced circumstances, but there had been affection at home while his mother was alive. Louisa had lost all that at the age of four. To be raised by Grace Westlake must have been a withering experience. It was a wonder Louisa was as warmhearted as she was.

"If you'll excuse me, I believe we are done. And I warn you again, Mrs. Westlake—I will not be a victim to what-ever machinations you or your minions decide upon to get rid of me. I'll be armed, and rest assured I know how to defend myself."

"You are talking utter nonsense!"

"Am I? Let's say we'll all be on our guard here at Rose-mont. While we are here." Charles hoped he'd left no doubt as to which of them was to go.

He left Louisa's aunt in a state of fury that no artful makeup job could conceal, whistling his way down the winding turret stairs. After only three wrong turns he found Louisa in their sitting room, pacing in front of a roaring fire. Several volumes and a newspaper were scat-tered on the table, as if she could not find one of them to concentrate on. Her face lit as he entered, causing an odd sensation in his chest. Did she view him as her champion?

She shouldn't.

"Well? Tell me everything!"

"I'm intact. She offered me money, but I'm afraid I have no specific amount to report of your worth—we never explored that far. She claims to have no knowledge of the little incident last night, and I almost believe her. And—you'd better sit down. You may not like what I have to say."

Louisa hesitated, then eased gracefully into a corner of the gray sofa. She had changed into a high-necked cream-colored wool walking dress after breakfast, and she looked very pretty. Her cheeks were pink, though her eyes were shadowed from their mutual lack of sleep. She folded her hands in her lap and gazed at him with clear, trusting eyes. She made him want to stand a little taller. Be a lot smarter—he may have tipped her hand too soon.

"Go on."

"I more or less invited your aunt to leave Rosemont. Told her she wasn't needed."

Louisa blinked. "And what did she say to that?"

"She didn't like the idea much. Said Rosemont was her home and even you would be grateful for all she'd done for you to let her stay."

She gave a little snort. "Grateful, eh? That's not a word I would use." Louisa looked down at her hands, which were knotted tightly, pale as the fabric on which they lay. "Rosemont *was* her girlhood home. I imagine she resented my father when he inherited it from my grandfather. It's not as if the property was entailed and had to go to the eldest male."

"How would two families share a house, even one this size?"

"True. I'm sure that's what my grandpapa was thinking. He expected Grace to marry—which she did, right out of the schoolroom. She had a substantial dowry, even if it didn't equal Rosemont's value."

"What was her husband like? I'll bet he was glad to die young." Somehow Charles could not imagine Grace allowing a hair on her head to be disordered. Lovemaking would have been fraught with complications, much too messy for fastidious Grace Westlake.

"I can't really remember him, but he wasn't so young. Uncle Harry was a good two decades older than she was— my grandfather didn't really approve of the match even if Harry's brother was a viscount, but there's no stopping Grace when she wants something."

"Kind of like her niece," he teased.

Louisa gave him a wobbly smile. "I should call you out for that."

"Pistols at dawn? There are things I'd much rather do

with you at that hour." The words were out before he had a chance to think. My God, he was flirting. And picturing Louisa in bed, her robe parted, her lovely white body open to his invasion. They had agreed that last night, no matter how superbly satisfying it had been, was a mistake. It would not do for Charles to lust after his employer.

But the horse was already out of the barn. Or, in homage to Louisa, perhaps the automobile was out of the garage. It was difficult to return the genie to the lamp. The toothpaste to the tube. He could think of a thousand metaphors, but it wouldn't change the attraction he had for her. Louisa was looking delectable indeed, a rosy flush on her face from his words. It would be so easy to lean over and kiss her wide mouth, toy with the little chocolate drop at its corner, seek a friendly war with her warm tongue.

"Charles—," she warned, but he couldn't seem to stop himself. He bent and cradled her cheek. Her skin was soft and pink, as though she bathed in honey and rose petals. Her lips parted in protest and he silenced her with one swift kiss.

It didn't matter that she was seated and he was standing at an awkward angle, because she was kissing him back despite her initial reluctance. Kissing him with some enthusiasm. Hell, there was no point to being modest—she was eating him right up, her lashes flashing, her hands unknotted and grasping at his jacket. Charles toppled down onto the ugly couch on one knee and took her in his arms. He could not see a ready way to unhook her from her dress, so he just shut his eye and enjoyed her trembling against him, the scent of violets heady. If he had money, he'd see that she always had a nosegay of them, their color deep and lush against her fair skin. He'd cover a bed with the tiny flowers and crush them beneath their bodies as they sought their pleasure.

Charles was getting carried away, plain and simple. And he didn't much care where he wound up as long as Louisa was somewhere within reach.

Chapter

❦

19

This was not supposed to be happening. They had agreed last night—this morning—to put the brakes on any further intimacy. It was just that she was so tired, so anxious, so unsettled to be back "home" where someone was trying to frighten her, and Charles was so . . . so—oh, words failed as he kissed her, the satin of his black eye patch smooth against her temple, his fingers disarranging her hair as he held her close.

Kathleen would be annoyed, both at the ruination of the chignon and the wicked kiss. Somehow her maid had gotten it into her head that Charles was not a good influence on Louisa, and she was right. All those lonely years, Louisa held herself apart from passion, and look what one night with him had done to her. She was ready to go back to the bedroom and take up where they'd left off.

The fine wool of her dress itched against her neck and every lace of her corset was a taunt. Louisa was hot all over. Breathless. Well, what could she expect when the captain covered her lips with such skill?

It didn't seem like he was thinking of his unhappy past,

or thinking anything at all. Louisa resolved to do the same. She'd just concentrate on the little licks, the sweep of tongue against tongue, the taste of Charles's toothpaste. The rough pads of his fingertips as they tickled her cheekbones. The breadth of his chest as she pressed against it. The warmth and strength of him. Louisa felt . . . safe.

She opened her eyes. Charles's vivid blue eye stared back at her. She could fall into its depths, plummet right beneath his skin. Never leave. But what did she know about him, really? Only what he'd chosen to tell her, and that all might be false, according to Kathleen as she'd ratted Louisa's hair up this morning. Designed to garner him sympathy—a poor boy who'd pulled himself up by his bootstraps. Who'd suffered unimaginably in wartime. She pulled back a little, and he sensed the kiss had wandered off course.

The loss of his lips on hers caused her heart to stutter. He sat back on the couch, his breathing ragged. "Sorry I overstepped my bounds again. You really must stop being so kissable."

"I can't seem to help it around you," Louisa said grudgingly. "Thank you for dealing with my aunt. I wasn't sure how to broach the subject about her leaving with her, and now you have. She won't go, of course."

"How can she stay if you want her out? Can't you call a constable or something?"

"It's not that easy. People here are loyal to her. I get on well with Cook and Griffith, but Mrs. Lang the housekeeper is Aunt Grace's creature. It wouldn't be much fun trying to run Rosemont with the staff against me."

"For heaven's sake, Louisa. Fire them. Don't you know a thousand people are standing on the breadlines wanting to take their place? This is *your* house. *Your* money supports it."

He was cross with her, rightfully so. She was a coward. But she couldn't shake the helplessness she felt in Grace's long shadow.

"I have to talk to Mr. Baxter."

"Fire him, too. He's in your aunt's pocket. The doctor—the lot of them. She wanted that fellow Fentress to divulge your medical history to me. For God's sake, isn't that illegal? Even if I were really your husband, he owes his allegiance to you."

She sighed. "I know you're right, Charles. It all seemed so clear when I was in France. But now that I'm back . . ." She trailed off. What was the matter with her? She had tasted freedom this past year. Surely she didn't want to go back to being under her aunt's thumb. Or worse, run away again from her rightful responsibilities.

Charles got off the couch and walked to the window. Louisa couldn't help but notice he had to adjust the fit of his trousers. Even in his annoyance with her, she stimulated him. That was rather satisfying—maybe she wasn't so powerless after all.

"You need someone to help you. Someone who knows more than I do. Why don't you ask Mrs. Evensong to recommend a good solicitor? Confide in her. She might come up with a plan to get rid of your aunt. The woman is renowned for fixing problems, isn't she?"

"Charles! What a brilliant idea! I shall write to her at once."

"And then we are going for a ride. Not in the blasted car but on a good, solid horse."

Captain Cooper would look delicious in tight riding breeches, his muscled thighs encased in fawnskin. And fresh air would be a welcome change. "We'll miss luncheon."

"Get your friend the cook to pack us something. It's not too cold out for a quick picnic."

Louisa wasn't so sure about that. The wind blew off the Channel at a brisk clip, but perhaps they could ride in the other direction to the Hermit's Grotto. There had never been a real hermit, but her grandfather had renovated an ancient hut into an elaborate faux cave, guarded by its own gargoyles, which she'd enjoyed exploring as a child with Hugh and their governess. And then, of course, with Sir Richard. Best not to think of that.

But now that the idea was lodged in her mind, she saw the horses tethered outside, the sheltering walls of the little building, the sturdy wooden furniture within. Louisa wondered what had become of the carpets and pillows— probably all riddled with mildew and mold. She'd have a saddle blanket, though—

Damn. Charles Cooper was doing it to her again, insinuating himself in her fevered imagination. What had happened to her good intentions? She'd kept herself chaste for nine very long years. Granted, it had almost been easy, as she had been basically locked up at Rosemont. Last year on the Continent she may have done a few cork-brained things, but she never broke her self-imposed celibacy.

She wasn't a prisoner now, except to her own lust. And there was Charles Cooper, tall and tantalizing, gazing out the leaded window at the white-capped waves. He was as fascinated by his view as she was of hers. Really, she could look at him all day—looking was not touching now, was it?

"Give me an hour." That should be time enough to notify Cook, get Kathleen to repair and redress her, and dash off a letter to Mrs. Evensong about the oddities at her bank. She would even invite the woman to inspect Rosemont, as she'd been keenly interested in the property and all its annoying inhabitants when they had met. "I'll meet you in the stable block. You'll find your way there on your own?"

Charles turned to her. "I thought we were going to stick together. I'm your bodyguard, remember?"

Louisa had almost forgotten. "No one will dare attempt anything in broad daylight. It's the nights we need to be worried about."

"Aye, that we do." There was something in his voice that told her he had quite another worry other than being hit on the head. She felt her cheeks warm—she'd never blushed so much in her life as she had around Captain Cooper.

"An hour," she repeated, then shut herself in her parents' bedroom and rang for Kathleen.

*T*he stable block was, as Charles expected, top-notch. A large brick complex, it also housed the Daimler at one end, with the chauffeur's apartment above it. He received a brief nod from Robertson from the open bay as the man attacked the car with a chamois cloth as if his life depended upon it. There was vacant space beside it for Louisa's car when it was returned after its repair. Charles could only hope it would take a good long while for the mechanic in London to secure the necessary parts. He was not ready to turn his life over to Louisa just yet. Several carriages in various styles and sizes were also parked, ready for their next outing.

The horses were far more interesting to him than shiny metal. He'd been horse-mad even when he lived in factory housing in London. He missed his steady old army mount, but he'd been in no financial position to keep a horse.

The smell of hay and harnesses and horse shit mingled with the sea air, forming a pleasant aroma. If he lived at Rosemont, he'd ride every day, down to the shingle or across the dull green fields they'd passed coming in.

A groom popped out onto the stone courtyard. "What can I do for you, Mr. Norwich?"

Charles stared at him blankly until he realized that of course any good servant would know who he was . . . or who he was supposed to be. "My wife and I are going riding. If you could saddle up her usual mount and find a horse for me, I'd appreciate it."

"Miss Louisa—that is, Mrs. Norwich hasn't ridden since I've worked here," the young man said. "But she pays particular attention to Emerald when she visits the stable."

He looked Charles up and down as if calculating his weight. "I think Mr. Hugh's Pirate Prince would suit you, sir. If you'll give us a moment, we'll have both horses ready for you and your lady."

Charles sat down on the weathered mahogany bench outside one of the bays. He would have offered to help, but upper crust Maximillian Norwich probably was not expected to saddle his own horse. Charles bit back a smile—Pirate Prince indeed. Was it the eye patch? he wondered. Charles had not ridden for pleasure often, though any jaunt on a horse was enjoyable, even into battle. Some sort of magic melded human with animal. He'd been lucky in his mounts—they'd carried him to safety most of the time.

The sun was warm on his face, though there was a pleasant nip in the air. It was always warmer on the coast, he reminded himself. One might not even know it was December save for the bare vines that climbed the brick. Roses here, too, even for the horses. Relaxing, he watched the activity in the yard. Robertson gave up his manic polishing of the car and disappeared into the building. Charles heard the steady wash of the waves, the cry of gulls, the whicker of horses. Rosemont really was a little paradise, despite Aunt Grace and the gargoyles.

So he was to ride on Cousin Hugh's horse. Charles hoped the groom would not get into trouble. From all he'd heard of Hugh, he was a man best not crossed. Charles was absolutely itching to meet him and cross him as soon as possible.

He was being petty. Childish. But the longer he stayed at Rosemont, the more he wanted to restore Louisa to her rightful position. He'd begun to think of himself as a Cavalier, and Rosemont's residents as Roundheads sucking all joy out of life. Time to put the young queen on her throne.

There was a vulnerability to Louisa that was not apparent at first. She was so pretty, so voluble—really, she could talk the bark off trees once she got going—that one did not see the hesitant girl within unless one looked. It might take her a while to find her feet at Rosemont, but Charles was willing to stay until—

What in the hell was he thinking? He'd been engaged as her companion for a month only. Plenty of time to roust out the relatives and fall into some mysterious decline and die, as Maximillian was destined to do. Charles wasn't sure about his own demise anymore—maybe Mrs. Evensong could find him something useful to do. This rescuing a damsel in distress business was very gratifying.

A couple of grooms eventually led out two prime specimens. Charles was so entranced with old Pirate that he failed to see Louisa round the corner of the building. And when he did—

Lord have mercy. She was hatless, her hair falling down her back in a loose braid. She wore a thick plaid scarf around her neck, a heavy wool hacking jacket, and men's riding breeches. There was not a loose fraction of fabric encasing her thighs. The young grooms both turned bright red and Charles remembered to close his mouth.

"Hello, darling! Hello, Jimmy! Angus! Emerald, my beauty. You have no idea how excited I am to go riding here again. I rode every chance I got on the Continent this past year, of course, but never on such fine animals as these." Louisa dug into her jacket pocket for a sugar lump and fed it to the mare.

Emerald was indeed a beauty, silver gray, with a glossy black mane and tail. Her saddle and harness were edged in bright green leather piping to match her name. Louisa frowned.

"Jimmy, a regular saddle if you please. Max, you don't mind a little delay, do you?"

So, no sidesaddle for Louisa. For the chance of seeing Louisa ride astride, her beautiful bottom rising and falling in front of him, Charles could wait all day. He gave her a loopy grin. "Whatever pleases you, my dear."

Chattering away in a friendly fashion, Louisa followed the boys back into the stable to replace the tack, which gave Charles the opportunity to inspect Pirate. The horse was massive, black and steady. Hugh Westlake had a good eye for horses. Charles stroked Pirate's nose and talked quietly to him as if the horse could understand his words. Some might think him a little mad, but Charles was of the opinion that horses were more intelligent than many people.

He turned when Louisa rode out of the stable into the courtyard. He would have loved to help her mount but had been deprived of that singular pleasure. She was not an especially tall woman, but her legs looked very long indeed against Emerald's flanks.

"We'll just ride over to the kitchen door. Cook will have our basket ready."

Charles let Jimmy help him up and tossed the lad a coin for his trouble. That's what Maximillian Norwich would do, wasn't it?

The basket turned out to be a lumpy linen sack that Louisa slipped into her saddlebag. "Where to next? The water or the woods?" she asked him.

"The water, I think. I never knew until I came here how restful it is to watch the waves. I never much enjoyed the ocean in transport, but that might have something to do with the company I had to keep."

"Hm. I'm afraid I don't share your serenity. I had to force myself to swim in the Mediterranean. The family curse. My parents and grandparents all drowned, remember."

He did. "Just don't go sailing."

Now, swimming—Louisa in a short bathing costume was another thing altogether. Her legs would be covered in dark stockings, but he'd be able to see every inch of them to the knee. He could circle his arms around her as she bobbed in the shallows, her skin glistening with wet diamonds, sodden fabric clinging to her neat figure.

Better yet, they could swim naked in the privacy of their very own beach. Charles would be at her side if her confidence faltered, take her into safety and make love to her in the sand until she forgot her tragedies.

"Did you hear what I said?" she asked.

It was a very good thing she was not a mind reader. "I'm afraid I didn't catch it. The wind, you know."

"I said, I will never go boating. Kathleen even had to dose me to get on the steamer to come home. I suppose you think I'm a nervous ninny. Oddly enough, I had no trouble getting on a ship to flee England."

"A Channel crossing is not so bad. But hopefully you won't be going on one again anytime soon. Unless you want to, of course. The lure of your Parisian dressmaker will be hard to resist, I imagine. "

Louisa lifted a golden brow. "Do you really think we can uproot Aunt Grace?"

"Count on it," Charles said with more confidence than he felt.

They picked their way down a steepish path to the narrow strip of beach below Rosemont. Pirate seemed nervous and Charles gave him a reassuring pat.

"Race you!" Louisa cried once they got into the soft sand. She took off before Charles could agree.

Minx. He watched awhile as her lovely round rump bounced ahead. For a man who had sworn off women, he was backsliding in a major way. One night with Louisa didn't mean he was cured of his grim dreams, however. But it was hard to feel sorry for himself in her presence.

Hard was the operative word. His cock twitched, waking to the image ahead of him. Rather far ahead of him now, scarf and pigtail flying. Cavalry officer Charles Cooper wasn't going to be beaten by some *girl*. He dug his heels into Pirate.

Pirate would have none of it. The horse whinnied and circled, and with total deliberation it pitched Charles right off into the sand.

Chapter

❦

20

Exhilarated, Louisa turned to taunt Charles once more. Her victory was short-lived. Charles Cooper was flat on his back on the shingle, Pirate Prince nosing him in the ribs.

He'd fallen off his horse? He'd been in the cavalry, for heaven's sake! She turned Emerald and rode back as quickly as she'd ridden away.

Louisa scrambled off Emerald and knelt at his side. Charles's bright blue eye was wide open, which was a good thing, wasn't it? "Charles! What happened? Are you all right?"

"More or less. The horse threw me. I guess he knows I'm not Hugh and doesn't like me much."

"Does anything hurt?" she asked, anxious. Charles's hat had rolled away, and waves were licking at it. "Your wound! Do you still have the bandage on?"

Charles shook his head to evident pain. "Took it off. Didn't want Grace to know the attack had been so successful."

"Oh, Charles." Louisa unwound the scarf from her

neck. "Can you lift your head? Or better yet, sit up. I'll clean the cut."

Charles struggled up on his elbows. "Woozy. Damn. Wasn't expecting to land on my arse so early in the day."

"Here, lean against me." He didn't argue. The back of his head was bloody again, but nothing like last night. She brushed the sand away gingerly with a corner of the scarf. "I think we should go back to the house."

"What, and miss the picnic? Nonsense. I just had the wind knocked out of me. I'll be fine."

He didn't look fine—too pale beneath his tan. "If you can bear it, let me pour some salt water on the cut. It's reopened and needs to be rinsed."

"I'll try not to howl like a baby."

Louisa left Charles swaying slightly and went to Emerald and rummaged through the bag. Cook had packed heavy tumblers for the wine, and Louisa took one out and dipped it into the sea. She fished his ruined hat out of the water and brought it and the glass back to Charles, who was squinting in the sunlight.

"Here. Hold on to your hat and tilt your head forward. This might sting."

"There's no 'might' about it. Do your worst." He gritted his teeth as she trickled the water on his scalp.

"There. It might actually help you to heal faster."

"Yes, Dr. Stratton. Damn horse. And I spoke to him so nicely, too." He gave the hat a vigorous shake and tucked it under his arm.

Pirate Prince stood sentry, his head down in what looked like shame. "I don't understand. Hugh has never complained about him."

"Maybe I'm out of practice. It's been a while since I was on a horse. Anyway, odd as it is, I'm hungry again. Thirsty, too."

"Let's walk a little ways. There are some rocks ahead that will shelter us from the wind. We'll tie up the horses and try again after lunch."

"You're in charge." Charles got to his feet without her help.

"Hold still." Feeling quite daring, she took her scarf and rubbed the sand off the back of his clothes, paying particular attention to his taut bottom. Louisa wished she could confide in Kathleen how splendidly he was made, but she knew her maid did not approve of the turn their arrangement had taken. Well, there would be no more turns. No more kisses. Louisa would exercise self-control if it killed her. They would just have lunch and plot the imminent overthrow of Grace Westlake.

It didn't take long to lead the horses and get to the wall of rocks that had been one of her favorite spots as a child. Like the grotto, it had afforded privacy where Louisa's imagination could run wild. The rocks became her castle fortress, where she ruled supreme. Despite the grumblings of her governess, she had scaled them and jumped to the white crescent of sand below a thousand times.

No one would be jumping today. She pulled the waxed linen lunch bag out. "Charles, in my hurry to change saddles I didn't put a blanket on Emerald. Could you get yours off Pirate Prince so we can sit down?"

"Aye." Charles made short work of the buckles even though the horse was skittish. He set the saddle down on the ground and unfolded the blanket. "I'll be damned."

"What?"

"Screws. Five of them, all bunched together." He pulled one from the weft of the wool and held the pointed end out to Louisa.

"*Screws?* How odd."

"Is it? No wonder Pirate didn't want to haul my carcass around." He ran a gentle hand on the horse's back, searching for injury. "It's all right, old boy. I don't hold it against you. Someone was out to get us both."

"Jimmy wouldn't do such a thing, Charles. I'm sure of it. He'd never hurt a horse deliberately. I've known him since he was a little boy. His grandfather is the stable manager."

"Hm."

"He must not have noticed. If the blanket was folded and the screws were already embedded somehow—"

"I'm sure you're right." Charles did not sound convinced.

"You don't think it's another attempt to scare you off?"

"I don't know what to think. Except if someone has it in for me, I'd rather die with a full stomach. What's in the bag?" He took the rest of the screws out and put them in his pocket, then shook out the blanket and placed it on the sand.

He was too calm. "Charles, I meant it when I said you could go."

"And leave you alone here? Don't talk rubbish."

He was seated now, his long legs crossed in front of him in Indian fashion. His riding boots were so new they were barely scuffed on the soles. He extended a hand. "If you're not going to join me, at least give me the bag. I'm starving."

Louisa sat. How freeing it was to wear pants. She mirrored Charles's position and spread out the lunch between them. It was a very simple repast—ham sandwiches, cheese, apples, and fruitcake, but the wine was an excellent vintage. Charles needed no direction as he picked up the corkscrew.

"To us," he toasted, after filling the tumblers. Louisa noted he took the one she'd filled with salt water and downed the contents in one long gulp.

"You *are* upset."

Charles took a bite of his sandwich to avoid the discussion.

"Maybe we *both* should leave Rosemont," Louisa said, fiddling with a bit of cheese.

He wiped his mouth with the back of his hand. "Not this again. You are not leaving. This is your home. I don't care how many screws or bolts or nails I sit on. I'll not be driven away."

"Th-thank you, Charles. I'll speak to Jimmy when we get back. Angus, too."

"Don't expect them to admit anything. Anyway, maybe you're right and they knew nothing about the blanket. It may have been some sort of odd coincidence. Now, when people start shooting at me, I'll get worried."

Louisa could feel the blood drain from her head. "Don't joke about something so horrid. We must remember to visit the armory later. I'll ask Griffith for the key." Nervously, she glanced up at the rocks, half expecting a villain to pop his head up and put an end to them both.

"Fine by me." He poured another glass of wine but merely sipped this time. "You are not eating."

She really should. Free of her confining "health" corset for once, she could stuff herself with no pain. But the reminder that they might be in danger was an appetite suppressant. Louisa took a grudging bite of fruitcake. It was exceptional, laced with brandy and studded with glistening bits of fruit. An early taste of the Christmas to come.

"Hey, that's dessert."

"I can do as I please, can't I? This is, as you pointed out, my home. You're welcome to my sandwich."

"I'll take you up on that."

They were quiet for a spell, the only sounds the steady lap of the waves, the huff of the horses, the slosh of wine as Charles replenished their drinks, and Louisa's crunching on her apple. She was satisfied with her cake and fruit. The wine, too. The sun radiated off the circle of rocks and gradually she felt her anxiety ebb. It was a pleasure to watch Charles eat—he was neat and Spartan in his approach, taking uniform bites, slicing his apple with brutal efficiency with a small knife that had appeared from his riding boot. He rose and divided the fruit between Emerald and Pirate Prince.

"No hard feelings?" Louisa asked.

"It wasn't his fault. Look, he hasn't even tried to topple

one of these rocks onto me with his long nose. You're a good fellow, aren't you?" Charles turned to her. "When are we expecting Hugh to join our merry band?"

Hugh. Louisa had forgotten all about him. "I'm not sure. Aunt Grace didn't say."

"Tell me about him."

Louisa repressed a shudder. Hugh had been the bane of her existence for years. "I dislike him intensely. But he's handsome."

"Handsomer than I?" Charles teased.

Right now no one was more handsome than Charles Cooper in her mind, but she'd never admit to it. Louisa shrugged. "He's above average height and fair. He resembles his mother."

"So, he could pass as your brother. Think of the beautiful children you could have if you married him."

Louisa tossed her apple core at him, hitting him squarely on the chest. He looked down at her and laughed. "I'll have to add you to the list of suspects who wish to see the back of me. Perhaps *you* set those screws into the weave."

"Don't be provoking. I could never cause discomfort to a dumb animal."

"Oh, couldn't you?" Charles murmured. "Anyway, about Hugh."

"I discussed him on the train coming down. Didn't you pay attention?"

"I have to confess I was not altogether focused on your every word."

"Why not?"

"Because, my dear, you talk too much. And you're too beautiful to make a man pay attention."

"That makes no sense at all. If you think I'm beautiful—which is ridiculous, by the way—all the more reason for you to listen to me." She knew she was blushing again. Damn.

"Tell me again. I promise to be a good student this

time." He returned to the blanket and folded his hands in expectation, like a proper schoolboy waiting for his lesson.

Louisa licked her lips nervously. The thought of Hugh always made her nervous. As a child he had tormented her, shutting her into dark closets, pulling her braids, putting insects in her bed—all the usual things little boys did to little girls. But when he got to be a big boy, instead of insects she often found Hugh himself in her bed, trying to persuade her to surrender her virtue. He'd been perfectly wild when she'd tossed said virtue away on Sir Richard Delacourt. He did not understand why she didn't want to do the same with him until she had held a gun on him.

"Aunt Grace encouraged Hugh to court me. To keep the fortune in the family, so to speak. After a while, his courting crossed the line. Several lines. I—I did not feel safe. I suppose I thought Sir Richard would marry me and solve my problems."

"The swine. Both of them."

"Well, to be fair we were all very young, and Hugh was heavily influenced by his mother. If he'd been successful in compromising me, then I could have no objections to the marriage, could I? My brief affair with Sir Richard threw a spanner in the works, and then he did not come up to scratch. He'd met my friend Lady Blanche Calthorpe here at Rosemont, who was richer even than I, and well connected besides. Her father is an earl." Louisa took a breath. She had not been asked to be a bridesmaid.

"But I still refused to marry Hugh after Richard wed. No matter what he tried—and failed—to do. After a while, he went back to university and I stayed locked in my room. His efforts recently have been very halfhearted. I think he's given up, even if his mother hasn't."

"I don't understand. You say the Westlakes are well-off."

Louisa nodded.

"Then why do they want your money?"

"Don't you know, Charles? One can never be too rich. And I think for Grace there is a certain justice in getting back her childhood home through her son and grandchildren. Quite frankly, I'd just as soon sell Rosemont to them and start fresh somewhere else."

Give up her home? Where on earth had that idea come from? It must be the wine talking.

Though why not? It was not as though Louisa had many happy memories of being raised here. She could build a new estate and gather her own collections of paintings and furniture and china. Modern things—she loved the graceful Art Nouveau styles she'd seen in Paris.

Charles stared at her. "Really? You'd give up the gargoyles? And I don't mean your Aunt Grace."

"Rosemont is just bricks and mortar. I expect the relatives and hangers-on wouldn't want to move with me, though I'm not sure about Isobel. Grace has put up with her this long, but not always cheerfully. She loathes Americans. And Isobel is . . . Isobel."

A flutter within told her she might have accidentally come up with the perfect solution to everything. Hell, she could *give* Rosemont to Grace—it wasn't as if Louisa needed the money once she got her little banking difficulty straightened out. "But don't say anything yet to Grace or Hugh. Let this idea percolate a little."

"Louisa." He was still looking at her intently. "Why would you give up your inheritance? This was your parents' home."

"And they died right out there." She gestured beyond the rocks. She had not let herself think about her parents drowning on her doorstep all day.

He reached over and took her hand. "Don't do anything rash. Rosemont could be a happy home for you, for your children. The past doesn't have to—"

He stopped and gave her a twisted smile. "Who am I to lecture you about the past? I've got my own demons."

Louisa smiled back. "Maybe we should lecture each other. Take turns."

"Remember, you're too beautiful. It's impossible for me to pay attention to you."

"Silly man." He continued to hold her hand, rubbing his thumb across her knuckles. It was comforting, and Louisa wished they could stay in this sheltered spot all afternoon. Just as friends. Good friends. She liked Charles Cooper very much.

But after a gentle squeeze, he dropped her hand. "I'll help you pack up. Now that Pirate's equine equanimity has been restored, we should explore the rest of the estate. You have no specific plans for the afternoon, do you? No sticking Aunt Grace with a knitting needle over tea?"

"I don't knit. I'm afraid I don't possess the usual feminine arts."

"You're feminine enough for me," Charles said, sweeping up the wrappers from their lunch and returning them to the bag. Louisa was sorry to see him put his gloves back on—there was something very attractive about his broad, warm hands, nicked and scarred though they were.

He did not have a gentleman's hands, she realized with a start. Would they give his identity away? Maximillian Norwich was a man of leisure and refinement.

Louisa much preferred Charles Cooper.

Chapter

21

It had been a near thing after lunch. All Charles had
wanted to do was tip Louisa back on the blanket and
kiss her senseless.

Do more.

He'd never removed trousers from a lady before, but
how hard could it be? After all, he undressed himself every
night. But he had promised Louisa—promised himself—to
avoid unwanted intimacy.

Well, *he* wanted it, that was certain. He wondered if
she noticed how hard he was as he lifted her on top of
Emerald. Charles had held her longer than was strictly
necessary, even after she assured him she could mount the
horse perfectly well by herself.

For a long hour, he'd watched her bite into the white
flesh of her apple and imagined those teeth somewhere
else. Watched her tip her golden head back and swallow
her wine. Watched her lick the sticky fruitcake off her
fingertips.

Lunch had been agony. For a man who had been dead

to women's charms for more than a year, he was suddenly—uncomfortably—alive.

Time to tame the unruly beast within. He had a job to do—to support her against her family. Charles had made the first inroads and would continue to behave as Louisa wanted, though he wasn't sure she should give up her home so easily. If he possessed an estate like Rosemont, it would pain him to sell it.

Of course, he'd never own such a place. He'd be lucky to get his old room back at Mrs. Jarvis's when this was all over.

What would he do with the rest of his life? For Charles was fairly certain he didn't want to put a period to his existence now. Funny how one night with a beautiful girl could cheer him up so. He felt almost happy—sexually frustrated, of course, but it was exhilarating riding across Louisa's property.

They'd climbed up the beach path and set off to the west over the fields. The landscape spread before them like a gray-green quilt, marked here and there by tenant cottages and hedgerows. Charles's heart had been in his throat as Louisa had sailed over bushes and fences. She was an excellent horsewoman despite the fact she'd been deprived of riding for so long. He let her get ahead of him, enjoying the view of her flying braid and her occasional backward glances. The sun felt as warm as summer, and Christmas seemed very far off.

Red-cheeked, Louisa waited for him beneath a copse of trees. "I am going to take you to the Hermit's Grotto now. It was a folly of my grandfather's design. I think truly it started out as an abandoned shepherd's hut, but he made improvements to it. It's just over the rise."

Charles couldn't help but laugh when he saw the collection of rocks and stunted trees hard against a small hill. An amazingly ugly gargoyle stood sentry in front of a low opening to a stone and daub outbuilding. There was no door, but a window covered thick with ivy gave a hint to the building's original purpose.

"That's Randolph," Louisa said, pointing to the winged creature.

"What was your grandfather's fascination with gargoyles? They're everywhere."

"I'm not sure. He even put them on his bank building in London. There's an architectural reason for them, you know—they divert rainwater from running down the building and damaging the mortar. And in medieval times, churches used them to frighten their illiterate congregation. If one didn't behave, one need only look at the image of evil everywhere and reform. Technically Randolph is a *grotesque* since he's not a waterspout."

"Very interesting. I never learned that at Harrow."

"I didn't learn anything in school, either. I only went the one year to be 'finished,' and it was incredibly insipid. Walking around with books on my head instead of reading them. Whitework. Organizing menus. I ask you."

"Sounds gruesome."

Louisa clipped him on the arm. "Don't mock me. I had a governess, but she didn't know much. I've had to educate myself."

"Brava." That might explain her interest in newfangled ideas, Dr. Freud and such.

"Women *should* be educated," she went on. "How can one raise a family when one is ignorant?"

"Do you want a family?" Charles asked carefully.

Louisa looked away. "I used to, as all girls do. But I've since realized my freedom is more important."

"You think women should have the vote."

"Of course I do! And we will."

"You ladies will just vote for the most handsome face." She was so easy to tease. He felt the immediate poke of her riding crop to his ribs.

"Women can already vote in some local elections and serve on boards. We need universal suffrage. The male sex does not hold exclusive rights to intelligence and industry."

"No, we do not. I've met my share of dunderheads." What an understatement that was, Charles thought.

"There. You see." She looked disappointed that he wouldn't argue with her.

"I do see." She was so lovely, bristling with indignation. Tiny damp curls framed her forehead. Charles longed to test their springiness between his fingers. Instead, he touched Randolph's spiky granite wing. "What is he guarding?"

"Nothing much. There's just a little room inside. We'd have tea parties here when I was little."

"We've still got some wine left. Why don't we go in?"

Charles didn't wait. He ducked his head below the open entryway. It was dark inside, with a strong scent of damp and earth. A crude hand-hewn table sat in the middle of the low-ceilinged room, with only one dusty chair beside it.

Louisa trailed a gloved finger on the table's surface. "Huh. There used to be four chairs here."

"Someone has helped themselves." Charles gave a violent sneeze.

"I haven't been out this way in years. It is very different than I remembered. There were cushions. An old rug."

"Carted off or rotted away, I expect. Randolph is not a very trustworthy watchdog. Or should I say watchlizard? He does have a reptilian look about him." He took his handkerchief out of his pocket and dusted off the seat. "Perfect for the princess. I'll go get the wine."

Once outside, Charles took a great gulp of fresh air and went to the tethered horses. There was a little less than half the bottle of burgundy left. No point to bringing it back home.

When he returned to the little hut, Louisa was not sitting but was peering out the ivy-covered window. "I used to meet Sir Richard here," she said, her voice dull.

"If the place holds unpleasant memories for you, we should go."

"No. I need to face them. Who I was. What I did."

"Louisa, you didn't do anything that a thousand other curious girls haven't done. You were lucky there were no consequences, except, of course, for your imprisonment. You've suffered enough, don't you think?"

"I suppose. I know my problems are nothing to most people's. I had a roof over my head. Clothes and food. A library."

He put his arm around her. "So you could educate yourself. You'll have to show me your favorite books later."

She leaned into him, warm and fragrant with violets, perspiration, and horse. Charles would not have expected the scent to be so arousing. "All right. Do you like to read?"

"I used to." It had been a long while since he'd taken pride in besting the other boys at Harrow. He'd not been able to find any solace in books since Africa. Couldn't afford them anyhow.

"There are many tempting books at Rosemont."

He looked down at her lovely flushed face. "There are many temptations at Rosemont. Starting with you."

The wine was forgotten as he kissed her, this time with more tenderness than desperate urgency.

Though Lord knew he was desperate enough.

She opened to him, shivering a little in the cool dark of the grotto. This kissing business was getting to be habitual. Charles supposed they should save the affection for when they could be observed, to continue to perpetrate their fraud, but these private exchanges of tongues were far more satisfying.

Louisa tasted of hope and regret and fruitcake. He was afraid he was going quite, quite mad, for surely hope and regret were not flavors. But her emotions blanketed him in drugging honey. Charles knew her now in a way that would have been inconceivable just yesterday.

There was no place to toss her down to have his wicked way. The rough table was out of the question—her arse was much too lovely for splinters and grime. They should ride back to the house. Seek the huge bed and pleasure each other until dinnertime.

He detached with reluctance. He had promised. As a gentleman, he could not compromise her further. If their deception was exposed, she never would live it down. Charles had no doubt that this time, Grace Westlake would have her way, possibly lock up Louisa somewhere far more grim than Rosemont, with real, white-coated gargoyles to keep her confined.

Sweet Jesus. Maybe he should really marry her. They wouldn't have to live together, but if he were her legal husband he could protect her from the predations of her family.

Louisa looked up at him. "Why did you stop?"

"I stopped because I didn't want to stop."

"Th-thank you. It seems I lose my head around you."

As it should be. Charles's own head was rolling around somewhere in a fantasy land. "Let's finish off the wine. But not in here—the air's too close." The memories too fresh and unpleasant even after all the time passed.

He led her outside and leaned against Randolph, setting the wineglasses against the gargoyle's flat head. "You pour. I'm about to sneeze again." He fished out a handkerchief—monogramed MN—and trumpeted. Her hands shook a little as she filled the tumblers with the last of the garnet liquid.

Charles took a sip, then put the glass down. "Have you ever thought of marrying? I mean, since you were a naïve young miss with stars in your eyes over that rotter Sir Richard."

She shook her head. "Never. I'll not be bullied by some man."

"What if the man was not a bully, someone you could trust to keep you safe?"

"I've never met anyone like that."

"Never?" He gave what he hoped was a reassuring smile.

She put her drink down, too. "What are you saying, Charles?"

"I'm not sure. I'm worried about you. If we made this real"—he waved his arm between them—"then no one could bother you."

"Except for *you*."

Damn. She was being logical. What could he expect? This was hardly a romantic proposal.

"I wouldn't bother you. We wouldn't even have to stay together. You could have your independence—I know how important that is to you. But you'd have the protection of my name. Grace couldn't touch you or your fortune."

Her face was very pale. "You're not joking?"

"On my honor, I am not."

"Is this because of last night? Do you have some ridiculous need to do your duty after—after what we did? I should tell you, I set out to seduce you. Quite deliberately." She raised her chin and gave him a challenging stare.

He grinned. "You succeeded. You don't have to give me an answer now. Perhaps you can arrange things without the drastic step of marrying me or anybody else. But I'm offering my support."

"But not your love."

Charles didn't think he had any love to give. But he was awfully fond of Louisa Stratton despite his best intentions to resist her. "You could look upon it as an extension of our current contract. I wouldn't expect any access to your money, however." *Or your bed.* It might kill him, if her relatives didn't accomplish the job first.

"I'd be a *feme sole* anyway, no longer a *feme covert*. My money belongs to me. The Married Women's Property Act passed in 1882."

"I see you know more about the legalities than I do."

"I've had to look them up. Though if I married Hugh, I know he'd try to do something tricky."

"You are not going to be pressured into marrying Hugh."

"I'm not going to be pressured into marrying anybody, including you." She'd gone from being soft in his arms to prickly. He'd done this all wrong. The idea was so new to him he should have given it more forethought.

He'd never asked anyone to marry him before. What would a chap like Maximillian Norwich do? There was no Seine to row her about in, just the ocean, and she was afraid of it. No Rembrandt to stand in front of, just a grotesque *grotesque*. He wasn't offering her much—he was poor, half blind, and half deranged. She was right to not fall at his feet in gratitude.

"I won't pressure you, Louisa. Just think about it. I realize we don't know each other all that well, and you might suspect me of being a fortune hunter. But I can *be* a real Maximillian Norwich, be a buffer between you and your family. I wouldn't expect anything in return."

"Why? If you don't love me."

He stiffened. "I hold you in the highest regard."

"I won't have you feeling sorry for me. I can fight my own battles!"

"Yes, yes, of course you can." He'd offended her somehow when all he wanted to do was help.

The argument was interrupted by the distant sound of a motor. "Is that a car?" Charles asked.

"The road is not far. We should be getting back."

That was that. Louisa leaped up on Emerald with no assistance and took off. It was up to Charles to pack up the glasses in his saddlebag. He left the empty bottle at Randolph's feet as some sort of offering. He doubted the gargoyle had any sway over Louisa. It would take more than a granite creature to inspire Louisa to reform.

Chapter

✣

22

$\mathcal{C}$harles found his way back, navigating by the dust Emerald threw up as Louisa raced her home. The joy of the day had been snuffed out, and it was his fault entirely. What the hell was he thinking, proposing marriage to an heiress like Louisa? He thought of Tom and Fred gawping at Rosemont's six turrets. They'd beat him to a pulp all over again for trying to rise above his station.

What would Louisa think if she saw where he grew up? Could he ever bring her home to his brothers and their wives? Not unless she wanted to be lectured about workers' rights and the evils of capitalism.

The odd thing was that Louisa might very well agree with Tom and Fred. She had far too many radical ideas. Hell, she wouldn't make anyone a comfortable sort of wife at all, despite her fortune. A man would long to be deaf within hours of the ceremony. She did *talk* so.

Charles resolved to take a vow of silence himself. Speak only when spoken to. Let the household think Maximillian Norwich was a man of mystery. He'd already said too much to Louisa and did not want to dig himself a deeper hole.

His good intentions shattered as he entered the stable yard. Louisa was still mounted, talking down to a handsome blond fellow who leaned negligently against the Daimler, a suitcase at his feet. Robertson hovered, probably waiting to rub off the smudge to the car's luster. He must have just come from picking up the guest at the railway station.

"Ah! There is your bridegroom now. I trust no harm has come to my horse, Norwich?"

Charles slid from the saddle in what he hoped was stunning grace. Foolishly pleased to see he topped Louisa's cousin by a few inches, he extended his hand.

"Hugh Westlake, I presume? Delighted to meet you." He squeezed and pumped with unnecessary zeal. "There was, in fact, a bit of a mishap with Pirate earlier. His blanket was laden with some screws. But no harm done."

"Screws? What the devil! Jimmy!"

"Gone to the village for his grandda," Robertson said in his Scottish burr. "Angus with him."

Hugh Westlake fussed over his horse, forgetting Louisa and Charles completely.

"May I help you dismount, darling?"

"I can get d—oh, yes. Of course, dearest." An old man Charles hadn't seen before came out for the horses, Hugh blistering him for the screw incident. The fellow didn't look like he understood a word of Hugh's tirade. Either he was innocent, or a very good actor.

Charles was beginning to think no one was as good an actor as he. He pretended touching Louisa did not affect him in any way.

"Well, this is good news," he whispered into Louisa's shell-pink ear. "Hugh seems to prefer his horse to you."

"Just as I prefer Emerald to you," she replied sweetly, taking his arm.

"Is that so? You may ride me anytime you like and discover my superiority."

She had sharp elbows for one so plush. "Charles!"

"You mean Max. Watch yourself, my lovely."

"Max, then. Let's escape while we can."

Arm in arm, they nearly ran around the corner to Rosemont's imposing entrance. Griffith stood, waiting. They almost made it to the open front door before Hugh came huffing up behind them.

"A word, Norwich. If you would be good enough to meet me in the library in an hour, I would appreciate it."

Charles turned to Louisa. "Darling, are we free?"

"Louisa's presence is not required."

"I'm sorry, Westlake. I don't do much of anything without Louisa at my side, particularly since there have been a few odd occurrences here since we arrived."

Louisa made a great show of yawning. "It's all right, Max. I think I'll have a nap before I dress for dinner."

"Coward," he whispered. "But something for me to look forward to after my talk with your cousin." He waggled his eyebrows at her.

Elbowed again.

"If you have no objection to the scent of horse and leather, why don't we just get to it now, Westlake?" Charles asked.

"Very well." Hugh looked Louisa up and down with an insolence that made Charles want to pummel out of him. "Louisa, I see you've lost none of your nerve. Trousers? Really?"

"Doesn't she look divine in them?" Charles interrupted before Louisa could fly off at Hugh. He hugged her and kissed her forehead. "Pleasant dreams, my dear. I'll be upstairs before you can miss me."

To his delight, Louisa brought his face down so she could give him a very thorough, very public kiss for the benefit of her wretched cousin. A kiss that involved her gifted tongue invading his surprised mouth just long enough to garner a disgusted snort from Hugh. Griffith was much too well trained to respond in any way.

"Hurry, Hugh. I can't bear it when Max is not with me."

All three men watched as she ran up the stairs, her hips

wiggling shamelessly. Louisa Stratton was a handful who would drive the average man to drink. Hemlock, if it was handy.

"She hasn't changed a bit," Hugh mumbled.

"Why should she?" Charles asked cheerfully. "She's nigh on to perfect."

"If you think that, I have a large clock to sell you at Westminster. Come, let's talk in the library over a brandy. Griffith, I presume the drinks cabinet is stocked?"

"Of course, Mr. Hugh. Would you like me to pour?"

"No, we'll need our privacy. See that we're not disturbed."

Charles followed Hugh down the marble hall, passing enormous rooms filled with blinding gilt furniture. Everything at Rosemont was far too grand. Maybe Louisa was right—she could build a cozy Arts and Crafts cottage, surround herself with comfortable furniture and painted pottery instead of Versailles reproductions and Sevres.

The library walls were lined with at least a thousand books. If Charles hadn't been asked to sit down, he would have roamed by the shelves with genuine interest. Hugh sat behind the massive mahogany desk, which must have belonged to his grandfather. Very lord of the manor. Charles curbed his annoyance and waited. He who spoke first lost, so they said. He was hoping that was true.

"Oh! The brandy. Be a good chap and fetch us some. It's just over there."

And now Hugh was trying to reduce him to servant status. Little did he know how true that was.

"I'd just as soon keep my wits about me, Westlake. It's early in the day. But you help yourself if you want."

Hugh grimaced. "Never mind then. I don't expect us to bond over brandy. I don't expect us to bond at all. I've had you investigated, Norwich. No one seems to have heard of you in France."

Louisa should have expected as much. Charles shrugged. "It's a big country. I assure you, I exist."

"My cousin is headstrong, and hopelessly naïve. You look like just the sort of adventurer that would take advantage of a helpless woman."

"Familiar with the type, are you? Louisa's told me some interesting tales of her girlhood."

Hugh's face darkened. "Don't believe everything you hear. She's not a very reliable source."

"I spoke to your mother this morning as well. No matter what either one of you has to say about Louisa's character, I am not interested. She is my wife, and I—" He paused. He was about to say "I love her." Well, why not? "I care for her very deeply. It seems to me neither you nor her aunt have similar feelings, which is why your time at Rosemont will be coming to an end."

"W-what?" Hugh sputtered.

"If Louisa and I are to live here, she doesn't need to be saddled with daily reminders of her unhappy past. This is *her* house. If you both hold her in such aversion, why would you even want to stay here? You and your mother cannot tell her what she can and cannot do anymore. She's twenty-six, not still a girl to be bullied by those who do not have her best interests at heart."

"What would you know of anything? You're a parvenu, a jumped-up fortune hunter! I assure you my mother did the best she could through Louisa's stubbornness and scandals. She managed the family fortune well enough to attract *you*, didn't she? If Louisa thinks she can just throw us out—"

"That is exactly what she thinks. What I think as well. No amount of threats or 'accidents' will make us change our mind. Enjoy this Christmas at Rosemont, Mr. Westlake, because it will be your last one."

Hugh shot up, knocking over the desk chair. "We'll see about that."

"Yes, we will. Louisa's new solicitor will be contacting you." Charles would write to Mrs. Evensong himself to inform her of the urgency of the matter. "Now, if you have nothing else to discuss, I believe I'll join my wife upstairs. Good day."

Well, Charles was earning his pennies today. Two unpleasant discussions with Louisa's relatives, a hard fall on his arse, and a severe case of blue balls. Perhaps the latter could be attended to once he returned to the bedroom suite, but he wouldn't count on it. Louisa's mood had been mercurial all day, almost odd enough for him to believe the aspersions cast against her.

Charles had an urge to take a bath to wash Hugh Westlake's blond perfection away. He would do so after he reported to Louisa. But once he entered the sitting room, he found the bedroom door locked against him. Vixen.

She couldn't possibly be asleep yet—he'd made very short work of his talk with Hugh, going in with guns blazing, no subtlety whatsoever. At least everyone knew where they stood now. It would be entertaining to watch it all play out over dinner if he didn't have to don confining evening clothes to do so.

Charles turned back into the hall and entered his own chamber. Everything appeared to be in order just as he'd left it, but the superstitious part of him ran a hand under the covers and pillows, looking for more screws, or something even more dangerous.

Nothing. That was good so far. Maybe the pranks would be limited to one a day. He picked up a book from the pile at his bedside and flipped through the pages, unable to concentrate. A lot had happened in the brief time he'd arrived at Rosemont, and so far he wasn't making much sense of any of it.

Time to wash his jumpiness away. Charles entered the echoing white-tiled bathroom and turned on the tap. Hot silver water splashed into the immaculate porcelain tub, quite a difference from the communal pump at his family home, or bathing in leech-infested waters in Africa.

It would be summer there now, the sun hot, the flowers blossoming where they hadn't been trampled. All the fires of Kitchener's army must have brought cleansing and growth to the empty savannah. His first Christmas in a tropical climate with thousands of men had been a strange affair, but no stranger than the Christmas of 1903 was bound to be at Rosemont.

Charles shed his riding clothes and eased his sore body into the bathtub. He'd used muscles today he'd forgot he had. Likely the stableboys would be cautioned not to let him ride Pirate Prince again now that Hugh was home, but there were plenty of other animals to choose from. Rosemont had everything.

Too much. Every bibelot and boulle cabinet was a testament to Louisa's grandfather's success. There were *things* everywhere—the house must be a nightmare to dust and polish, Charles thought, chuckling as he pictured Louisa in a starched white apron with a feather duster. She might even be game, but there was a fleet of well-trained servants to handle the domestic chores. Running an operation like Rosemont was not for the faint of heart—no wonder Grace Westlake made such a good job of it.

Charles plunged his head beneath the water to clean his wound, then soaped himself. He took a sniff. Violets. He'd smell like Louisa. His own body would drive him mad with unquenched desire. He lay back in the tub and closed his eyes, fisting his bobbing cock. Just the thought of her made him hard. In breeches, her pert bum rising above the saddle. Certainly out of breeches, her golden hair tickling his chest as she glided over him, her own eyes closed in bliss.

He was close to his peak when the doorknob turned.

Chapter

❦

23

$\mathcal{R}$obbie pretended he didn't see Kathleen crossing the courtyard, her arms folded over her lovely little bosoms. He was about to experience her Irish temper again—twice in one afternoon!—and it wasn't fair. He'd tried—it was a damn stroke of genius to fiddle with the horse blanket on such short notice.

That captain fellow was too hard to hurt.

All afternoon Robbie had expected Miss Louisa to come flying home on Emerald in a tizzy. He'd been prepared to drive the motorcar as a makeshift ambulance to carry the poor fellow home. The captain was young—his bones would mend in no time. What was the harm to a broken arm or dislocated shoulder?

But no. The man had fallen on his rump in the soft sand, almost immediately after mounting Pirate Prince. Kat had come to tell him after she put her mistress to bed for the afternoon, practically hissing and spitting like her namesake. She'd had several hours now as twilight stole upon them to stew over his inability to put Louisa's hireling out of commission.

Well, he'd stewed, too. Mr. Hugh was home, and they'd all better watch out.

"There's been another telegram. I told Griffith I'd come find you. Mrs. Westlake wants you to pick up Mrs. Lang on the evening train."

"Damn. The old bat." There went Kathleen's freedom.

"I have an hour before I get Louisa dressed for dinner. If you can stop cleaning the car long enough."

"Is that a proposition, Miss Carmichael?"

"It is not. I thought we should strategize. Just talk."

Robbie tossed his chamois cloth on a bench. "You can't come up to my room. Someone will see." The yard was crawling with grooms, and old Hathorn, the stable manager, was a Westlake loyalist. They'd both be out on their arses if it was discovered Kathleen had a follower.

"Meet me on the beach in five minutes."

"We'll bloody freeze to death. The sun is low in the sky and the wind's picked up." The day had been unusually mild for December, but the temperature was dropping as night fell.

"Button up, Robbie." Kathleen turned on her heel and left him standing there.

He should just leave Rosemont before he got into trouble. Kathleen was trouble. Her mistress was trouble. He was a fool to let a skinny freckled redhead lead him around by his pecker.

Unfortunately he loved her. The last year had been hell without her, but Robbie was afraid all his future years would be hell with her, too.

If he wasn't hanged so he could live them.

Robbie tied his scarf tighter to remind himself of what might happen to his neck, and squashed a cap on his head. He slipped away from the garage and ambled across the spacious lawn, hoping there were no prying eyes up at the house. There were about a hundred windows and anyone might see him skulk down to the shore when he should be working, or trying to look as if he was.

The stone steps to the beach led him straight to Kathleen, who was wearing a track in the sand.

She shook off his embrace. "Took you long enough."

"I went by my watch."

"I didn't mean five *exact* minutes. Walk with me."

They headed toward an outcropping of rocks. Gulls cried and circled overhead, and Robbie was reminded of his awe when he first took this position. He couldn't believe his luck—an estate like Rosemont right on the water, a young heiress and her maid to carry about. But then Louisa had run off and taken Kathleen with her. The ocean lost its luster while the mostly unused car shone as if it were still in its showroom. Driving Grace Westlake's son back and forth to the London train was not the pleasure he'd dreamed of.

Once inside the circle of stones, Kathleen stamped her foot. "I don't know what to do! I think she's falling in love with him! After just a handful of days' acquaintance! She says the stupidest things against him, but I know she doesn't mean a word. It's like that saying from Shakespeare—'the lady doth protest too much.'"

Robbie had never read Shakespeare, but he knew all about Lady Macbeth—what Scottish lad didn't know about the Scottish play? He didn't want any more of Cooper's blood on Kathleen's hands. "Maybe you—we—should do nothing and let nature take its course. I fell in love with you, too, in less than a week, remember. Fool that I am. I can't keep dreaming up ways to incapacitate him. You should give me credit, really—I thought the bit with the horse was genius on such short notice. Jimmy's not easy to distract."

"Pah. It didn't work. But I reckon you're right. We're apt to get caught. Louisa is talking about carrying a gun! I ask you, where can I conceal a gun in her evening gown? She wants pockets sewn into all her dresses! They'll spoil the lines, and if Mr. Worth weren't dead already, he'd kill himself when I mutilate his clothes. Maybe she should just marry this man in reality—I hear he gave Grace and Hugh terrific set-downs today."

"'Grace and Hugh'?" he mimicked. "Aren't you a cheeky girl. Where's your respect?"

She sniffed. Damn, her nose was just an adorable little button, covered with golden spots. Robbie stuck his hands in his pockets so he wouldn't give in to tweaking it.

"I don't have any for the likes of *them*. So anyway, Robbie, I'm calling off our plan. We'll just have to trust that Mrs. Evensong knows her business and the captain is a good man. After all, she brought you here to me, didn't she? Cooper must have passed muster with her. She's very thorough."

"Aye, she is that." And the woman knew a great deal about automobiles, too, for someone so elderly.

"So kiss me, then."

Robbie had no objection. Some men might find Kathleen a bit too bossy, but when she ordered him to do what he wanted to do anyway, what was the difficulty?

She tasted of tea and peppermint. He'd skipped his own tea with the grooms and Hathorn, afraid to meet anyone's eye. The stable was in an uproar over the screws, and Robbie felt some guilt, though it had all been for a good cause.

But Kathleen had abandoned it, and Robbie was perfectly willing to follow wherever she led him, as long as her next scheme was not as harebrained. He was a peaceful fellow at heart, and it was a relief not to be required to hit Captain Cooper anywhere else ever again. The man had suffered enough, losing an eye and being damned watchful with the one he had left. There was a weight to the man— oh, not physically, as Cooper was whippet-thin, but something rested heavily on his shoulders that was obvious to the grandson of a Scottish witch. Not that Robbie believed his old gran was really a witch, but she *knew* things and sometimes he thought he did, too.

Robbie knew, for example, that now that Mr. Hugh was home it was just as well Mrs. Lang was coming back tonight to lock the maids in. Robbie didn't trust the man an inch. Kathleen had never said anything to confirm his suspicions, but he'd bet his next quarter's salary that Hugh would try to interfere with one of the girls—or more than one—before too long.

Hugh might have an easy time of it. Robbie had turned down several offers while Kathleen was away. Some of the girls were no better than they should be, but he'd made a promise and he intended to keep it.

He held Kathleen tight against him, protecting her from the damp wind that swooped between the rocks. She could always count on him to protect her. The sooner they married, the better, because kisses like this were the beginning to his end. Robbie would go mad when she pranced off to the house to attend Louisa in her Worth gowns when she should be attending him—fixing his dinner on his little stove, sharing it, looking across the candlelit table with her hazel eyes twinkling at him. He'd help her wash up and take her straight to bed, though she'd probably want to read one of her romance books first. Robbie wasn't against reading per se, but he could think of things he'd much rather do of an evening than read about imaginary people and their plights. Why waste time reading three hundred pages when the hero and the heroine were going to get into bed by the end anyway? Real people he knew had enough to contend with without borrowing fictional trouble.

Och, God. Her hand was slowly moving down his front and she would know how lost he was to her in about four more inches—*ah.* He felt her lips curl up in triumph under his, the little wench. He was just a man, a randy one at that. Robbie could get hard just *thinking* about her. Having her wiggling in his arms was pure torture when there wasn't the time or the place to finish the job. Well, there was, for he probably wouldn't last above a minute, but he wasn't about to take her outside up against a cold, rough rock, no matter how tempted he was.

He took a couple steps backward and wiped his mouth with his sleeve. "You've got to go before I forget myself."

She grinned. "I can remember for the both of us."

"Kat, don't tease me so. You've got your duties, and I've got to pick up the old hag."

"Mrs. Lang is in mourning, mind. Be nice."

"Her mother must have been a hundred. Mrs. Lang is well past seventy."

Kathleen straightened her lace-edged cap. "And she's spent all her working years here at Rosemont. Imagine being in one place for your whole lifetime."

"That's not for me, Kathleen. I told you I want to better myself. Someday we'll see the back of this place."

"And what will we do?"

Robbie took her arm and they retraced their footsteps in the wet sand. "I'll have my own garage. You'll be home with the babies."

Kathleen stopped. "The babies?"

"Aye. We'll have as many as I can afford, and as I'm planning on being a very successful man, shall we say eight? But we'll take what the good Lord gives us."

"Eight children?" Kathleen shrieked over the wind. "Are you daft? I'll be dead or deranged! No more than three, and then you'll keep your trousers fastened if you know what's good for you."

Something went very still within him. "You'd deny me my rights?"

"You'd deny me mine? I don't want eight babies. Or six. Or four. My mother had a dozen children. Only seven of them lived for any worthwhile length of time, and I saw what happened to her. Her hair was white at thirty, and she was dead by thirty-five."

Robbie swallowed. He'd been careful, or as careful as he could be the too few times they'd done the deed. The thought of Kathleen's glorious red hair white before its time was not a happy one. "There are ways—"

"Aye, and we'll use them, every one. I've been to France

and heard things, you know. I won't wind up like my mother, no use to anyone. And if it means we have to exert some self-control when we marry, we'll manage."

"Kathleen, I've spent the last year managing."

She gave him a saucy look. "See? Your hand hasn't grown hair or fallen off."

"Brat." He supposed she made sense. What did he want eight children for? He wasn't a farmer with fields to cultivate. But he'd spent the past year dreaming of spilling inside her as a man was supposed to do to avoid sin. As his church insisted, although he guessed the church wanted them married first. Damn, sin was everywhere and most inconvenient. "All right. But talk to Miss Louisa. I want to marry you. Soon."

Kathleen stood up on her toes to kiss his cheek. "I will. Thank you, Robbie, for understanding. You're a good man."

I'm an idiot, he thought as he watched her skip up the steps to the lawn.

But he was Kathleen's idiot, and he didn't think that was going to change.

Chapter

✦

24

"Oh-Charles?"

Charles snatched his hand away and willed his pending orgasm away. It was a very, very near thing. He slapped a sea sponge over his penis and sat up, sloshing water on the tiles.

"Do you have need of the toilet? I'll be out of the tub in a moment," he said gruffly.

"I'm sorry I disturbed you. I didn't know—the door wasn't locked."

"I must remember to lock it in the future." God, how embarrassing was this, to be caught with his hand around his cock like some adolescent schoolboy. How long had she been standing there anyway? Long enough, judging from her bright pink cheeks. Even through his visual fog, he saw her well enough. She wore a wrinkled linen nightgown banded at the neckline and cuffs with lace. It was a modest garment, but she was as tempting to him as if she'd entered the room naked.

He'd imagined her napping barefoot in her riding breeches, but this was better. She looked rested, the lavender smudges under her eyes fading. Charles wished he'd chosen to sleep rather than read or bathe. He was bone-weary and in agony thinking too much of what was not to be. For Christ's sake, he'd asked this girl to marry him this afternoon! The blow to his head must have done more damage than he realized.

She was still standing there, making puffy little bunches in the fabric of her nightgown with her fingertips.

"Oh, what the hell," she mumbled, then pulled the nightgown over her head.

"Louisa!" He was so shocked her name came out a croak. He closed his bad eye and gazed at her in openmouthed wonder.

"I lied. I knew you were in here—I heard you splashing about. Moaning, too. You are rather noisy when you seek your satisfaction. It—it excited me. I couldn't go back to sleep."

Charles knew he must look like a landed fish, even though most of him was still underwater.

"May I join you in the bath? I'm not sure what can be accomplished, but I mean to try."

"Louisa!" Monsieur Grenouille was still present, croaking away. Fish, frogs, and his own mermaid, with her rippled golden hair fresh from its braid.

"It *is* a large tub. I think my parents sometimes bathed together, shocking as it is to imagine one's parents in flagrante delicto. They were very—spirited—together. Perhaps that's why Aunt Grace disliked them so. I can't see her bathing with my uncle, but they must have had intercourse at least once—there is Hugh to consider."

Even croaking was beyond him now. Charles watched as she lifted a long white leg over the side of the tub. "Scoot back a bit, won't you?"

Like a mindless drone, he slid back as far as he could go. The sun was setting, but he'd lit the lamps in the bathroom so he could shave off his afternoon stubble properly. Every smooth bit of her skin was visible. What he'd imagined last night in the firelit room could not even begin to compare with Louisa in the fading daylight. She had a faint sheen of silver-gilt hair on her arms and legs, the triangle between her legs a little darker. She sank down into the tub and they were knee to knee.

"I think there are hairpins in the soap dish. Could you pass them to me? My hair will never dry in time for dinner and Kathleen will be irritated with me."

Hairpins? Soap dish? Did that mean he'd have to stop staring at her? He glanced down to the metal basket that was fixed to the lip of the tub. Sure enough, there were a few long hairpins in it. He fumbled at picking them up, then watched as she wound her waist-length hair into a loose coil and pinned it up.

No more mermaid. But her neck was long and elegant, marred only by the livid kiss he'd inflicted on her last night. He leaned toward her and swept his thumb across it. "Does it hurt?"

"Oh, no. But Kathleen was furious when she saw it. She seems to have taken against you."

Charles had been perfectly polite to the redheaded maid as far as he could recall. He'd have to try harder to be as charming as Maximillian Norwich.

"What will she think when she comes up to help you dress for dinner and finds us in the tub together?"

"*I've* locked the door. Besides, I think she's busy with Robertson. They really should get married."

So should we. But he kept those unwanted words to himself. He'd only known her a couple of days, for God's sake.

"Well, now what?" Louisa asked brightly.

"Wh-what do you mean?"

"I had trouble falling asleep, but once I made my decision, I slept well for the first time in ages."

Charles's heart gave an erratic lurch. Did this mean she accepted his proposal after all? "What decision?"

"I've decided it's stupid not to make full use of you

while you're here. Who knows when I shall ever encounter such an honorable, attractive man again? I'm determined to be a spinster, you know. Isn't that the awfulest word? One pictures crooked spectacles, the scent of mothballs, and bad hats. But there's no reason I shouldn't enjoy myself where I can. The rest of Rosemont can go hang, but I've got *you* for the month."

"*Awfulest* is not a word," Charles said repressively. So, she thought to "make full use" of him, did she? He was not a stud, nor was she a mare to be covered. He might want to lift her up from the water and plunge her down on his still rock-hard cock, but he had standards. He was hired to do a theatrical job, not to fornicate. She made him sound like some sort of male prostitute.

"Don't talk grammar to me when we have so little time."

Charles squashed the sponge more firmly on his aching cock. "Louisa, this is most unwise. Not to mention one would have to be very acrobatic to have intercourse in a bathtub."

"I'm sure it can be done if we expend a little effort. Why, you need do nothing but sit there. I can climb on top of you and—"

"Louisa!"

She didn't bat an eye or blanch, when any of his recruits would have recognized that tone and acted accordingly terrified. Louisa Stratton was not terrified. She gave him a seductive smile and actually batted her eyelashes at him. Had she been practicing in a mirror?

She was impossible. And irresistible. Hadn't he been thinking of just such a thing when she waltzed in in her virginal nightgown? Of course in his fantasy, her hair was down, but she was right to be practical. One wouldn't want to annoy one's maid now, would one?

"The water is getting cold. We should be getting out."

She swiveled behind her and turned on the tap.

"We'll flood the house!"

"Don't be such a worrywart. Rosemont must have fifty rooms. What's one wet ceiling? Now, where were we?"

Charles grabbed hold of the edge of the tub and pulled himself up. "We were nowhere." Unfortunately, he looked down at Louisa when he spoke, and saw that pink, pointed tongue at the corner of her lips through the blur of swirling black particles in his bad eye. Her mouth was almost at the level of his manhood, and every single one of his good intentions went down the bathtub drain.

Charles shut his eyes. "Louisa," he begged.

He heard the squeak of the tap being turned off, then felt her hands grip his thighs. He caught himself before he fell back into the water. Gooseflesh now covered his body, but the cold didn't seem to have any effect upon his rampant penis.

"I'm not sure I'm very good at this. I only tried it once and we were interrupted," she said apologetically.

"Oh good Christ," he growled. She never knew when to stop talking. The last thing he wanted to think of was Louisa Stratton pleasuring some other man with her luscious mouth.

She was *his*.

He shuddered at the first tentative lick, the blood in his groin alive with heat. She grew bolder and licked harder as he moaned all over again, taking him a little ways between her wide, expressive lips. Her mouth was warm, exquisite, and her unpracticed touches of tongue and teeth had him on knife-edge in seconds. Her lack of experience was the purest gift she could give him, but Charles simply could not spill like this no matter how generous she was.

"Louisa," he rasped. He longed to be seated deep inside her, but that wouldn't do, either. He pressed his fingers against her jaw and gently detached her. "You must let me keep some shredded semblance of being a gentleman. Give me the sponge, please."

Her face showed no disgust, only innocent curiosity. Nodding, she fished the floating sponge out of the water and handed it to him. He slid down into the tub, protecting her from the spurt of his completion, the release so strong and swift it took his breath away.

Her brown eyes were wide, watchful, boring into the well-placed sponge. "Does it hurt when it—when it's over? You look like you're in agony."

She was ridiculously adorable. For all that she had an alleged wicked reputation, it seemed she really knew very little. "Did you not pay attention last night?"

"Not really." Her blush deepened. "I was concentrating on myself. I think my eyes must have been closed. And it was dark."

"It's dark now." The sky beyond the bathroom windows was slate gray, and Charles was pretty sure a star winked at him through the leaded glass. Was he in pain? Not physically, but his heart felt too big for his chest.

The water was getting cold again. Before he'd stepped into the tub, he'd lit the little brazier and arranged some towels on a nearby tufted bench, but the tiles held the chill. He reached for his eye patch atop the bath sheets and tied it back on, righting his world. Louisa sat across from him, her arms now crossed, depriving him of a clear view of her beautiful breasts.

"Let's get out before we get into any more mischief. I'll dry you off and you can face Kathleen."

"That's it?"

"Louisa, my dear, what would you have me do? I've disgraced myself and taken advantage of you. Kathleen is right to detest me." He stood again and offered his hand.

She took it and climbed out of the tub. "No she isn't."

She stood still as he swathed her like a mummy. He squeezed her shoulders and brought her closer. "What you said. About us carrying on an affair while we're here. I know you think it's a good idea, an opportunity for discovery, if you like, but it may prove dangerous to us both."

Louisa looked up at him. "Dangerous in what way?"

"For one thing, I could get you with child, even if we

take precautions. Then we really would have to marry, and you say you don't want that. And what kind of honor would I have to exchange sexual favors for money? For that's what it comes down to, you know. I'm your employee. I've only just begun to make peace with myself. I—I haven't liked myself in a very long while. If we continue this—whatever it is—I'll be back in the dumps and grow to resent you."

She looked stricken. "Oh, Charles! I didn't think. This is not a lark to you, is it?"

"No," he said softly, wishing he could kiss away the wobble from her lower lip, "it's not a lark at all."

Chapter

❦

25

Clearly, she should be locked up somewhere. Returning to Rosemont had addled her beyond the usual addlement. Addlement. Was *addlement* even a word? She'd add it to the awfulest list and call it good.

Or maybe, instead of Rosemont, it was Charles Cooper. He was sending her mixed signals, like a telegraph wire gone awry. He wanted nothing to do with her now, but this afternoon he'd asked her to marry him!

He hadn't really meant it, of course. They barely knew each other. And they were from completely different worlds, with nothing whatsoever in common. He was a hero, and she was just a silly heiress, no matter how much she claimed otherwise. He'd made a difference in his world, and she had merely rebelled against hers.

Coming to him in the bathroom was rebellion. A proper sort of woman would have pretended not to hear him or understand what he was doing in there. He hadn't really been all that noisy, despite what she said. A few gasps. A grunt. Some rhythmic splashing. If her ear had not been pressed against the door, she might not have heard a thing.

But she had been unable to ignore him, having come to the conclusion she should just seize the day. Make hay while the sun shone. Enjoy every inch of Charles Cooper while he was handy. She really liked him, even if he was a man.

Because he was a man.

He'd been magnificent standing in the tub, his swollen member unavoidable. It had seemed the most natural thing in the world for her to open her mouth and taste him. He seemed to like it very much, and Louisa had to confess she had, too—she'd felt rather powerful scrambling up on her knees and kissing him with such wicked wantonness. After all, he'd done much the same thing to her last night. She was only returning the favor.

But she was greedy, empty, throbbing between her legs, her breasts still pebbled with desire. Or maybe she was just cold, as Charles had warned.

His eye patch was tied on crookedly, his hands still resting on her shoulders. She couldn't meet his perfect blue eye.

"I'm sorry."

"For invading my privacy or tempting me beyond reason?"

"I tempt you?"

"Need you ask? I've never met anyone like you, Louisa, and I don't quite know what to do with you."

You could touch me, just once more. Like you did last night. With your hand.

Or your tongue.

There would be no babies then, would there? Touching wasn't intercourse. One touched one's pets, patted and stroked them, tickled behind their ears and raked one's fingernails down their backs so they arched—

"Louisa? You have a most peculiar look on your face."

"It's nothing. Well, it's not nothing. Suppose you help me one last time." One more time would hurt neither of them, would it? Then they could pull the brake and go on with their deception.

"Help you?"

"Like I just helped you."

He released her shoulders. "What are you talking about?"

"I understand your reluctance to be my paid lover, I do. What is a man called when he assumes that position, anyway? Women are called mistresses."

"I have no idea. Fancy man? Stallion? Whatever the name, I'm not going to become one."

"No, no," she said hurriedly, "I quite agree. It would be pure folly. I don't wish your conscience to be taxed any further than it has been. You are completely in the right to refuse to do my bidding in the bedroom."

"But? I know there's a but. Do you know when you are thinking, your tongue wiggles at the corner of your mouth like a tender little worm?"

Louisa retracted her tongue and sealed her lips, then objected. "Tender little worm? How horrid!"

"See for yourself." He spun her to the mirror over the pedestal sink. "Go on. Think."

"I cannot think on command!" He towered behind her, a smirk on his face.

"Oh, can't you? You've been trying to convince me you're not some empty-headed deb."

"I'm too old to be called a deb," Louisa said, feeling mulish.

"Contemplate the sorry state of the world. The suffragist cause. Why the sky is blue."

This was ridiculous. Louisa could think of nothing but kissing the smug quirk from Captain Cooper's lips and getting him to put his hand up her towel. If she wiggled a little, she might just be able to unfasten the tuck and have the damn thing drop on the floor. Then he could put his hand around her hips and discover she was *weeping* with need.

He was still naked himself. For a man who wanted to protect himself from her lust, he was doing a damn poor

job of it. Glistening drops of water snaked down his muscled arms as he pushed her toward the mirror. Charles was
a little too thin, but well made. What a pleasure it would
be to share something rich and delicious with him—cake
and fruit and mulled wine in the privacy of their own
bedroom, curled up in the covers—

"There it is. See?"

Louisa blinked into the mirror. By God, the man was
right. Now she'd spend the rest of her life trying not to look
like she was chewing on a worm.

She met his gaze in the mirror. "Charles, I would appreciate it very much if you could put me out of my misery."

"Shall I hit you on the head like our unknown assailant,
or do you have something more creative in mind?"

"Do you remember last night, when you climaxed without me? Well, you've done it again. You made up for it
later, and very nicely, too—I'll grant you that. But today
you've rediscovered your principles. Now we are supposed
to pretend nothing ever happened. You've explained your
reasoning, and I respect your decision, truly I do. But I
wonder if you could just postpone your born-again virtue
for about ten minutes. I really don't think it will even take
that long. All I have to do is concentrate, and if you touch
me in the right places—which you've already demon-
strated you can do with a considerable degree of deftness
and dexterity—I'll be able to resign myself to a lifetime
of celibacy. Or at least a month of celibacy. I suppose once
our charade is over there will be nothing stopping me from
finding a willing partner in the future." Though doing the
various things she'd done with Charles with someone else
somehow did not hold that much allure.

She watched his face in the mirror as she babbled on.
At first, he'd simply looked indulgent as he pointed out the
habit she was unaware of. Then his face went through
several subtle convulsions—one would have to look hard
to see them, and Lord knows she was looking hard because
the man was so damned handsome. Charles looked a bit

thunderous at the end. Could he be jealous? That might be a good sign, mightn't it?

He spun her again so they were face-to-face. "What are you asking?"

"Well, you're all relaxed now. Or you were. *I* feel quite tense. Being alone with a gorgeous naked man tends to have an effect upon me. You could—finish me off, I believe you called it last night. It will be difficult to get through another family dinner as nervous as I am."

"Nervous."

"Yes. You know. Throbbing a little *down there*. My breasts feel funny, too, like little surges of electricity are running through them. Hm. I wonder if I should get Rosemont electrified if I stay. That might make it less gloomy."

Charles's expression was comically confused. Louisa did not know why she was discussing home improvements with him at the moment—she really had other priorities.

"I won't ask for any attention from you again. We'll go back to having a strictly professional relationship. Friendly in public when you pretend to be Maximillian, but conforming to strict guidelines in private when you're just Charles."

"Oh, shut up, Louisa." He grabbed her face and kissed her with a kind of fury. She was ever so happy when the towel slid from her body and she was pressed against his clean, violet-scented skin. Somehow he didn't smell feminine at all. Charles Cooper was all man—why, his enormous penis was poking into her belly even after he'd just climaxed so recently. Maybe they could finish each other off, though Charles would still be in the lead for orgasming. Was *that* a word? Goodness, her vocabulary was expanding. Being with Charles Cooper was like going to some sort of erotic finishing school.

Heavens. *Finishing.* She giggled.

Damn. Charles stopped kissing her. "What's so funny? Crowing because you're going to get your way again? I'm just some poor chump who can't seem to stand up to you."

"Oh, no. I'm not laughing at *you*, just something foolish I thought of. You know how foolish I can be—you tell me often enough. Don't you think we should go to your room? Not mine, because Kathleen might come up. The sink is digging into my back."

Charles sighed. "I think I must be a patient for your Dr. Freud. I will be totally mad before the month is over."

"But it will be worth it; I promise you." At least she hoped it would be. If they only had this one time, Louisa would throw herself into the process with as much enthusiasm as she could summon.

This time Charles locked all the doors against invasion. His bed was rumpled, a book facedown on the coverlet. Louisa picked it up, and Charles snatched it away from her.

"Look here. We don't have much time. We shouldn't even be doing this. But if we are going to do this, you're not going to start off by reading some damned book."

"Yes, Charles," Louisa said meekly. "What do you want me to do?"

"Nothing! This is supposed to be for you—to relieve your tension. Do not touch me."

"Not at all?"

"Not one finger. In fact—" An odd look crossed his face, and he stalked to the draperies framing the mullioned windows. Faint stars twinkled in the gray sky. "Yes. These should do the trick." He untied all the gold cords from the faded brown curtains. "Lie down."

"Wh-what are you going to do with those?"

"I am going to tie you up, and cover your mouth with one of Maximillian Norwich's silk neckcloths so you will be quiet for once. And *then*, Miss Stratton, I am going to make you much less nervous. You'll be lucky if you'll be able to walk downstairs to dinner."

"Yes, Charles. That sounds lovely."

Louisa didn't understand why he growled so at her words, but then she understood very little of the male psyche. She lay down on the bed and spread her arms and legs helpfully toward the bedposts, where he lashed her with complicated knots about her wrists and ankles. As if she'd try to escape. This was all rather intriguing, as long as he remembered to untie her afterward so she could get ready for dinner. She was getting hungry.

Louisa was less certain about the cravat he wrapped about her mouth, but it did have a practical aspect—if Charles's ministrations caused her to make unseemly noise, the household would not know of it. She hoped Kathleen was still busy with Robertson and would wait for Louisa's ring before she came upstairs.

She could still see, and Charles looked very fierce indeed. His lips were set in a grim line, as if he was angry with her for asking him to relieve her this one last time. It was a shame he was so upright, but that was also his appeal. She really liked him very much.

What would it be like to spend more than a month with him? Goodness, if they were married they could play games like this all over Rosemont and not worry about the consequences. There were lots of windows and lots of drapery cords. But his wasn't a serious proposal. It was all part of Charles's honorable nature to want to protect her from her family's villainy.

Louisa did not want to get married. She still might have control of her fortune, but she would lose herself and probably her heart. It was one thing to be muted and tied up for amusement, but marriage really robbed women of their own voices and bodies.

She decided it was easier to shut her eyes than to see the shadows flicker across Charles's stern face as he examined his handiwork. So when he joined her on the bed, it came as a surprise. The mattress dipped, and she could feel the heat of him even if no part of him was touching her. What was he thinking? She was in such a vulnerable position. Did he realize how much she trusted him?

Where would he start? She was as tight as a bowstring, waiting.

The answer came soon enough. Charles parted her already-spread thighs and slicked his tongue over her center, then sucked her clitoris firmly into his mouth. He toyed with it using his tongue, slipping a finger inside her at the same time. She was soaked and he experienced no difficulty when a second finger joined the first. His blunt nose was buried in her nether curls and it sounded like he was humming, each note sending a current from her little shame tongue somewhere deep within—she'd read those words somewhere in a naughty book she and Kathleen had taken turns reading aloud on hot summer nights. It had prompted her to get a mirror to see the accuracy of the description, without Kathleen's knowledge, of course. My, but women were made in secretive fashion. Every important inch was buried treasure, unlike men who were designed for all the world to see.

Tongues, shameful or otherwise—she'd have to remember to retract hers when she was thinking, but there was no chance of doing much proper thinking now—*oh!* She would have been thrashing about with sensation if she could, yet somehow her immobility was even more of a stimulant. Louisa could do nothing but lie still and feel every touch, hear every breath.

Just as she'd promised, a scarce few minutes passed before she was completely mindless, vaulting off the bed and nearly knocking poor Charles off the field. If this was the last time they would do anything like this, Louisa wished he'd been less efficient, but she really could not complain of the decadent, luxurious tremors shooting down to her tethered toes.

She opened her eyes to see him untying the braided cords. "There," he said, removing the gag and brushing a thumb across her lips. "That should hold you a little while until you can get your next lover. Do be more discriminating in the future—neither Sir Richard Delacourt nor I are appropriate consorts for you. You deserve more."

"I do?"

He grabbed a pillow to cover his rigid erection. "Enough. You got what you came for. I'm not handing out any more compliments. Now get out and go get dressed. I'm sure Kathleen is skulking about with her ear at the door. As of this minute and forever more, I am simply the man you hired to pretend to be your husband. No more kissing. Anywhere. Let's behave like a normal society couple—I understand there's a good reason for separate bedrooms. Pretend to loathe me. That way when you kill me in January you won't have to simulate grief."

He sounded so final. Louisa supposed he was right—somehow they had switched roles. Hadn't she been averse to having a "real" pretend marriage with him? She'd been adamant about displays of unnecessary affection. And now she just wanted to pull him down onto the bed and kiss him.

Anywhere.

Louisa rubbed her wrists. "I'll meet you downstairs. Shall I have a footman sent up to help you dress?"

Charles snorted.

"I'll take that as a no." She cleared her throat. "Thank you for your—your kind assistance with my difficulty. I feel much better now."

"Bully for you. Now scamper off, would you?"

Louisa scampered. She paused in the bathroom long enough to pull the plug out of the tub and pick up the towel that had dropped. Catching a glimpse of herself in the mirror, she thought she looked too well tumbled to escape Kathleen's notice.

And then she heard a muffled, agonized shout. Her name, if she was not mistaken. Poor Charles. She could have helped him with that if only he'd asked.

Chapter

❦

26

A malevolent undercurrent ran all through the evening
from the obligatory predinner drinks in the drawing
room to pudding at the table. Charles could find no fault
with the food or the German wines, only with the company, which consisted of just the odd assortment of family
and Dr. Fentress, who seemed to be a fixture. Even Louisa
was subdued—the exuberance she displayed with him
was buttoned up fast beneath a high-necked sky-blue
satin gown that showed no pulchritude whatsoever. Whether
she was avoiding stimulating Hugh or himself he wasn't sure.

He was beyond stimulated. The taste of Louisa was still
on his tongue, and he hadn't a clue how he was to stick to
his resolution for the rest of the month.

No sexual congress. It was imperative he keep his distance, for he couldn't allow himself to be used in such a
way again, no matter how delicious Louisa Stratton was.
He had feelings for her that would not be assuaged by the
occasional slap and a tickle by her fiat. If she couldn't see
her way to marry him—and really, why should she? He
had nothing much to offer an heiress—then he was not

going to break his own heart by falling ever deeper under her spell.

Charles was placed next to Isobel again, but thankfully Grace had Hugh and Dr. Fentress for dinner companions tonight. She had given him one brittle smile over her glass of champagne and then ignored him with a steadfastness he could only admire. He avoided Isobel's wandering hands as best he could and tried to make conversation with an ancient woman who had at one time been Louisa's father's and Grace's governess. Evidently she was past governessing by the time Louisa and Hugh came around but still supported by the family. Perhaps Grace was human after all, though he wouldn't want to bet the bank at Monte Carlo on it.

Charles gazed around the table. Several leaves had been removed since last night, though the table was set as formally. There was Miss Popham, the retired governess; crusty old Great-Uncle Phillip, who sat at the head of the table tonight; Louisa; Miss Spruce, Grace's secretary; Dr. Fentress; Grace; Hugh; and the grabby Isobel. One of these people might have hit him on the head last night—except for Hugh, who had not been home—though none of them looked at all capable or dangerous under the chandelier. Of course, Hugh could have instructed one of the servants to get Maximillian Norwich out of the way.

Grace blotted her lips on a linen napkin and rose. "Gentlemen, we ladies are leaving so you may discuss the boring issues of the day that would simply confound the weaker sex. Do join us when you've solved the world's problems."

So, was Grace Westlake a secret suffragist? Interesting. Louisa rolled her eyes at her aunt's speech and waved at Charles before she was shepherded out of the room. His thigh finally free of Isobel's imprecations, he relaxed a fraction in his chair. Hugh raised a finger and a footman sprang to it with the port and walnuts.

Griffith materialized at Charles's side with a humidor. "Would you care for a cigar, Mr. Norwich?"

Louisa didn't care for smoking. It was one of her rules. Charles shook his head. The other three gentlemen had no such scruples or orders. Soon the dining room air turned blue with smoke, and Charles realized he'd smell like a chimney anyway.

A sullen Hugh puffed away, and deaf Phillip couldn't be bothered to make conversation with anyone, so it was up to Dr. Fentress to be amiable. "So, Mr. Norwich, what do you think of Rosemont? I heard you say you explored the property on horseback today."

"It's a remarkable place. Were you acquainted with Louisa's grandfather?"

The doctor nodded. "I set up my practice locally at his invitation. I was fresh out of medical school when George Stratton approached me. His wife was sickly, and he wanted someone he could depend on. He was often in the City, and worried about Louisa being alone here. Oh, that was your Louisa's grandmother—she was named for her, but you probably know that. I've served all the family ever since. I delivered your wife, you know."

"Did you deliver Mrs. Westlake, too?"

Fentress twitched. It must be rather strange to carry on a quasi-romantic relationship with a woman you pulled from a birth canal. "I did. But not her brother Byron—he was a few years older. Nor young Hugh here, either. Mrs. Westlake resided at Marbury Court then, Viscount Marbury's estate in Herefordshire. The late Mr. Westlake was the viscount's brother."

"Don't bother with the genealogy lesson, Doctor. Norwich won't be here long enough to add to the Stratton family tree," Hugh sneered.

"Oh? Why do you say that, Westlake?" Charles asked mildly.

"You'll soon tire of Louisa's antics. Or she'll tire of you. Dr. Fentress here can tell you she's not right in the head. Hysterical. Isn't that right?"

The doctor examined the ruby liquid in his glass. "I

shouldn't like to say without closer observation. Perhaps she's changed this past year. But there's no question she was highly strung before she left. Impulsive. She was a great trial to poor Grace. I sometimes had to prescribe medication to make her see reason."

"You drugged her to shut her up."

"Now, now, Mr. Norwich. That's most unfair. Louisa's manic episodes were a harm to herself and the household. Her aunt only has her best interests at heart. We understand Louisa. You've known her, what, a few months? We've known her all her life. And you think you're in love with her. I find love colors one's perception. One cannot be a reliable witness when one is in love."

That was certainly true in the doctor's case, as he let himself be led around by Grace Westlake.

"Love. Bah. The girl's mad." Phillip surprised them all by inserting himself in the conversation.

Hugh laughed sourly. "I quite agree, Uncle Phillip."

"What's that?" the old man barked.

"I said I agree. Louisa is mad and there's no such thing as love. Whatever you think you feel for my cousin won't last, Norwich. You'd be better off accepting my mother's offer before Louisa breaks your heart."

Charles was fascinated. It was as if he'd fallen down the rabbit hole like Alice into an alternate reality. These people, who all claimed to know her so well, described a Louisa he didn't recognize. Yes, she was impulsive, outrageous really, when she begged Charles to relieve her sexual frustration. When she rode off hell for leather across the downs. When she came apart beneath him. But that's what he liked about her—her honesty. Her energy. Her vulnerability.

But what if he'd got the wrong end of the stick? Charles had to admit he was dazzled by the heiress. Maybe he wasn't the best judge of character. His experiences in Africa had warped his perspective for months now. Years.

Charles spun a walnut on the tablecloth with a blunt

fingertip. "I'll take my chances, gentlemen. A month with Louisa is as good as a lifetime. We'll see what the New Year brings."

"If you live that long. You'd better watch out. Your wife is handy with a pistol."

Charles looked up with interest. "You sound as if you have reason to know, Westlake."

"The girl has tried to kill me any number of times. She's dangerous."

"It sounds like you did something to earn her wrath."

"Who knows what sets Louisa off? She's unbalanced."

According to Louisa, Hugh had tried to compromise her repeatedly. Too bad Louisa didn't plug him right between his golden brown eyes. "I expect it will take more than a girl with a gun to kill me. I've faced more firepower in Africa than that."

Charles realized his mistake at once.

Hugh's eyebrows lifted. "Africa?"

"On safari," Charles said quickly. "Years ago. Lions."

"I wasn't aware they provided lions with guns," the doctor chortled.

"You're right. Their teeth and claws are enough to deter any righteous man. But some of the other hunters were inexperienced," Charles extemporized. "Careless. That's how I received my injury." *Oh, shit.* Wasn't he supposed to have been a boxer? Too late to backtrack now. Maximillian the Great White Hunter popped a walnut into his mouth, hoping to prevent any further faux pas.

"What an interesting life you've led," Dr. Fentress said. "I suppose compared to lions on the savannah, our Louisa is relatively harmless."

"I'm sure old Max here has already felt her teeth and claws." Hugh smirked, and Charles controlled his desire to fling the silver bowl of walnuts in his face.

"I have no complaints regarding my marriage," Charles said, hoping to shut down any further aspersions against Louisa.

"It's early days yet," Hugh replied. "Don't say we didn't warn you."

Charles stood. "I've had quite enough of this male camaraderie. I must warn you, Westlake, if you keep insulting me or my wife, my Christian charity may not extend to allowing you to stay through Christmas. You have no official standing at Rosemont save as Louisa's childhood tormentor. And when you grew up, you were little better—some might say much worse, trying to importune an innocent girl into your bed."

Hugh's face suffused with color. "Rubbish! If Louisa told you that, she was lying. As usual. And anyway, she hasn't been innocent for years; it's a wonder she didn't whelp a litter of bas—"

The rest of his sentence ended as Charles rounded the table and punched Hugh in his aristocratic nose. He tipped backward in his chair and fell with a satisfying thud. The man resembled a turtle on his back, legs kicking frantically to right himself. Charles couldn't be bothered to see if he succeeded. He closed the dining room door with a flourish and made his way to the drawing room.

Tonight there was no music, just Louisa looking miserable standing alone by the window holding a cup of tepid tea, the other women clustered together on the sofa and chairs.

"Come upstairs with me at once, my love," he said, holding out an unfortunately blood-spattered hand.

Grace shrieked, but Louisa didn't blanch or bat an eye. "Of course, Max, darling. If you ladies will excuse me."

"What have you done?" Louisa whispered as they ran up the staircase.

"Only what needed to be done. Your cousin will not be smelling any roses or anything else for some time."

Louisa tripped on the step and he caught her. "You *hit* him?"

"I did. I'm sorry if you object, but he was insufferable."

"He's always insufferable. If this was another century,

he'd be fighting duels left and right. *I* could have happily skewered him any number of times."

"No duels. No boxing matches, either. Which reminds me, apparently I was on safari somewhere in Africa and some idiot injured my eye."

This time Louisa stopped still on the stairs and glared at him. "I told my aunt it happened in the boxing ring."

"I know. I remembered too late to keep the story straight. Lying does not really come naturally to me, I'm afraid." What about Louisa? Was Hugh right in accusing her? She'd certainly dreamed up Maximillian Norwich with no difficulty. What if everything she'd told him was *her* truth but not *the* truth?

There was that bit of tongue again, as well as scrunched eyebrows on her worried face. "Maybe Aunt Grace will forget."

"Not bloody likely. Grace does not strike me as someone who glosses over details. Well, I can't do anything about it now. We can hardly explain that a shell landed a little too close to me for comfort. What would Maximillian Norwich be doing in the middle of a war? Better that I was hunting elephants or some such."

She staggered on the stairs again. "Never say you would kill a defenseless animal."

"Oh, certainly not. I much prefer to shoot people, but only if they're armed and shooting at me. Though you're a fine one to talk. Where do you think your fur coat and fur muff came from?"

"Charles!"

"Hush. The walls have ears. There may be a footman crouched behind that curtain on the landing. Come on. Let's lock ourselves in before Hugh comes dashing up the stairs to call me out." He took Louisa's elbow and hurried her up the stairs.

Once in their suite, he methodically locked all the doors that led to the corridor, then for good measure shoved furniture against them. Louisa paced before the sitting room fire.

"Kathleen won't be able to come in."

"So what? What do you need her for?"

"She—she helps me undress."

Charles looked at Louisa. Her blue dress had a great many satin buttons running down the back. "I can do that."

"Oh. We usually talk a bit, too. About the day. She's my best friend, you know."

"You'll have to talk to me instead. Although I know how the day has gone." Pretty much straight to hell.

"Don't you think you should wash that hand?"

Charles had forgotten. To Louisa's credit, she hadn't fainted dead away when he stormed into the drawing room dripping Hugh Westlake's blood. He walked through her bedroom to the bath, but not before catching sight of the lacy pink nightgown spread out across the counterpane, placed there by the evil Kathleen in a plot to drive him entirely around the bend. The thought of Louisa in it and out of it was too vexing to contemplate.

Charles scrubbed Hugh away with vicious determination. If he were smart, he'd continue on to his room and bolt the door. But he'd lost his wits sometime in the past two days, and he had buttons to unbutton.

Chapter

❦

27

They were safe, barricaded in, not that Louisa thought Hugh would come bounding up the stairs after Charles. Hugh was probably tattling to his mother right this very minute. She pictured their two gilded heads in the flattering candlelight, complaining and plotting against them.

Louisa had anticipated that things would be unpleasant at Rosemont on her return, but somehow she'd not imagined fisticuffs and attempted murder. Fortunately her letter had been posted to Mrs. Evensong, so it was simply a matter of days before all this would be sorted out. In the meantime, she and Charles could settle into their own little kingdom in her parents' suite. There was no reason to join the others for meals—she could arrange food to be delivered. Goodness, it would be like old times, when she was confined to her room for weeks after some minor infraction.

This time, she was confining herself.

Charles returned from his washup, his jacket and waistcoat shed. "I could use a nightcap. Do we have anything up here?"

He had spoken of his reliance on alcohol before Mrs. Evensong employed him. Was working for Louisa so stressful he would backslide after two days of moderation?

Yes, it probably was.

Two days. That's all it had been, with a few extra hours at his boarding house and tea at Mount Street. Louisa couldn't believe so much had happened in so short a time. They had confided in each other. Been physically intimate. Escaped assault. It was them against the world now, or at least against the residents of Rosemont.

She opened the corner cupboard. It was well stocked with decanters of brandy and whisky and several bottles of Madeira. "We're in luck. Pick your poison."

"I don't suppose there's gin."

"People like us aren't supposed to drink gin."

"But I'm not people like us, Lulu."

"Please don't call me that horrid name." She grabbed a corkscrew, the wine, and two stemmed glasses. It would be less harmful than the stronger spirits. She had no interest in seeing Charles foxed—if he wanted to protect her as he'd promised, he'd better be clearheaded. Her hands shook a little as she poured. Charles stood before the mullioned window, staring out at the black ocean and blacker sky.

"Here you are. Chin-chin."

"To us. The real us, not 'people like us.'" Charles tipped back the glass and drained the wine in one swallow. "I wonder what tomorrow will bring."

"Nothing, I hope. We can stay right up here all day and be comfortable." Not that being in Charles Cooper's presence was exactly relaxing.

He turned to her. "What do you mean?"

"We needn't go downstairs." She tried for a cheeky grin. Let him think she was trying to get him back into her bed.

Charles frowned. "You want to hide?"

Louisa, knowing she was a coward, nodded.

"Balderdash. I won't let you mope about in the suite all day. We've got things to do."

"We do?"

"Yes. Didn't Reverend Whosit ask you to do the flowers for Sunday's church service? We can ride over tomorrow—on a proper horse, not place ourselves at the mercy of your taciturn chauffeur. And while we're in the village, shouldn't we buy Christmas presents for Grace and Hugh?"

"You can't be serious."

"What, are you saying lumps of coal are unavailable locally? I didn't get to see much of the High Street when Robertson brought us home from the station, but I swear there's a store or two."

He was teasing again. When he looked down at her like that, all she wanted to do was kiss him.

That wouldn't do. They were done with all that.

But oh, she didn't want to be.

"I don't think you should do any more fighting. They'll think you're uncivilized."

Charles set his glass down. "And so I am. I can't stand by and let them hurl such vile insults at you, Louisa. They make me so angry."

"Thank you."

"Don't thank me until I get rid of them. Anyhow, didn't you say Hugh boxed at university? Maybe I should take him on. The loser leaves Rosemont."

"No!" Louisa had no interest in seeing Charles's beautiful face beaten to a bloody pulp. She had no faith in her cousin sticking to sportsmanlike conduct.

"As you wish. But I'm willing to run into shot for you."

She placed a hand on his arm. "I couldn't bear it if anything more happened to you. I'm already so guilty about last night's mischief."

"I'm hard-headed. Hard in other places, too," he muttered.

She knew Charles could be very hard indeed. Now that his image was lodged in her mind, he popped up with distressing frequency. Louisa started at the sound of the doorknob rattling. "Kathleen?"

"Yes, Miss Louisa. I can't seem to open the door."

"N-no. We—we've locked ourselves in. Because of what happened last night. There may be villains afoot."

There was a conspicuous silence from the hallway. Then her maid said, "Will you be needing anything from me?"

"I think we can shift for ourselves. Thank you." Louisa waited to hear Kathleen retreat, feeling a little strange talking through the door.

Instead there was a furious little rap. "You have to let me in, Miss Louisa. And then I suppose you'll want to fire me."

"I beg your pardon?"

"Open the door, and I'll explain everything. Oh, Robbie's going to kill me. I've ruined our lives."

Louisa looked at Charles in confusion. He nodded, then pushed the chair away from the door.

Kathleen entered, her face as white as her starched cap. "You'd both better sit down. Please." She stood in front of the fire, twisting her hands.

Louisa chose a chair while Charles claimed the gray sofa. Louisa had never seen her maid so nervous, except when she was a passenger in the car.

"I've done a wicked thing, Miss Louisa, and I owe the captain an apology. N-no one is out to hurt you anymore. It was me. I mean, it was I."

Charles's hand went to the back of his head. "*You* hit me?"

Her freckled chin lifted. "It may not have been my hand, but at my direction. I wanted to protect Miss Louisa, see. I could tell something was happening between you, and I thought if you had a little accident you wouldn't be interested in any folderol."

"Folderol?"

"You know what I mean, sir. And anyway, your injury didn't stop you from"—Kathleen blushed scarlet, then continued—"acting upon your animal impulses. It was just as I feared. I—I came back to see if you were all right and heard you two going at it like a pair of rabbits."

"Kathleen!" Louisa was stunned at the betrayal. Her trusted confidant had almost murdered Charles and compared her to an animal, no matter how cute! Did rabbits even make noise during sexual congress? Louisa rather thought they only screamed when they were killed. It was supposed to be a terrifying sound, like a baby's wail. She'd have to ask some gardener or other, but she was quite sure she had made no noises of that nature last night.

Although she'd lost her composure completely in those two short days. Anything seemed to be possible, except to keep track of her wandering mind.

Time to focus. Was she angry at Kathleen? Oh, yes, she was.

Charles, on the other hand, looked amused. "Did you think I was such a gay Lothario? Out to take advantage of your mistress and break her heart and her bank?"

Louisa had seen Kathleen's self-righteous face many times in the past five years, and here it was again. "You're a good-looking man, sir, and Miss Louisa is not always sensible. Why, if you knew the things she did this past year, you'd be worried yourself."

Worse and worse. "Don't talk about me as if I'm not here!" Louisa cried.

"Sorry, miss. But you know you tend to make a mistake here and there. I was only trying to protect you. They told me how the captain kissed you at dinner—George the footman said he thought you were going to be ravished right on the lace tablecloth in front of all the guests. Wicked, it was. Indecent. I love you like a sister—better, because some of my sisters are spiteful cats and you've always been so kind to me. I've been a fool to risk the best job I could ever have, but I didn't want you to get hurt."

"So you decided to hurt me instead." Charles spoke in

a remarkably calm voice, as if he got hit on the head every night.

"I am sorry, Captain Cooper. Mr. Norwich. Whoever."

"Who was your partner in crime? Robertson?"

Kathleen's eyes dropped to the carpet. "I shouldn't like to tell."

"But you already did," Charles countered. " 'Robbie's going to kill me,' I believe you said in the hallway. I suppose he stopped polishing the Daimler long enough to put screws in the horse blanket, too."

"I didn't tell him to do that! He took it upon his own initiative."

"An enterprising fellow. He should go far in life. Well, Louisa, what shall we do with this pair of miscreants? I confess I wanted to finger Hugh for the crimes—I'm rather disappointed."

"How can you take this so well, sir?" Kathleen asked. "It's rotten what we did. I know that now. You're not really a bad sort."

"I appreciate your confidence in me, Kathleen. It's somewhat a relief to discover I'm not doomed to die at Rosemont. I find I'm really not interested in dying anywhere at the moment. Thank you for putting my mind at rest."

"I'll start packing. But please, miss, take pity on Robertson. He really didn't want to do it."

"Packing!" Louisa swallowed hard. What would she do without Kathleen? Even if Charles could help her with her buttons, he would be leaving in a few weeks. And angry at her or not, Kathleen was really her only friend.

"Yes, Miss Louisa. I won't expect a reference. And if you decide to arrest me, I'd understand. But Robbie is almost innocent."

Charles rolled his eyes. "Kathleen Carmichael, you're something of a siren, aren't you? You lure men to their doom."

"Not men, Captain. Just one man. Robbie and I want to get married. When I go, he may give notice and come after me. I don't know how we'll manage—"

"Oh, shut it, Kathleen. You're not going anywhere. And you think *I'm* half-cracked. Your idea was preposterous! What if Charles had been seriously injured? Captain Cooper is no danger to me." What a whopper that was. In two days, Charles had penetrated not only her womanly core but her heart. Which was ridiculous. She hardly knew the man.

"I'm so sorry, Miss Louisa. Captain. I'll make sure nothing happens to you ever again. I already talked to Robbie, and he feels even guiltier than I. He loves me, you see, and will do anything for me, even if it goes against his principles."

"You're a lucky woman," Louisa said tartly.

But then, so was she. Charles Cooper was ready to serve her in any capacity she asked—save one. Plus, he'd asked her to marry him, too. Maybe they should all have a double wedding. A cackle of laughter escaped along with the tension that had been building since last night. Both Charles and Kathleen looked at her with alarm, but once Louisa started laughing, she couldn't seem to stop.

She was surrounded by people who resorted to violence to protect her, and they thought *she* was the crazy one. There were elements of French farce and Gothic intrigue rolled up together—no wonder she'd been off-kilter since she'd come home. She was in the wrong play.

Kathleen's slim hand pushed down on her shoulder. "Sit down, Miss Louisa. I'll fetch you a cold cloth to calm you."

"That's all right, Kathleen. I'll take care of your mistress."

"And I know just how you'll try," Kathleen said with asperity. "Just because I don't plan on incapacitating you anymore doesn't mean I approve of you interfering with her."

Charles was no longer amused. "I'm not going to

'interfere' with her! I've given her my word not to touch her again, and I can't believe I have to pledge to you as well."

"St-still here," Louisa hiccupped from her chair.

"Perhaps I should mix up some of Dr. Fentress's elixir in a nice hot cup of tea for her."

"That's right. Drug her until she doesn't know whether she's coming or going. That should do the trick," Charles said, his sarcasm obvious. "No wonder she's so unhappy."

Louisa wiped the tears from her cheeks. "*Still* here. And I'm not unhappy!"

"You're hysterical then."

"I am not! Anyone would find this all too"—what was it, exactly?—"too much. I want both of you to leave me alone. No cold cloths, no elixirs. Certainly no lovemaking. I can take care of myself, as I always have. Go away!"

Neither Kathleen nor the captain moved one inch, each staring at her with concern. What would it take for them to obey her?

"You *are* fired, Kathleen. At least for tonight. And Ch-Charles, I release you from your service. P-please pack up and Robertson can drive you to the train tomorrow morning. I'll say we quarreled. And then send myself a telegram in a day or two. You'll meet with an unfortunate accident in London. A robbery on the street gone awry. Maximillian wouldn't part with his purse easily—it was his father's, made from the hide of a very rare sort of cow. The Norwich family crest was on it—"

"No." The word was said in unison from both maid and man, although Charles growled it more than spoke it.

"I'm going to put her to bed, Captain Cooper. When she gets into those stories of hers, it's clear to me she's got a fever of the brain. Such an imagination. I'm sure she'll tell wonderful stories to her babies, but right now she's very tired."

"I'm not tired," Louisa said, sulky. And she was not having any babies to tell stories to. Not that she'd ever given children much thought before—she was never getting married now, was she?—but suddenly they didn't seem quite so sticky and unpleasant. A dark-haired boy, a golden-haired girl—oh, what was the matter with her? Charles was right. She *was* hysterical.

"At least you should be able to sleep well tonight," Charles said in a soothing tone that got on her last nerve. "No intruders, right, Kathleen? Robertson will keep to his quarters like a good boy and we'll all feel jolly in the morning." He left her sitting there and set to going through the suite, removing obstacles from doorways. She could hear furniture sliding and clunking away in the next room.

Jolly. Ha. Louisa glared at her maid. "I don't know if I should forgive you." She was rather hoping to be trapped up here with Charles for the foreseeable future.

"I am sorry, truly I am. We meant only to keep you from falling prey to a fortune hunter. You're usually on guard against such men, but the captain seems to interest you. Am I correct?"

Louisa felt her face grow hot. "He's a very interesting man."

"Good in bed, is he?"

"Kathleen!" She really did not have much to compare him to, but she was pretty certain no sane woman would have any complaint over Charles Cooper's caresses.

"Well, you be careful. You wouldn't want to get in the family way. I don't suppose you have one of those clever Mensinga diaphragms we learned about in Germany—you would have told me."

Louisa restrained herself from sticking her fingers in her ears. "You're right. I'm exhausted. Put me to bed."

She tried not to mind that Charles never returned to her or their nightcap as she sat at her dressing table in a prim nightgown, Kathleen brushing out and braiding up her hair. Once her maid finally left—after boring her stiff with praise of Robbie Robertson's prowess—Louisa made her way through the bathing chamber and tentatively turned the captain's doorknob. It was unyielding. Locked against her.

Just as it should be.

Chapter

28

Saturday, December 5, 1903

At least he wasn't going to be trapped in temptation too near a bed with Louisa in the suite all day. No one was out to kill him, Charles thought as he nicked his cheek with his razor. He was doing a good enough job at that all on his own. He blotted the blood up on a pristine white towel, hoping he wouldn't incur the permanent wrath of Rosemont's laundress.

He'd just about finished bleeding and dressing when Louisa rapped on his sensibly locked door.

"Charles, breakfast has been brought up to the sitting room." She sounded brisk. Imperious. The old Louisa Stratton was back.

"Thank you. I'll join you in a moment." He'd dressed to ride, thinking it would do them both a world of good to get away from the estate and visit the village. He knew nothing about flowers but could stand about as she poked things into vases in the church vestry.

Satisfied that his tie was straight, he exited through the hall door and strolled down the corridor to the sitting room, just in case Louisa was still in dishabille in her room. The scent of sausages would have drawn him even if he didn't want to see her this morning.

He was rewarded by a vision of both silver domed dishes and his "wife." There were two other people in the room as well. A footman, not William today, was arranging the food on the table in front of the window under the watchful eye of a slender, distinguished-looking older woman. The missing housekeeper, Charles presumed. He plastered a sober expression on his face and prepared to offer his condolences once they had been introduced.

Louisa sat before the crackling fire, wearing a neat burgundy riding habit. So she remembered his proposition. It was another glorious early December day, milder even than yesterday, he'd thought as he stuck his head out of the window earlier. It seemed warmer outside than it was in the mausoleum-like house.

"Good morning again, darling," Charles said, slipping into his Maximillian mode.

"Max!" she said with false brightness. "May I make you acquainted with Rosemont's sterling housekeeper, Mrs. Lang? Mrs. Lang, my husband, Maximillian Norwich."

Charles extended a hand. "I am most happy to meet you, Mrs. Lang, and compliment you on the superb state of my wife's home. And you have my sympathies on the loss of your mother."

Mrs. Lang's mother must have been ancient indeed. The housekeeper was wreathed in wrinkles herself. She nodded regally back at him but did not take his hand. No doubt Maximillian Norwich should not be in the habit of shaking hands with the servants, so Charles stuffed his paw into a pocket.

"Thank you, sir. Congratulations on your nuptials."

The woman did not smile, so Charles was unable to see

if the crone had all her own teeth left. He remembered Louisa saying the housekeeper was in Grace's camp, so there probably was very little value in trying to charm her to show her teeth. He'd be most happy to toss the woman out on her bony arse, if it meant fewer headaches for Louisa.

"Breakfast looks lovely, Mrs. Lang," Louisa said, moving to the linen-draped table. "Please give Cook our compliments. We can serve ourselves as we did yesterday. Are you as hungry as I, Max?"

"Hungrier."

"Will you or your husband require anything else? The staff is at your disposal. Mrs. Westlake tells me you wish to make some changes at Rosemont."

"Nothing that concerns *you*, Mrs. Lang," Louisa said hurriedly. Good Lord, Louisa was frightened of her own housekeeper. Charles was a little, too. When the servants left, Charles felt his spine relax a fraction. Oddly enough, he was more worried about being found out as a fraud by the Rosemont staff. Class differentiation was ingrained so deeply in British society his every vowel was suspect. He'd worked hard to overcome his working-class background and accent, but the scrappy boy within would never be totally eradicated.

He sat, noting that Louisa had resorted to artificial color on her cheeks. He had passed an indifferent night as well, imagining he could hear every sigh and rustle of her bedcovers through three doors. Had she touched herself in thwarted desire as he had? At this rate, he'd be blind in both eyes by the end of the month.

But he wasn't going to leave. Not until Louisa got the upper hand over her household, even if it meant his hands grew hairy. Not that he believed such nonsense. The boys at Harrow would have resembled apes if such tales were true.

He speared a pair of sausages from the platter. Once again there was more food than two people could possibly eat. Louisa contented herself with buttering a perfect toast triangle, avoiding the meat and eggs altogether.

"You're going to fade away," Charles said, passing her a cut-glass dish of raspberry jam.

"I doubt it. Have you ever noticed how much people like us eat?"

"'People like us' again."

"You know what I mean. All this food can't be good for one."

"Didn't you tell me your aunt went on some sort of slimming regimen?"

"She's rabid about her figure. For a while, she would only eat green things."

"I presume that's what sent her to bed too weak to be mean." Charles popped a sausage chunk in his mouth. "An army can't move without meat, you know."

"I have no objection to a nice joint—just not at breakfast."

"You really should try one of the sausages. They're very good. There's some sort of spice I can't identify."

"Cook makes her own. I've watched her. One should never watch sausages being made."

Charles laughed. "So you know your way around the kitchen?"

"I would never say that—I'm no cook, though I believe I can boil water and roll out biscuit dough with the best of them. I did spend a lot of time in the kitchen when I was young, but as I grew older I moved on to the conservatory. I should show it to you before we leave for our ride. Griffith tells me he took care of my plants personally with the help of the head gardener." Her eyes rested on the ceramic urn they had been given as a wedding present, which still rested on the sill. "We can bring that downstairs. I'm sure something can use repotting."

"So you have a green thumb."

"And all my other fingers as well," Louisa said with a grin, wiggling them. "Minding my plants is the only feminine domestic skill I've got. Don't ask me to paint or sing or play the piano. Sewing is absolutely out of the question."

She was more than feminine enough for him. Charles reached for another sausage. "I've heard you sing, remember. You're not so bad."

"There are excellent acoustics in the bath. All that tile. And one can't go wrong with Christmas carols."

They lingered over breakfast, Louisa succumbing to some fruit and a small bowl of porridge while Charles worked his way through the eggs and mushrooms and every last sausage. He might have overdone it a bit, but in a little while he'd get sufficient exercise. Until he'd come to Rosemont, he'd been on limited rations for a very long time, partly out of economy, mostly out of sheer lack of appetite. Nothing had interested him but his gin bottle and its longed-for obliteration. When he'd remembered to eat, he'd subsisted on tinned food and weak tea over a spirit stove in his room at Mrs. Jarvis's. He couldn't afford to pay her board, not that the scents coming from her kitchen were at all inviting.

Once he was done here, he'd have enough money to rent decent lodging. Since it seemed he was not going to kill himself after all, he might even take up George Alexander's offer for suitable employment. Charles wasn't sure what he was qualified for, but he was willing to work hard, fill up his days with something useful.

What would Louisa be doing a month from now? Would she be back in Paris or Vienna or Berlin, or up to her eyelashes in the conservatory, forcing some bulb to bloom out of stubborn will, her apron freckled with dirt? The poor plant would have no choice but to bend and thrive to her desire.

Just as he had. She was a force of nature, plucking him out of his gloom and setting him back on his feet with a few judicious words and a cloud of violets.

He pushed himself away from the table with some

reluctance. She had been relaxed with him this morning—they had chatted as if they were old friends. Were, in fact, husband and wife. But that was not to be, even with his precipitous proposal.

"Show me this jungle of yours." He picked up the planter from the sill and hefted it into the crook of his arm. Now that he looked at it, he saw it was not painted but covered in tiny mosaic tiles. The pattern was faintly Arabic and quite lovely, its brilliant blue glaze contrasting with pure white. Orientalism had been all the rage in the last century—he'd learned that in his art history book.

Once he followed Louisa downstairs to the lush indoor garden, he recognized exactly why the staff had chosen the urn. The wall adjacent to the house was covered with blue and white tile squares, with occasional touches of green. Birds and flowers and leaves joined together and repeated themselves, their detail quite remarkable. A shallow pool set into the floor shimmered in the sunlight, reflecting the design. Small braziers were lit at regular intervals along the brick floor, and three long tables teeming with plant life ran the length of the building. White iron fretwork decorated the arched windows, and the glass ceiling vaulted heavenward. It was hot enough in the room to strip and plunge into the little pool.

"Oh! The fountain is turned off," Louisa said. "It's very soothing to work in here when it's running."

Charles let out a low whistle and set the heavy urn on a table. "This is amazing. It's almost like some kind of church."

"The Cathedral of the Holy Orchid? That's what my favorite specimens are. Orchids are notoriously difficult, and I've lost more than I care to count. But I think Griffith has done a spectacular job. The conservatory was the only thing I missed about Rosemont while I was away, really." With a gloved fingertip she touched a pale petal of something Charles couldn't identify. "I guess I should cut some flowers for the altar. The roses should travel well, and I'll mix them with greenery and ribbon and some dried grasses."

She picked up a pair of secateurs and a basket from a neatly organized shelf and went to a row of potted rose-bushes that flanked the south-facing window. Charles watched as she snipped tightly closed rosebuds, laying them carefully onto the wicker, the bright sunlight limning her body. He missed her breeches, but there would be another scandal for her if she entered the church in them.

"I'll just wrap up the stems and we'll be off."

The air was humid and thick—too thick—and suddenly Charles felt light-headed. He gripped the edge of a table and gulped for air. Heat invaded his lungs, reminding him of Africa. A palm tree in a corner completed the illusion, its fronds somehow vacillating in the still air. The sight in his good eye blurred, then tiny black spots began to dance a demonic jig. A sharp pain divided his body, doubling him over. Too many sausages. Served him right for being a glutton. But damn, they had tasted good.

Louisa was across the room at the sink, oblivious to the fact that he was slipping to the floor. Good grief, he was fainting like some gothic heroine. *Fainting.* He slumped onto the brick, cushioning his head from the blow with an arm. So he had some sense left, but precious little. His stomach twisted and he felt the bile rising. He was going to lose his breakfast, and not a moment too soon if it would alleviate the agony that possessed him. Best to turn himself over so he wouldn't choke on his own vomit—that would be unpleasant, and leave Louisa unprotected. The bricks could be hosed down; there was a drain right there—

Charles lost the rest of his thought as he rolled under the table and retched onto the floor, spilling the lurid contents of his stomach in a very undignified, un-Maximillian way.

Chapter

29

*L*ouisa was startled by an odd gurgle behind her. She turned, but Charles had disappeared.

"Max? This is no time to play hide-and-seek." She turned off the tap, then bundled the roses into a damp towel and gently rolled them into loose brown paper, tying them up with the twine she used to stake her plants. "Are you ready to go?"

Sunlight streamed in through the roof, dust motes swirling. Charles was not sitting in any of the wicker chairs, nor was he examining the trays on the tables. "Max? Charles?"

Another wet noise, and then she heard him. "D-down here."

"What do you mean? Where are you?"

"Floor. I'm d-dying."

"You are not!" Louisa dropped the parcel and skirted around the first table. Beneath the table in the middle Charles lay near what looked and smelled suspiciously like a puddle of vomit. "Charles! You're ill!"

She sank to her knees and was immediately sorry. Louisa had never been good with sickroom evidence or its aroma. She'd had to drench herself in scent so she could sniff her wrists and handkerchief all the way through the Continent to avoid the un-Englishness emanating from foreign bodies, too. Well, technically *she* was the foreign body, but her nose was very particular. She pinched it just now and thought of summer roses. Thought hard. Lots of roses in riotous color, perfuming the air, lush blossoms that in no way resembled the chunks of undigested sausage she quickly closed her eyes to.

"Can you get up?"

"N-not sure. Head. Stomach. Knives."

"Oh, you poor man. But I did warn you against all that meat."

"No lectures."

"Shall I call for some footmen?"

"Maximillian Norwich would never be caught in this state."

"Forget about Maximillian Norwich." Charles's face was the color of lamb's ears, that peculiar gray green that was soothing in a plant but disconcerting on a human. Louisa really did have to move him before she joined him in his disgrace—the contents of his stomach were a vivid olfactory reminder of his gluttony. "If you cannot stand, suppose you move a little ways away from your current position." She covered her face with a sleeve and desperately inhaled wool and violets.

He chuckled. "Just like maneuvers. Duck and cover. They won't get me. They didn't before, even when I wanted them to." He made some shooting noises, which alarmed her.

"Whatever you can manage."

Poor Charles crawled away as slow as a centipede. How did people deal with nursing? Of course, she had not blanched at the sight of his wound the other night, or last night when he had Hugh's blood on him, for that matter. Louisa was not entirely fainthearted, she assured herself, trying hard not to gag. "Keep going if you can." The next county was preferable.

She rose from her knees and went back to the sink, wetting a towel and washing her own face with it first. She ripped open the roses and breathed deeply, tucking one into her bodice for emergency relief. He had cleared himself away far enough down the aisle between the tables, then collapsed. She got down on the floor so she could wipe his face and feel his forehead. "No fever."

"Small mercy. I do not feel well, Louisa. I think—I think I've been poisoned."

Louisa almost let Charles's head fall back to the brick floor. "What? Don't be ridiculous! Kathleen promised no more tricks."

"Maybe it wasn't Kathleen this time. I've made no shortage of enemies. There they are, the devils." He pointed in the general direction of a large *Schefflera arboricola*.

"It was just the sausages, Charles. How many did you eat? Six? Seven? Anyone would suffer for that."

"Eight, but who is counting? I see two of you. Not clearly, I might add. Your edges are fuzzy. Everything's moving. Look there—can't you see that table leg? Won't stay still. Watch for falling plants. Oh God." Charles giggled, actually giggled, as if he'd already been hit in the head and lost his wits.

"This is not funny, Charles."

He only laughed louder. "White light—so, so bright. Need some dark spectacles like that Evensong woman. To see you better. You are an angel, Louisa. No wings, though. But by Jove, your tits make up for their lack. Wings are no good in bed. Feathers tickle. Tits—now, they're a different story. Soft and plump. Like peaches. Want to kiss you, my darling."

Louisa reared back from his breath. "Not until you chew a mint leaf." Perhaps the whole plant. What had come over him? His symptoms were not like any stomach upset she'd ever had. He seemed almost . . . drunk. Silly. Certainly amorous when she least welcomed his attentions.

"Fuck you into next week. So, so hard."

And clearly he didn't know what he was saying. He'd resolved not to touch her again, and she felt sure he was a man of his word, no matter how much she didn't want him to be. "Do you think you can stand up?"

His eyelid fluttered shut. "Not a chance. Your lap is so comfortable."

"Be that as it may, I'm going to put you back on the floor and ring for some help." She took off her riding jacket and wedged it under his head. Rising a bit unsteadily, she yanked the bellpull near the door and prayed for swift delivery.

An unfamiliar footman entered, one of Aunt Grace's new hires. "Yes, Mrs. Norwich?"

"I have a problem. My husband is not well." And not in possession of his faculties. "You'll need to fetch William to help you carry him upstairs. Alert Mrs. Lang to send in some maids to clean the floor, and send Cook upstairs to our suite at her first opportunity." No one else should eat any of the suspect sausages, else they would find themselves in Charles's pickle. "I'll need a pot of strong tea as well. Perhaps some paregoric."

The footman took a sniff and wrinkled his nose. "Yes, madam."

Kathleen could help her undress Charles—if she was innocent of any mischief. Louisa would soon find out.

The next quarter of an hour was a busy one, with Charles quoting snippets of ribald poetry as the men carried him through the house. He insisted the footmen stop on the landing so he could examine the figured wallpaper, which he claimed was speaking to him.

Kathleen had been picking up her mistress's room when they trooped in, and she swore she and Robertson had nothing to do with Charles's bizarre behavior. She looked as worried as Louisa felt. Between all of them, they removed his riding clothes and put him in a pair of monogrammed silk pajamas. Once he was finally safe in her bed with a basin nearby, Louisa told William to fetch Dr. Fentress, who happened to be paying his daily visit to her aunt.

"What do you think about my arse now that you've seen it, Kathleen?" Charles mumbled.

"It's prime, sir, and no mistake," Kathleen replied, rolling her eyes. "Men. Even when they're out of their heads they're a vain lot, aren't they?" she whispered.

"What can be wrong with him? He said he thought he was poisoned," Louisa whispered back.

"That may be. If he were fevered, that might explain his delusions, but he's almost cold to the touch. His eyes look funny."

"My eye, you mean," Charles said, sounding cheerful, his hearing still as acute as ever. "But I can't look as funny as you girls. Did you know you have bugs in your hair? Little pink spiders, I think."

Louisa restrained her impulse to run screaming to her mirror. He was seeing things that didn't exist. Hearing things that made no noise. Saying things he wouldn't ordinarily say.

"Wish I could vomit again. Should stick a finger down my throat—"

"No!" Louisa cried. "Dr. Fentress will be right here. I've ordered tea, too."

"A girl like you probably thinks a cup of good English tea will cure the clap."

"Charles!" My God, he wasn't diseased, was he? She'd heard of people going mad from syphilis. But surely Mrs. Evensong would have discovered such a thing.

"Max," he corrected. "You are forgetting our little play. I am but an actor, hired at your whim."

Oh dear. What if he forgot in his present state of confusion? Dr. Fentress would run straight to Aunt Grace.

"Just try to be quiet, Max. Close your eyes so you don't see things that trouble you."

"Eye, you mean. And you are the only thing that

troubles me," he said, then laughed maniacally. But he did shut his blue eye.

He looked perfectly innocent. There was a tiny cut on his cheek where he cut himself shaving. Was the blade rusty and he had some form of blood poisoning? One didn't lose one's mind from eating too many sausages.

Dr. Fentress entered without knocking. "William says we have an emergency. But I see the patient is asleep."

"Am not," said Charles, not opening his eye.

"What seems to be the problem, Mr. Norwich?"

"Drugged, I should think. Mushrooms."

Louisa's mouth dropped open.

"Can't be sure. Sausages may have been tampered with as well. Tasted different. But the hallucinations are consistent with ingesting a certain type of mushroom. Went to visit my grandmother once in the country when I was a boy. Brothers and I picked mushrooms and got sick. Can't remember much about it except Fred laughed himself hoarse, and Fred is not one to laugh a lot."

Heavens. Charles was unexpectedly eloquent about his condition. Dr. Fentress nodded. "I remember a case like that written up in an old issue of the *London Medical and Physical Journal*. Ask Cook to come up, Louisa."

"I already have. What can we do?"

"Make him flush his system. Kathleen, get someone to run down to the beach and fetch a good quantity of seawater. That should do the trick. And then he must be watched so he doesn't harm himself or anyone else. The effects should wear off by this afternoon."

"This afternoon!"

Charles grinned up at her. "What's the matter, wife? Afraid to spend the day in bed with me? I don't want some damned footman. I want you, pink spiders and all."

"I'll help you, Miss Louisa, uh, Mrs. Norwich," Kathleen offered. "William can wait in the hall if we need him." She hurried out of the room.

Both Cook and Mrs. Lang entered as the maid left. Cook's usually rosy face was as white as her apron.

"Oh, Mrs. Norwich! I can't believe there's poison in my kitchen."

"We think he ate some bad mushrooms at breakfast. Where did you get them?" the doctor asked.

"My girls picked them from the woods, where they always do. I'm so, so sorry!"

"I don't blame you," Louisa assured her, though she supposed Cook might be just as treacherous as Kathleen and Robertson. "But if there are any left, throw them away. I wondered about the sausages, too."

"The sausages?"

"Just because Ch-Max ate so many of them. But they're probably all right."

"I should think so. They're made to my special recipe and I've never had one complaint."

"Hush, Miriam. No one is casting aspersions on your cooking," Mrs. Lang said. "Mrs. Norwich, I suppose after this little upset you will want to leave Rosemont and return to France."

"Well, not right this minute," Louisa snapped. Poor Charles was in no condition to travel anywhere.

"What can we do to help?" Cook asked.

"I don't know. What besides seawater should he have?" Louisa turned to Dr. Fentress.

"Nothing else until he's emptied his stomach. I doubt he'll be hungry again for a while, and when he does eat, make it the simplest of nursery food. Just make him as comfortable as you can, and don't be alarmed if he sees and says odd things. As you know, he's delusional—he's invented brothers when you said he was an only child. Like the imaginary playmate you used to have—isn't that right, my dear? What was his name . . . Melvin? Malvern? My goodness, I believe it was Maxwell! What an odd coincidence that you've married a man with almost the very same name! I'll stay the day to keep an eye on him. Call me from your aunt's quarters if you need me."

Louisa hadn't thought about her invented friend in a long while, and she hoped Dr. Fentress would not give any more thought to him, either. Damn. Trust him to have paid attention to her when she was a little girl when no one else in the household did. He was a good-hearted man, save for the fact he was under Grace's thumb. The doctor seemed more than delighted to have an excuse to spend more time at Rosemont today with her aunt.

Louisa sent everyone away, stationing William in the hallway. Charles did not appear violent, but she might need help to escort him to the bathroom. She placed a hand across his brow, and his eye whipped open.

"I want you naked, right next to me where you belong."

She'd thought he was sleeping, he'd been so quiet. "Not now, Charles. When you're better," Louisa lied. She wouldn't hold him to things he didn't mean when he was under the influence of some toadstool.

"Promise?"

"You might change your mind. When you're better."

He clasped her hand and held it over his erratic heart. "I've been a fool, Lulu. Marry me. Please."

It was just the toadstool talking. "You don't mean that."

"I do. If I live."

"Of course you're going to live. Oh, where is Kathleen?"

"I don't want her. I want you. Do you know I've never really wanted anyone before? And who should I fall in love with but an heiress who's miles above me? Come down to earth, Lulu. I'll spend the rest of my life trying to make you happy."

Louisa's eyes welled with tears. If only he was in his right mind.

Chapter

❦

30

Kathleen, who had perhaps one head too many, hovered over him. She bore a glass bottle of vile-looking, gray-green liquid.

"I tried to strain most of the sand out of it."

"I'll pour it into a teacup. Can you sit up, Charles?"

It would be so much easier to stick his fingers at the back of his throat. Now that he'd figured out what was wrong with him during a brief lucid phase, the sensations he was experiencing weren't too awful. Yes, it was disconcerting to see the random flashes of color and the wobbling objects, but he felt like he was floating in a warm, calm sea. He really didn't want to have to *drink* the sea to bring him back to reality.

But he wanted to wipe the look of worry off Louisa's face, so he dutifully swallowed all the saltwater in one gulp and asked for more.

A mistake. Well, he supposed that was one way to look at it—perhaps the purging was necessary. He made use of the basin several times, having difficulty aiming since poor Louisa's hands shook so.

"Let Kathleen do this. You're not made for this kind of thing," Charles murmured.

Louisa passed the bowl to Kathleen, who, as she dashed off to the bathroom, looked just a fraction less affected than Louisa did. "I feel responsible."

"Why? Because some kitchen maids picked the wrong mushrooms? It could happen to anyone."

Louisa left the bedside and went to the bank of windows. To his one working eye, she was lit up like a Christmas tree, tiny bursts of light flickering all around her like some kind of twentieth-century saint painted by a grand master.

"I don't like mushrooms, you know. They taste rubbery."

"You are a finicky girl. No sausages. No mushrooms." His stomach gave a rumbling lurch. Kathleen had better hurry back with the basin.

"What if the poisoning was deliberate? They know my likes and dislikes in the kitchen."

"What? You're accusing your poor cook? The woman was in a terrible state."

"Maybe it was guilt. Or someone else could have mixed the odd mushrooms into our breakfast tray."

"This business with Robertson's pranks has unhinged you. No one's out to 'get' me, Louisa." Though if they were, Charles would like the job to be finished. He was feeling most unwell. The hallucinations had abated some, but his innards were in an uproar.

What a waste. Here he was in bed, with a beautiful woman just yards away. The thought of intimacy, while compelling, was down a rather long list of things that took precedence. "I have to get up, Louisa, and I'm not sure I can. Will you get William to help?"

*S*ome hours later, Charles awoke from remarkably pleasant if confusing dreams to a dim, hushed room. Louisa was curled up on a chair in her wrinkled riding habit, a book facedown in her lap. She was watching the fire, her face lit in the ordinary way. She had never looked more beautiful.

"Hello, Lulu." His voice sounded like sandpaper had roughed up his vocal cords.

"Charles! How do you feel?"

"I see only one of you, which is rather a shame. The more, the merrier. What have I missed?"

Her cool hand swept across his brow. "Even Aunt Grace came down to check on you. She wants to fire all the kitchen maids."

"That seems extreme. I'm sure it was an accident."

"Dr. Fentress is spending the night in case you take a turn for the worse. Cook asked me what your favorite foods are to make up a light supper tray, but of course I didn't know. I hope you like creamed chicken and rice pudding. That seemed suitable for an invalid. Hugh sent up a bottle of his best brandy and says he hopes you recover soon so he can challenge you to a boxing match. I think you broke his nose—it looks like a potato."

"Something to look forward to."

"The fight or the food?"

"Both. I think a good sparring match might clear the air here. I hope the rice pudding has raisins."

Louisa closed her book and stood. "I can go ask Cook—"

"Please don't go. I much prefer your company to the possibility of raisins."

She sat back down, tucking a loose tendril behind her ear. "Are you really all right?"

Charles felt as if he'd been sandblasted from within. "I believe there's not an ounce of evil left inside me. Thank you for bearing with me. It couldn't have been an easy job."

Louisa's cheeks turned pink. "I wasn't especially useful."

"Just the fact that you were near helped. You ought to give William a raise."

"He tells me he's seen his brothers in worse condition after Harvest Home." Louisa smoothed her skirt, and Charles wished she'd decided to smooth his brow again. "Cook tells me she won't let anyone else touch your tray. She feels terrible."

"Really, tell her it's all right. I'm still kicking." He wiggled a feeble foot under the covers.

"You can tell her yourself. She'll be bringing dinner up—or at least accompanying a footman so no one can make any mischief."

Despite his nap, Charles was too tired to argue that it was probably all a harmless mistake. He dragged himself up to a sitting position, sliding easily in his silk pajamas. *Silk pajamas.* He'd never worn anything like them and wasn't sure he liked the way they felt against his skin. Despite the masculine forest green color and blocky gold monogram, they seemed more appropriate for Louisa.

"You must be exhausted. Why don't you get undressed?" He patted the vacant space next to him. "We can have supper in bed."

"That wouldn't be proper."

"For Mr. and Mrs. Maximillian Norwich to dine in bed together? Of course it would." Charles gave her what he hoped was a confident grin.

"That's just it." Louisa looked back into the flames. "I think we should tell the truth. You've only been here three days, and each day has brought disaster of one kind or another. Rosemont is not lucky for you. I think—I think you should go. I must have been delusional myself to think all this was a good idea. The make-believe."

"Louisa—"

"I'll pay your full fee," she said hurriedly.

"I don't care about the money!" And he didn't, at the moment. "We can make the pretense true if you want to. Why don't you marry me?"

"You don't really mean that."

"I don't? I asked you yesterday. I believe I asked you

earlier today when I was off my onion. You need someone, even if you don't think you do."

She rose, the book dropping to the floor, and almost ran to the windows. "I don't need anyone! I've never had anyone, and I'm perfectly fine."

"You are a stubborn girl."

"I'm not a girl. I'm a woman. And I do not need a man to tell me what I need or don't need." Her nervous fingers traced a pattern on the dark glass.

He was going about this all wrong—no surprise, for proposing to independent heiresses was not his specialty. "What if I told you I loved you?"

She turned to him, her face scornful. "I wouldn't believe a word."

"Why not? Are you unlovable?"

"I—you don't even know me."

Charles wondered if he had the strength to walk to the window. Deciding to risk it, he swung a leg out of bed.

"What are you doing? You're meant to stay in bed and rest."

"I find being with you unrestful, Lulu. Which is a good thing." The room spun, but he continued his mission. Once he got to the window, he clutched at her hand to steady himself. She didn't pull away. "Do you know before I met you I wanted to die?"

Her brown eyes widened. He could look into them all night. "Wh-what?"

"I've told you what happened in Africa. I could not get it out of my mind. Couldn't sleep. Couldn't eat. Couldn't care about anything. But when I'm with you, I care. I think of nothing but you. You've invaded me."

"Th-that's ridiculous."

"I suppose it is. My feelings make no sense at all. How can someone like me hope to have a life with someone like you? It's absurd. We have nothing whatsoever in common. When your aunt finds out about my background, she'll have an apoplexy."

"Class shouldn't matter."

He kissed her fingertips. "Oh, but it does, my naïve darling. Everyone will say I married you for your money."

"We are not getting married." There was no force behind her words, and Charles allowed himself to feel some hope.

"Give me a week to change your mind. What's the worst that could happen?"

"You could *die*. And Aunt Grace could have me locked up."

"The princess in the tower. If you were my wife, I'd rescue you. You could live just as you pleased—I wouldn't interfere with whatever cork-brained scheme you dreamed up." He took her in his arms. She fit so beautifully against him, it was the most natural thing in the world to kiss her. He had brushed his teeth after his last bout with the basin so had no reservations about limiting their contact to one respectful peck.

Louisa melted into him, opened her mouth, met him more than halfway. Charles tasted both her yearning and her reluctance. He would prove he loved her if she gave him some time, tell her with his body and his actions. Let her use him physically—he'd use every weapon in his arsenal to convince her, no matter how it injured his male pride.

"I was so frightened," she said, her heart beating against his when he ended the kiss. "You were quite mad. How do I know this is not another manifestation of the mushrooms?"

Charles laughed. "*The Manifestation of the Mushrooms*. Sounds like a gothic thriller. I can only tell you my head is relatively clear, or as clear as it can be when you are so near to me. You bewitch me."

"I'm not sure that's a compliment."

"Oh, it is. Louisa, I'm not asking you to give up your autonomy. I think you'll find me an understanding husband—I have no wish to give orders left and right. I did enough of that in the army."

She pulled away a little. "I can't think right now."

Good. He hoped he had the same effect on her as she had on him. "You needn't give me an answer, just seven more days for us to get to know each other better. I will tell you how my older brothers bullied me and you can complain all about that bastard Hugh."

"I've done that already. And it's not pleasant to dwell in the past."

No, it was not. It was only because of Louisa that he could even think of a future.

But if she refused him, he was not going to succumb to his previous misery. He'd been weak, drowning himself with drink and self-pity. All that must end. Surely he had something to give, some skill to hone.

And if she did agree to marry him, he couldn't live off her income as a kept man—he was no fortune hunter. Charles would have to find some sort of occupation.

Mr. and Mrs. Charles Cooper would scandalize English society. He didn't mind for himself, but Louisa might be hurt by wagging tongues. Any children they might have would have difficulty establishing themselves despite the Stratton fortune, too.

Those problems would be faced head-on when the time came. Together, Charles was sure they could survive anything. Tonight, he just needed to get Louisa into his bed.

Wait. He was already in hers, or would be if he went back and collapsed into it. What a marvelous idea. He felt a sinking spell coming on.

Chapter

❦

31

Charles had rallied a little at supper, sitting up and consuming a gigantic portion of chicken à la Keene in puff pastry and a cinnamon-topped rice pudding studded with enough raisins to satisfy the most avid raisin aficionado. But he seemed listless afterward, responding to Louisa's conversation half a tick behind his usual sharp wit. So out of concern, or so she told herself, she had agreed that he should sleep in her bed again.

Kathleen had suggested he return to his own room, and volunteered Robertson's services to play watchdog through the night. The chauffeur himself had come up with the idea to atone for his previous bad behavior, but Louisa had rejected it. Charles was her responsibility.

And besides, lying next to him all night was hardly a hardship. He had bathed after dinner—by himself even though Louisa had offered to help—smelled delicious, and sported a fresh pair of striped silk pajamas. Navy this time, which brought out the deep blue color of his visible eye. She watched as he readied himself for sleep, fiddling with the knot of his eye patch.

"Can I help you with that?"

"My fingers feel like sausages tonight. Oops, there's the dreaded word. I'm afraid I won't be able to face Cook's sausages anytime soon."

He sat still as she untied the black silk string. She smoothed the faint red lines the patch had left on his skin with a fingertip. "It was just as well you were a glutton. Nature relieved you of some of the poison to your system."

"And the seawater did the rest. I may never go swimming again, either." He turned down the lamp wick on the bedside table, plunging the room into darkness save for the firelight.

Louisa would like to see him swim next summer, his sleek body cutting through the waves. "Next summer" would mean he'd successfully convinced her to consider his suit. They might be married, living at Rosemont, sharing this bed every night.

Captain Charles Cooper would have his work cut out for him—Louisa had sworn off men for close to a decade. It would be enjoyable to watch him try to seduce her, not that she'd resist him with much determination. He had proven to be very adept at stimulating her senses, had awakened desire within her that she'd thought long dormant.

But marriage was forever. Unless you believed in divorce, which was still expensive and difficult and scandalous despite all the dissolution of American society unions across the pond. Better not to marry at all and live in sin if there was some doubt of fidelity.

Why couldn't she and Charles have an affair? She could run up to London once a month. Stay at Claridge's or the Savoy. Indulge themselves in a few nights of pleasure. No strings. No obligations.

Charles would never do it. He'd think she was using him, and he'd be right.

Marriage. Louisa peeled back the covers on her side of the bed as though she'd done it for years. There was familiarity and comfort with Charles, which on its face was absurd. She'd known her plants longer.

They had been through quite a bit together over the past few days, however. Louisa had seen him at his worst and at his best. His best was certainly very, very good.

"This is cozy, isn't it? I can see stars twinkling right from the bed."

Charles was still at least a foot away from her, and his voice was low. Louisa wiggled down so she could see the night sky. It was breathtaking, whether one knew one's constellations or not.

"It's a clear night. We've been very lucky with the weather for December."

"Louisa Stratton. You have a man in your bed and you are talking about the weather?"

She heard the sly smile behind the words. "You are recuperating from a terrible ordeal."

"I know a way I could feel better much faster."

"Really? What do you have in mind?"

She expected him to turn toward her and sweep her into an embrace. But Charles Cooper was a man of surprises. "Sing to me."

"I beg your pardon?"

"My mother used to sing me to sleep when I was a boy. Until my brothers teased me about it. Called me a baby. I asked my mother to stop and I think I broke her heart."

"How old were you?"

"Four or five."

"You *were* a baby!" Louisa was four when her parents died. She'd still sucked her thumb and slept with a ratty old stuffed bear. Grace had called the toy disgusting and had thrown it away, and coated her fingers with something vile-tasting so she couldn't stick her thumb in her mouth anymore without gagging. Louisa had Grace to thank for her straight teeth, but it had been a cruel loss of self-comfort.

"In my world, I was almost old enough to go to work,

Louisa. George Alexander wouldn't have hired me, but others would have."

"Unconscionable. I thought there were laws against such things."

"Perhaps in the textile industry. But families have to eat, and many children are put on factory floors at an early age. I started at eight. And didn't have it easy since my father was the foreman. He never wanted anyone to accuse him of favoritism, you see."

"Poor Charles."

"I got clouted like clockwork for no reason, from my dad and my brothers. So you see, I deserve a song."

"I suppose you do. I don't know the words to many nursery songs." She couldn't remember her nurse singing to her often—probably that was one more thing that Grace had forbidden.

"Here's a hint—look out the window." He hummed a few rough bars.

"Of course." She took a breath, and her gentle alto broke the silence.

> *"Twinkle, twinkle, little star,*
> *How I wonder what you are.*
> *Up above the world so high,*
> *Like a diamond in the sky.*
>
> *When the blazing sun is gone,*
> *When he nothing shines upon,*
> *Then you show your little light,*
> *Twinkle, twinkle, all the night."*

There were more verses, but she couldn't remember the words. So she just repeated herself several times until she felt a bit foolish. Charles was a grown man, not a four-year-old, but she sensed his body relax beside her.

"Thank you—that was lovely. Sweet dreams, Louisa." He made no move toward her.

After a few minutes, she cleared her throat. "Don't you want a kiss good-night?"

"I couldn't stop at one kiss."

"Who says you have to?" she asked boldly.

"Remember, I'm meant to be wooing you. Taking things slow. Getting to know you. I don't want to pounce on you—and anyway, I may not be quite up to it." He rolled to the side, putting his lips out of bounds.

Louisa could do all the work—in fact, that would suit her to the ground. Charles could lie flat on his back and she'd ride him to the finish line. But she didn't want to impugn Charles's sense of honor and restraint. She'd kind of forgotten where he stood on their physical relationship. When he'd been out of his mind, there was no question that he wanted to—well, he'd used that blunt Anglo-Saxon word, hadn't he? She'd shivered when he'd said something about fucking her into next week. That sounded very, very naughty, even if next week was just tomorrow.

Hell, she'd have to go to church with the family. She hoped someone else had taken the initiative to do the flowers.

And *now* she was thinking of flowers and church instead of weather with a man in her bed.

Louisa lay still, listening for his breathing. She was much too keyed up to sleep, the air practically vibrating with Charles's silk-clad maleness. How was she supposed to check on his welfare in a dark room? He might have a relapse, have more bad dreams. She was tempted to turn a light back on.

That might disturb him—he needed his rest after the day he'd had. Tomorrow they'd start fresh—maybe he'd be well enough to join her in the little fifteenth-century church in the village. There would be no more accidents, and she and Charles could live happily ever after.

Nursery rhymes and fairy tales. Sometimes one never outgrew one's childhood, the longing for safety and warmth. Louisa did not expect to find such things at

Rosemont, but she'd never had Charles Cooper as her champion before.

He wanted to marry her, and said he wouldn't try to interfere in her life. Was that possible? In her experience, men ruled the roost. Even her father, who'd loved her mother madly, had the final say in their lives. The seascapes on the wall of this bedroom were *his* collection. They'd died on *his* boat. If Grace deferred to anyone, it was to Hugh, her own son. Some would say a man's dominance was the natural order of things. They were, after all, bigger, stronger, louder.

But a tiny bee could fell a man. Louisa felt a determined buzz coming on.

"Charles," she whispered. "Are you asleep? I want you. That is, if you want me."

In seconds, she had her answer. He flipped so he was facing her, his white smile gleaming in the dark, his fingertips on her cheek.

"I thought you'd never ask again. I was kicking myself for clinging to my virtue earlier."

"To hell with your virtue. Virtue is vastly overrated."

"I quite agree. Well, my darling, where exactly do you want me?"

"Everywhere," Louisa replied, thanking the star she wished on.

Chapter

32

Sunday, December 6, 1903

harles was much improved, his color good and his spirits high. He was dressed already for church, whereas Louisa was still lounging about in her diaphanous peignoir over the breakfast table. The sausages had been resolutely ignored, and mushrooms of any kind were absent.

She felt deliciously decadent, or as decadent as one ought to feel before one went to church. The evening had been a great success as far as she was concerned. The deepest part of the night as well. Several times. She grinned inwardly, trying not to gloat. It wouldn't do to think she'd maneuvered to get Charles right where she wanted him, although to be honest they'd probably maneuvered each other.

"Well, my dear, I think that's about all my dicky stomach will take this morning." Charles had left a corner of toast crust but had eaten some eggs and bacon, and drunk two cups of coffee. Cook had come upstairs with the footman, swearing she'd had a taste of everything on the tray herself. The poor woman said she'd set a watch on the larder all day and night so that everything coming from the kitchen was fresh and wholesome.

"How many of me do you see?" Louisa teased. She could almost laugh about it now, but yesterday had been rather terrifying.

"Only one, but one of you is enough for any man. Can I help you dress?"

"You know if you started where we'd wind up, you wicked man," Louisa said. "I'll ring for Kathleen."

"I'll mope about in my room until you're ready."

Louisa put her teacup down. "Have you written in your journals since you've been here?"

"I have not. We've been a trifle busy, haven't we? And somehow"—Charles sat back, fiddling with a monogrammed cufflink—"I don't have the urgency anymore. The despair I felt. It's almost gone, a mere shadow of itself. Really, it is the oddest thing. I have been sleeping, and when I'm awake, I quite like my life as Maximillian Norwich. He's been to Africa, but just on safari. Much more fun." He gave her a shrug and a crooked smile.

"I would like to read your journals sometime, though. If it wouldn't be an invasion of your privacy."

"You would not like what's in them, Louisa."

"I daresay, if you spoke of doing away with yourself." If Charles was serious, if he truly meant to have a life with her, they would have to face his past. She'd been reckless, but he'd faced true demons and almost let them win.

He gazed out the window, taking his time to speak. "You know, I don't think I ever really meant it. I simply couldn't see my way out of the hole I'd dug for myself. I'd killed my career, was half blind, alienated my family—I felt pretty damned sorry for myself. I feel now as if I've woken up from a bad dream—it's as if *I'm* Cinderella and *you* are Prince Charming."

"Surely I'd be Princess Charming. Mrs. Evensong must be the fairy godmother." She pictured the odd little woman with black wings to match her neat black dress.

"Whoever she is, she's bloody brilliant. I owe her quite a bit. Do you think we'll hear from her soon?"

"Oh! I forgot to tell you. I received a telegram from her yesterday while you were sleeping. She got Mr. Baxter to open up the bank. On a Saturday! Can you believe it?"

"I do. I think Mrs. Evensong can get anybody to do anything. She got me here, and that in itself is a miracle."

Louisa remembered the squalid flat he lived in, bleakness in every corner. How depressed he must have been to accept that smelly room as his due. He'd been a war hero, for heaven's sake. Charles Cooper had a fine-honed sense of honor and obligation, an instinct to protect. Lord, look what he did with his ghastly landlady when he thought they were under attack.

Louisa wondered where her explosive little car was at this moment. She'd love to drive Charles about the countryside before it got unbearably cold. This warm weather was bound to change soon.

Christmas was almost upon them. Grace would have arranged the festivities already, inviting the Merwyns, the Naismiths. Dr. Fentress and Mr. Baxter, too. Those familiar faces had surrounded her and hemmed her in most of her life.

"You know Mr. Baxter was one of my trustees, and he's managed my account since I came into my fortune."

"He hasn't managed it very well if what you've told me is true."

"That's what Mrs. Evensong's determined to find out before she goes to the trouble of finding someone else for me. If worse comes to worst, I could transfer my funds to another institution, but that might mean a run on Stratton and Son. If *I* don't have confidence in my own family's bank . . ." Louisa let the sentence hang. Her grandfather would roll in his grave at her disloyalty. He'd worked hard to provide the standard of living the Strattons had enjoyed for the last fifty years.

"I see. It's tricky, isn't it?"

Louisa nodded. "Mr. Baxter was my grandfather's friend. Perhaps in his advancing years, he's not as sharp as he used to be. I know Grace has him wrapped around her little finger. Dr. Fentress, too. She can be utterly charming when she likes."

"I'd like to live long enough to find that out for myself," Charles said.

"Of course you're going to live a long life!" The thought of killing him off as Max had made a complete retreat in her mind.

"I hope so; I truly do." Charles took her hand in his. "Thank you for last night. Even if all this proves . . . temporary, I've learned something I won't forget."

His hand was warm. Safe, yet not safe. Louisa felt a flutter in her chest, reminding her to send him away so she could dress before they wound up back in her bed.

"I really must ring for Kathleen. We'll be late for church, and Aunt Grace will have a conniption. She's probably already taken the brougham with Miss Spruce and Isobel."

"I assume Robertson will be driving us."

"Yes. You won't be too fierce with him, will you? He's awfully penitent."

"I've managed not to bite Kathleen's head off, haven't I? It was all her idea, anyway."

"Yes. You've been a brick. Kathleen is quite in awe of you now."

"I somehow doubt that. She's seen me at a considerable disadvantage." She'd held the bowl at least once while Louisa averted her eyes.

"Even when you'd lost your senses, you were very sweet."

"What exactly did I say?"

"Never mind." She really couldn't repeat his sexually suggestive language on a Sunday morning. She wriggled her hand away from his. "I have *got* to get dressed."

"I'll meet you downstairs, then. Maybe I'll get lucky and run into Hugh."

"Don't pick a fight with him."

"I wouldn't dream of it." Charles rose and straightened his jacket. "It's been a while since I've attended a church service. I hope I remember what to do."

The little chapel seemed unusually full to Louisa. She got the distinct impression that absolutely everyone in the vicinity had come to gawk at the prodigal daughter and her new husband. It had been a while since either she or Charles had sat through a church service—Louisa and Kathleen had explored the great cathedrals of Europe as art tourists, not worshippers. It had been novel to lie abed in a swank hotel sipping chocolate on a Sunday morning, listening to the church bells echo throughout Paris. Kathleen had said she was dooming her immortal soul, but Louisa hadn't believed that. God must know her heart, bruised as it was.

The altar flowers today resembled spiky dead weeds. She would make sure nothing interfered next week with a proper arrangement of Advent greenery. Charles had had a rocky welcome to Rosemont, but surely the next week would be uneventful. She'd have time for flowers, time to do some Christmas shopping in the village to give the local shops her custom. Maybe even go to London for a day or two to escape the atmosphere at home.

Aunt Grace was not precisely filled with Christian charity when Louisa and Charles turned up in the family pew seconds before the service started. Thank heavens Hugh was not present, for fisticuffs in church would frighten poor Mr. Naismith right out of his cassock.

Louisa listened with half an ear as he delivered his sermon, sang with little more enthusiasm as Mrs. Naismith pumped the old organ. Advent hymns were so dreary. Charles had a pleasant baritone, and it was temptation itself to stand so close to him to share the hymnal. Louisa's thoughts strayed somewhat far afield from the "deeply wailing, deeply wailing, deeply wailing" lyrics. She really had nothing to wail about. Even if her homecoming had not been all it should have been, she hadn't faced it alone. Charles had been at her side.

Louisa glanced across the aisle at the Delacourt pew. Sir Richard held his own hymnal, but he was not singing. He looked bored but fortunately was not canvassing the church with his cold gray eyes and did not notice Louisa. His wife, Lady Blanche, did. She gave Louisa a shy smile, then busied herself with the next gruesome verse. Louisa had not really spoken to her old friend Blanche in nine years about anything of consequence. No more girlish confessions or giggling.

Almost immediately after Louisa's disgrace, Blanche had been wooed and won by Sir Richard, who'd suffered no apparent social ill effects from debauching Louisa. At first Louisa felt betrayed, but now she considered she had made a very lucky escape. It was poor Blanche who had to live with the horrible man, after all.

There were two little girls between Blanche and a woman who must be their governess. The heir to the Priory was under a year old, and in his nursery this morning. Sir Richard had the perfect life—a rich, pretty wife, healthy children, and a fine ancestral home, and he was probably busy breaking his marriage vows with impunity.

He hadn't been locked in his room, denied company and forbidden to ride for years and years.

Louisa was not feeling much Christian charity with the world at the moment. As if he sensed that, Charles put his hand on her waist and drew her closer. She now was snug against him, which warmed her body in the chilly church, and her spirits, too. Aunt Grace clucked her disapproval, but Isobel caught Louisa's eye and winked.

When they returned to the hard wooden pew, Charles kept his arm around her. Mr. Naismith didn't object to this display of affection and rattled out the final blessing, looking squarely at Louisa. That warmed her, too.

Louisa hadn't expected the Delacourts to linger after church, and they didn't. Perhaps someday she'd be friends with Blanche again, if Richard permitted it. If Louisa stayed at Rosemont, they'd bump into each other now that Louisa was free to go where she pleased. Not that the parish women's group held any interest for her. She got antsy just thinking about sitting through a meeting with all Aunt Grace's friends looking down their lorgnettes at her.

"What's on the agenda this afternoon?" Charles asked as he helped her into the Daimler.

"We always have a huge lunch that feels like it's going to last until suppertime. Sunday may be a day of rest, but not for the servants. Aunt Grace makes them all go to the early service so they can come back and work their hearts out."

"Shall we say I'm not up to it yet?"

Louisa knew he was saying that for her, giving her an escape route. She shook her head. "We must be brave."

A half hour later, they were in the sunshine-filled dining room. Hugh was still missing, but the relatives and retainers were in full force. Once again, poor Charles was seated between Isobel and Grace, but he seemed to know how to handle them. Louisa heard honest laughter from her cousin, not the usual flirtatious trill. Charles ate sparingly under the watchful eye of Dr. Fentress opposite, and engaged her aunt in conversation that appeared relatively civilized. In fact, the whole meal was the most pleasant since she'd come home. It almost made Louisa think they could all live in harmony.

Almost.

Chapter

❧

33

Charles had been persuaded by all concerned that he should rest the afternoon away, as if chewing his excellent lunch had been an arduous task. He would have preferred to "rest" with Louisa, but she had plans to steal the Daimler away from Robertson and ride around her property while the weather held. Though Charles trusted Louisa with his life, he was not prepared to get into a moving vehicle with her at the wheel just yet.

So here he sat in the leather club chair in his shirtsleeves, an unread book in his lap. The waves below sparkled in the sun, inviting him to take a walk on the beach. He didn't wish to incur Louisa's opprobrium, however, so he leaned back and shut his eyes.

He'd almost convinced himself to fall asleep, was in that half-life between relaxation and slumber, when there was a knock on his door.

"Come."

Griffith entered, looking pained. "I do hate to disturb you after all your trials here at Rosemont, Mr. Norwich, but there is a lady downstairs who says she has come from London to speak with you and Miss Louisa."

Charles knew no ladies, from London or anywhere else. Somehow he couldn't see Mrs. Jarvis riding the train through Kent, not that she knew where he was anyway.

"Did she give her name?"

"Oh, yes, sir. She's most respectable. We've had dealings with her agency before, but of course I've never met her in person. It's Mrs. Evensong."

Mrs. Evensong was *here*? Louisa said she'd received a telegram. Whatever the woman had found at the bank must have been urgent for her to visit unannounced on a Sunday afternoon.

"I'll be right down once I make myself presentable, Griffith."

"Do you want me to valet for you, Mr. Norwich?"

"I still remember how to dress myself. Please make Mrs. Evensong welcome. I'll be down in less than a quarter of an hour."

Charles would change his shirt—in fact, he'd dress from the skin out, because somehow he was afraid Mrs. Evensong would suspect he was not wearing the fine linen smalls she'd ordered in such quantity for him. He'd gotten a little too casual with his clothing of late, especially when he'd had to do his own laundry. His underwear had been so ragged they barely did the job. Like a Scotsman, Charles didn't have much under his trews.

Charles crossed the room and opened the drawer. He suppressed a yelp as a flea landed drunkenly on his knuckle. He smacked it, doing himself an injury in the process, then stared down at the neatly folded clothes. The white fabric was dotted with tiny black bugs, all of which were, thankfully, dead. The drawers were lined with cedar and pennyroyal and rosemary, which had done their job. Someone had played a mean trick, but the kitchen cat was undoubtedly grateful its fleas had been transferred upstairs.

Charles scooped out the clothes and tossed them out the window, where they blew across the lawn like giant snowflakes. Someone could fetch them and take them to the laundress, but just in case there were any survivors, he hoped they liked to fly. His skin began to itch from an imaginary attack and he wondered if he should toss the dresser out the window, too.

Wait. There were his journals. Gingerly he pulled them out and shook them over the windowsill, the pages fluttering. They appeared undisturbed, for which he was thankful. Charles put them into the empty monogrammed trunk and turned the key. If the prankster had read the pages, surely the journals would have been taken to blackmail him with.

So, no underwear in honor of Mrs. Evensong. He hoped she was not in possession of Röntgen's experimental equipment. He dressed in haste, wiping himself down first to ward off any errant fleas, and raced down the stairs.

Griffith was hovering in the hallway at the bottom of the staircase, and Charles explained about the bug infestation and asked that his room be inspected and cleaned thoroughly. The butler's white eyebrows shot up when Charles confessed what he'd done with his underwear, and the man very nearly smiled.

"That was quick thinking, Mr. Norwich."

Charles had been in the army long enough to be acquainted with fleas, body lice, and a host of other unpleasant creatures. "There is someone at Rosemont who doesn't like me, Griffith. Perhaps several someones. See if you can't ferret out who is behind this recent mischief. Louisa tells me you are the center of Rosemont's universe."

Griffith rubbed his white-gloved hands together. "I don't know as I'd say that, sir. But rest assured, I'll try to discover the culprit. This sort of thing puts us all to shame. Cook and Mrs. Lang and I as senior staff have a responsibility to the family that we take seriously. Nothing like this has ever happened here before."

"I would imagine not. But so far, no one's died, right?"

The butler shivered. "And so we hope no one will. Mrs. Evensong is in the small blue drawing room. Do you know where that is? I'll take you there—it's a bit cozier."

Small was a relative term, but the furniture in the blue drawing room was sturdier and more comfortable than the grand gold room they met in before dinner. Mrs. Evensong sat on a sofa with a teacup in her hand. She waited until Griffith withdrew before she spoke.

"Good afternoon, Captain Cooper. I trust things are going well?"

Charles joined her on the couch. "Not really. Oh, no one suspects I'm not who I'm supposed to be, but things aren't quite right here. Someone put fleas in my dresser drawer, and yesterday I was poisoned with hallucinogenic mushrooms."

"What!"

Charles had a feeling it took a lot to shock Mrs. Evensong and was proud of himself for succeeding. "Not to mention that the chauffeur tried to kill me, but that was all a misunderstanding. So you see, I'm earning every penny, not that I want Louisa's money. I understand you have some news about that."

It took her a moment to digest Charles's speech, and then she rallied. "That's for Miss Stratton's edification," Mrs. Evensong said primly.

"I'm not sure when she'll be back. She's out driving at the moment, causing terror to sheep and small animals everywhere."

"So Griffith told me. I can wait. In fact, Miss Stratton invited me to spend some time at Rosemont, although she neglected to tell her staff I might arrive at any moment. Understandable, what with all the fuss here. How do you feel about motorcars, Captain?"

"I know next to nothing about them, except that Louisa loves them. I suppose I should be open-minded for her sake."

"It was not an idle question. Before I left London, I had a meeting with George Alexander."

"How is old George?" Interfering as usual, he'd bet. George probably had another plan for Charles's future, all wrapped up with a shiny bow.

"He's very well. Mr. Alexander has presented me with an investment opportunity. You may not credit it, but I'm very interested in automobiles myself."

"Are you now?" Charles pictured Mrs. Evensong behind the wheel, her proper black hat blowing off on the road.

"I am. Are you aware that Mr. Alexander has purchased the Pegasus Motor Company?"

Charles had always been aware that George had more businesses than his pottery works, but he did find this news surprising. "I am not. Bully for him."

"He's asked me to approach you—"

Charles raised a hand. "While I know George means well, he cannot continue to keep rescuing me. As I said, I don't know anything about cars."

"But you do know how to command men. And you are honest to a fault, when you're not pretending to be Maximillian Norwich. Mr. Alexander wants to build a manufacturing plant outside New York City, and a showroom on Fifth Avenue. He'd like you to be in charge of the American operation with all that it entails—hiring workers, sales personnel, an architect, meeting with engineers and the design team to ensure that Pegasus is in the forefront of twentieth-century transportation."

Charles laughed. The idea was absurd. Better he should be asked to glue wings on a real horse. "He's asking the wrong person. You should be talking to Louisa."

"Perhaps *you* should do that." Mrs. Evensong's expression was inscrutable behind her gray lenses.

"Wait a minute. What do you mean?"

"It's obvious you've formed a *tendre* for her, even after so short a time. If you went to New York, you might ask her to go with you."

The woman had been with him less than five minutes. How could she *know*? "Mrs. Evensong," Charles said slowly, "are you playing matchmaker?"

"Do I need to again? I rather thought I was successful the first time."

"You thought that Louisa and I—that we would—" He struggled to avoid the words *love* or *lovers* or, God forbid, *fuck*.

"Become close? I did. You were both ripe for dalliance. Miss Stratton deserves someone special."

"Believe me, I'm nobody special," he sputtered. "You *did* investigate me?"

"Oh yes. Quite thoroughly. The Evensong Agency is no fly-by-night business."

Charles got up and walked to the window, his legs shaky beneath him. His head was spinning again, and he'd come nowhere near a mushroom. One of the maids was fishing an undershirt out of the bushes.

"Miss Stratton has had difficulty with her family. There may be no mending the rift. I work miracles, but Grace Westlake is a challenge even for me. It might do Miss Stratton a world of good to remove herself from Rosemont again, this time with someone who values her for her many good qualities. You do value her, don't you, Captain?"

Charles's mouth was dry as dust. He nodded. What he felt for Louisa couldn't be put into words anyway.

"Excellent. Well, we shall see what happens. I have a letter here in my bag from Mr. Alexander that explains the particulars. His terms are very generous, certainly more than enough to support a wife and family in some style." She handed Charles a thick envelope, which he put in his coat pocket. He'd read it if his head ever cleared.

A wife and family. Would it be possible? If he had prospects, could Louisa see her way to marrying him? He'd asked, but he knew she didn't take the offer seriously.

"May I pour you a cup of tea, Captain? You look a trifle disconcerted."

"Yes, you may, Mrs. Evensong. You'll be happy to know lately tea satisfies me as much as gin used to."

"I am not at all surprised. Like George Alexander, I recognized the silver beneath the tarnish. Ah! I hear a car coming up the drive now."

For an old woman, her hearing was excellent. In a few minutes, Louisa joined them, her cheeks pink and eyes shining. She looked almost—*almost*—as beautiful as she did after Charles brought her to orgasm.

"Mrs. Evensong, you came! Welcome to Rosemont."

"I told you I would as soon as I had news to impart. May I speak frankly in front of Captain Cooper?"

"Of course! I trust him implicitly," Louisa said, smiling at Charles with an openness that pierced him to the core.

"Mr. Baxter and I spent several hours going over your account books yesterday. He sends his apologies, by the way, for it was clear to him at once that he should have paid more attention. Your suspicions were correct— someone was diverting your funds."

"Who?" Louisa asked.

"I will be in a better position tomorrow to reveal that. Mr. Baxter is interviewing the person even as we speak. Now, don't be concerned. The missing money is hidden safely in another account bearing your name. Nothing has been stolen."

"I don't understand."

"As I said, we'll explain it tomorrow. I might use my time at Rosemont today to discover who has been targeting Captain Cooper."

Louisa's golden brows knit. "Charles, I thought you believed the mushroom business was just an accident."

"Maybe, but that doesn't explain the fleas."

"Fleas!"

"Don't worry. Most of them were dead. But someone put them in with my smalls."

"What? When?"

"I couldn't say for sure. You know I don't wear them, Louisa."

Well, there went his discretion. Louisa blushed but didn't show one inch of shame in front of Mrs. Evensong.

"You *have* been getting along well," the woman murmured.

"Extremely," Louisa said. "Oh my goodness. You don't suppose bugs were put in my lingerie drawer, do you? Kathleen will have a fit."

"I'm sure she would have noticed. I would guess someone entered my room yesterday when I was in yours, or this morning when we were at church."

"I'd better find Kathleen. Mrs. Evensong, you'll excuse me, won't you?"

"Of course, my dear. It's time I explored Rosemont on my own. You two young people should enjoy what's left of the daylight."

"Let's go for a walk in the garden, Charles. If you're up to it."

Charles was up to anything if it involved Louisa Stratton.

Chapter

❦

34

The sky was smoke gray. Dusk was approaching, but Louisa was in no hurry to return to the house and dress for dinner. She wanted to give time to the squadron of maids who were turning out their rooms in search of six-legged creatures.

It wasn't the six-legged creatures that worried her. Who was the two-legged villain behind this latest insult to Charles?

If Hugh were a twelve-year-old boy, he would fit the profile perfectly. But no one had seen Hugh all day, and fleas seemed too foolish even for him.

Kathleen and Robertson felt guilty, and so they should. They'd started all this with their misplaced concern for Louisa's virtue. It was like opening Pandora's box—what would happen next to poor Charles?

He didn't look poor as he examined one of her grandfather's gargoyles with an appreciative grin on his face. It guarded a circle of old roses, bourbons and damasks and gallicas, which were now just thorns and canes. This gargoyle, or *grotesque* if she were to be accurate, was almost as tall as Charles, with horns and hooves and a forked tongue. It was remarkably hideous, and it had always been her favorite.

"What's this ugly fellow's name?" Charles asked.

"Lambkin."

"No, really."

"It is Lambkin. He is quite terrifying, so I gave him a name to neutralize that. I always imagined he was soft-hearted inside all the granite. Sad because he was judged on his appearance."

"Appearances can be deceiving," Charles agreed. "I was dazzled by yours, of course, but thought you were—"

"Just a 'silly society girl,'" she finished. "Yes, I remember."

"It's hard to believe it was only a few days ago." He tucked her arm in his and continued walking on the crushed stone that connected all the gardens. Louisa wished he could see them in bloom—the gardens were romance spelled out in roses.

Did she want romance from Charles? Yes, she did.

She was very, very close to accepting his offer of marriage. He was solid, someone she could depend on, someone who laughed with her and not at her. When she was with him, she didn't feel the need to invent Maximillian Norwich or anyone else. Charles was somehow enough, and she felt "enough" with him without resorting to her usual flights of fancy.

"Are you cold, Louisa? It's getting dark."

She squeezed his arm. "I'm fine. I have you to keep me warm."

"Let me go back and get you a warmer wrap. Why didn't you wear your fur coat? The night's finally feeling like December."

"Sometimes I don't feel right wearing it. All those beautiful little snowy animals killed and sewn together just to cover my body."

"So you won't eat the roast lamb at supper tonight," he teased.

"That's not the same thing. One doesn't eat ermine—that would be like dining on rats."

"I hear rats taste like chicken."

"Charles!"

"Well, prisoners sometimes consider themselves lucky when they catch one. The Boer women—" A sudden shadow fell over him, deeper than the dusk in the garden.

They walked in awkward silence, the only sound the pebbles scattering under their boots and the gulls calling over the rushing sea. What could she say to ease him?

"You will never forget."

He didn't look at her. "How can I?"

"You can't. You shouldn't. What you can do is publish those journals of yours so that others will know and not let it happen again. I can help you with that. Find a publisher. Pay to have it printed if I need to."

He pulled away and sat on an iron bench. "I don't want to spoil what we have, Louisa. I'm afraid if I read over it and relive it all again, I'll kill the happiness I feel now. The first true happiness of my life, really. The guilt will always be with me, but when I'm with you, it's not so—not so sharp."

"Aren't you the one who said we can't let past mistakes determine who we are?" If those were not his exact words, it was at least the lesson she'd learned from being with him.

"That makes me sound much wiser than I am."

Louisa sat down next to him. "We can try to be wise together. My aunt Grace will never see me as anything but the wild child I was. And truthfully, I deserve her criticism. I went out of my way to break all her rules, and look where it got me."

"Hey, wait a minute. You're with me in the twilight,

with the waves breaking beyond the hedges. I'd say you didn't do too badly."

"Exactly. Every misstep led me to you."

"Oh, Louisa." He took her face in his hands. "I love you."

His kiss proved it—hot, dark, full of longing and hope. If she married him, she'd make him kiss her like this every twilight, every dawn, and the hours in between.

I love you. No one had told her that and meant it, except perhaps for her parents so long ago, and she couldn't remember that.

She lost herself in the moment, oblivious to everything but his steady touch and the sure sweep of his tongue. She felt much more than the desire to have him possess her body. Though that thought was not far off, the bench in view of the bank of windows made it impractical. Louisa wanted to pledge herself to this man, heart and soul, and realized he'd just given her the words to do it.

That would mean she'd have to stop kissing him, which she couldn't possibly do. She had time to tell him how she felt. All the time in the world. Right now, she would kiss him as if her very life depended on it.

The kiss had both hard edges and blurred lines, so she was never sure where it would go next. It was electrifying— no, comfortable. Sweet, then so sensual she found herself tugging at Charles's buttons. He covered her shaking hand and pressed it against his rigid cock. *She* did that to him— they did something magical to each other, for she was wet beneath her lacy bloomers. If only the hours would fly by until they were in their bed alone.

But there was family to endure, and Mrs. Evensong to entertain. With the greatest regret Louisa inched away from Charles and smoothed his eye patch in place. His visible eye was midnight blue, so deep and dark with lust she shivered.

"Louisa." He said her name with breathless reverence, and she felt warm. Kissed all over.

"I love you, Charles. I'll marry you."

Surprise, joy, and fear, too, flashed across his face. He kissed her again, this time so gently she thought she would weep. His thumb brushed her lashes, and Louisa realized she *was* crying, just a little. She had never in her life felt so happy, not even when she'd run away.

"You won't regret it, I swear."

"But you might," she said, laughing shakily. "I'm quite a handful."

"And you fit so perfectly in mine. When can we marry?"

"Oh my goodness. The family thinks we already *are* married. I guess we could sneak away somewhere. Obtain a special license. But damn it, it's Advent. No minister will agree to marry us."

"So," Charles said, grinning, "we'll have to continue to live in sin. Lots of it."

She gave his shoulder a friendly slap. "You are very wicked."

"So I've been told. What about a registry office? Or have you always had your heart set on a church wedding?"

"You know perfectly well I never planned to marry at all. My heart wasn't set on anything."

"Until you met me."

"You are growing increasingly smug, Charles. I might just change my mind."

He held her hand to his heart. "You wouldn't be so cruel."

No, she wouldn't. A life with Charles was bound to be interesting. Louisa didn't have the first idea how to be a proper wife, but she had a feeling Charles would not want her to be especially proper.

However, she couldn't see him navigating through the fussy gilt French furniture at Rosemont. They'd have to sell it all. Aunt Grace would howl—

"Why are you frowning? You're supposed to be delirious with happiness," Charles chided.

"I am happy. I was just thinking very housewifely thoughts."

"Well, stop. I prefer your smiles."

Louisa gave him one—it was effortless when she looked at his handsome face. He was ever so much more handsome than Maximillian Norwich, who would not have to die after all.

"Oh my goodness."

"Again?"

"What will we tell my family about your name when we really marry? You can't go through the rest of your life being called something you aren't."

Charles sat back on the bench, still clutching her hand. "My darling, just tell them this was a hoax—that they'd been so rotten to you that you had to make up Max to keep them at bay. You should be honest with them."

Louisa swallowed, imagining Grace's fury. "I think we should marry first. Then my aunt can't have me committed to some insane asylum. You'd put a stop to that."

"I might. If you made it worth my while."

"Charles!" She couldn't mistake the slow, burning look he gave her. It was plain what she could do—gladly—to keep him on her side.

"Let's worry about all this when we have to. You're getting goose bumps, Lulu. Let's go in the house and see if we have any more pests in our rooms. Besides Kathleen, I mean."

She didn't even mind his calling her Lulu anymore. What on earth was wrong with her? "I'll tell her you said that."

"Do. I'm anxious to see if she'll keep her promise to not hit me on the head again." He gave her a quick hug and pulled her up from the bench.

It was nearly dark now. Lights blazed from Rosemont's ground-floor windows, casting bright rectangles on the gray-green grass. Louisa could see the servants laying the dining room table, Griffith in the middle of everything making sure it was perfect. Sunday supper was usually lighter fare, but that didn't mean the silver stayed in its velvet trays.

A French door at the end of the west wing squeaked open. Odd. The gun room was in darkness, yet Louisa thought she saw a shadowy figure step out onto the lawn. She turned to Charles to ask if he saw it, too, but before she could frame her question, there was a report, a whizzing noise, and Lambkin's head exploded in front of them, sending shards of granite flying over the path.

Charles pitched backward, dragging her to the ground with him and rolling on top of her. Poor man—he'd done the same with his awful landlady when Louisa's car engine misfired.

"It's all right, Charles. I'm fine," she said in a soothing voice.

He was dead weight on top of her. Quiet. Too quiet. Louisa touched his temple, staining her gloves with something dark.

Blood.

Charles had been shot. Her screams were enough to get the servants running, but not enough to wake him up.

Chapter

❦

35

No, no, no. This couldn't be happening. Louisa had spent her whole life making up stories and changing them around to suit her. In them, her parents never died, her aunt was warm and loving, Hugh didn't pull her hair or put spiders in her bed.

So Charles was *not* lying in her bed still as death, a jagged gash through his left eyebrow. Dr. Fentress had *not* been summoned to stitch it. She was *not* pressing a clean cloth on Charles's forehead to stanch the bleeding.

Instead, she and Charles were still on the garden bench, entwined in each other's arms, professing their feelings with perfect words when they weren't sharing perfect kisses. Planning to marry. They would rise in a few minutes and take a different path to the house, one where there were no gunshots and shattered grotesques. They would have a convivial meal with her relatives, where there was no subtext of disapproval.

When Louisa was a little girl, she'd clasp her hands in front of her and screw up her eyes, almost seeing those alternate lives she'd constructed. A tear escaped and she brushed it away with impatience. Now was not the time to lose herself in fairyland.

Kathleen and Robertson stood behind her. It was Robertson who'd come running first, picking Charles up as if he weighed nothing and carrying him all the way upstairs to their suite. The maids had still been armed with cleaning solvents and rags, but they'd scurried away at Kathleen's orders.

"Why won't he wake up?"

"Now, Miss Louisa. He's got a right hard head, we all know that. Give him some time. I'm sure he'll be fine. Better than new when he comes to."

Louisa wasn't fooled by Kathleen's little speech. "What if he's not? What if he doesn't recognize me or even know who he is?"

"You've been reading too many books. Amnesia is much rarer than those authors would have you think. It's a lazy plot device, if you want my opinion."

Louisa didn't. She was much too heartsick to argue about low forms of literature. "What can be keeping Dr. Fentress?"

"The poor man only just got home a few hours ago. It's not easy being at Rosemont's beck and call twenty-four hours a day. Your aunt keeps him on a short leash."

"Maybe he should just move in." Aunt Grace had never been sick until recently, but the doctor had been underfoot for years. If they were courting, they just should get on with it at their age and make it legal. "Look! Did you see that? His eyelids fluttered! Charles! Can you speak? It's Louisa. Lulu."

Charles gave no indication that he heard her. At least his breathing was steady, although he looked like the marble effigies she'd seen in churches all across Europe.

"Maybe it's best he's unconscious, miss," Robertson said. "I've been stitched up a time or two and it's not much fun."

"And he's very lucky he wasn't actually shot," Kathleen added. "Just hit with a chunk of rock."

Yes, there was that. But someone had shot *at* him. Or her. Louisa cursed herself a thousand ways for coming back home.

"Robertson, I want you to stay up here with us. You can sleep in Charles's room. He needs a bodyguard. Kathleen, I want you to go to the village inn tomorrow and fetch all our food. I don't want to take any chances."

"What about tonight?"

"I'm too upset to eat anything, and if Charles wakes up, he's likely to be sick again. Nausea happens with head injuries. Oh, I can't believe this is happening." She wrung her hands, feeling just like a distressed heroine in some grisly gothic novel.

There was a knock on the door. "It's Griffith, Miss Louisa. Mrs. Evensong would like a word with you if it's not too inconvenient."

Louisa had hoped for Dr. Fentress. "I'll meet with her in the sitting room. Kathleen, stay with him and let me know if there's any change." She bent and gave Charles a lingering kiss, hoping he'd waken just like Sleeping Beauty or Snow White. Alas, her mouth was just an ordinary thing, not capable of rousing him in any visible way.

Mrs. Evensong had dressed for the dinner that was now delayed, if not canceled altogether. She wore a handsome black velvet dress spangled with jet and black lace gloves. Louisa was surprised to see how neat her figure was for an older woman.

"Let us sit down, my dear. You must be worried to death."

Louisa followed her to the sofa. "He asked me to marry him, and I said yes," she blurted. "I can't lose him."

"My, you have had a busy few days. I won't keep you from his bedside for long, but I wanted to let you know I am doing everything in my power to get to the bottom of the rot at Rosemont. We can't have any more accidents, can we? If I'm not successful in the next day or two, it might be best for you both to leave when Captain Cooper is sufficiently recovered."

Louisa nodded. "I agree. But Charles is so stubborn— he thinks it would be cowardly for me to go and leave Aunt Grace in charge. But if anything happens to him—" She could not finish the sentence. Charles had become so important to her in such a short time she simply didn't know how she could go on without him.

"I sincerely hope nothing else will. You watch yourself as well—that bullet might have been meant for you. Now, I'm off to have a sherry with your aunt in a little while. She doesn't quite know what to make of me, nor I of her, but I expect we'll sort it all out. But first, I think a visit belowstairs is in order. Do you know I've placed quite a few of your servants here? I'll just check on how they're doing, and perhaps someone will tell me something useful about all these attempts of mischief. Servants always know everything."

Mischief. An understatement if there ever was one. A bullet escalated everything. She might never forget the sight and feel of Charles lying inert and insensate on top of her.

But it might have been so much worse.

"I have an idea."

"What is it, my dear?"

"When Charles wakes up, he could pretend to be more badly injured than he is." Louisa prayed he'd wake up fully intact, his mind sharp and all his perfect body parts in perfect working order.

Mrs. Evensong's brows knit. They were rusty, nothing like the silver hair on her head. "Go on."

"If the person who shot at us knows they were nearly successful, they might let their relief show. Gloat. Show guilt by making some sort of suspicious comment to you. Even, God forbid, get careless and make another attempt to kill him. We'd protect Charles, of course. I can't let anything else happen to him."

"Your idea has quite a lot of merit. I'm disappointed that I did not think of it myself," Mrs. Evensong said. "Now all we have to do is hope he wakes up soon so he can conspire with us. Good night, Miss Stratton. Keep your young man safe."

Impulsively, Louisa gave the woman a hug. Without her monstrous black hats and umbrella, she was much less formidable. "Thank you, Mrs. Evensong."

"There, there." Mrs. Evensong fished out a handkerchief from the little jet-beaded bag at her wrist. "Keep it. I have another in there. One can never be too prepared, can one?"

"I *hate* to cry," Louisa said, after blowing her nose in a most unladylike manner.

"Don't view tears as a sign of weakness. They just show your strength. You care a great deal—that's a good thing. Many people just float through life not attaching themselves to anything." There was a wistful look on Mrs. Evensong's remarkably unwrinkled face. She gave Louisa a quick hug and left her on the gray sofa.

It was a comfort to know that the businesswoman would stay a few days. When Louisa had invited her to Rosemont, she really had not expected her to come. Mount Street had been a hive of activity the day she'd taken tea there—the Evensong Agency had a network that probably extended to the household of King Edward himself. Mrs. Evensong employed a great many people of her own at the employment agency. The offices were crammed to the corners with desks and typewriters and eager young people talking on cast brass telephones. Louisa wondered who was in charge with Mrs. Evensong away, but then, Mrs. Evensong was always prepared, wasn't she?

Louisa returned to the bedroom, where she was relieved to see Dr. Fentress there and closing Charles's wound. "There you are, Louisa. Don't you worry; I haven't lost my touch. There will be the faintest of scars. Looks like he's already had some work done in the area before. How was his eye injured? On safari, wasn't it?"

"Um. Yes, I think so. Well before we met. One of his companions had an itchy trigger finger and poor M-Max got in the way. Lucky for the lion," answered Louisa. Kathleen, who was holding the doctor's tray of surgical instruments, rolled her eyes.

"That's what he said at dinner. Odd. I thought Grace said it was a boxing match. Hugh is raring to test your husband's skills in the arena once his health is restored."

"Uh, there was a boxing match, too. I was confused. But he doesn't box anymore. I won't let him." She really should stop prevaricating. Charles was right. It was time to tell the truth. Keeping the lies straight was an all-day affair.

"Then you'd better speak to him again. Mr. Norwich decked your cousin the other night without much warning. I will say Hugh *was* being provoking—what can you expect from the boy when all his dreams are dashed?"

"What do you mean?"

"Surely you know he wanted to marry you. It was the fondest wish of his mother also."

"I can't see why," said Louisa. "All they ever do is criticize me."

"Only because they care about you, my dear."

Louisa didn't want to waste time arguing when Charles's life was in danger. "When will we know how he is?"

"That's hard to say. Kathleen told me what you told her—he took a sharp blow to the head and then fell backward, hitting his head again before he rolled you to safety. He should be monitored. I'll spend the night, but I expect you'll want to do the actual monitoring. My housekeeper will be delighted to be rid of me again."

Housekeeper. Damn. Mrs. Lang was probably put out with her for not telling her about Mrs. Evensong's visit, but she hadn't expected it herself. When Louisa had a free minute, she'd apologize to the old dragon. Not that she wanted to—she'd just as soon show the woman the door. While Rosemont was beautifully run, Louisa could not feel comfortable under the housekeeper's disapproving glare. She'd never measure up to her aunt.

Oh, she wished she'd never come home. But then she never would have needed a real fake husband, and never hired Charles. She'd never know what it was like to be kissed and so masterfully touched. Treasured. She wouldn't have laughed half so much or felt such compassion. Louisa had been racketing about and avoiding reality this past year, but now she had a reason to be still and listen to her heart.

It was rather a surprise to find out she had one. After Sir Richard, she'd locked it up as securely as Aunt Grace had imprisoned her at Rosemont.

"Thank you, Dr. Fentress. If—when—he wakes, I will call for you."

"It looks like you have plenty of support. Take turns during the night and get some rest of your own," the doctor said, patting her shoulder. "I'll leave my bag and instruments here in case they're needed, but no doctoring him yourself, my dear, except to change the dressing if necessary. He might thrash about and loosen it in his sleep."

Louisa nodded. Once the doctor left, the three of them stood somewhat helplessly around Charles's bed. "Kathleen, why don't you and Robertson go down to the servants' hall and get some supper? I'll take the first shift."

"If you're sure you'll be all right by yourself. Shall I bring up tea when I come back?"

"Only if you're positive it's not poisoned. Perhaps I'm being foolish. The mushrooms may have been an accident. But the fleas did not find their way into Charles's underclothes by themselves, and I hardly think a poacher was in the garden." She sat down on a chair close to the bed and touched Charles's cheek. "Oh, if I care anything about him at all, I should send him away."

"He won't go, miss."

Louisa looked at Robertson in surprise. "How do you know?"

"He came to talk to me this morning before church. I offered to hold still if he wanted to punch me to pay me back for the other night. He's a fine fellow, miss—said he knew you'd not had an easy time of it even if you did have pots of money, and Kathleen was right to be worried about you. We talked about this and that, man-to-man. It's my opinion he cares about you something fierce. I ken how the captain feels—I care about my Kathleen the same way."

"Hush, Robbie."

"I do. I'm not too proud to say it. We'd like to get married, Miss Louisa, once things here are settled. I know it's not the right time to bring it up, what with you fretting about the captain and all. But things will be all right—wait and see."

"I hope you're right." Louisa wondered if she looked quite so stupid as Kathleen did as she grinned up at her lover. Probably so. Love had a way of knocking sense and dignity right out of one.

"Oh!" Robertson slapped his forehead. "I meant to give this back to the captain. You may have need of it tonight." Sheepishly, the chauffeur reached into his jacket and pulled out Charles's missing gun. "Sorry," he said.

"I know, it's all Kathleen's fault," Louisa replied, shoving the revolver in a drawer. "Go on, you two. And don't hurry back. I probably won't sleep a wink tonight anyway."

The truth was, she wanted to be left alone with Charles. She clenched her fists together and squinted as she'd done so many times when she was a little girl, imagining him leaping from the bed and striding to the window to watch the whitecaps below. He'd invite her to walk on the beach in just her nightdress. Louisa hastily changed the time of year in her mind to high summer, where the breeze from the sea would be temperate and the sand still warm from the day's sun. They would walk awhile, the water rushing around their bare feet. Charles would give her a look—she could see his expression clearly under a full moon—and pull her night rail up over her head. His head would dip to tug her swollen nipple into his hot mouth. Her knees would buckle and he would hold her fast, working his fingers and tongue and teeth on her sensitive flesh until she didn't have a coherent thought in her head. His hand would find her needy center and prepare her for what was to come—what she craved—and the scattered stars would flash inside her eyelids before he thrust within her.

The image was so real, her pulse sped and her breath quickened. Wake up wake up wake up, she begged. Make this waking dream true someday. *Please, Charles*—

Suddenly, he shifted and thrashed on the bed as if he were under attack. "No, goddammit, no!" There was an unearthly howl, and then Charles—her strong, steady Charles—began to sob as if his heart were shattered.

"Charles! You're dreaming! Wake up, love." She tried to hug him, but in his nightmare he pushed her away.

It took a long moment for him to come to, sitting up in the bed, his face a mask of pain.

"My God." He was so quiet, Louisa feared he'd gone under again.

She grasped his hand, which was dead weight in hers. "What is it? What's wrong?"

A full minute passed. "I don't know. Nothing. Everything. Did I hurt you?" He slipped his hand free.

"No, of course not. You'd never hurt me," Louisa said, smoothing the sheet back down on his chest. Never intentionally, of that she was certain.

"Oh, wouldn't I? You really don't know what I'm capable of." He cocked his head, then shook it, wincing at the movement. "What happened to me?"

"Someone shot at us. Or at Lambkin, really. Pieces of the statue flew everywhere and one hit you."

He touched the bandage that partially covered his bad eye. "Move the lamp closer."

She did as he asked, although she knew bright light bothered him when he wasn't wearing his eye patch.

"I can get you an eye patch. Not the one you were

wearing—I'm afraid it was torn and covered in a little bit of blood." What an understatement, but she didn't want to alarm him. "You have a cut over your eye, but Dr. Fentress sewed it up quite neatly. You'll be as handsome as ever."

"I don't care what I look like, Louisa. For a second I thought I could see, but now it's back to the way it was. Maybe even worse. I—I don't think we should marry after all."

Chapter

36

he army doctors had told him he might get better someday, but he couldn't keep living on hope.

Someday was never coming.

He could live with the loss of his sight. But he couldn't live with his dreams.

When he'd opened his eyes from the nightmare, his vision had been sharp. Brilliant. And then—

Maybe it had been wishful thinking. An old memory from his previous life when the world was in vivid color instead of shades of gray.

But the dream before waking . . . Let's just say he might never allow himself to fall asleep again.

Louisa dead beneath him. At his hand.

Like Marja.

He might do anything at night and never know it. How could he expose someone he loved to what he was?

Broken.

Louisa was blessedly alive, blurry, hovering at his bedside. How he wanted to see her clearly just once.

It was unfair to her to be saddled with someone who

couldn't see, who couldn't provide for her properly, or really, provide for her at all.

And possibly even kill her, just as he'd killed Marja.

What had he been thinking?

The job offer from George might amount to nothing, even if his vision was good enough to take it. If he couldn't tally up profit and loss columns, what use would he be in New York? And not everyone was as enamored of cars and had as much money to indulge in them as Louisa Stratton. What if he couldn't sell any, the workers went on strike, and the company went bust?

More importantly, how could he ask Louisa to leave Rosemont?

It was her home. She'd gone through enough anguish to hold on to her rightful place here. Nothing should stop her now, especially marriage to a half-blind beggar with delusional pretensions to better himself. He was just a factory foreman's son.

Borrowing trouble, as his mother would say, but he couldn't overcome the feeling of helpless panic that washed over every inch of his skin. The dream had peeled back all the civilizing Norwichian layers he'd tried to paste on. There was something frightening underneath.

Charles had a roaring headache. There were dozens of black spots swirling about, and the gray shadow that always hung at the edge of his vision loomed even larger than ever.

"Don't be ridiculous!"

"It's you who's being ridiculous. You can't—shouldn't—make a life with me, Louisa. You deserve more."

"Oh, you tiresome man! Don't tell me what I deserve! I know what I want, and you're it."

"Maybe you were the one hit on the head," Charles grumbled.

She was slowly coming into focus. Her dress was splotched with blood, and her topknot had unwound in a precarious bundle at one side of her head. His pristine princess looked as if someone had dragged her through a hedge backward.

This is what came of spending time with him. Destruction.

And possible death.

"So, someone shot at us," Charles said, looking away. She was too beautiful even in her disarray. "Who? This seems a trifle more serious than fleas in the drawer and screws under the saddle."

Mischief had turned to attempted murder. When he left, would she be safe at Rosemont?

Who was he fooling? He hadn't been able to protect her to start with. He'd spent half his time here with Louisa taking care of *him*.

"It *is* serious, and Mrs. Evensong and I have a plan. I'll tell you all about it, but don't think I'll let you get away with crying off our engagement, Charles. We'll discuss it when you are more yourself." She was actually wagging a finger at him, or maybe two. It was hard to tell.

Charles felt his lips turn up against his will. "I assure you, I am myself. Mostly blind and finally awake to the impossibility of our union. It's—it's unequal, Louisa. Unsuitable. Implausible. I was an utter fool to propose."

"And was I an utter fool to accept, Mr. Walking Dictionary?"

Yes. Yes, she was, an utterly adorable, lovable fool.

Charles shut his eyes, but the spots continued to waltz on his eyelids. "I'm not going to start calling anyone names." Perhaps if he went to New York on his own and made something of himself—

No. He really wouldn't ever be worthy of her.

"Coward."

He opened his eyes. "I beg your pardon?"

"You are lying there feeling sorry for yourself again. I thought we had done with all that."

"Had we?" Charles couldn't hide his bitterness. It was as if the past few glorious days—well, more or less glorious despite all of the assaults—had never happened and he was wallowing in self-pity. At least this time his sheets were cleaner and he was stone-cold sober.

He could feel Louisa's disapproving stare, even if he couldn't quite see it.

"As I said, we shall discuss the marital issues later. Right now—"

"There are no marital issues to discuss. I withdraw my offer, and you should be doing cartwheels."

"You know I don't like to be told how to think or what to do, Charles. I've had enough of that to last two lifetimes. You are being very provoking at the moment."

"Even more reason to thank your lucky stars that we are done. Now that Mrs. Evensong is here, you'll get to the bottom of the bank business and my role here will be superfluous." Not long ago, they were looking at the stars in the winter sky from their bed. Charles had been the lucky one then.

Louisa gave a world-weary sigh. "I can see there's no point in reasoning with you. Very well. I hired you to be an imposter. You'll have another opportunity in the next day or two to expand your role and earn your fee. And then if you wish to go—" She shrugged and spread her hands wide. "I can't stop you now, can I? You're a grown man. Go back to London and live in—in—"

"The word you're searching for is *squalor*."

"Whatever you say. You know all the words today. I'm not going to waste my breath arguing with you. I can only hope someone else will shoot at you again and knock some sense back into you."

Damn. She thought this would all blow away—that he was simply in a black mood. What would it take for her to realize he was not the man she thought him to be?

"So tell me what game we are playing next, Miss Stratton—you and Mrs. Evensong and I. What do you want me to pretend now? And will I earn more money? Now that I'm not to be kept by an heiress, I'll need every penny."

Brutish. Blunt. That would show her. He went in for the kill when she sat silent at the bedside, still unmoved by his show. "When can I expect your old lover to show up? Sir Richard is the local magistrate, is he not?"

Charles spotted the worried tip of her tongue, the only sign his words were beginning to disturb her. "Oh! I don't think anyone's thought to call the authorities, such as they are. And yes, Sir Richard is magistrate. I certainly don't want *him* here to muck everything up." Clearly she was not ready to see Sir Richard Delacourt twice in one day. Or ever.

She should be furious with Charles. His behavior toward her was horrid, but he didn't dare to press his boorish act any further. With each hostile word, the pain deepened in his head.

And heart.

Eventually she would have to see the error of her ways.

"Someone shot at us, Louisa. Someone in this house. They need to be punished." He wasn't angry for himself, but something could have happened to her. Charles might not deserve her, but that didn't mean he was indifferent.

Didn't mean he didn't love her.

He wished he could take her hand back. On it was the plain gold band Mrs. Evensong had acquired for them. He had wanted to place it there himself one day, pledging his troth, whatever that was.

Louisa shook her head. "I don't think they really meant to shoot *us*. We were very far away from Lambkin at the time."

"It was dark. If we're dealing with an inexperienced shooter that might explain it, too." He paused, knowing his next words might be more wishful thinking—he was itching to get at Hugh Westlake and pummel him senseless. "And if one is a marksman, one can shoot to miss. I presume your cousin Hugh is handy with a gun."

"Y-yes. But I can't believe he would do such a dangerous thing! The fleas are much more his style. He was forever putting bugs in my bed when I was a little girl."

"All of these 'accidents' have been warnings, Louisa, even from Kathleen and Robertson. People want me—or us—to go away. Even your housekeeper asked if we were ready to go back to France."

"Well, we should go then. I can't bear to have anything else happen to you."

"You are wasting your concern. This is your home, but I'll leave as soon as I'm fit to travel, or whenever this ruse is finally at an end." Judging from the way he felt now, that would be never.

But he had to go. Louisa would be fine. She was an heiress. Spirited. Beautiful. She would find someone, a better someone. A man of her own class and background. A healthy, whole man who wouldn't hurt her.

Be a burden.

"What crackpot idea do you have now to unmask our villain?"

Out came that tongue again. "I think you should pretend to be blind."

Charles laughed harshly. And it hurt. "I don't think there will be much pretense involved. I told you, things are worse than they were."

"I am sure they will get better, though."

Of course she did—she was off in her fantasy world. "Have you been to medical school while I've been unconscious?"

Louisa ignored the jibe. "We will see who takes pleasure in, or advantage of, your disability. Mrs. Evensong will interview everyone, and I will help her. She is very canny, and has been responsible for the new hires. I've known the rest of the staff all my life."

And they were complicit in keeping her a prisoner in her own home. Charles fought back a comment—she shouldn't think he cared about her in any way.

The Sherlock Holmes idea was absurd. "So, you will talk to them and ferret out all their secrets. Am I to walk into walls and trip over furniture while you do it? You *will* have to pay me more."

"You needn't do actual harm to yourself. And Robertson will be your constant companion in case the shooter strikes again."

"Wonderful. We'll both get killed and then you'll have to deal with Kathleen. I don't envy you *that*."

*L*ouisa wouldn't leave him alone, even after he'd said a host of rude things. Stubborn little witch. She was curled up on the chaise, sound asleep.

It was past midnight. Charles was nowhere close to joining her. The blanket across his chest felt like a vise and his head ached.

He'd leave tomorrow after he performed his circus act. Louisa could say their "marriage" was at an end—who would want to be married to a blind man?

Kathleen and Robertson had already spread the rumor belowstairs that he couldn't see, and Louisa had given them the night together in Robertson's quarters. Old Mrs. Lang didn't need to know that Kathleen wasn't sleeping in their suite and try to lock her into the maids' wing.

Outmaneuvering the housekeeper had pleased Kathleen enormously. She said it was only fair since the woman had been on the warpath lately. "Sour as a crock of that nasty pickled cabbage stuff we had in Germany. I don't mind giving her the slip," she had said to Louisa with a mischievous grin.

Louisa thought Mrs. Lang must be upset by the danger and chaos at Rosemont. Kathleen had retorted the only thing the woman cared about was coddling Grace, and that the rest of them could all go hang.

Kathleen's words were still floating around in his head,

so when he heard the gentle knock on the door, he shot up in bed. "Come!"

Louisa slept on. How would she protect herself when he was gone?

Well, it wouldn't be his problem. He'd done a damn poor job taking care of her so far anyway.

Carrying a candle, Kathleen entered and quickly averted her eyes from his bare chest. "Begging your pardon, Captain," she whispered. "I need to wake Miss Louisa. Something's happened."

Louisa was still curled into a ball, half her face covered by the blankets.

"What? Is it something I can handle for her?" he whispered back.

"I don't think so. She'll need to know before she goes downstairs tomorrow morning."

"Tell me."

"It's her plants, sir. Someone's gone into the conservatory and wrecked it."

That beautiful room, teeming with lush life. Louisa loved her plants and had told him they were the only thing she missed while she was away. *The bastards.*

"Everything?"

"No, mostly her orchids. Her favorites. Like her babies, they are. Pulled out of the pots and thrown all over the floor and crushed. Griffith is practically in mourning. He took it upon himself to take care of them while we were gone, and a good job he did of it, too. Whoever did it didn't break the containers, so there was no noise to wake anybody up."

"Someone isn't satisfied with what they've already accomplished," Charles said grimly.

But how did Kathleen find out? She was supposed to be with Robertson ensconced over the garage.

Unless they had done it together.

"Mrs. Lang is waiting for her orders before the maids

clean it all up. She wonders if Miss Louisa will find something that's still salvageable," the maid said.

Kathleen didn't look guilty, just tired and a little love-flushed. "How is it that you're up?" Charles asked.

"I went down to the kitchen to make some sandwiches. I lied and said they were for you when Mrs. Lang found me. She was making the last of her rounds."

An explanation, but was it the truth?

Charles hated to expose Louisa to the destruction, but she wouldn't like it if they threw away plants that could be saved somehow. "Tell Mrs. Lang to wait. I'll wake Louisa and we'll be down shortly. Get all the indoor servants together, every one. Mrs. Evensong, too."

Kathleen's eyes widened. "*Now*, sir? It's after one o'clock in the morning! Most of them will have to be up to work by five. And Mrs. Evensong's a guest. I should hate to disturb her."

"Tell them they can sleep in an extra two hours."

"Mrs. Westlake won't like that one bit."

"I don't care. It's time we ended this nonsense once and for all. Strike while the iron is hot, so to speak."

Kathleen looked doubtful, but she nodded and left the room.

Damn Rosemont and all its inhabitants. He'd like to burn the place down. But that might be next on their tormenter's agenda.

Charles washed quickly and put on a pair of his fancy pajamas and a dressing gown. He stood over the chaise, forbidding himself to touch Louisa's bare shoulder.

"Louisa, wake up."

"Not quite yet," she mumbled. "It can't be morning."

"It isn't. I have some bad news, but not the worst it could be. Everyone at Rosemont is fine. Someone is *too* fine, actually."

She rolled onto her back, her lashes bent from the pillow. "What is it?"

"The conservatory has been vandalized. You're wanted

downstairs to see if there's anything left worth re-planting."

She sat up. "That's it. We're leaving today. I just can't fight this, whatever's going on. I—I *hate* Rosemont. I've never been happy here, except when I was a baby, and what do babies know?"

"I'm not leaving until I get a chance to test my acting skills, and *you* are not leaving at all. You wanted to interview the staff, and I've arranged it, right this very hour. Kathleen is rousing them all."

"I'm to talk to the servants *now*? It's the middle of the night!"

"Exactly. Whoever did this thing has not been asleep long. That is, if it wasn't Grace or Hugh. I can't see either of them getting their hands dirty, however, as much as I'd like to think they are behind your troubles. Get dressed."

"You are ordering me about again," Louisa said, a warning note in her voice that Charles paid no mind to. Any husband she'd have would risk being henpecked until he resembled a dart board.

"It's almost over, Louisa. Tonight you'll deal with the staff. Tomorrow Mrs. Evensong will give her report on the issues at the bank."

"I don't care anymore if I'm paupered!" Louisa cried as she tied her dressing gown.

"Don't be impractical. I want my payment. God knows, I've earned it." It was difficult to be a sneering, repulsive Charles, but he was doing his very best.

He tripped and bumped his way downstairs after refusing Louisa's guiding hand. It nearly killed him to stand aside as Louisa swallowed back her tears in the ruined conservatory. But he was playing his part and he couldn't see now, could he?

Chapter

37

*L*ouisa pulled herself together. It would not do to fall apart over *plants* in front of the Rosemont servants, for heaven's sake. They would think her mad, when people had real problems in this world.

There were so many of them, both shredded plants and sleepy servants. Grace had spared no expense making Rosemont comfortable in its largesse of personnel.

Louisa could replace the plants. She had plenty of money, even if some was being siphoned off her accounts. What she did not have at the moment was patience.

Charles—she must remember to call him Max in front of all these people—was being troublesome. She did not know what had gotten into him after this most recent injury, but she wanted it gotten out.

She hadn't decided to marry him on some whim. Louisa knew, or thought she knew, everything about him. He was not an easy man. Would never be. Things had happened to him that were too significant to be smoothed over with a few kisses. In that respect they had something in common, although she would never claim to be as fragile as he was.

Men didn't like to be fragile. Vulnerable. For some reason, they thought they had to march through life giving orders, smashing things and then putting the pieces back together inexpertly. Always be in control. Be strong, and too silent when they were not huffing and puffing.

Louisa had given up on men years ago, but she had made a reluctant exception for Charles and was not about to let him go.

So what if his vision didn't ever get back to normal? He didn't need to see her to touch her—so far, he'd done rather magnificently in the dark and the daylight. And he didn't need to seek employment—she had enough money to support him and his entire family.

But Charles, damn him, was probably not seeing things her way at the moment. Actually, he was committed to not seeing anything at all. His performance so far was alarming the clot of servants who were standing in the library, awed by the spectacle as if they were watching a Shakespearean tragedy. His hands flailed out before him, and Louisa was suspicious that he'd *chosen* to poke poor old Mrs. Lang.

Her keys had rattled as she leaped back away from him. *Of course.* All the servants were locked into their respective dormitories at night. Louisa had sometimes worried over that—what if there was a fire or an emergency? But Grace had been implacable. No one was to wander Rosemont after hours. There would be no male-female hanky-panky in *her* house.

Louisa believed Grace just liked the power of locking people up.

Louisa gave her little speech and introduced Mrs. Evensong to those who had not made her acquaintance. She apologized for dragging them all out of bed and explained Mrs. Evensong would want a few minutes with each of them.

"Griffith, I trust all the footmen and other male servants were secure in their wing?" Louisa asked. Mrs. Evensong lifted one of her reddish brows, then smiled. Louisa basked briefly in her approval.

"Of course, Miss Louisa. And I saw to all the outside doors myself and checked them again before I came here. No one has breached the locks."

Well, Kathleen had come in from the garage, but Louisa wouldn't want Griffith distressed. Kathleen was a clever girl and probably had a bunch of keys herself, which meant that other people might be equally resourceful.

She looked at the white, sleep-rumpled faces. No one looked particularly sly or secretive, and as far as she knew, none of them had a quarrel with her.

Destroying her plants was very personal. Spiteful. Grace could have put someone up to it, but somehow Louisa didn't believe that.

What had Charles said last night when he forgot to be mean? *If Hugh and Grace had hired an assassin, they were not getting their money's worth.* She nearly smiled.

Louisa turned to Mrs. Evensong. She was sitting on a tufted couch, her gray hair still up in its elaborate style as if she'd never been to bed. Goodness, *she* was not the guilty one, was she? Louisa almost smiled again.

"So you will vouch for all the men," Mrs. Evensong said to Griffith.

"Aye, Mrs. Evensong. With my life. I may be getting older, but I know my duty. I cannot tell you how sorry I am, Miss Louisa. I babied those plants the year you were gone."

The butler looked devastated, more upset than she herself was. "And will you do the same for the women?" Louisa asked, turning to Mrs. Lang.

"Of course. Except for your maid. I found her in the kitchen. She says you sent her down for sandwiches for your husband."

It was clear from the tone of her voice that Mrs. Lang had decided on the culprit. It was a good thing Robertson wasn't here to defend his love, but over the garage, probably wondering where his sandwiches were.

"As I did. You all can ascertain that Cap—uh, Mr. Norwich has been grievously injured again. He cannot see a thing after this latest attack. It was the least I could do to give the man a sandwich, something he could hold easily." Louisa clasped his hand. Even if he'd wanted to withdraw it, he was conscious of the role he was to play and let her touch him.

He frowned. "Who is this?"

"It is I, my darling. And you're not to worry. I'll take care of you. I know my duty, too. For better or for worse, for richer or for poorer, in sickness and in health until death do us part."

There were audible sighs throughout the room at Louisa's romantic gesture. She hoped Mrs. Evensong was studying the servants' expressions. Who was touched? Who looked disgusted?

Charles squeezed her hand so hard it hurt and bent down in a lover-like position. "You're overdoing it," Charles whispered into her ear, causing the hairs to lift off the back of her neck.

He was so close, and yet so far away.

"*You* should talk. Was it necessary to break that vase in the hall?"

"You wanted a show. I'm giving it. And the vase was damned ugly."

She stroked his cheek with her free hand and he stiffened. "Are you watching for signs of guilt or triumph? No one will suspect if you stare at them."

"I have my suspicions."

"Who?" asked Louisa eagerly.

"Not now." Charles's face shuttered. Before she touched him, Louisa thought he was quite enjoying himself.

She asked the servants to leave and wait in the hallway for their turn. There was nervous shuffling. Some of them looked stricken, others belligerent; some were simply too exhausted to care what their beleaguered employers were up to. Louisa would have a chance to examine the entire gamut of emotions as the night progressed.

Charles sat silent and glum by her side as, one by one, a parade of individuals came in as organized by Griffith. Few had access to the gun room, unless they, like Kathleen, had secreted away keys, but the conservatory was open to all. Mrs. Evensong's questions were few but pointed. To a man and woman, they all swore they had nothing to do with any of the incidents targeting the Norwiches.

With every oath of innocence, Louisa grew more frustrated. What had she expected? How lovely it would have been if someone had fallen on the Turkey carpet prostrate with remorse and confessed. She had been naïve to think her plan would work, and now she was just plain numb.

Mrs. Evensong had left them alone some time ago, moving smartly for a woman her age in the middle of the night. Louisa didn't stir from the sofa. It was a comfort to have Charles against her. He had fallen asleep four fruitless interviews ago.

In his blissful ignorance, he had sagged against her and his head was resting on her shoulder. Louisa knew soldiers were trained to fall asleep anywhere when they could snatch a few moments, so she didn't flatter herself that he meant anything by it. It was not a secret message to her that he really cared. He was still as determined to leave, just as she was determined to forbid it.

Well, one couldn't *forbid* Charles to do anything. But how to persuade him that they had a future together?

The man couldn't be bribed, and she wouldn't want him if he could be. She was not above using sex to seduce him, but that seemed underhanded, and a little desperate. It was not as if she knew what she was doing anyway.

Louisa was forced to conclude that she had to tell him the truth—that she'd fallen in love with him and simply couldn't do without him. She'd told him before, but he needed to hear it again. They could face their demons together.

He wasn't the only one with bad dreams.

The clock chimed three. "Charles," she said, her voice soft. She wasn't worried anyone would hear his true name—the staff had all slouched off to bed some time ago with reassurances they could begin their day late. Louisa would deal with Aunt Grace.

Before heading to bed herself, Mrs. Evensong and Louisa had compared notes in hushed tones while Charles breathed heavily in his sudden slumber. She and Louisa agreed on a person who stood out from the others.

Motive. Opportunity. Words that before these incidents had belonged solely to the crime pages or penny dreadfuls. Louisa was cautiously optimistic. But if none of the servants were guilty, that left one of the family or Miss Spruce.

Insupportable.

"Charles, wake up." She couldn't leave him on the sofa all night.

She wanted him in her bed. She had begun her night sleeping on the chaise but was unwilling to return there.

His eyelids fluttered, and then he sprang away from her as if he'd touched a hot stove.

"I beg your pardon, Miss Stratton. My falling asleep was unforgivable."

Miss Stratton? Oh, Charles. As if that will keep me away.

"You've had a rather difficult day. What did you think?"

He stood, looking deliciously rumpled. "About what?"

"The interviews, silly. Mrs. Evensong and I are nearly certain that the culprit is—"

"Kathleen, of course."

Louisa leaped up. "Kathleen! Don't be absurd! Of course it isn't Kathleen!"

"We can't argue here," Charles said, the annoying voice of reason. "Anyone could hear us."

"And I certainly plan to argue! Where could you have gotten such a ridiculous idea?"

Charles put a finger to his stubbled chin. "Hm. Let's

see. A hit on the head. Burrs. Mushrooms. Fleas. I admit using a firearm is a novelty for her, but maybe she had Robertson do it for her. She leads him around by the nose as you used to do me. She was the only one about when Mrs. Lang locked everything up. It's obvious."

He sprinted up the staircase, this time not lurching into walls. Louisa had difficulty keeping up with him.

"It is not obvious!" she hissed. "Honestly, that blow to your head has affected you in more ways than one."

"Why? Because I can see clearly? In a manner of speaking, that is."

"If you had *three* eyes you couldn't be more wrong! Kathleen and Robertson apologized!" Out of breath and angry, Louisa slammed and locked their bedroom door.

"Words are cheap," Charles said, pushing a dresser against it.

"Well, you'd know all about that! Offering marriage and then reneging. T-telling me you l-love me!" Louisa flung off her robe and kicked one slipper into the corner.

"You're better off without me," Charles growled.

"Says who?"

"I do, you ninny! I don't know how I ever thought we could get along long enough to make it through the wedding vows."

"We get along fine!" Louisa shouted. "Better than fine! What has come over you?"

He stalked across the room and grabbed her by the elbows. "Good judgment at last, my dear. I can't marry you. I can't protect you, but then that won't be necessary. You and Mrs. Evensong will solve this little mystery; you'll run Rosemont and find some poor sap who will knuckle under your thumb and listen to your constant babbling."

Louisa looked up into his lovely, weary face. "Stop it, Charles. Just stop it. Nothing you can say will make me love you any less. Please tell me what this is about."

Chapter

✦

38

He sat down on the bed. Would this night ever end?

"What is there to say? I've already told you."

Louisa sat down beside him. "No, you haven't."

If he spoke his nightmare vision aloud, surely that would cure her of her girlish hopes. But his tongue thickened. Words might be cheap, but they had power. He didn't want to unleash his hell-born images. She would look at him with pity.

Fear.

He shook his aching head. "I can't."

"Charles, I spent years having no one to talk to. Then Kathleen came, and things got a little easier. It helps to have someone to share your worries with."

"Ah, now you're an alienist."

"Don't mock me. I love you, and nothing you can ever say will drive me away. Unless you don't love me back."

How simple it would be to tell her that. But it would be the vilest lie.

He took her hand. "You know of my dreams."

She nodded.

"Sometimes they seem more real than reality, if that makes any sense. I never know when they'll occur. They are—they are horrible. I'm afraid I'll harm you, Louisa."

She blinked. "That's all?"

"Isn't that enough? But no, that's not all. We come from two different worlds. You'd lower yourself by marrying me." He wasn't fit to fetch that slipper from the corner.

"Oh, for heaven's sake. You're such a snob, Charles."

He was stung. "I am not!"

"Don't talk to me of class barriers. This is not India, and you aren't an untouchable. The twentieth century is ahead of us. Things are going to change."

She spoke with such certainty. Which one of them was more delusional?

"Louisa, don't you see? It doesn't matter if I love you. We cannot be together."

Her fingernails dug into his skin. "Love is the only thing that matters, Charles. The rest is . . . dust. Inconsequential. I know you suffer—you've seen things I don't even want to imagine. And you don't have to talk about them unless you want to. We can sit silently beside each other for the rest of our lives, as long as we *are* beside each other."

"What if I murder you in my sleep? You might regret that 'beside' part."

She had the audacity to laugh. "I suppose we can have separate bedrooms if you insist. As long as you visit me occasionally."

"Louisa, this isn't funny. I can be—I *am*—violent."

"I know."

She was absolutely exasperating. "If I told you I was Satan himself—"

"I'd have to sin some more to ensure we could spend eternity together. Charles, I *love* you. What happened in the past only served to bring us together. I am not the same careless girl and you are not the hopeless fellow you once were, but if we hadn't been those people, would we love each other?"

"I didn't say I still loved you," Charles said, stubborn.

"I know. But I *know*."

There she was again. "I cannot get rid of you, can I? Not even for your own good."

"I'll be the judge of what's good for me, and you, Charles Cooper, are good."

"Oh, Louisa." The tiniest flame kindled in his heart. Was it possible to be happy?

He didn't know anymore. This afternoon when he learned about George's offer, he had been optimistic that he and Louisa could start a new life in that shiny twentieth century she was so sure of. He knew nothing about New York or cars or business, but he could learn.

But could she leave Rosemont and its towers and gargoyles and roses?

"If you could go anywhere, start anew, where would you go?" he asked her.

"Well, I thought before all this—before *you*—that I'd like to go to New York next."

This was welcome news. "Really?" he said, trying to keep his burgeoning excitement at bay.

"My mother was from New York, you know."

"Yes, you've spoken of that."

"But I don't want to keep living out of a steamer trunk for the rest of my life, wandering about the world, so you won't have to worry I'll drag you to strange places when we marry."

"When we marry," Charles repeated. She seemed so sure. Was it really so easy?

"I'd like to settle down. Make my own home to my own specifications. And Kathleen is really not that fond of travel. Now that she's to marry Robertson, I don't expect she'll want to go anywhere. You know you are completely wrong about her, by the way."

Maybe he was. His head was spinning. "Perhaps you're right."

"What's this about, where I want to live? Can it be I've convinced you to change your mind and marry me?" she asked, grinning.

He squeezed her hand, feeling his resistance to her ebb like the tide outside. "You are very convincing, Louisa. But I'll explain later. When we get to the bottom of everything. And then, if you want to leave Rosemont, I think I know just the place."

Charles wouldn't tell her yet. He hadn't quite made up his mind. One couldn't head up an automobile division without firsthand knowledge of the machines.

He could ask Louisa to teach him to drive. Talk about the blind leading the blind.

Charles would have his old life back. No, his old life really wasn't worth much. A new life. He was done drinking to blind himself to his blindness and deaden his memories of the dead. He'd be with the woman he loved, have a second chance to make things right.

He would talk to George about the journals. His old friend might not be keen to have one of his employees expose the unheroic underbelly of British army life. But war would come again, and if Charles's words could change one small thing for the better, it would be worth the notoriety.

"What do you mean?"

"It's my secret for now. And no matter how many kisses you give me to worm it out of me, I'll never tell."

"You want to kiss me." Louisa looked a little surprised.

"I thought you knew everything," Charles teased.

"Are we finished talking?" she asked doubtfully.

"Oh, I think so."

"And we'll marry?"

"Perhaps."

She elbowed him. "Will you or will you not marry me?"

It was time to throw caution to the wind. They could have separate beds. If necessary, he could get Robertson to tie him up and gag him every night.

After he'd shown Louisa how much he loved her, of course.

"I'm not sure. I think I need a kiss to decide me. Or two. One may not be enough."

"You don't know the power of my kisses." There was a martial gleam in her dark eyes.

"Oh, I think I do," Charles said softly. "But perhaps you should remind me."

Louisa gave him an arch look. "Captain Cooper, I believe you're trying to trick me."

"Are you trickable?"

"When it comes to you, yes."

"Excellent." He shimmied up the pillows, feeling only a little light-headed. Her lips brushed too shyly against his, as if she thought he might break. Someday he would be fully in possession of all his strength, but considering everything he'd gone through in the past few days, he wasn't doing too badly.

For one thing, he had the sense to let Louisa control the kiss, to see where she'd go with her newfound power over him. Not quite far enough, but he wouldn't complain, couldn't anyway with Louisa's tongue wrapped pertly around his. Her hands were on his shoulders and Charles wished she'd become a bit more creative with them.

His pajama top had been removed and he felt the warmth of her palms and the slight quiver of her fingertips. *Go exploring,* he said silently. *I won't mind. I need this. I need you.*

He quivered himself when she somehow knew to circle his nipples, her fingers matching the swirl of her tongue in his mouth. It was like a dance only she knew the steps to, and Charles relaxed into her lead. Dancing was something that had never been taught to him in his father's factory cottage, but an officer had to learn to be good company. Nothing had ever prepared him for Louisa Stratton, however.

He sat as still as he could as her hands moved lower, tangling with the pajama pants he still seemed to be wearing. She paused over the buttons, twisted one, then stopped kissing him.

"Will you tell me now?" she asked, breathless.

"Tell you what?" Charles had almost forgotten there was a point to this seduction.

"You are a very vexing man."

"Maybe you haven't been convincing enough for me to spill my secrets. Remember, I've been trained not to break under torture."

Although he'd tortured himself long enough.

"I have not yet *begun* to torture you, Charles Cooper."

"You sound positively savage. I am terrified, Miss Stratton." And delighted to see what she'd do next.

What came after the kisses wiped any worry from Charles's mind, at least temporarily. She found all the buttons and took him in her mouth and with utter selflessness brought him to the most exquisite agony. A man couldn't think of practical matters under the circumstances. He wouldn't waste a minute in doubt under Louisa's spell.

This woman loved him and was proving just how much. If he'd ever felt unworthy of her before, he was aware now he was as base as base could be and wouldn't have it any other way. Charles belonged to Louisa as he never had to another—she could do precisely what she wished because it seemed their goals were mutual.

Lucky stars. Lucky man. Things might even be *too* good. Charles was superstitious, as were many soldiers. When the stars aligned so perfectly, they were bound to shower down on one's head and knock one unconscious.

He'd already spent some time tonight in that state. It was getting to be habitual at Rosemont. He wanted to be aware of every lush lick, to encapsulate this precious moment in time so *this* Louisa would be present in his dreams as well as beside him in life.

Louisa was to become his wife—again—once they could figure out how to accomplish the thing. Charles wondered if they could get someone to marry them aboard the ship that would bring them to New York—not the captain, for he had no authority to marry anyone despite the popular misconception. Maybe there'd be a parson on his way to minister to the wild frontier.

Oh, those damn practical matters when Louisa's warm mouth was all that mattered. He and Louisa were unlikely partners, but for the first time in years, Charles felt whole. Human. And he had his heiress to thank for the rest of his life.

Chapter

❦

39

"I fixed everything myself, Miss Louisa, so you don't have to worry. It's just toast and tea. Took the bread and butter right from the servants' table since nobody croaked at breakfast. Cook wanted to do up something proper for you, but I wouldn't let her. I think you'll have to mend some fences there—I left her in tears, talking about quitting and going where they didn't think she was a murderess. Even Mrs. Lang stuck her long nose in—says she has a jar of jelly that's ideal for invalids. I told them both we'd be taking care of ourselves from now on until Mrs. Evensong's meeting."

Their "invitation" to it had been on the breakfast tray. Eleven o'clock in the drawing room.

"What's the old bird up to this morning?" Charles asked, crunching into a slice of dry toast. He and Louisa had not slept much, and his stomach was unsettled.

But there had been no dreams, and that was the important thing.

"Like a regular Scotland Yard inspector she is. She has a way about her—she was down in the servants' hall at dawn even if she was up most of the night chatting up the staff in the most natural way. Even old Griffith poured his heart out. He's very loyal to you, Miss Louisa, and upset that someone is causing all this trouble on his watch. Do you want me to stay to help you dress?"

"I'll do the honors, Kathleen," Charles said, dismissing the maid. "Let's go down in a blaze of glory, Lulu. Wear all your diamonds in the daytime. I'll make sure old Max looks sharp, too."

"You're right, of course. It's so annoying when you're right."

"I've only been right since I met you. You've been the making of me."

Louisa gave him a wobbly smile. "You're sweet to say so."

"I'm just telling the truth." She looked so tired. Nervous. The stress of the past few days was taking its toll, and she'd disappeared early this morning without telling him where she was going. Charles couldn't wait to get her out of here.

If she wanted to go.

He poured her a cup of tea. "Will I still be blind? I have a hankering to knock a few more of Grace's atrocities over."

"Behave yourself."

"Impossible. You inspire me to misbehave."

There. He'd earned a smile from her.

"I think your performance last night produced the necessary results. Just be normal."

Ha. He'd seen himself in the mirror this morning and wondered how Louisa could look at him without shrieking. He'd put the sticking plaster back on to cover the wound and his eye patch was fastened securely, but he looked nowhere close to normal. Lambkin had not been gentle.

The drawing room was not crowded once they arrived. The staff was represented by Griffith and Mrs. Lang standing at attention. Grace sat in her usual gilt chair, with

Dr. Fentress beside her. Hugh was present, as was Mr. Baxter.

"Excellent. You're all here," Mrs. Evensong said.

"I fail to see what authority you have to call a meeting here in my home. My niece's home," Grace amended. "You are just a guest."

"I invited Mrs. Evensong to come, Aunt Grace. I'm sure whatever she has to say is important."

"Humph. Well, get on with it."

"Calm yourself, Grace, dear," Dr. Fentress said. "You know your constitution is not strong."

Charles kept his own *humph* from escaping. Grace Westlake was a bejeweled battle-axe who would outlast them all.

"Miss Stratton—that is, Mrs. Norwich—has employed me to look into some discrepancies at her financial institution," Mrs. Evensong began.

"Our bank?" Grace said, her outrage visible. "Stratton and Son has an impeccable history of service."

"We'll get to that later," Mrs. Evensong said. "At present, I wish to discuss the odd occurrences that have plagued Mr. and Mrs. Norwich since they arrived at Rosemont last week. Mr. Norwich, if you would be good enough to observe something?"

Charles nodded.

"I thought he was blind," Mrs. Lang said with some confusion.

"I'm slightly improved today, no thanks to my attacker." His vision *had* increased a little, enough to make him think he'd be back to his old self eventually. His "old self" was not perfect, but he was used to his limitations by now. "They say one's other senses become more acute when one cannot see, Mrs. Lang. I'll be happy to help."

Mrs. Evensong reached for Mrs. Lang's hand, and Louisa gave him a little push forward. The housekeeper's hand trembled under the inspection. It was immaculate, save for a fleck of dirt under a split thumbnail.

"Potting soil, I believe."

"Yes. I helped the maids clean the conservatory."

"That seems only fair, as you caused the mess. And there is still the faintest scent of gunpowder, even after all the scrubbing I imagine you did. Do you agree, Mr. Norwich? You've had experience with firearms."

Charles inhaled, but his nose was not as keen as Mrs. Evensong's. He pretended to agree. "Gunpowder. Definitely."

Mrs. Lang stiffened. "How absurd."

"Is it? I wonder," Mrs. Evensong said thoughtfully. "When you returned from your mother's funeral, you heard all about how Mrs. Norwich's new husband had threatened to toss out the Westlakes. You didn't like that—you've been here since Grace Westlake was a little girl here. You're fond of her, and young Hugh, too. You also heard that Mr. Norwich had been attacked twice—it was all the talk of the servants' hall.

"There was already mischief afoot," Louisa piped up. "So when you welcomed us home the next morning, you slipped some bad mushrooms onto the breakfast tray when you brought it up. You know I don't eat mushrooms. I imagine it was more out of spite than any true desire to cause serious harm. Just to warn my husband off. Make his stay at Rosemont uncomfortable so he'd persuade me to return to the Continent and you could keep the status quo."

Charles watched as the color leached from Mrs. Lang's face. "You also tampered with the smallclothes in his drawer, not knowing that the gentleman"—and here Mrs. Evensong blushed rather prettily for an old lady—"declined to wear them on most occasions. All those little creepy-crawly things died, actually because you've trained your staff so well to line and powder the drawers against insects. So when Mr. Norwich didn't break out in welts or twitch himself around like he had Saint Vitus Dance, you upped the ante considerably.

"Grace Westlake and Mr. Griffith are the only ones

besides yourself that have the keys to the gun room. Mrs. Westlake was upstairs dressing at the time of the shooting, with both her maid and secretary present as witnesses. Mr. Griffith was supervising the setting of the table."

"Anyone could pick a lock," Hugh interrupted. "Even me, although I swear I didn't do anything."

"No. I know where *you* were, Mr. Westlake. Mr. Baxter can vouch for you. I've accounted for all of the residents and staff at the hour in question. But no one can place Mrs. Lang anywhere in the house. May I finish?" She gave Hugh a quelling look.

"Mrs. Lang, you went into that room, took a revolver, and shot at Mr. Norwich when he was walking in the garden with his wife. I believe you aimed to miss, but you were unlucky there. Or should I say Mr. Norwich was, poor man. When the gargoyle shattered, a fragment hit Mr. Norwich in the temple."

Mrs. Lang's lips were white but unmoving. It did not look like she was about to confess anytime soon.

"And then you made a serious mistake," Louisa said, stepping forward. "You took the gun back to your quarters." She pulled a revolver from her dress pocket and the housekeeper flinched.

A gun. In Louisa's pocket. Somehow Charles was not surprised. And it looked damned familiar—he'd had the selfsame gun for a decade. What in hell?

"I didn't! I put it right back—" Mrs. Lang realized what she had said, and collapsed into a chair that Charles was quick enough to get under her.

"My goodness," he said to no one in particular. "I guess I can see again."

"The destruction in the conservatory in the night was simple malice, born out of your frustration. Since your attempts at removing Mr. Norwich had gone awry—in fact had injured him so severely he was unfit to travel—you ruined the one thing you knew meant something to Mrs. Norwich. Petty, Mrs. Lang, very petty." Mrs. Evensong adjusted her smoky spectacles and turned to Hugh Westlake.

"As for the difficulty with Mrs. Norwich's bank account, Mr. Baxter and I went over the books with a fine-toothed comb on Saturday. When confronted on Sunday, Hugh Westlake admitted he manipulated the balance in order to bring Mrs. Norwich home for Christmas. She hadn't answered any letters, and then she married a stranger so abruptly. Grace Westlake was beside herself with anxiety, so much so she stopped eating and took to her bed. Hugh claims he fudged the figures to bring peace of mind to his mother, and I guess we should take him at his word." Mrs. Evensong did not sound entirely convinced.

"So, there you have it. A loyal servant run amok. A loyal son who took advantage of his position at the family bank to please his mother."

"You are a wonder, Mrs. Evensong," Charles said. She had ferreted all this out after less than twenty-four hours at Rosemont, and Louisa had helped. His "wife" was now training the revolver on Hugh and Charles hoped it wasn't loaded.

"Am I f-fired?" Mrs. Lang stammered.

"Yes," Louisa said.

"No," countered Charles. "It doesn't really matter what happens here. My wife and I are going to America."

Louisa blinked. "We are?"

"We are," Charles said firmly. He took the gun from her and handed it to Mrs. Evensong, who dropped it into her capacious black reticule without a qualm. Charles would get it back later. He'd made up his mind as he shaved this morning, remembering Louisa's words. She would never be happy at Rosemont—it simply held too many unpleasant memories. Perhaps once they had a family, they'd visit and make new memories. But now, Louisa deserved a place of her own.

"A friend of mine has purchased an automobile company and he wants me to oversee his New York operation.

I expect that there's an opportunity there for you, my darling. We can have adjoining desks. You know much more about cars and society people than I do and will be invaluable. I can see the advertisements in the glossy magazines now, a photograph of you bundled in your white fur coat—no, a good *cloth* coat—behind the wheel. You'll be an inspiration to Gibson Girls everywhere." He grinned at Mrs. Evensong.

"You are offering my niece a *job*?" Charles heard Grace's horror, but Louisa looked thrilled.

"I can test-drive the new models?"

"Once Robertson deems them safe enough. We can bring him and Kathleen with us if they want to come. He's an excellent mechanic, you know. A bit of an inventor himself."

"You're being awfully high-handed, Charles. I mean Max," Louisa said quickly. No one seemed to notice her mistake. "What if I don't want to go? You said you wouldn't order me about in this marriage."

"You can stay here if you want to, Louisa. But I'm counting on you coming with me to begin a new life. Our *own* life. Something we make together, without interference from family or society's rules. Somewhere where we'll be on a more equal footing—you know America is more democratic."

Louisa looked at Grace, her tongue disappearing from its thinking corner. "You really wanted me to come home?"

Grace's fair skin mottled. "I was worried about you, you foolish girl. I always have been. You haven't a brain in your head—look who you've married! A foreign adventurer who wants to drag you off to America and work in some *office* and put you in the newspapers!" She shuddered.

"*I* work in an office, Mama," Hugh interjected.

"But in the family bank! And only part-time. That's perfectly respectable. It was good enough for my father, after all."

"You care about me," Louisa said, her voice tentative.

"Of course I do! I've spent my whole life trying to mold you, for all the good it's done us both. I hoped to raise you as a proper wife for Hugh. He's loved you since he was a little boy—why, I haven't a clue. You are a sad disappointment, but then you always have been."

Charles kept his clenched fist to his side. It wouldn't do to hit a woman. Grace Westlake thought she'd done her best. Perhaps she had, within the limits of her abilities. He glanced at Hugh, whose cheeks matched his mother's. The man said nothing to deny his affection for Louisa.

Could it be true, that both the Westlakes cared for her in their own peculiar, awful way? Families were odd—he knew that from personal experience. His brothers had beaten the stuffing out of him, yet when he was at his lowest, he wanted to leave them an inheritance that would smooth their futures.

"I think I have to sit down," Louisa said.

"Right here, dear." Mary Evensong moved to the sofa and patted the cushion.

Louisa tumbled down next to her, a blank look on her pale face. It was a lot to take in—to discover she was loved, no matter how inexpertly, by people she thought hated her, to be offered a future in a strange country by a man she barely knew. No, that wasn't true—she and Charles had been forged together in fire this past week. She had seen his delirium and blood and vomit and stupidity and hadn't flinched, or not flinched much, anyway. They could make this work, given half a chance.

"Just think about it, Louisa. I don't have to leave until January. We can still spend Christmas at Rosemont."

Grace examined her diamond rings, her face still flushed. "I'd like that," she said, her voice brittle. "But I'd understand if you wanted to leave at once. Mrs. Lang, I'm going to have to dismiss you." She raised a glittering hand to stop the housekeeper from speaking. "I know what you did, you did for me. But the consequences could have been dire for my niece's happiness. She seems to love this man, though I cannot see why—there is something very odd about him to be sure, and it's not because he doesn't wear his smalls. You said your mother left you her cottage. You can go back there. I'll give you a generous pension—you've served the family for decades and deserve a good, long rest."

"Y-yes, madam. I'm sorry if my judgment was at fault," Mrs. Lang said. "I never meant to really hurt anybody, just scare them some and make them go back where they came from."

"I come from *here*," Louisa reminded the woman.

"We all of us have lapses from time to time," Grace replied. "Pack up your things. Mr. Baxter will see to the bank draft for you." She motioned the man to her side and whispered a figure in his ear that raised his gray eyebrows. "I don't know that I'm happy with you, either, Percy. You should have kept a closer watch at the bank. Stratton and Son's reputation is not to be trifled with. Hugh could be ruined—and the bank—if it's discovered what he tried to do."

"I'm sorry, Mama."

"Oh, be quiet, Hugh. You are a disappointment to me, too. But now that Louisa is finally out of the way, it's time for you to find a proper girl to marry. Someone who knows how to behave."

"Yes, Mama." Charles wondered how long Hugh would play the obedient son before the façade cracked.

But it didn't really matter. Louisa was safe, and Charles was almost sure she'd be on that steamship to New York with him.

Epilogue

> *Dear Aunt Grace,*

> *It is with the heaviest of hearts that I write to tell you my beloved husband Maximillian is dead and I have married Charles Cooper—*

Damn, that would never do, unless Dr. Fentress was sitting right next to her when she opened the letter to revive her. Louisa adjusted the delicate hair clip Charles had given her as a wedding gift. It was a tiny jeweled orchid made of backless enamel. Louisa could stare at it for hours, so it was just as well when it was on her head she couldn't see it and be distracted by it. If it had been a brooch or a bracelet, she'd never get a thing done.

And there was so much to do. In half an hour, she had to meet the architect downstairs to approve the renovations to the showroom. A small shipment of Pegasus cars was due in two weeks, and she planned a champagne reception to celebrate. She still had some furniture to buy for their brownstone, and Charles's side of their office needed a good painting. Now that he'd read that art book, he seemed to have decided opinions as they wandered through galleries on Saturday afternoons and was very hard to please.

The weekends were the extent of their honeymoon, but as Charles said, they'd had their holiday the month at Rosemont. Once they'd arrived in the States, they'd been so busy getting married and scouting for living quarters and an office space, they had no time for anything else.

Charles didn't even have much time for his nightmares. When they came, they were fewer and farther between, and Louisa held him fiercely until they passed.

The wedding ceremony had been at city hall, where no one had ever heard of the scandalous Louisa Stratton or the dashing Maximillian Norwich except their witnesses, Mr. and Mrs. Robert Robertson. Charles's family had been an ocean away, although Louisa had met them before they sailed. Hardworking people, who were surprised when Louisa's attorney set up trusts for all their children. Charles's brothers would never take a handout themselves, but it was damn difficult to deny your children opportunity, especially when charmed by Louisa Stratton.

So the wedding was quiet. But everyone would be hearing about Charles Cooper and his plans for the Pegasus Motor Company soon. Right this very minute Charles was inspecting a potato field on Long Island that would be the ideal site for an automobile plant. He had invited her to go out on the train with him, but she really, really had to write to Grace. She'd put it off long enough—the few lines she'd scribbled since she'd gotten settled did not begin to tell the story. Louisa pulled out a fresh sheet of paper from her office desk drawer.

Dear Aunt Grace,

This will come as a surprise, so I hope you are sitting down and have smelling salts nearby. Perhaps Dr. Fentress is somewhere about. If he isn't, he should be. Please give him my love. There is no reason why you should not accept the man's constant devotion and make him the happiest of men. Life is uncertain, and one should open one's heart to possibilities. Neither one of you is getting younger, if you will pardon my frankness. You know my runaway tongue, but I do mean well, just as I believe you do.

You were right about me—I am an impossible hoyden. Headstrong. Impulsive. But for once I did a silly thing, and it turned out to be very smart.

Last December, I hired a decorated war hero, Captain Charles Cooper, to pose as my imaginary husband Maximillian Norwich through the Evensong Agency. Yes. Imaginary. I invented him to make you think I was perfectly well taken care of. You said Max sounded too good to be true, but Charles is even better. We are now married in actuality and could not be happier. I hope you will forgive us for tricking you, but I'd say we were punished enough when we first arrived at Rosemont.

I know you are incensed that I am working alongside my husband, but I've discovered ways I can be useful to him—it is the oddest thing, but Americans love to hear English people speak. For some reason, they think we are far more intelligent than we are. I can rattle on for ages, and they hang on my every word!

Of course Charles truly is brilliant in his way. He went to Harrow. He is a positive whiz with figures, and a whiz at other things that would make a proper lady blush—but then I'm not a proper lady.

You don't care much for modern music, but I'm sure you've heard "A Bird in a Gilded Cage." That's where so many of us women wind up, isn't it? Protected "for our own good." Covered up at the end of the day. Charles doesn't want to put me in a cage, and views me as something more than an ornament on his arm. He still gives me all the protection I could ask for, but freedom and respect, too, although he is not quite so enamored of my voice as the Americans. Wish us well, if you are able. We can visit Rosemont at Christmas if you will have us.

> *With love to everyone,*
> *Your affectionate niece,*
> *Louisa Stratton Cooper*

There. That wasn't too awful. And she wouldn't be around to hear Grace scream. But it probably would be sensible if she didn't open Grace's letters for a little while until the dust died down.

Louisa blotted the letter and tucked it into an envelope. She closed her eyes and clenched her fists, trying to imagine what the next few months would bring, but her famous imagination failed her. Pretending just wasn't as much fun as it used to be.

She'd just have to wait and see, like any ordinary heiress who was married to an extraordinary man.

TURN THE PAGE FOR A PREVIEW OF MAGGIE
ROBINSON'S NEXT LADIES UNLACED NOVEL

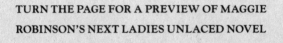

In the Heart of the Highlander

COMING IN OCTOBER 2013

FROM BERKLEY SENSATION

Mount Street
London, May 31, 1904

*M*ary Evensong was tired. Tired of wearing smoke-gray spectacles that covered her hazel eyes. Tired of wearing an itchy gray wig that covered her russet hair. Tired of the problems that came in by the sackloads every time the mailman rang her doorbell.

And most especially tired of her Aunt Mim, who was the original Mary Evensong and refused to stay retired.

Every day when Mary locked up the Evensong Agency offices and trudged upstairs to the elegant apartments above, she had to face Aunt Mim's questions and Aunt Mim's gouty foot. It was the gouty foot that had been both their undoing. Mim had been running both her employment agency and people's lives since 1888, after a successful career as house-keeper to a duke. Instead of relaxing in the handsome cot-tage the duke had provided once she turned fifty-five, after forty years of exceptional service to the family, Mim

Evensong sold it, took her savings, and set up her business in London. She knew what great—and not so great—houses needed in the way of reliable servants.

She also knew what flighty young society girls needed. She'd had experience helping to marry off the duke's five difficult daughters, and had sat up with the girls more nights than she could count discussing the vagaries of young gentlemen. Her cleanliness, canniness, and common sense made her uniquely qualified to solve various domestic disasters.

But one morning in 1900, just in time to herald in the new millennium, her big toe began to throb. Soon the other toes joined it. Her ankle, too. Now it was with the greatest difficulty that she rose from her chair and hobbled to the window to watch the traffic on Mount Street. There was no thinking of her going downstairs to her thriving business to interview footmen or to meet with a mama in her private office to discuss a daughter's slide into scandal with an impoverished musician who insisted on playing ragtime instead of Richard Strauss.

So four years ago, Mim had invited her namesake niece Mary to make her home with her and learn the ropes of the Evensong Agency. Mary was a spinster, just as Mim was—the Mrs' was an honorific that had been granted to her as the duke's housekeeper as she rose up the ranks.

Mary really had nothing better to do—both her parents were dead, her brother married and running their grocery shop. She faced a dismal future of keying the cash register and unpaid babysitting for her hellacious little nephews.

Mary was a sensible young woman, and looked forward to a new life in London, one without frogs in her bed and the constant chatter of her bossy sister-in-law at home. She would not miss the scents of overripe melon and problematic sausages at work, and so she hung up her spotless apron there with no regrets.

It was only when she arrived in town that Mim's plan for her looked less than sterling. Mim was harboring the fond delusion that one day her foot would miraculously reduce in size and she could return to the massive mahogany desk in her corner office. The fact that she was in her seventies did not dissuade her from feeling the company could not function without her and her vaunted wisdom. It was imperative to continue its lucrative services, and imperative that her clients trust the dispenser of those services as they had these dozen years.

Young Mary did not look especially wise. True, she had a broad forehead and shrewd hazel eyes, but her hair was reddish and some people thought redheads were unbalanced. She was short of stature, too, though Aunt Mim was of a similar height and her lack of inches had never stopped her from being terrifying when the situation called for it. If the agency was to carry on and prosper, a disguise was necessary. Thus Mary was bewigged and bespectacled—just temporarily, Mim assured her, until she could get back on her feet, so to speak. No one would really look at her—older women in large black hats were a dime a dozen, nearly invisible in their ancient ubiquity, so Mary should have no fear of discovery.

An army of doctors had been discreetly consulted, and Mim was no closer to waltzing than she was before they mounted Mount Street's steps. And poor Mary never got a chance to waltz at all—she was too busy pretending to be an elderly woman, and growing into the part more perfectly every day.

Something must be done. But not today. Today was . . . taken.

There was a rap on the frosted glass of her office door, and her secretary, Oliver Palmer, poked his head in. "Lord Raeburn is here to see you, Mrs. Evensong."

Oliver was a handsome young man with impeccable manners. He made an excellent impression at the reception desk and was totally discreet. If he suspected Mary was not exactly who she purported to be, he never gave any indication of it. He had secrets of his own.

Oliver had been frank about his unfortunate situation—
and his hunger—when Mary had interviewed him. Flat
broke, he'd come about another job, but Mary claimed him
for her own and he was now invaluable to her. Oliver's
finger was firmly on the pulse of all society gossip. It was
he who'd provided the newspaper clippings about Lord
Raeburn, not that she'd needed reminding. She remembered the grainy scowling photographs on the front pages.

Accident, though there had been invisible quotation
marks on the word. *Open window. Insufficient evidence.*

"Oh, dear. Do I look all right?" Mary could have bitten
her tongue. She'd never asked Oliver such a thing no matter
how noble her clients were, and he gave her an odd look.
Lord Raeburn was only a baron, after all. And after what
happened in Scotland, no decent woman should even give
his good opinion a second thought.

"Very handsome, as always, Mrs. Evensong. Your hat
is very becoming."

It was perhaps ridiculous to always wear her hat indoors,
but with judicious pinning, it kept her wig on straight.
"Send him in. We'll need a tea tray."

"If I were you, Mrs. E., I'd offer the fellow a whiskey."

"I'm sure you're right. See to it, would you, Oliver?"
There was single-malt whiskey in a cabinet somewhere.
The Evensong Agency always had everything at hand and
in hand. In the past four years, Mary Evensong had found
husbands for heiresses, valets for viscounts, and even a
dairymaid for a marquess who kept a Hertford cow in his
kitchen, much to the consternation of his cook. The agency
was famous for achieving the unusual—in fact, her aunt
had hit upon "Performing the Impossible before Breakfast
since 1888" as its motto.

Some members of the peerage, like that marquess, were
known for their eccentricity. Lord Alec Raeburn was not
one of them. What he was known for caused Mary's heart
to beat a little faster.

If he had a simple staffing problem, he would never

have bothered to come himself. So the nature of his visit must be personal. She doubted he was looking for a new wife—his old one had not been dead a year, and the scandal surrounding her death would take much longer to die down. Mary was not naïve enough to think he was celibate after all the rumors, but surely it was too soon to seek her matchmaking services.

Mary cleared her throat and drummed her gloved fingers on her desk. Her hands were nowhere near as wrinkled as they should be, so she wore her gloves at all times, too. And right now, her palms were damp with perspiration.

The clacking of the typewriter keys ceased in the outer office. Her girl stenographers were no doubt swooning—discreetly, she hoped—as Lord Raeburn made his way to her inner sanctum. It was with the greatest difficulty that Mary stopped herself from swooning along with them as Oliver opened the door to announce Lord Raeburn.

As if one wouldn't notice the man. A woman would have to be blind or dead not to respond to his physical presence.

For one thing, he was more or less a giant, but in the best possible way. Mary had been to a fair once that advertised "the tallest man in Britain," but the poor fellow had been the ugliest man in Britain as well. Lord Raeburn was not ugly, except perhaps for his attire. He wore a walking kilt in his family's tartan, an unfortunate combination of yellow and black that reminded Mary of angry bees. But his black jacket molded to his massive shoulders and matched his longish hair and neatly trimmed beard. Mary was not at all fond of beards, but somehow she didn't think Lord Raeburn was hiding a weak chin. His eyes looked black as well, giving her and her office intense scrutiny while she stumbled to her feet and extended a hand.

"Good afternoon, Lord Raeburn," she said briskly, hoping she could trick herself into feeling as confident as she sounded. "Won't you sit down? Oliver, bring us in the refreshments we discussed, please." She needed a stiff drink herself—she was feeling like a giddy schoolgirl. He was gorgeous. No wonder women fell at his feet.

And out his windows.

Lord Raeburn tucked himself into one of the leather client chairs. It was a very tight fit. "Thank you for seeing me on such short notice. I'm bound for home in a few days, and I have to know I have your help before I go."

"What can the Evensong Agency do for you, my lord?"

"I'm not sure you can do anything. But I'd like you to try. I won't beat about the bush. Do you think I murdered my wife?"

Mary took a quick breath, then stalled for time with a question of her own. "Does it matter what I think?"

"It might. If you just take my money and pay me lip service, there's no point in me hiring you now, is there? We Scots don't like to waste our time. Or our gold."

Her spine stiffened. "I can assure you the Evensong Agency does not take on clients merely to humor them and pad out account books. If we can perform a legitimate service, we do our utmost to fulfill our obligations."

"So you won't say if I'm a killer or not."

"I'm afraid I'm not sufficiently acquainted with the particulars of the case," Mary lied. Oliver kept scrapbooks filled with the most interesting articles under his desk. Lord Raeburn had one all to himself.

Oliver chose that moment to step into the office with a silver tray. There was not only a decanter of whiskey but a pretty china teapot on it. They were silent as Oliver arranged and poured. Mary reconsidered her thirst and decided to keep her wits sharp, settling on a cup of oolong. To her surprise, Lord Raeburn did the same.

"Thank you, Oliver. That will be all."

"I'll be just outside if you need me, Mrs. Evensong. Just outside."

Lord Raeburn gave Oliver a wry smile. "Don't worry, lad, I won't ravish your employer. I may be a blackguard in the eyes of the world, but I do have some standards."

Well. Could the man be any more insulting? She shouldn't be offended—she was meant to look like an old trout—but the twenty-nine-year-old woman beneath the black hat was inexplicably annoyed. Mary set her tea down, causing the liquid to splash on its saucer.

"Perhaps you'd better tell me why you are here."

"I need a woman for a month."

Mary rose to her full height—not that there was much of it—in umbrage. "We are not that sort of employment agency, Lord Raeburn. Good afternoon."

"Oh, get off your high horse and sit down. I didn't make myself clear. I need to hire a woman to infiltrate the guests of that new hydrotherapy spa. The Forsyth Palace Hotel. In the Highlands. Have you heard of it?"

Mary had. There had been full-page advertisements in all the London papers when it opened last year. It was built in the Scots baronial style, accommodating 200 guests and offering first-class accommodations for healthy visitors and various hydropathic treatments for those whose health was not so robust. Mary had even entertained the idea of sending her aunt there, but Mim would never leave the agency solely in Mary's hands.

To be fair, Mary had received amazingly astute advice from her aunt—Mim was sharp as a tack, especially when it came to the trickier clients. Lord Raeburn might be joining that list, if Mary could figure out what he wanted.

"You say 'infiltrate.' Why do you not employ an inquiry agent? I know several reputable agencies I can recommend."

"They're all men, Mrs. Evensong. I need a woman to lay a trap for the doctor who runs the place. The man responsible my wife's death."

Mary turned her teacup, wishing she had the ability to read the dregs. "Why haven't you gone to the authorities with your suspicions?"

"Och, what's the point? They think I'm guilty—it's just they don't have enough proof. But I'll tell you this—my wife was seduced by that piece of sh—slime. Dr. Josef Bauer," he spat. "I have my wife's diary. Everything's in there. She paid him a fortune to keep it quiet."

Mary looked across her desk at the baron. His color was still vivid through the light gray of her lenses. Judging from the expression on his face, he was in a state of controlled fury. She wouldn't want to see him lose that control. A man his size would frighten anyone with a modicum of sense. It was difficult to imagine his wife daring to be unfaithful. Surely she would know there would be consequences.

"What would you want this woman to do?"

"Pretend to be a patient. Toss around my money and attract Bauer's attention. Get cozy with him."

She shook her head. "As I said, we don't employ ladies to do that kind of work."

"She wouldn't have to fu—uh, fornicate with him. Just catch him doing something unethical. Like trying to kill her and pass it off as an accident after she made her will over to him."

"I doubt any one of my job seekers would be willing to make themselves a possible murder victim, Lord Raeburn," Mary said dryly.

"It doesn't have to go that far, of course. If he's accused of carrying on romantically with one of his patients, that should be enough to ruin his reputation. What husband or father would trust him to cure his wife or daughter? And anyway, I'd be there to keep your woman safe."

Mary's mouth dropped open a second too long. Goodness, she must look like the veriest imbecile. "You?" she asked, when she gathered her scattered wits.

"I've booked a suite of rooms there. I'm having some renovations done to Raeburn Court now that Edith is . . . gone. The hotel is not two miles away, and it's only natural I stay close to supervise. It's the only decent place to stay in the area. The only place, period. We're a bit isolated from the world."

Yes, that was the spa's attraction—unspoiled countryside. Pure air, high altitude, fresh water. Enough wildlife and waterfalls to thrill any amateur photographer. Yet there was train service to Pitcarran, a charming little town close enough for a day trip in one of the hotel's horse-drawn wagonettes.

It seemed Mary had committed the advertisements to memory. She wondered if Oliver had saved any stories about it.

"Bauer knows me. I make him nervous," Lord Raeburn continued. "He may slip and make a mistake."

"He also may be on his best behavior," Mary said. "Does he know he has you for an enemy?"

"Oh, yes."

Mary shivered at the glitter in Lord Raeburn's black eyes.

"Let me see if I understand this. You wish Dr. Bauer to be discovered in a compromising position with a patient, even though he knows you will be watching him."

"The man's ego—you are familiar with that alienist fellow Freud?—knows no bounds. He's full of himself. I think because I will be there he'll flaunt his indiscretions in front of me, knowing there's not a damn thing I can do about it. Who will believe anything bad I have to say about him? Me, a man who killed his wife? I have no credibility." Lord Raeburn sat back in his chair, looking vulnerable for the first time. Mary decided she had to reread all the newspaper accounts of Lady Edith Raeburn's death.

"Let me think about this."

"I don't have time for you to dillydally, Mrs. Evensong. If you can't get someone to do it, I'll have to hire some actress. I do know a few."

Yes, Mary had heard that he did. Lord Raeburn and his wife had lived apart for most of their marriage. No wonder the poor woman sought comfort in the arms of a sympathetic Dr. Bauer.

"Why haven't you already?"

"The girls I know—let's just say they're more suited to

the chorus line than playing an heiress. I need someone fresh. Innocent. Someone Bauer will think he can corrupt with no consequences. From what little I know, he only debauches virgins, who are then too mortified to confess their stupidity."

"Then why did Dr. Bauer target Lady Raeburn?" From the moment she asked the question, Mary knew she had made a mistake. She watched Lord Raeburn struggle to frame his answer.

Instead of the shout she expected, his words, when they came, were quiet. "My wife was very young when we married. Delicate. She had a disgust of the marital act. Or perhaps she just had a disgust of me. Josef Bauer somehow overcame her objections."

Mary Evensong was rarely surprised by anything her trickier clients had to tell her, but she was surprised now. Lord Raeburn had bared his heart. His pain. Somehow she knew he'd never told the truth to anyone before.

Edith Raeburn had been a virgin. And a fool.

Mary made her decision, and hoped she wouldn't be sorry. "I'll do it. That is, I'll find someone for you. When will she have to leave?"

"We wouldn't want to arrive at the hotel together—let's say, get your girl to come a week from Thursday. The sooner we can put a period to Bauer's villainy, the better. Do you have someone in mind?"

"Yes," Mary said, hoping Aunt Mim would approve of her madcap plan.

Mary wasn't madcap—she was steady. Sensible. Responsible. Boring. But that was about to change.

She pulled out a contract and discussed terms as if she didn't have black and yellow bees buzzing drunkenly in her head.

*He wouldn't settle for less than
her unconditional surrender.*

From *New York Times* bestselling author
MADELINE HUNTER

The Surrender of Miss Fairbourne

As reluctant business partners, Emma Fairbourne's defiance and Darius Alfreton's demands make it difficult to manage one of London's most eminent auction houses. But their passionate personalities ignite an affair that leaves them both senseless—until the devastating truth behind their partnership comes to light, threatening the love they have just begun to share . . .

"Hunter's books are so addictive."
—*Publishers Weekly*

madelinehunter.com
facebook.com/MadelineHunter
facebook.com/LoveAlwaysBooks
penguin.com

M1193T0413

LOVE
ROMANCE NOVELS?

For news on all your favorite romance authors,
sneak peeks into the newest releases, book
giveaways, and much more—

"Like" Love Always on Facebook!
 **LoveAlwaysBooks**

Enter the rich world of
historical romance
with Berkley Books . . .

Madeline Hunter

Jennifer Ashley

Joanna Bourne

Lynn Kurland

Jodi Thomas

Anne Gracie

Love is timeless.

berkleyjoveauthors.com

Discover Romance

berkleyjoveauthors.com

See what's coming up next from your favorite romance authors and explore all the latest Berkley, Jove, and Sensation selections.

See what's new

~

Find author appearances

~

Win fantastic prizes

~

Get reading recommendations

~

Chat with authors and other fans

~

Read interviews with authors you love